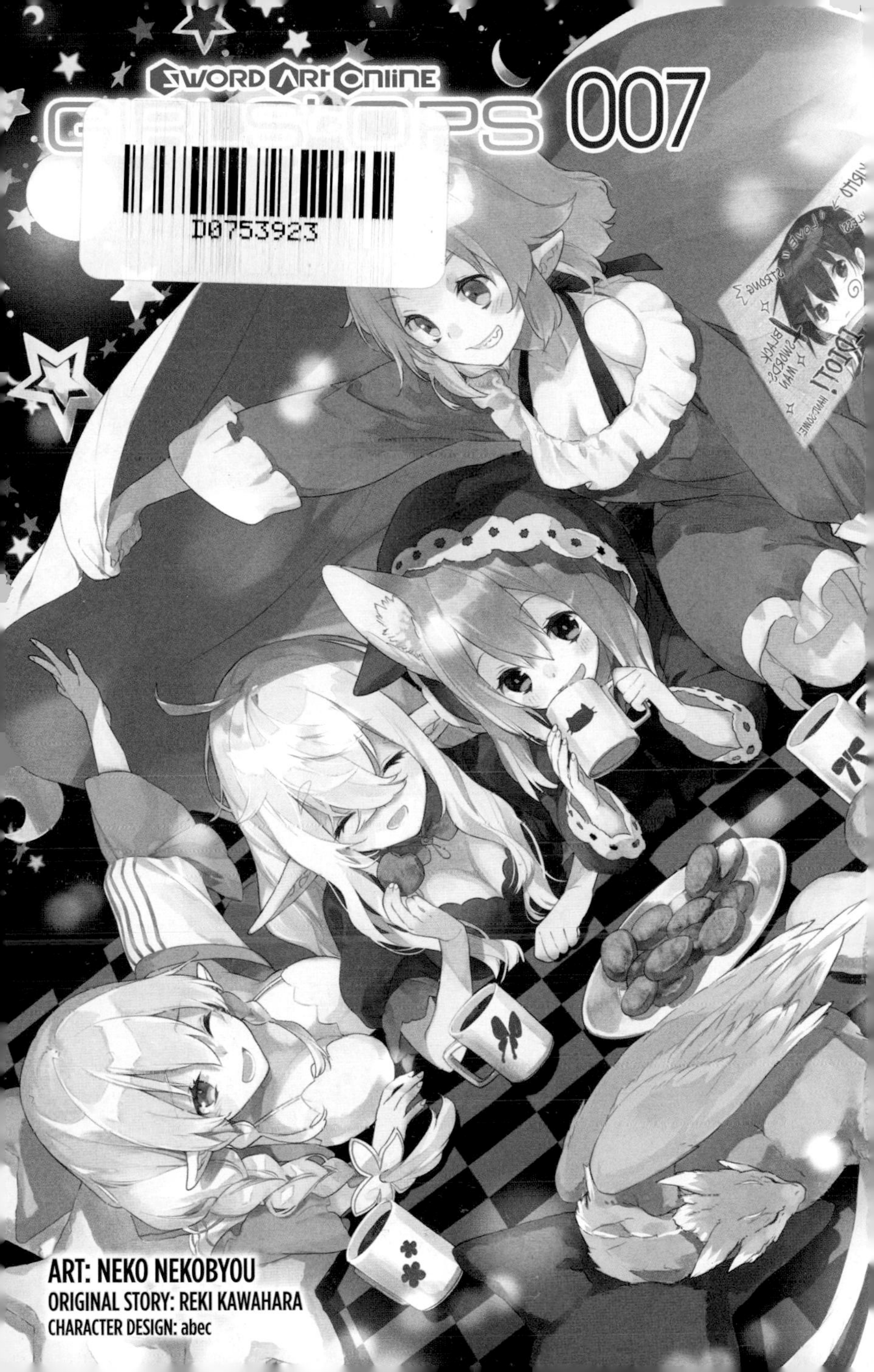
SWORD ART ONLINE
GIRLS' OPS 007
ART: NEKO NEKOBYOU
ORIGINAL STORY: REKI KAWAHARA
CHARACTER DESIGN: abec

007

SWORD ART ONLINE
GIRLS' OPERATIONS

art: Neko Nekobyou
original story: Reki Kawahara
character design: abec

Contents

Aaaaaaah!

WHO?

SWORD ART ONLINE
GIRLS' OPS 007

SWORD ART ONLINE
GIRLS' OPERATIONS

ART: NEKO NEKOBYOU
ORIGINAL STORY: REKI KAWAHARA
CHARACTER DESIGN: abec

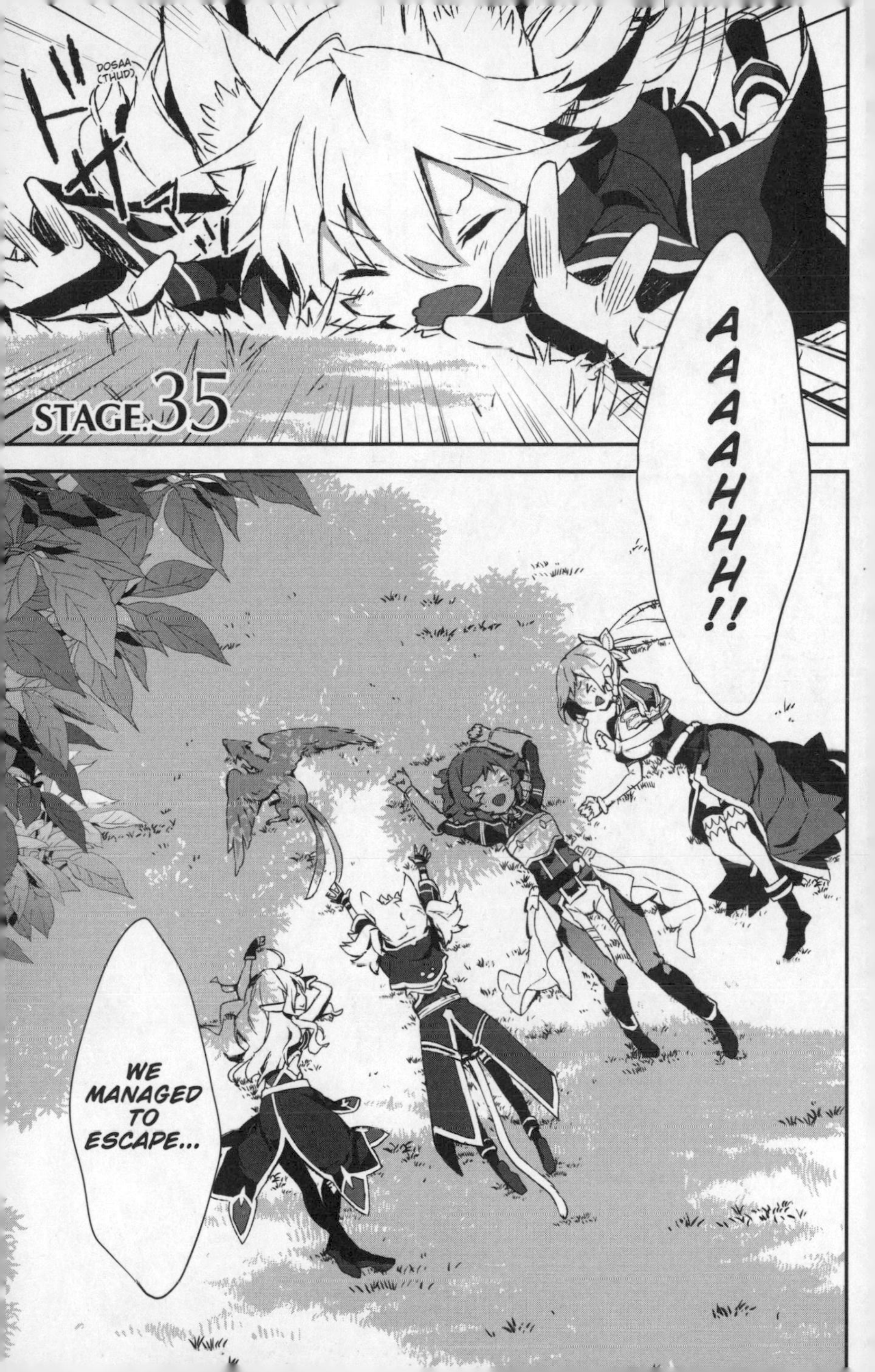
DOSAA (THUD)
STAGE.35
AAAAHHH!!
WE MANAGED TO ESCAPE...

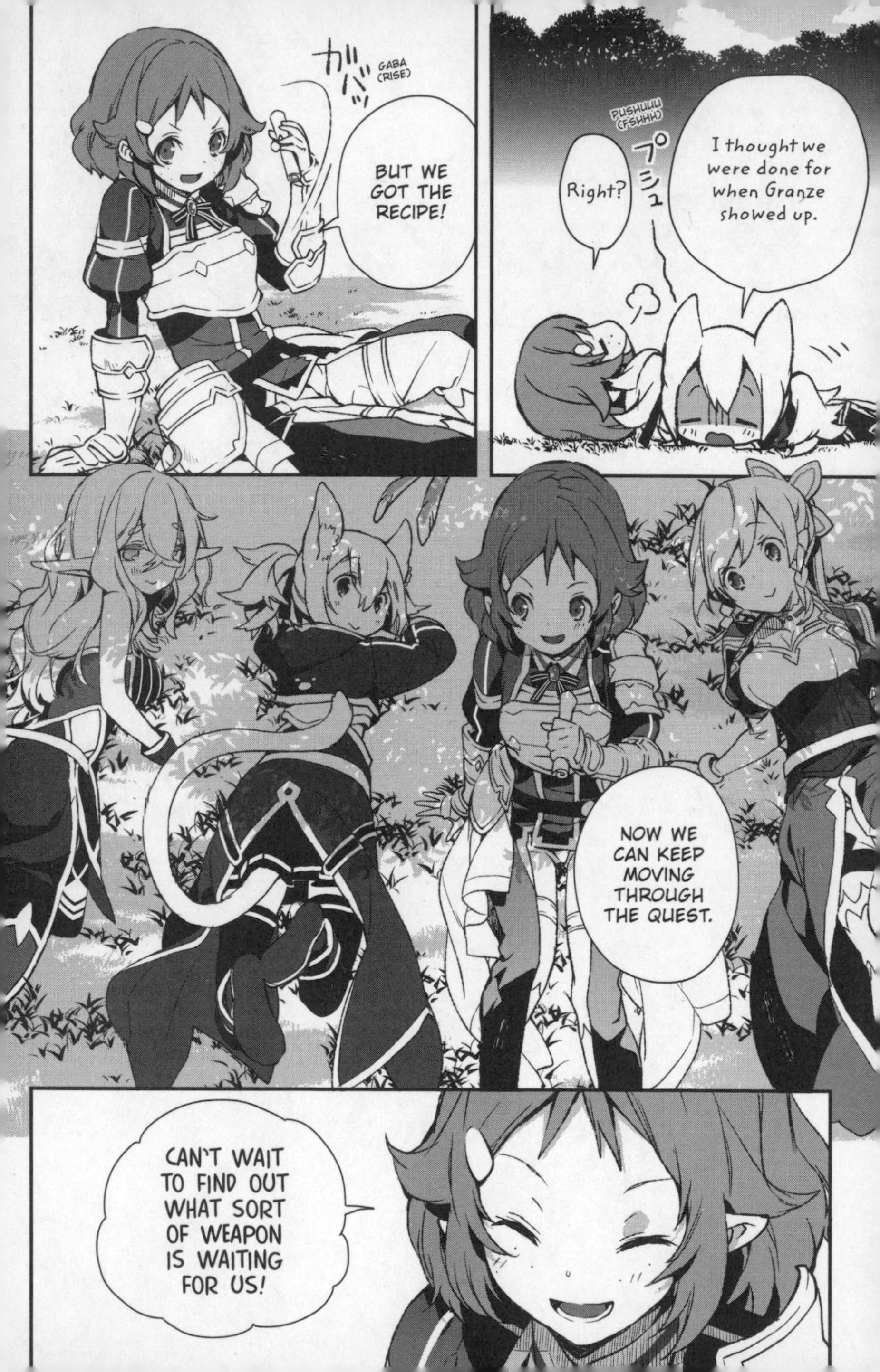

I thought we were done for when Granze showed up.
Pushuuu (fshhh)
Right?
Gaba (rise)
BUT WE GOT THE RECIPE!
NOW WE CAN KEEP MOVING THROUGH THE QUEST.
CAN'T WAIT TO FIND OUT WHAT SORT OF WEAPON IS WAITING FOR US!

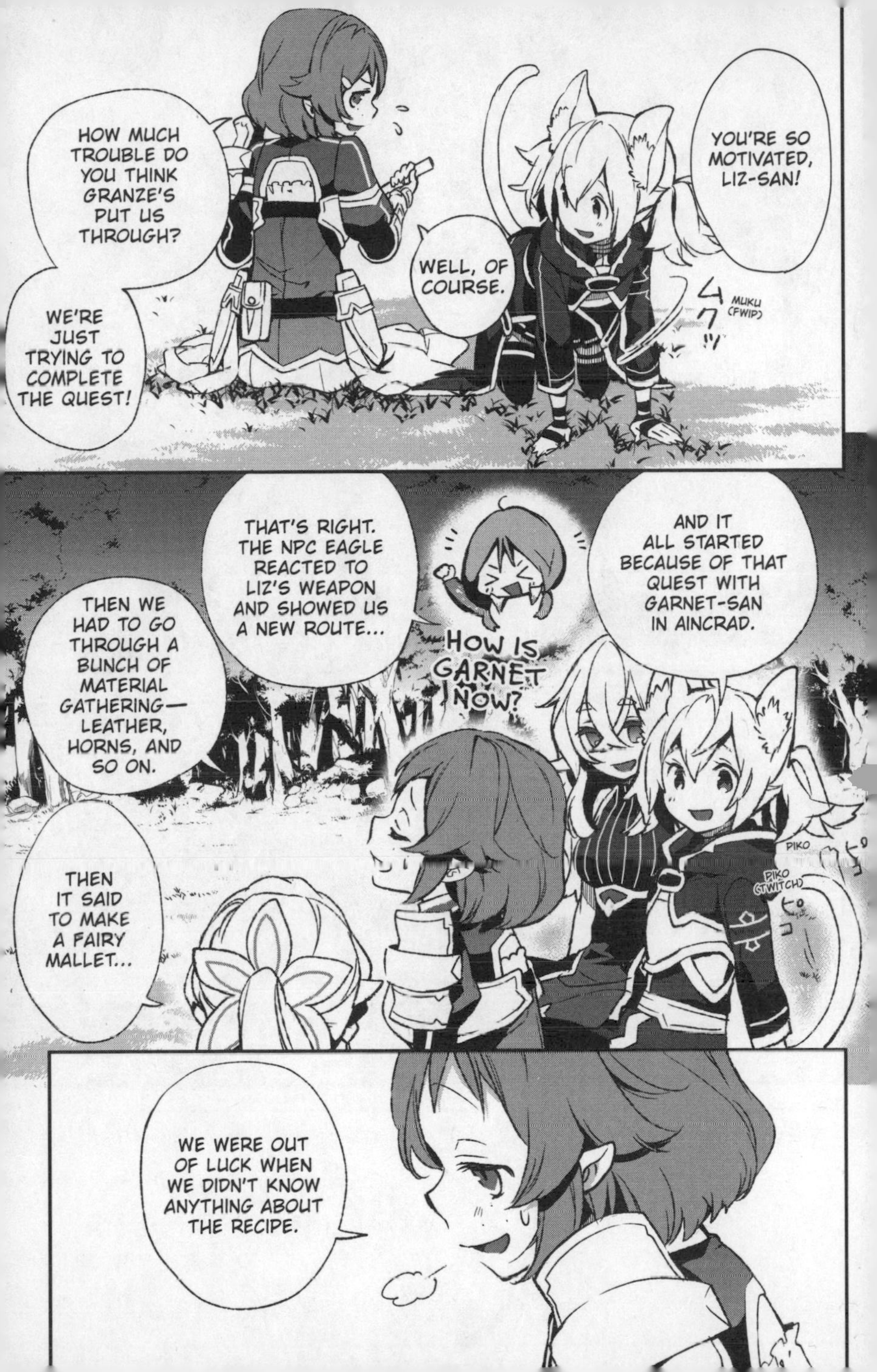
YOU'RE SO MOTIVATED, LIZ-SAN!
MUKU (FWIP)
WELL, OF COURSE.
HOW MUCH TROUBLE DO YOU THINK GRANZE'S PUT US THROUGH?
WE'RE JUST TRYING TO COMPLETE THE QUEST!
AND IT ALL STARTED BECAUSE OF THAT QUEST WITH GARNET-SAN IN AINCRAD.
HOW IS GARNET NOW?
THAT'S RIGHT. THE NPC EAGLE REACTED TO LIZ'S WEAPON AND SHOWED US A NEW ROUTE...
THEN WE HAD TO GO THROUGH A BUNCH OF MATERIAL GATHERING—LEATHER, HORNS, AND SO ON.
PIKO
PIKO (TWITCH)
THEN IT SAID TO MAKE A FAIRY MALLET...
WE WERE OUT OF LUCK WHEN WE DIDN'T KNOW ANYTHING ABOUT THE RECIPE.

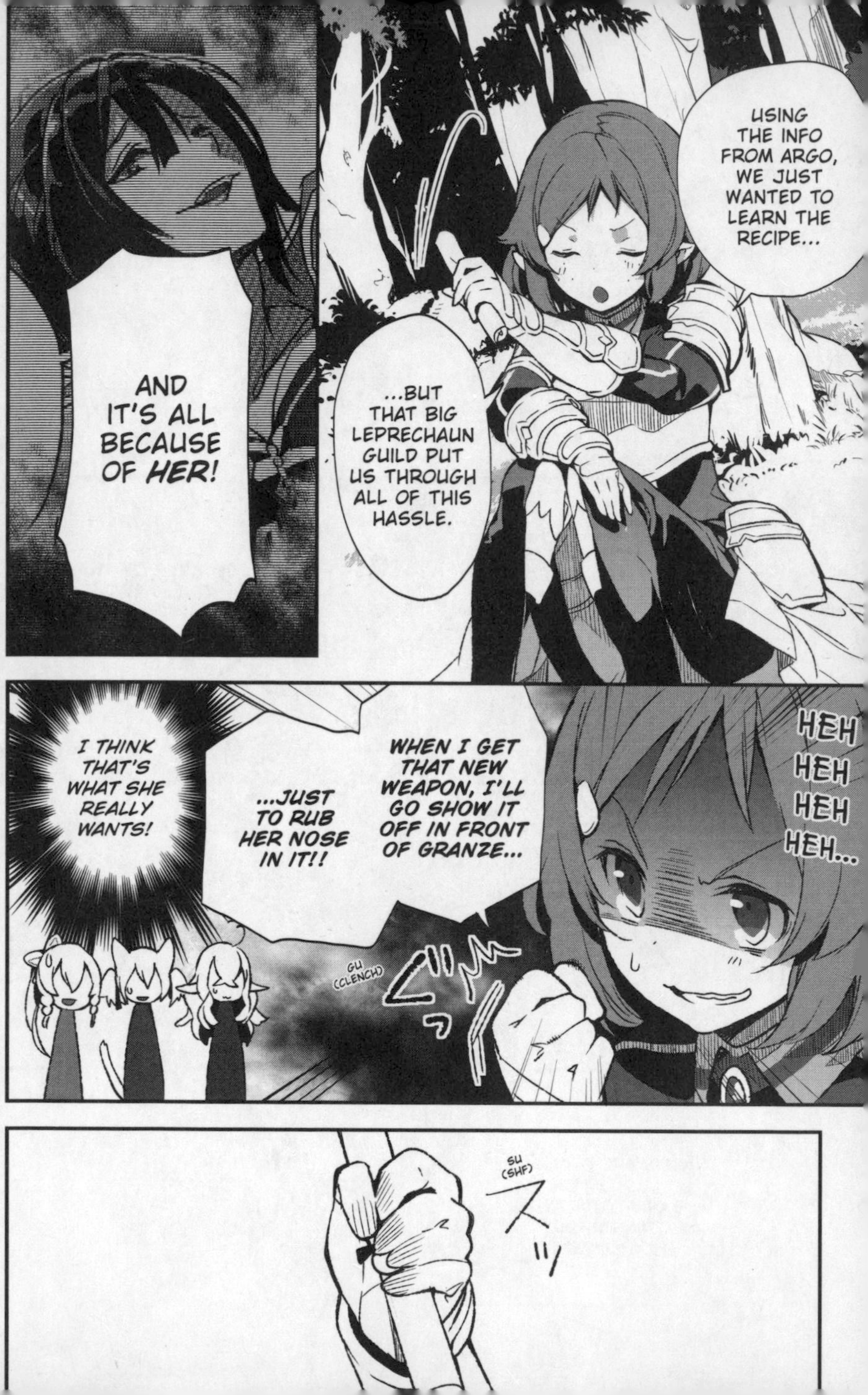
USING THE INFO FROM ARGO, WE JUST WANTED TO LEARN THE RECIPE...
...BUT THAT BIG LEPRECHAUN GUILD PUT US THROUGH ALL OF THIS HASSLE.
AND IT'S ALL BECAUSE OF HER!
HEH HEH HEH HEH...
WHEN I GET THAT NEW WEAPON, I'LL GO SHOW IT OFF IN FRONT OF GRANZE...
...JUST TO RUB HER NOSE IN IT!!
I THINK THAT'S WHAT SHE REALLY WANTS!
GU (CLENCH)
SU (SHF)

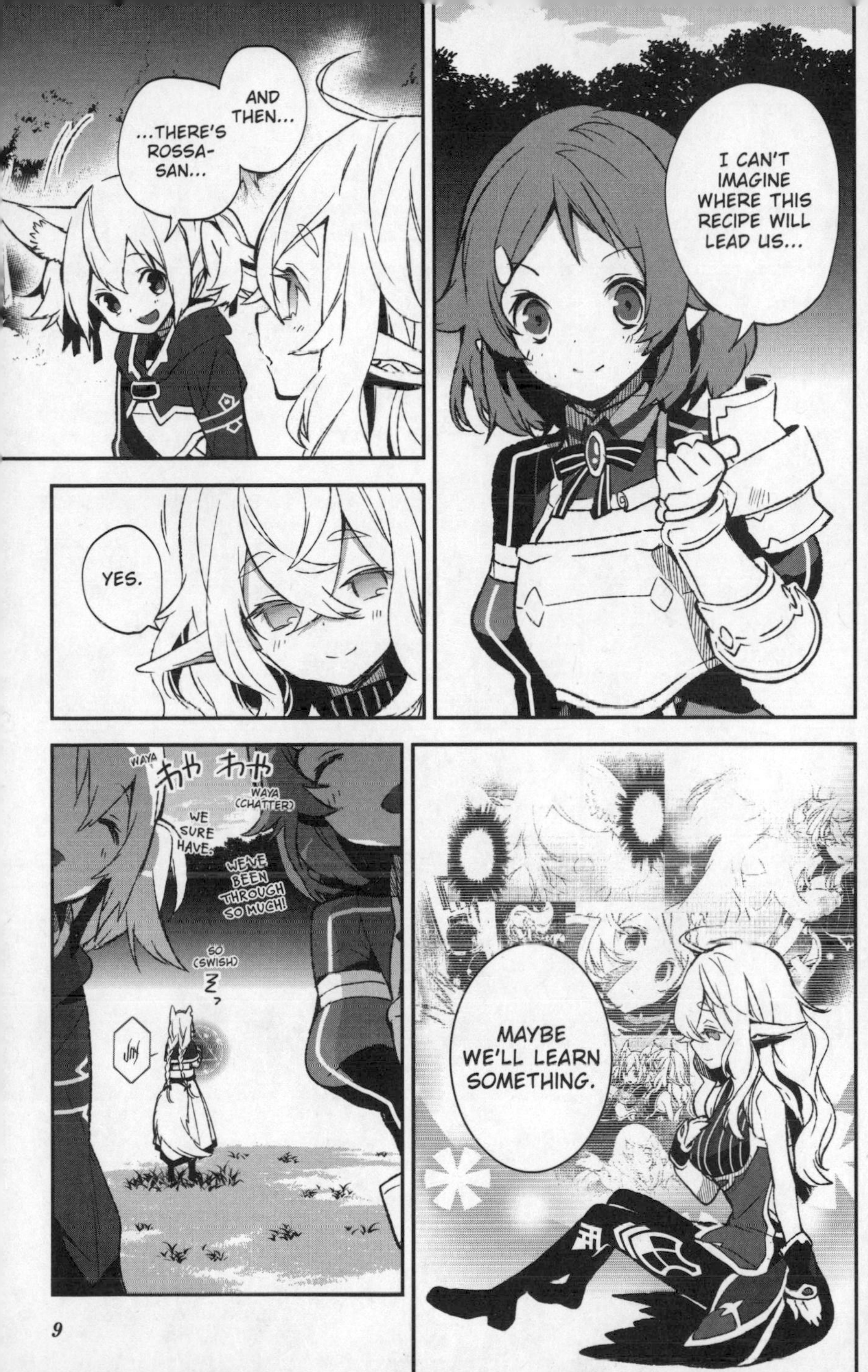
I CAN'T IMAGINE WHERE THIS RECIPE WILL LEAD US...
AND THEN...
...THERE'S ROSSA-SAN...
YES.
MAYBE WE'LL LEARN SOMETHING.
WAYA
WAYA (CHATTER)
WE SURE HAVE.
WE'VE BEEN THROUGH SO MUCH!
SO (SWISH)

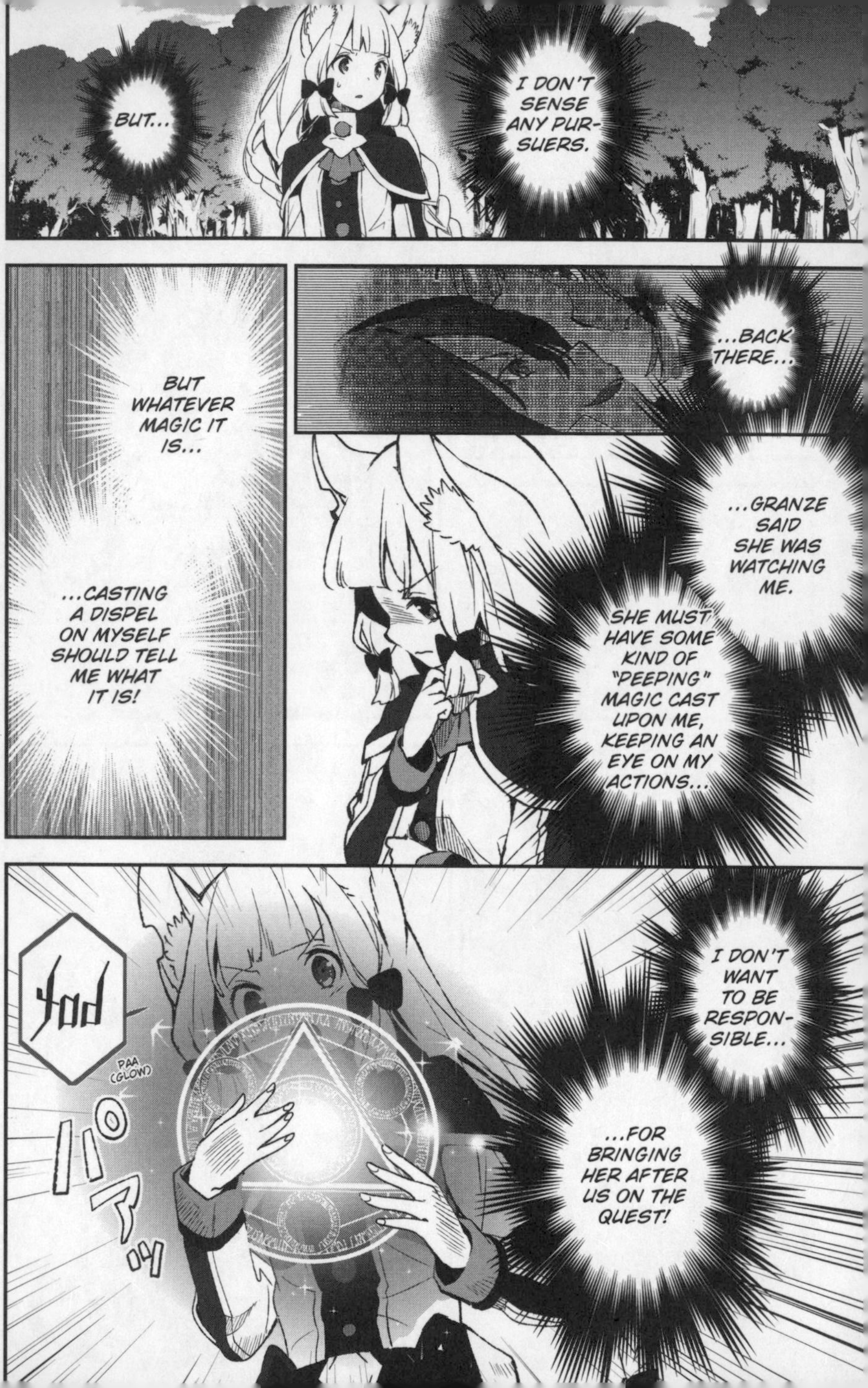
BUT...
I DON'T SENSE ANY PURSUERS.
...BACK THERE...
...GRANZE SAID SHE WAS WATCHING ME.
SHE MUST HAVE SOME KIND OF "PEEPING" MAGIC CAST UPON ME, KEEPING AN EYE ON MY ACTIONS...
BUT WHATEVER MAGIC IT IS...
...CASTING A DISPEL ON MYSELF SHOULD TELL ME WHAT IT IS!
I DON'T WANT TO BE RESPONSIBLE...
...FOR BRINGING HER AFTER US ON THE QUEST!
PAA (GLOW)

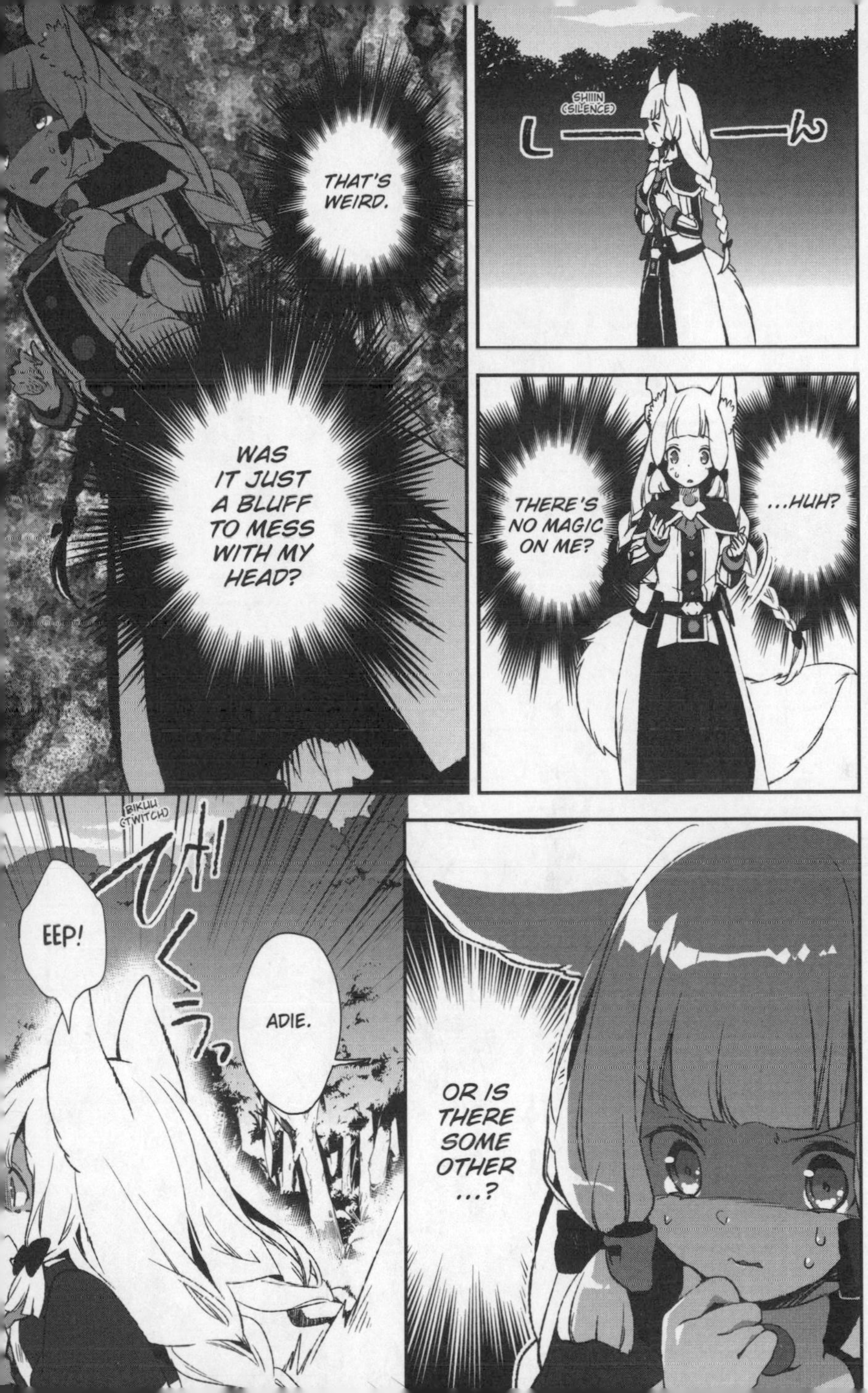
SHIIN (SILENCE)
し——ん
...HUH?
THERE'S NO MAGIC ON ME?
THAT'S WEIRD.
WAS IT JUST A BLUFF TO MESS WITH MY HEAD?
OR IS THERE SOME OTHER ...?
BIKUU (TWITCH)
ADIE.
EEP!

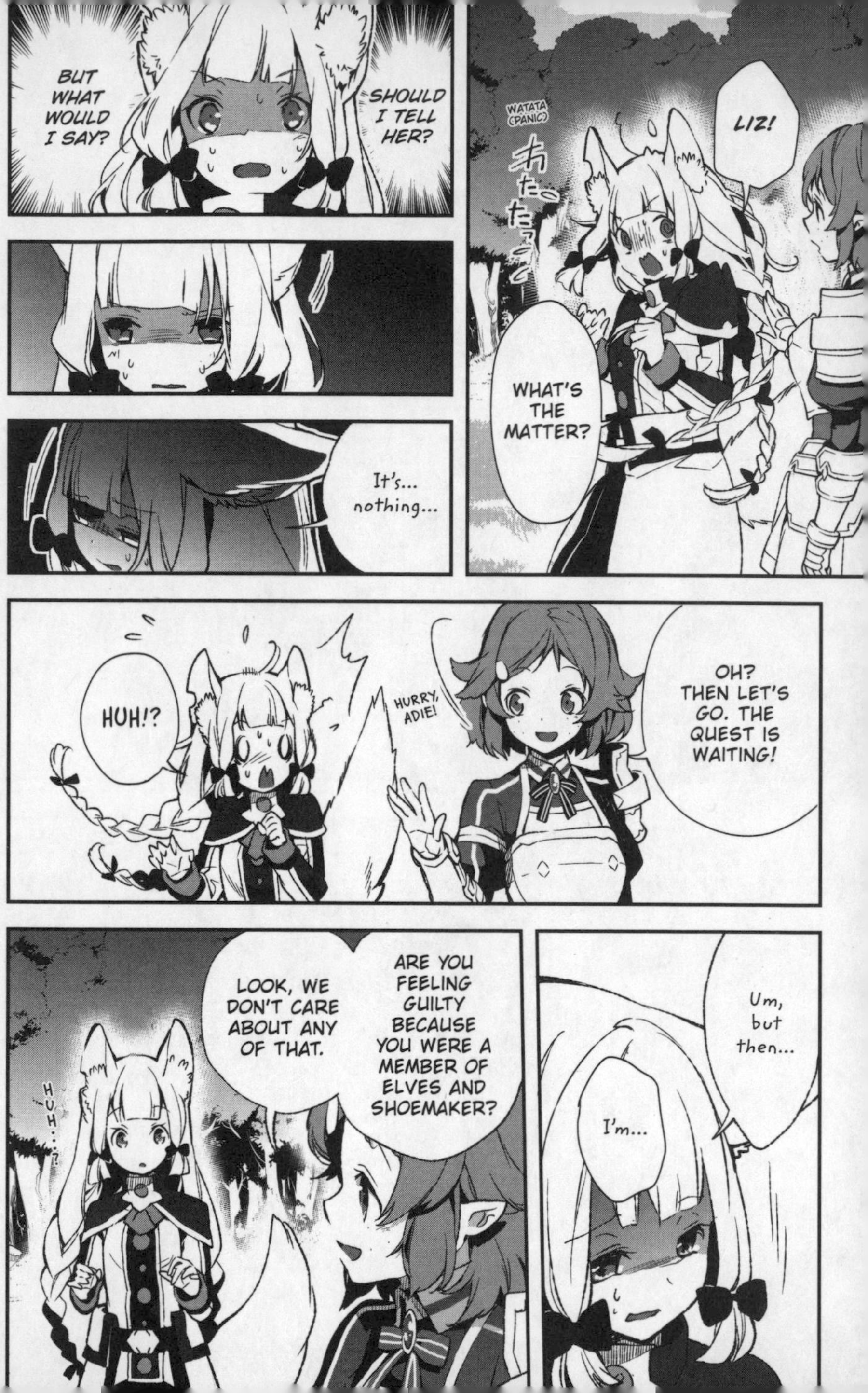
LIZ!
WATATA (PANIC)
あたたっ
WHAT'S THE MATTER?
SHOULD I TELL HER?
BUT WHAT WOULD I SAY?
It's... nothing...
OH? THEN LET'S GO. THE QUEST IS WAITING!
HURRY, ADIE!
HUH!?
Um, but then...
I'm...
ARE YOU FEELING GUILTY BECAUSE YOU WERE A MEMBER OF ELVES AND SHOEMAKER?
LOOK, WE DON'T CARE ABOUT ANY OF THAT.
HUH...?

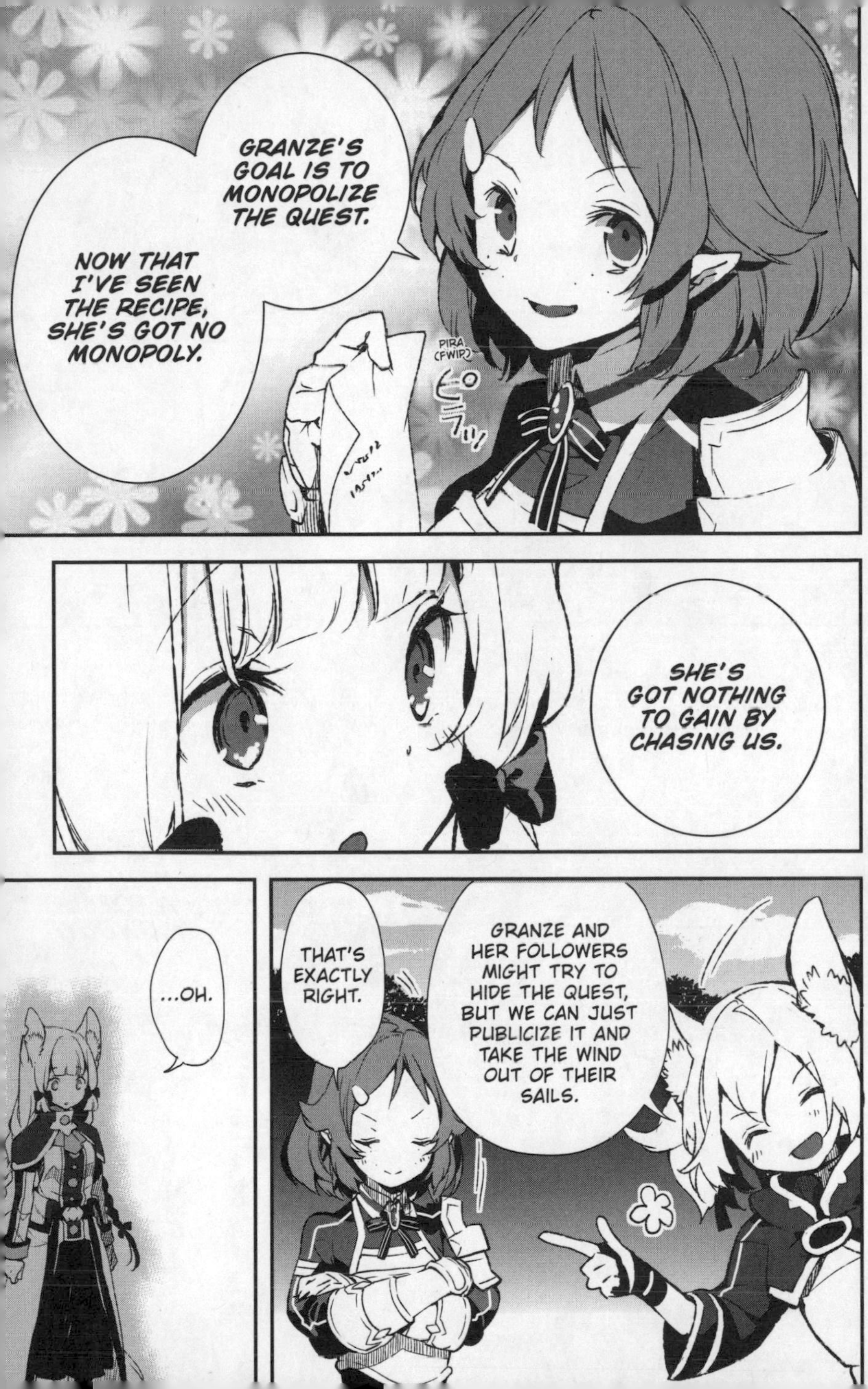
GRANZE'S GOAL IS TO MONOPOLIZE THE QUEST.
NOW THAT I'VE SEEN THE RECIPE, SHE'S GOT NO MONOPOLY.
PIRA (FWIP)
SHE'S GOT NOTHING TO GAIN BY CHASING US.
GRANZE AND HER FOLLOWERS MIGHT TRY TO HIDE THE QUEST, BUT WE CAN JUST PUBLICIZE IT AND TAKE THE WIND OUT OF THEIR SAILS.
THAT'S EXACTLY RIGHT.
...OH.

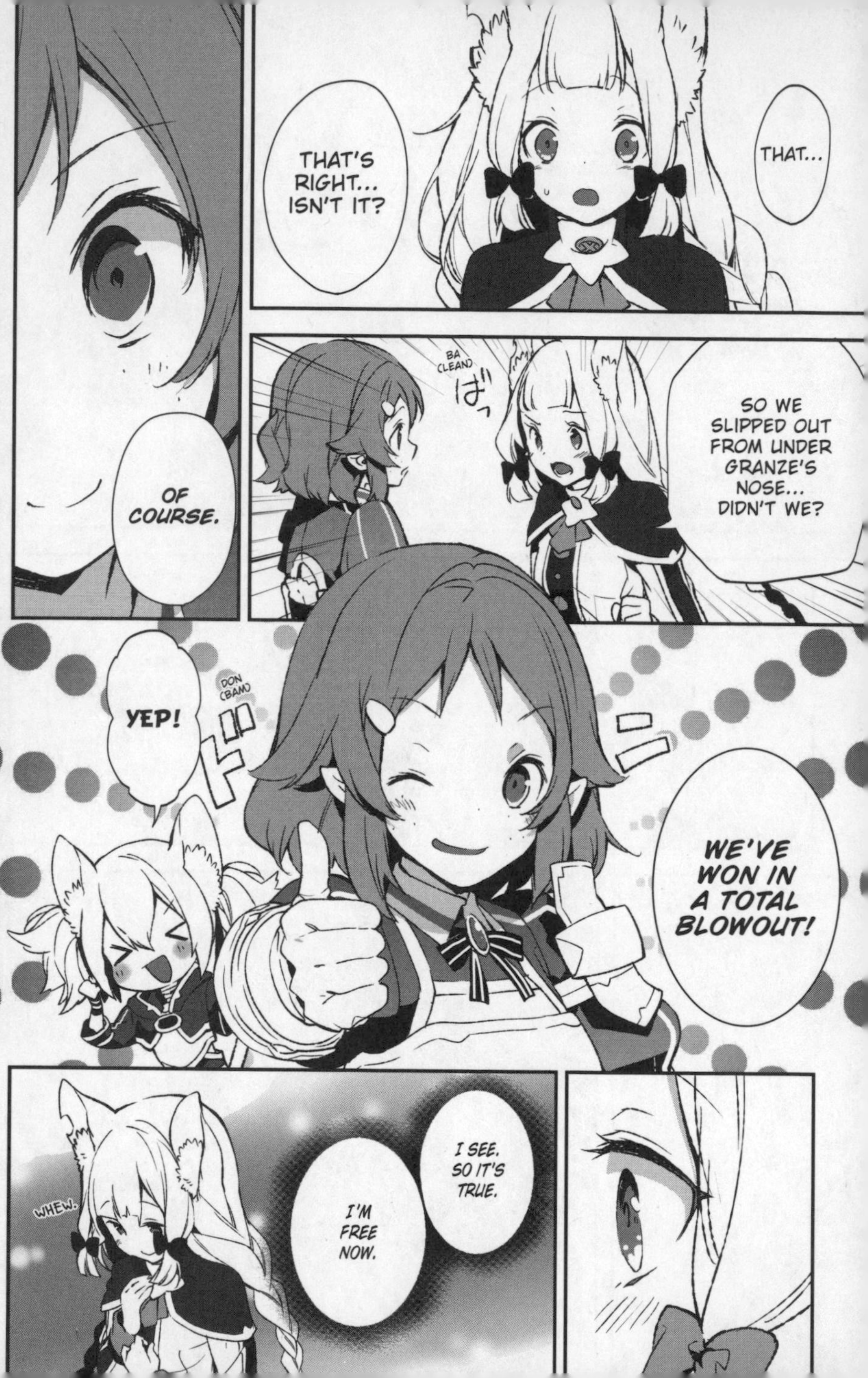
THAT...
THAT'S RIGHT... ISN'T IT?
BA CLEAND
ばっ
SO WE SLIPPED OUT FROM UNDER GRANZE'S NOSE... DIDN'T WE?
OF COURSE.
WE'VE WON IN A TOTAL BLOWOUT!
DON (BAM)
ドン
YEP!
I SEE. SO IT'S TRUE.
I'M FREE NOW.
WHEW.

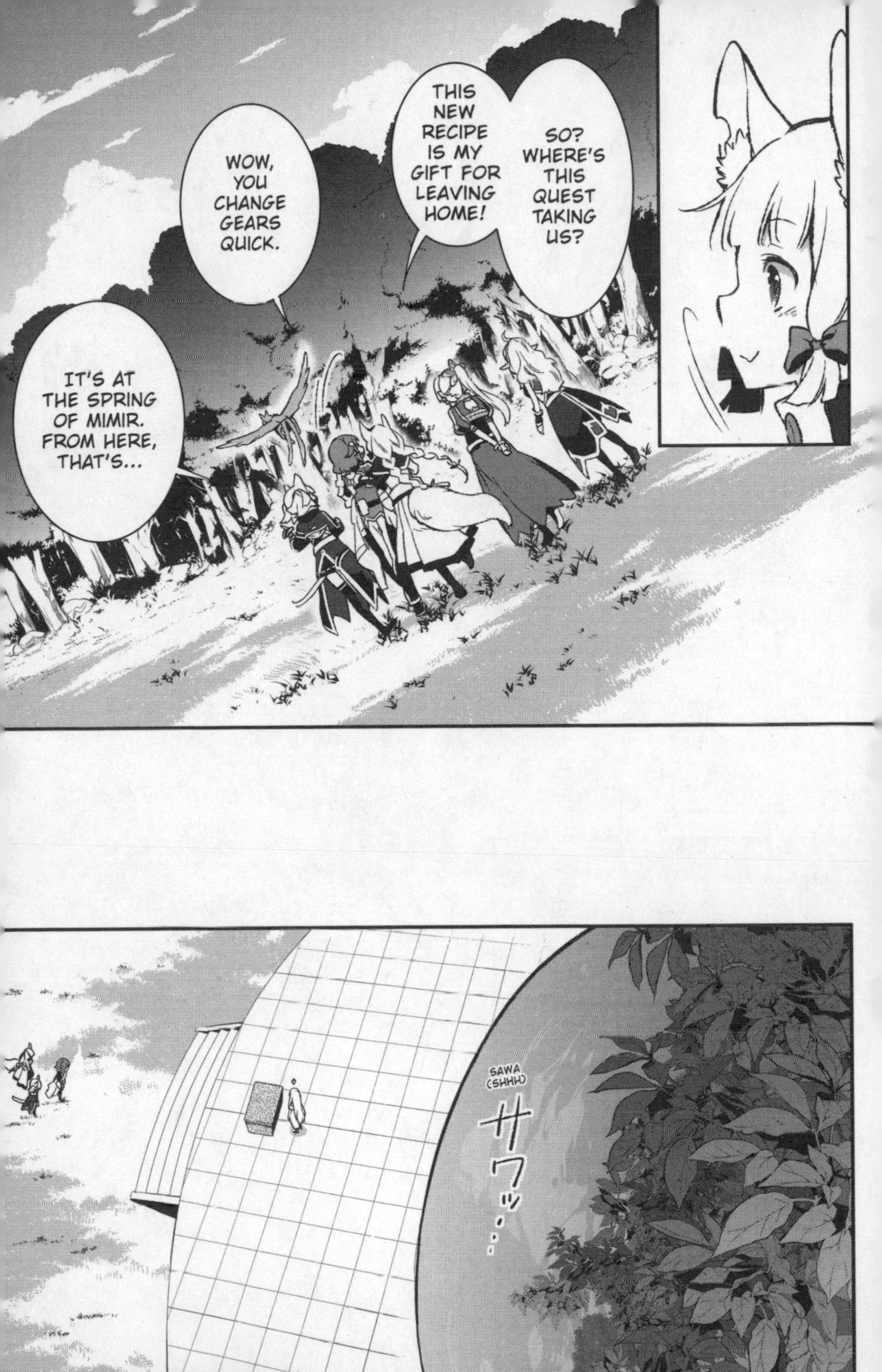
THIS NEW RECIPE IS MY GIFT FOR LEAVING HOME!
WOW, YOU CHANGE GEARS QUICK.
SO? WHERE'S THIS QUEST TAKING US?
IT'S AT THE SPRING OF MIMIR. FROM HERE, THAT'S...
SAWA (SHHH)
サワッ

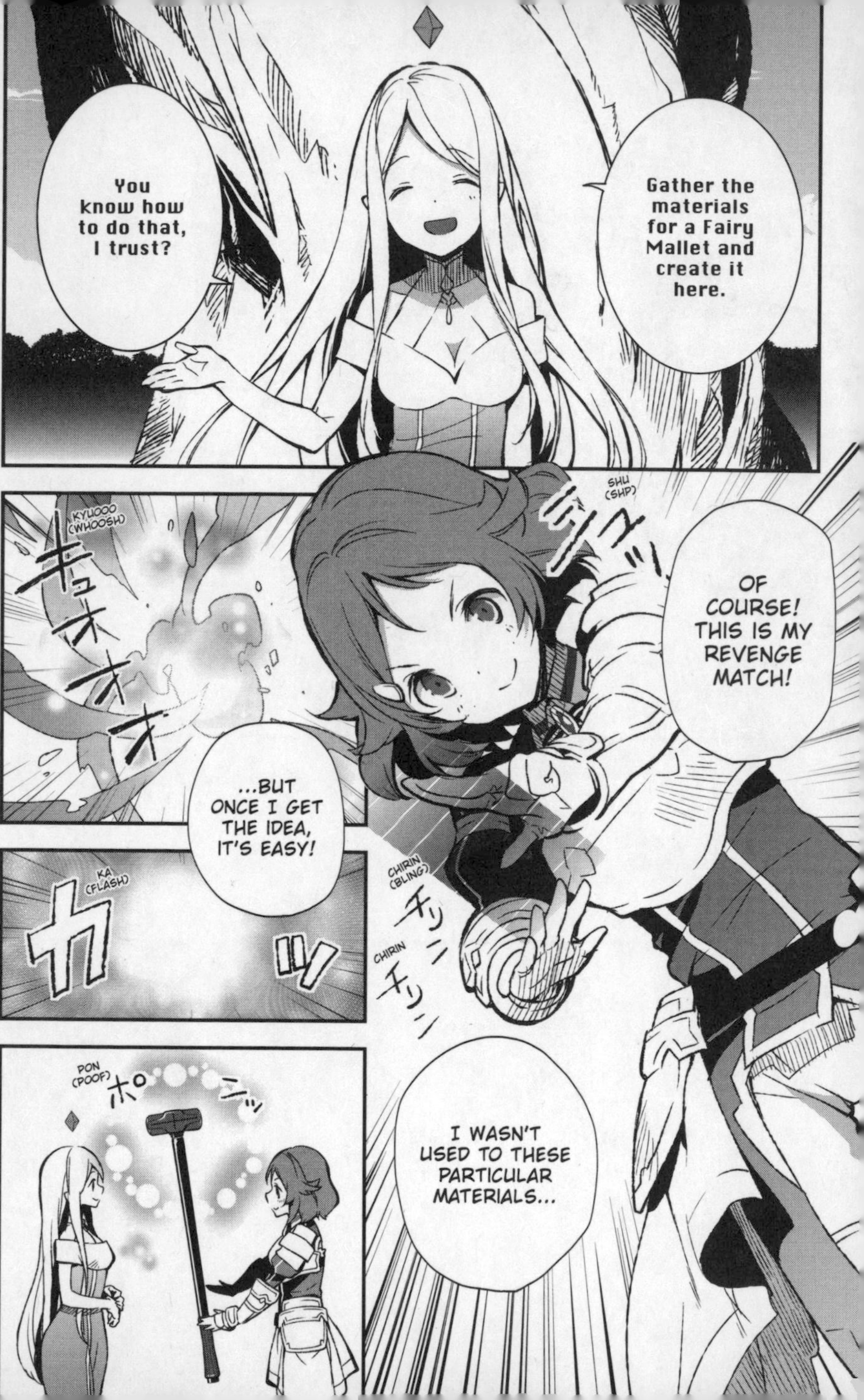
Gather the materials for a Fairy Mallet and create it here.
You know how to do that, I trust?
SHU (SHP)
OF COURSE! THIS IS MY REVENGE MATCH!
KYUOOO (WHOOSH)
KA (FLASH)
CHIRIN (BLING)
CHIRIN
I WASN'T USED TO THESE PARTICULAR MATERIALS...
...BUT ONCE I GET THE IDEA, IT'S EASY!
PON (POOF)

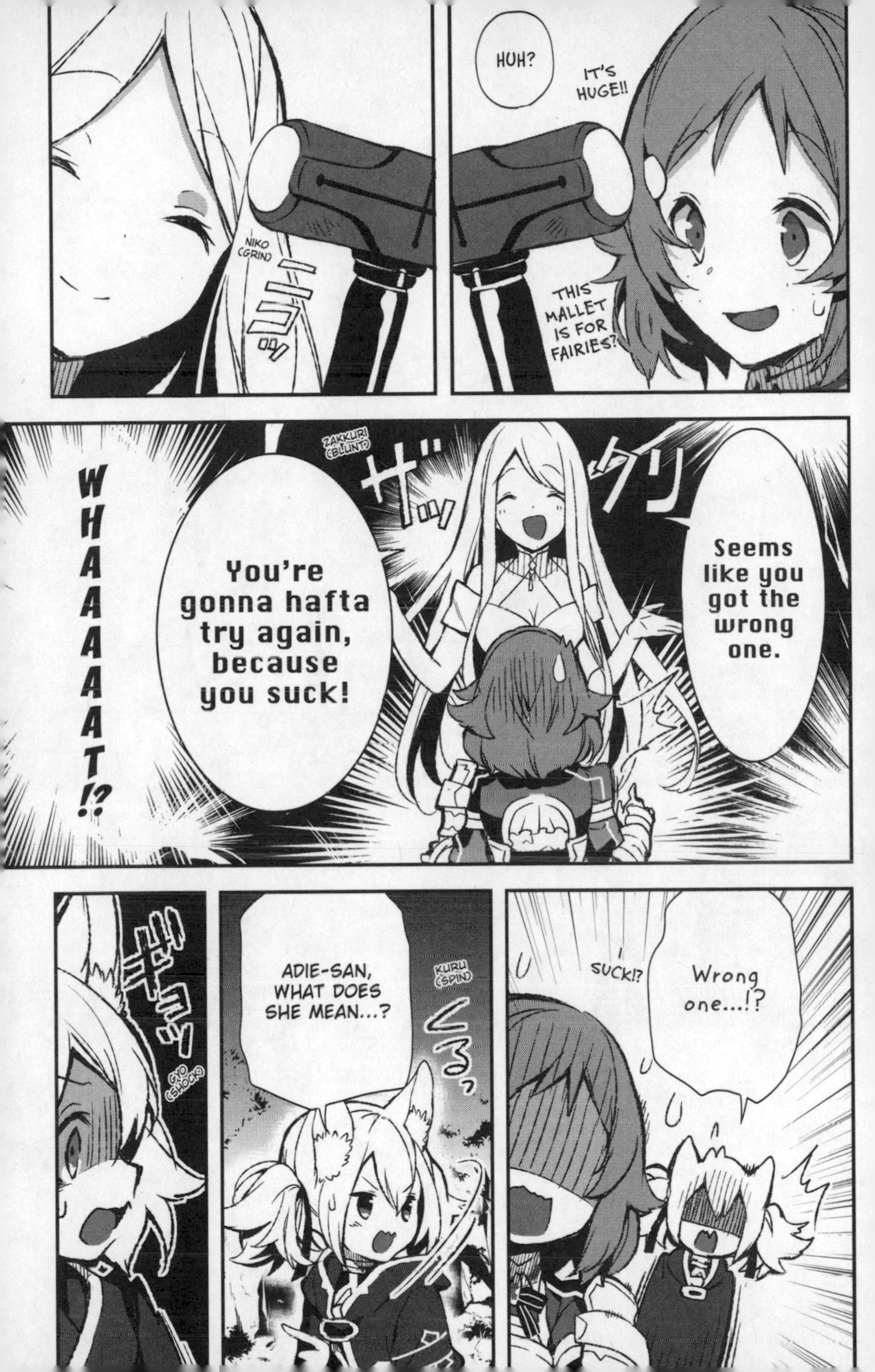
HUH?
IT'S HUGE!!
THIS MALLET IS FOR FAIRIES!?
NIKO (GRIN)
Seems like you got the wrong one.
ZAKKURI (BLUNT)
You're gonna hafta try again, because you suck!
WHAAAAAAAT!?
Wrong one...!?
SUCK!?
KURU (SPIN)
ADIE-SAN, WHAT DOES SHE MEAN...?
GYO (SHOCK)

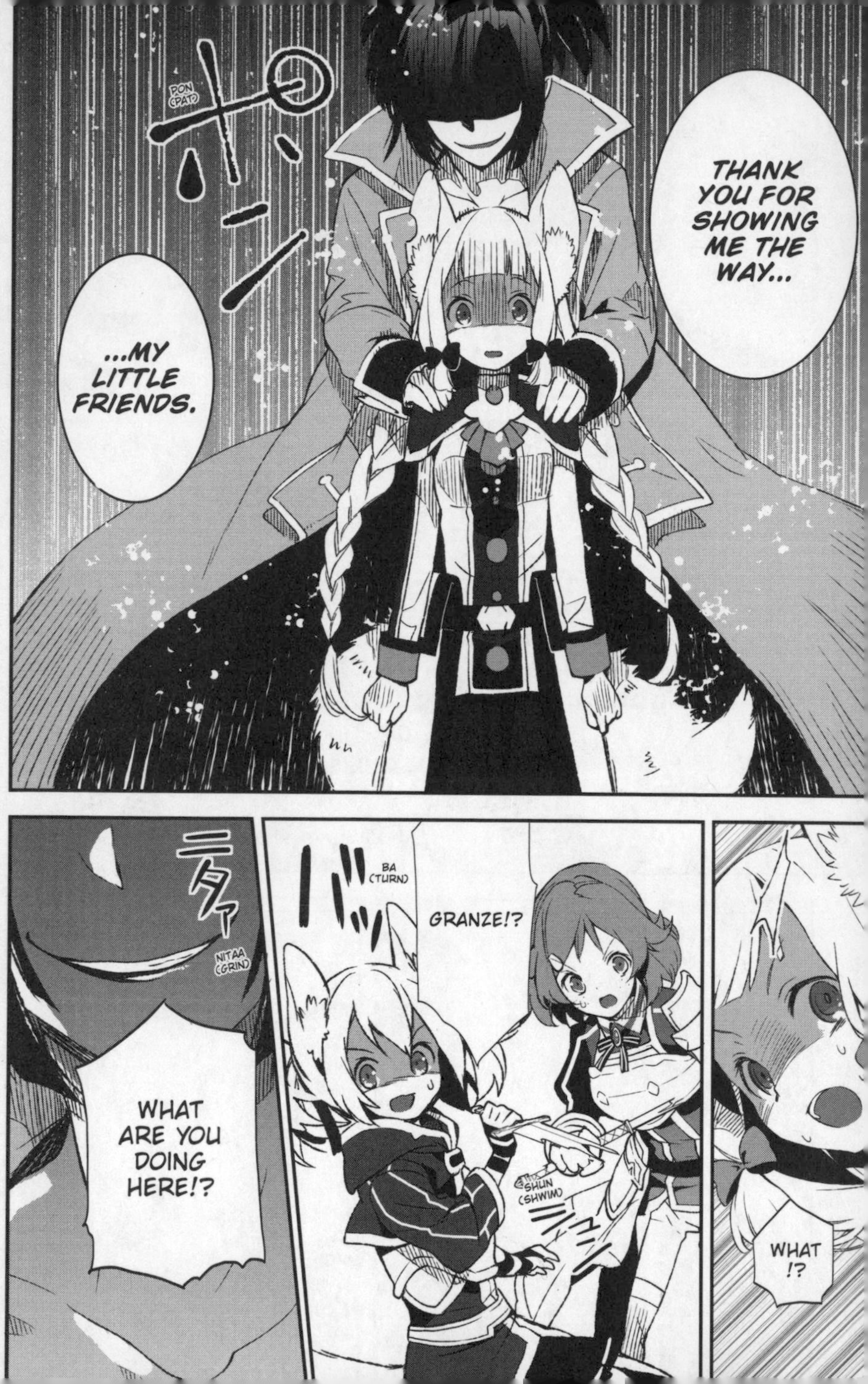

PON (PAT)
THANK YOU FOR SHOWING ME THE WAY...
...MY LITTLE FRIENDS.
WHAT!?
BA (TURN)
GRANZE!?
SHUN (SHWIM)
NITAA (GRIN)
WHAT ARE YOU DOING HERE!?

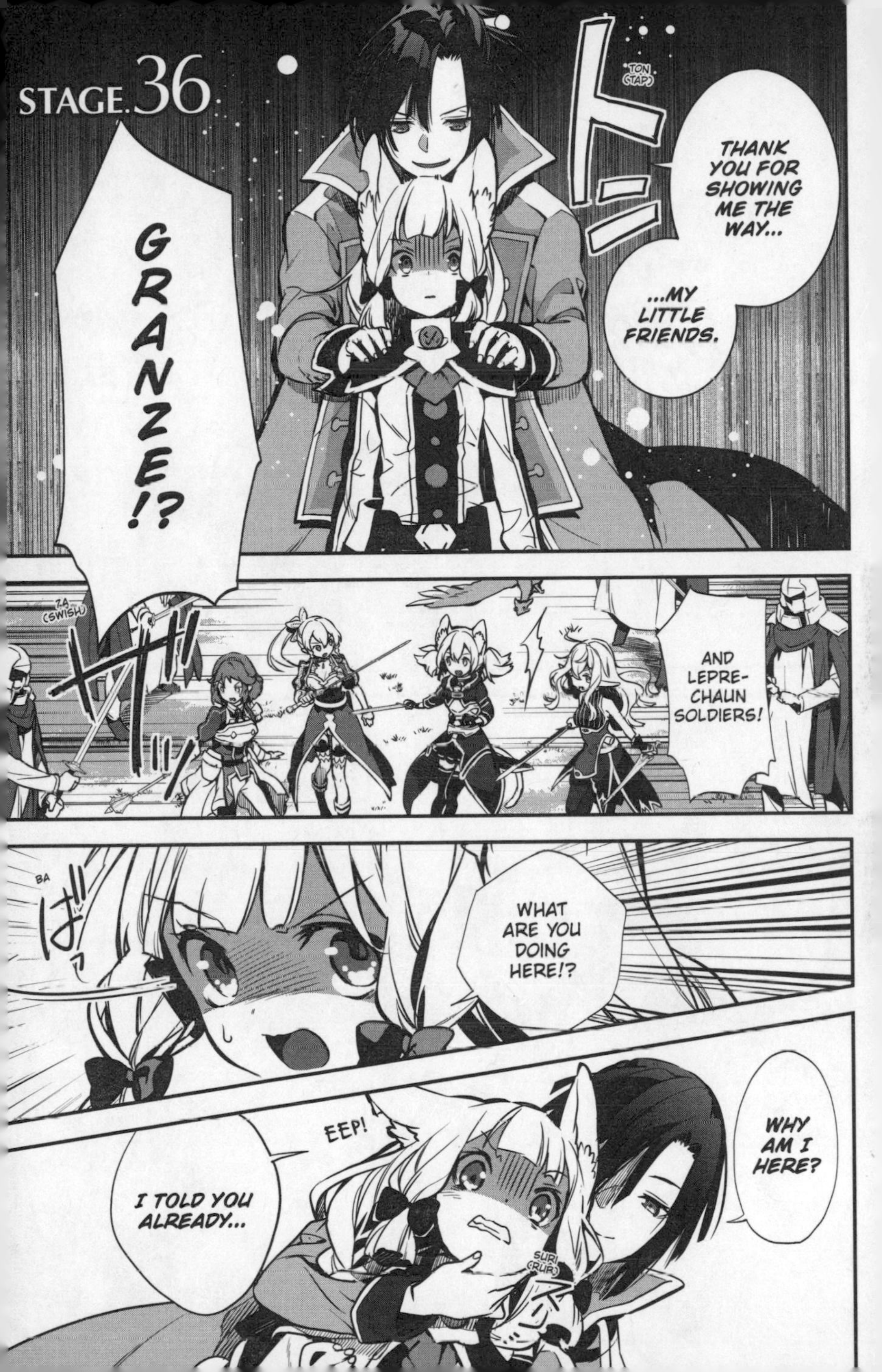
STAGE.36
TON (TAP)
THANK YOU FOR SHOWING ME THE WAY...
...MY LITTLE FRIENDS.
GRANZE!?
AND LEPRE-CHAUN SOLDIERS!
ZA (SWISH)
WHAT ARE YOU DOING HERE!?
BA
WHY AM I HERE?
EEP!
SURI (RUB)
I TOLD YOU ALREADY...

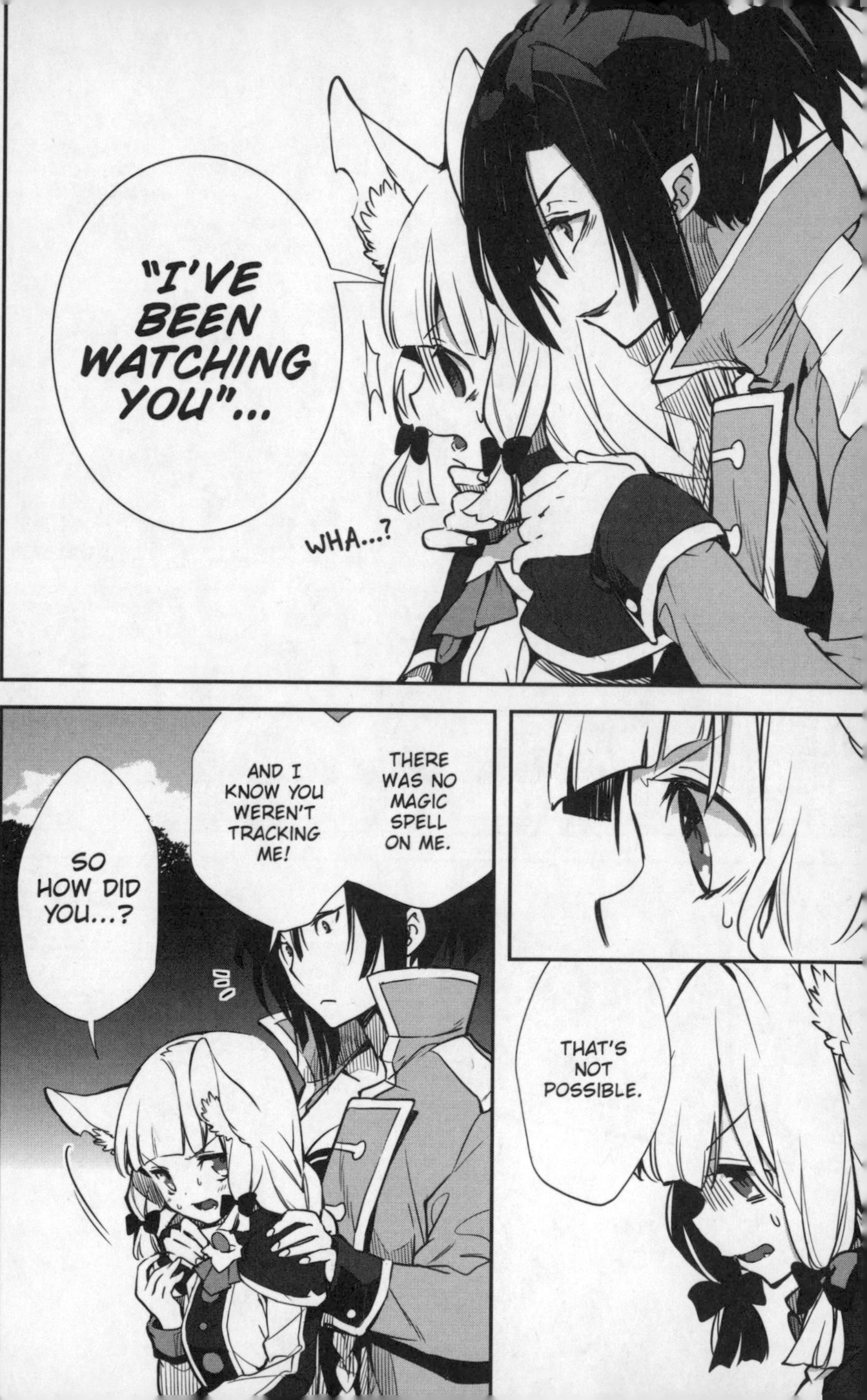
"I'VE BEEN WATCHING YOU"...
WHA...?
THAT'S NOT POSSIBLE.
THERE WAS NO MAGIC SPELL ON ME.
AND I KNOW YOU WEREN'T TRACKING ME!
SO HOW DID YOU...?

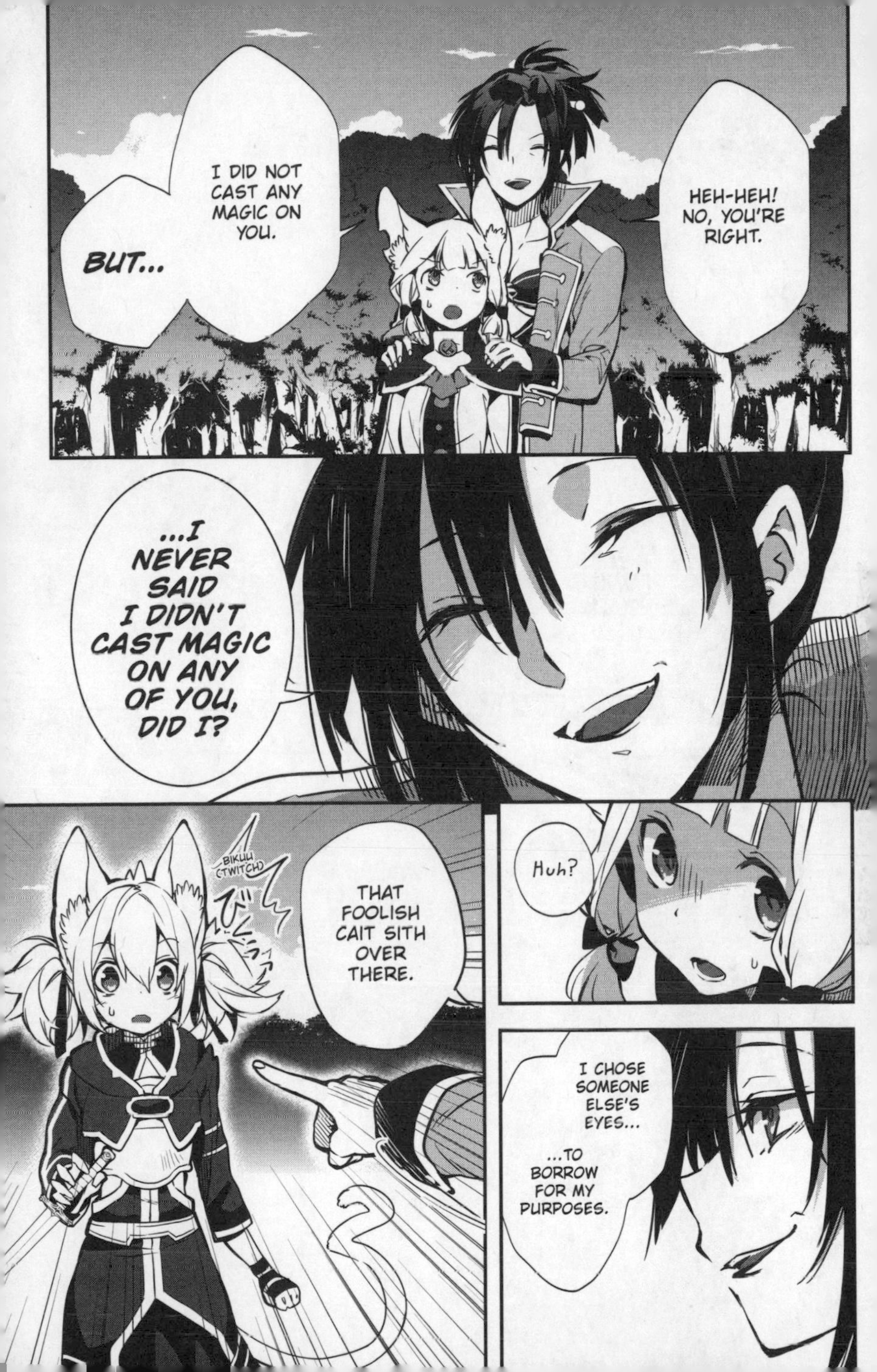

HEH-HEH! NO, YOU'RE RIGHT.
I DID NOT CAST ANY MAGIC ON YOU.
BUT...
...I NEVER SAID I DIDN'T CAST MAGIC ON ANY OF YOU, DID I?
Huh?
I CHOSE SOMEONE ELSE'S EYES...
...TO BORROW FOR MY PURPOSES.
THAT FOOLISH CAIT SITH OVER THERE.
BIKUU (TWITCH)

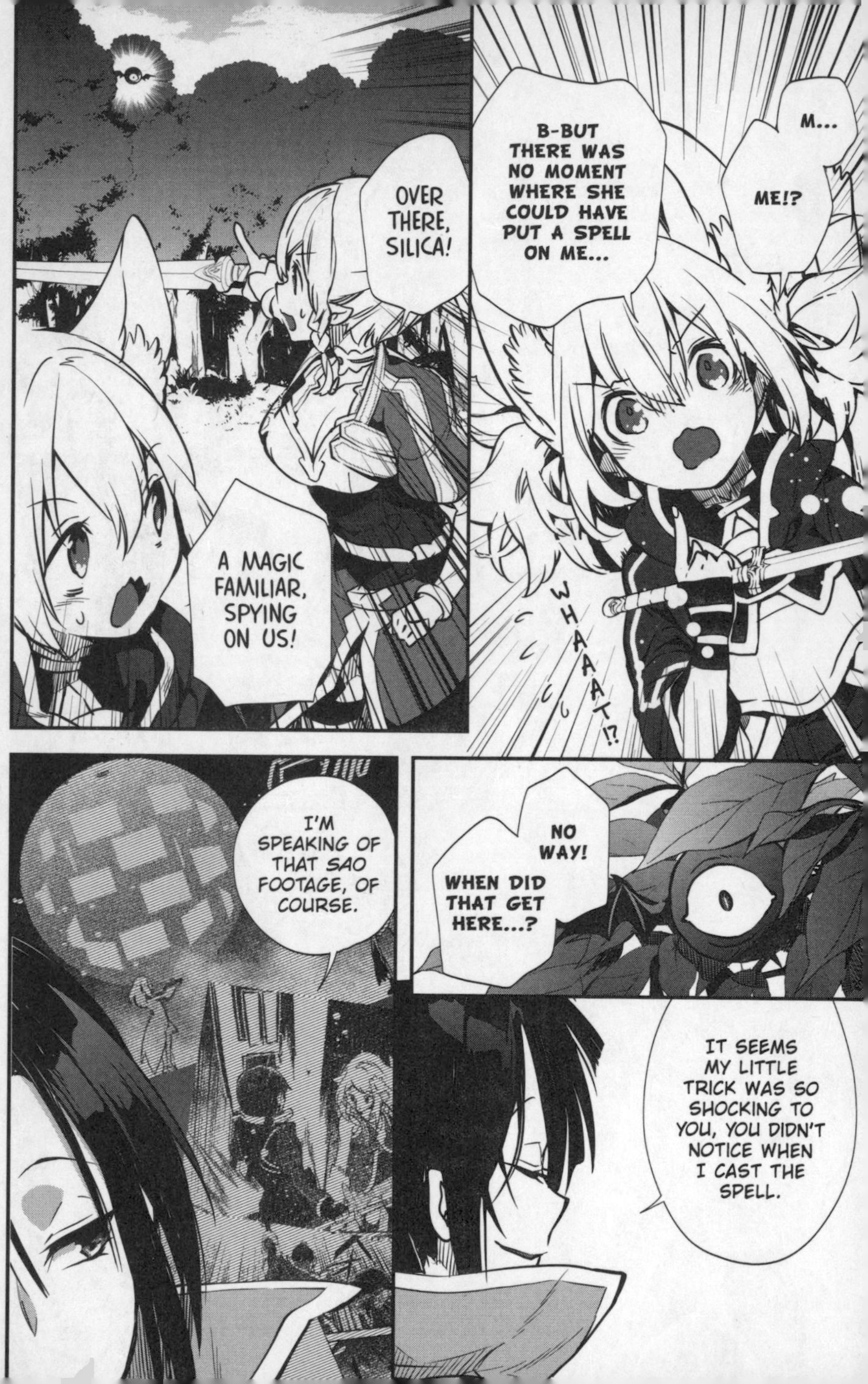
M...
ME!?
B-BUT THERE WAS NO MOMENT WHERE SHE COULD HAVE PUT A SPELL ON ME...
WHAAAAT!?
OVER THERE, SILICA!
A MAGIC FAMILIAR, SPYING ON US!
NO WAY!
WHEN DID THAT GET HERE...?
I'M SPEAKING OF THAT SAO FOOTAGE, OF COURSE.
IT SEEMS MY LITTLE TRICK WAS SO SHOCKING TO YOU, YOU DIDN'T NOTICE WHEN I CAST THE SPELL.

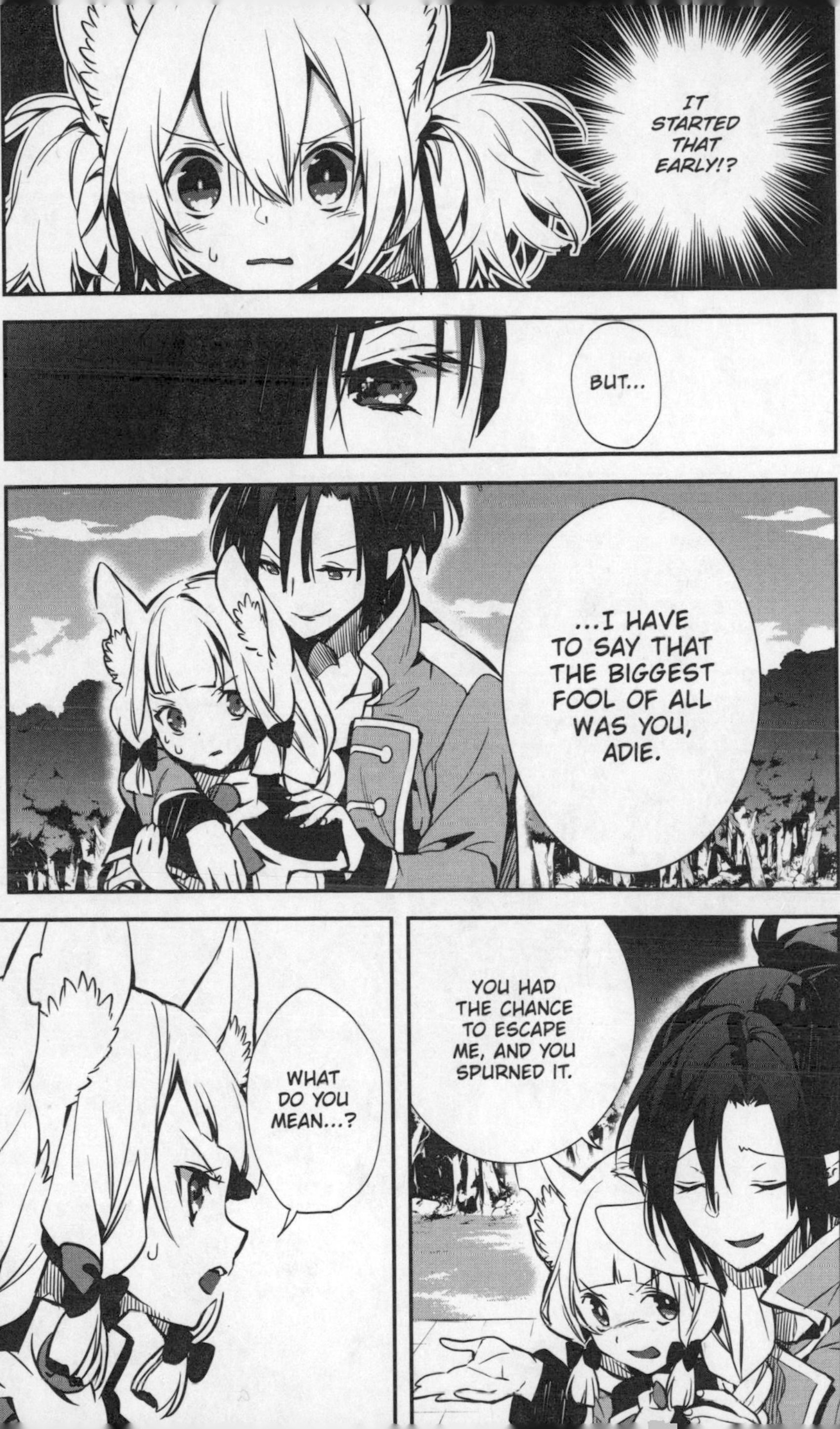
IT STARTED THAT EARLY!?
BUT...
...I HAVE TO SAY THAT THE BIGGEST FOOL OF ALL WAS YOU, ADIE.
WHAT DO YOU MEAN...?
YOU HAD THE CHANCE TO ESCAPE ME, AND YOU SPURNED IT.

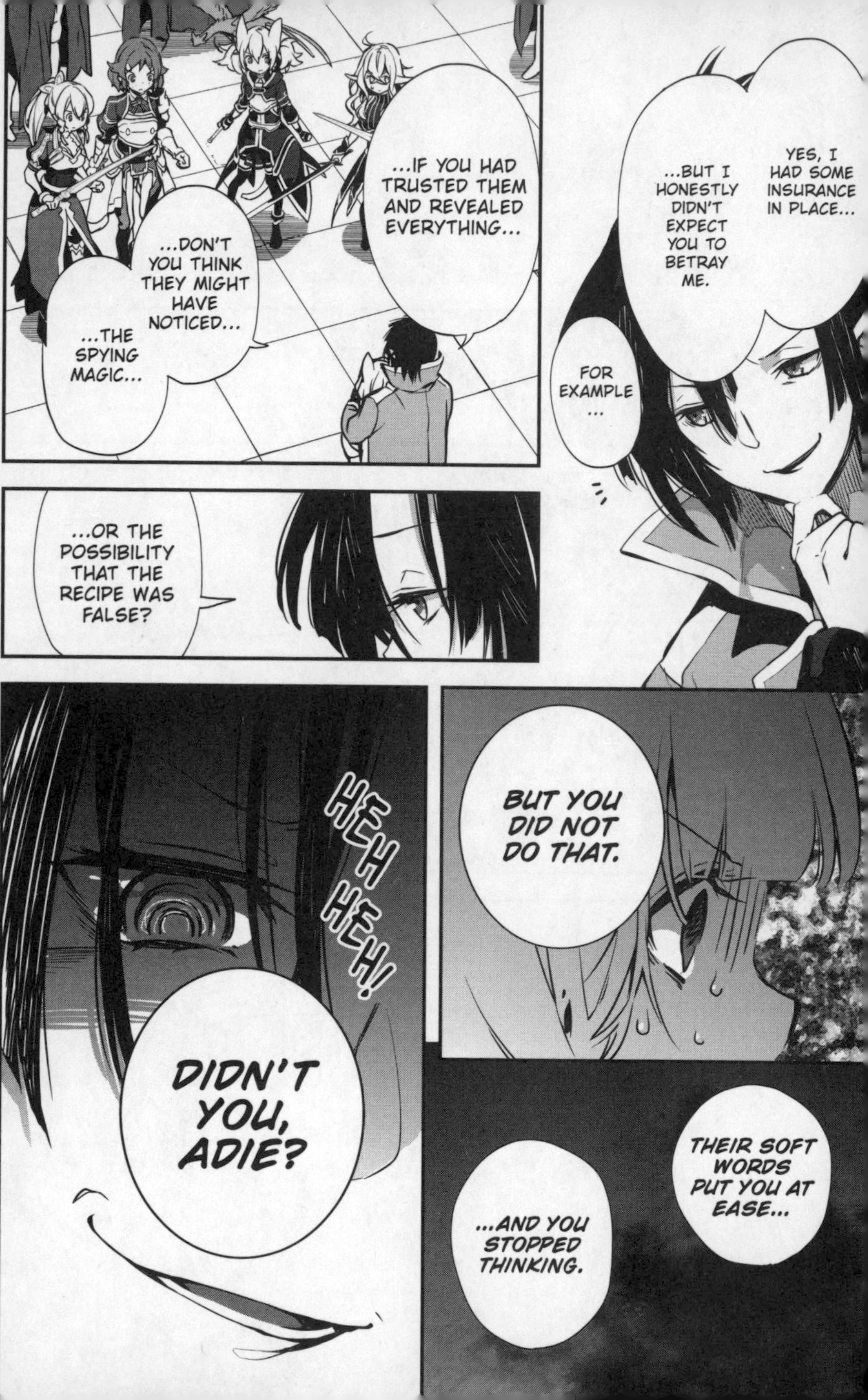
YES, I HAD SOME INSURANCE IN PLACE...
...BUT I HONESTLY DIDN'T EXPECT YOU TO BETRAY ME.
FOR EXAMPLE ...
...IF YOU HAD TRUSTED THEM AND REVEALED EVERYTHING...
...DON'T YOU THINK THEY MIGHT HAVE NOTICED...
...THE SPYING MAGIC...
...OR THE POSSIBILITY THAT THE RECIPE WAS FALSE?
BUT YOU DID NOT DO THAT.
HEH HEH HEH!
DIDN'T YOU, ADIE?
THEIR SOFT WORDS PUT YOU AT EASE...
...AND YOU STOPPED THINKING.

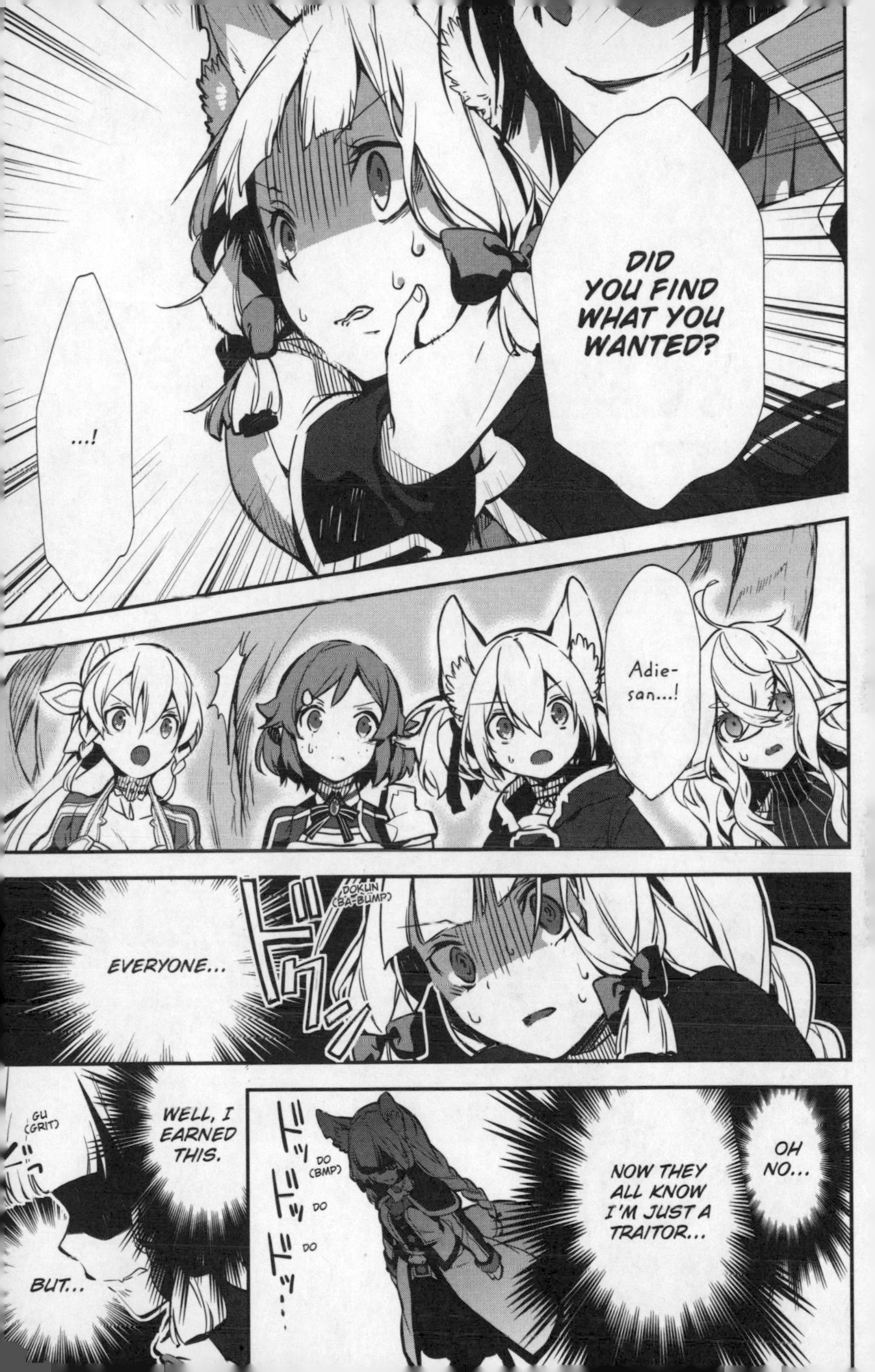
DID YOU FIND WHAT YOU WANTED?
...!
Adie-san...!
DOKUN (BA-BUMP)
EVERYONE...
OH NO...
NOW THEY ALL KNOW I'M JUST A TRAITOR...
DO (BMP)
DO
DO
WELL, I EARNED THIS.
GU (GRIT)
BUT...

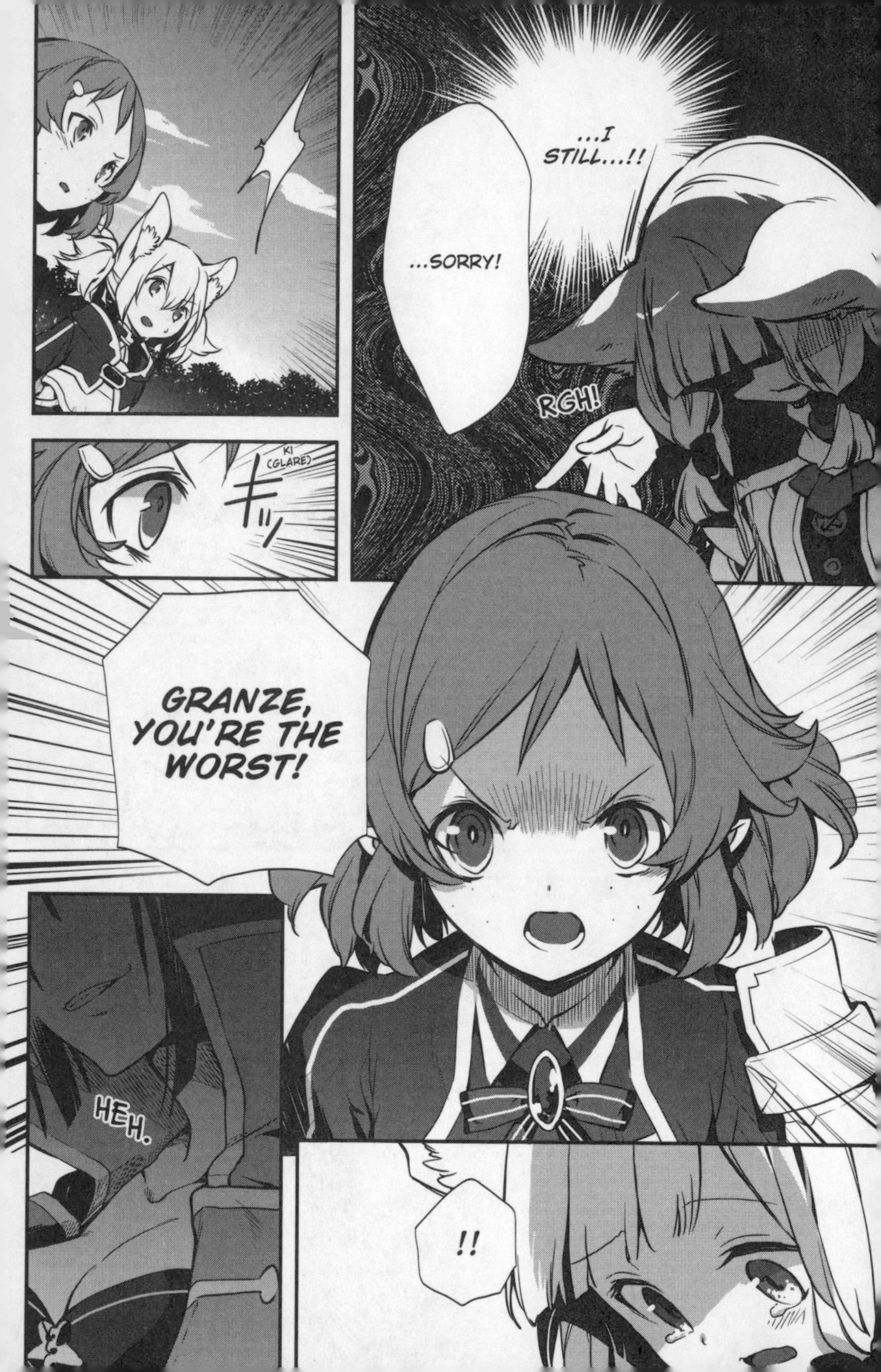
...I STILL...!!
...SORRY!
RGH!
KI (GLARE)
GRANZE, YOU'RE THE WORST!
HEH.
!!

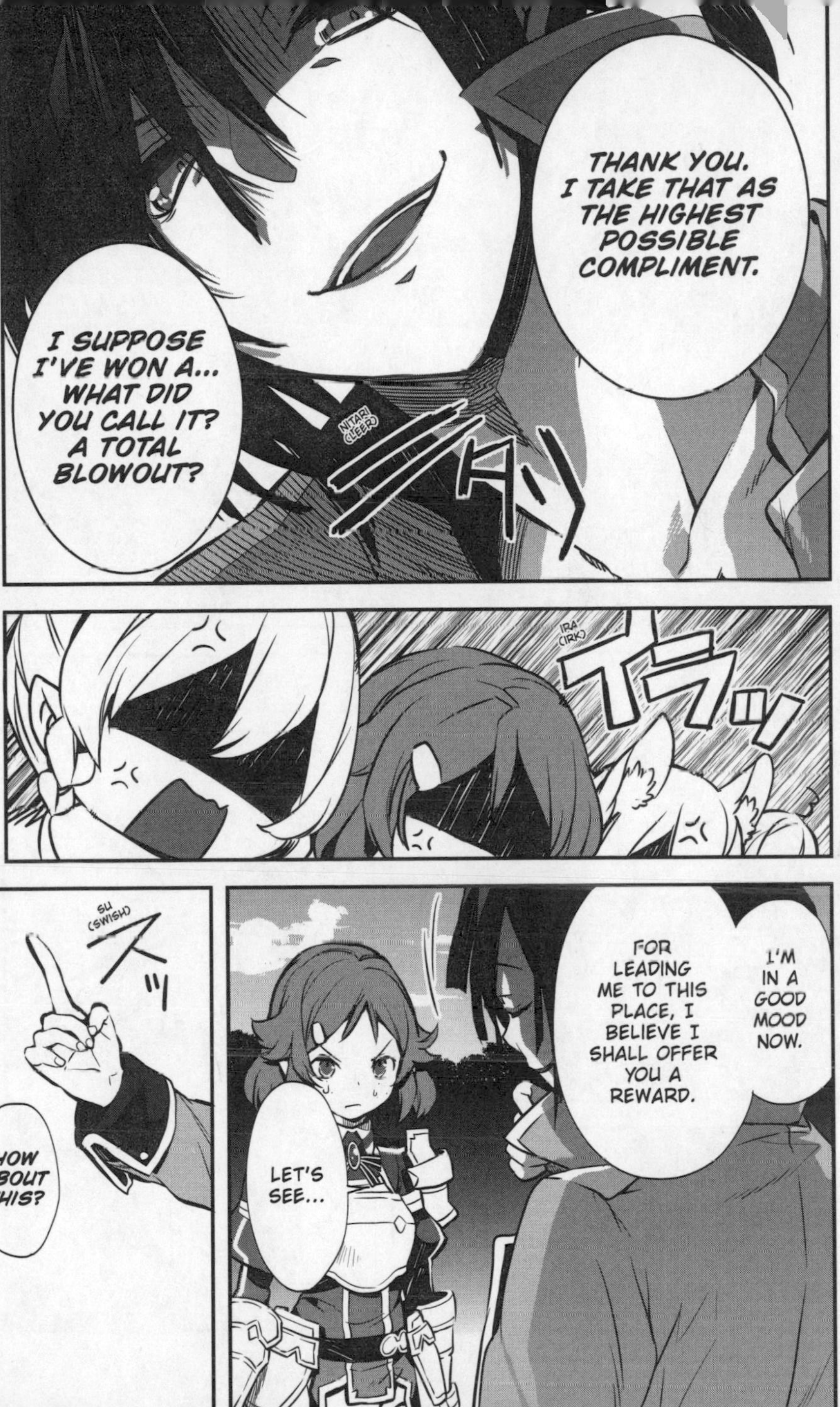

THANK YOU. I TAKE THAT AS THE HIGHEST POSSIBLE COMPLIMENT.
I SUPPOSE I'VE WON A... WHAT DID YOU CALL IT? A TOTAL BLOWOUT?
NITARI (LEER)
IRA (IRK)
I'M IN A GOOD MOOD NOW.
FOR LEADING ME TO THIS PLACE, I BELIEVE I SHALL OFFER YOU A REWARD.
LET'S SEE...
SU (SWISH)
HOW ABOUT THIS?

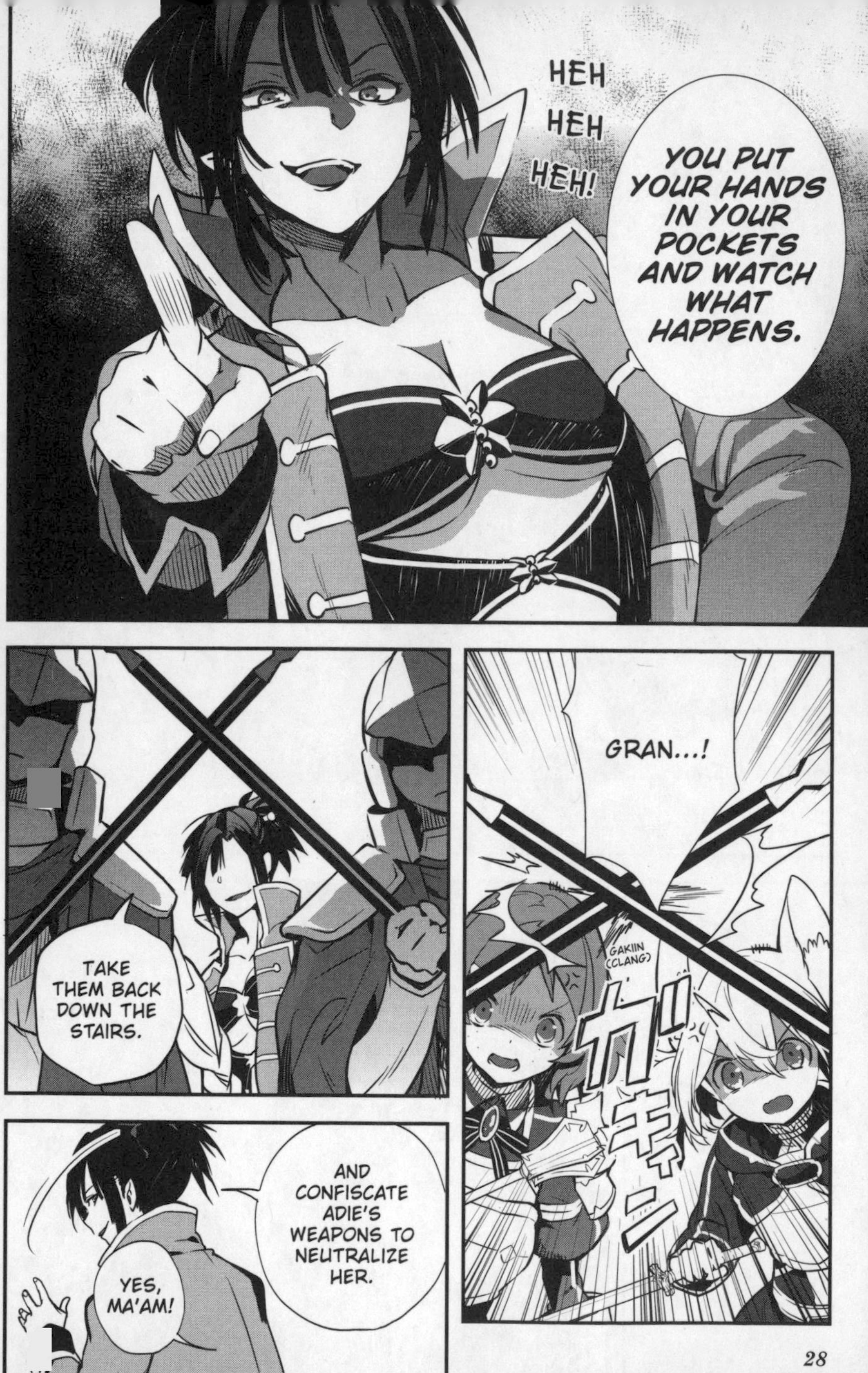
HEH HEH HEH!
YOU PUT YOUR HANDS IN YOUR POCKETS AND WATCH WHAT HAPPENS.
GRAN...!
GAKIIN (CLANG)
TAKE THEM BACK DOWN THE STAIRS.
AND CONFISCATE ADIE'S WEAPONS TO NEUTRALIZE HER.
YES, MA'AM!

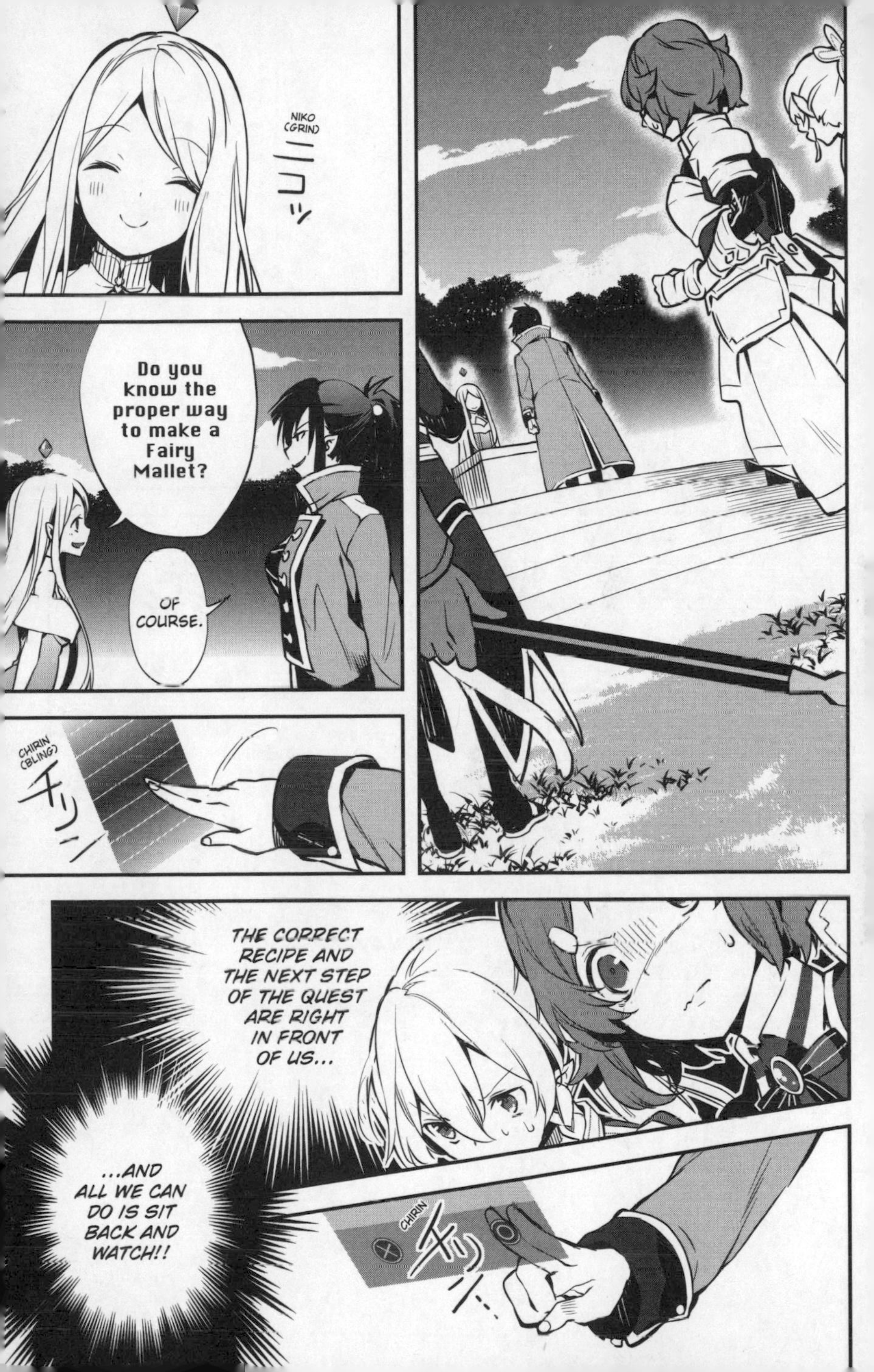
NIKO (GRIN)
ニコッ
Do you know the proper way to make a Fairy Mallet?
OF COURSE.
CHIRIN (BLING)
チリーン
THE CORRECT RECIPE AND THE NEXT STEP OF THE QUEST ARE RIGHT IN FRONT OF US...
...AND ALL WE CAN DO IS SIT BACK AND WATCH!!
CHIRIN
チリン

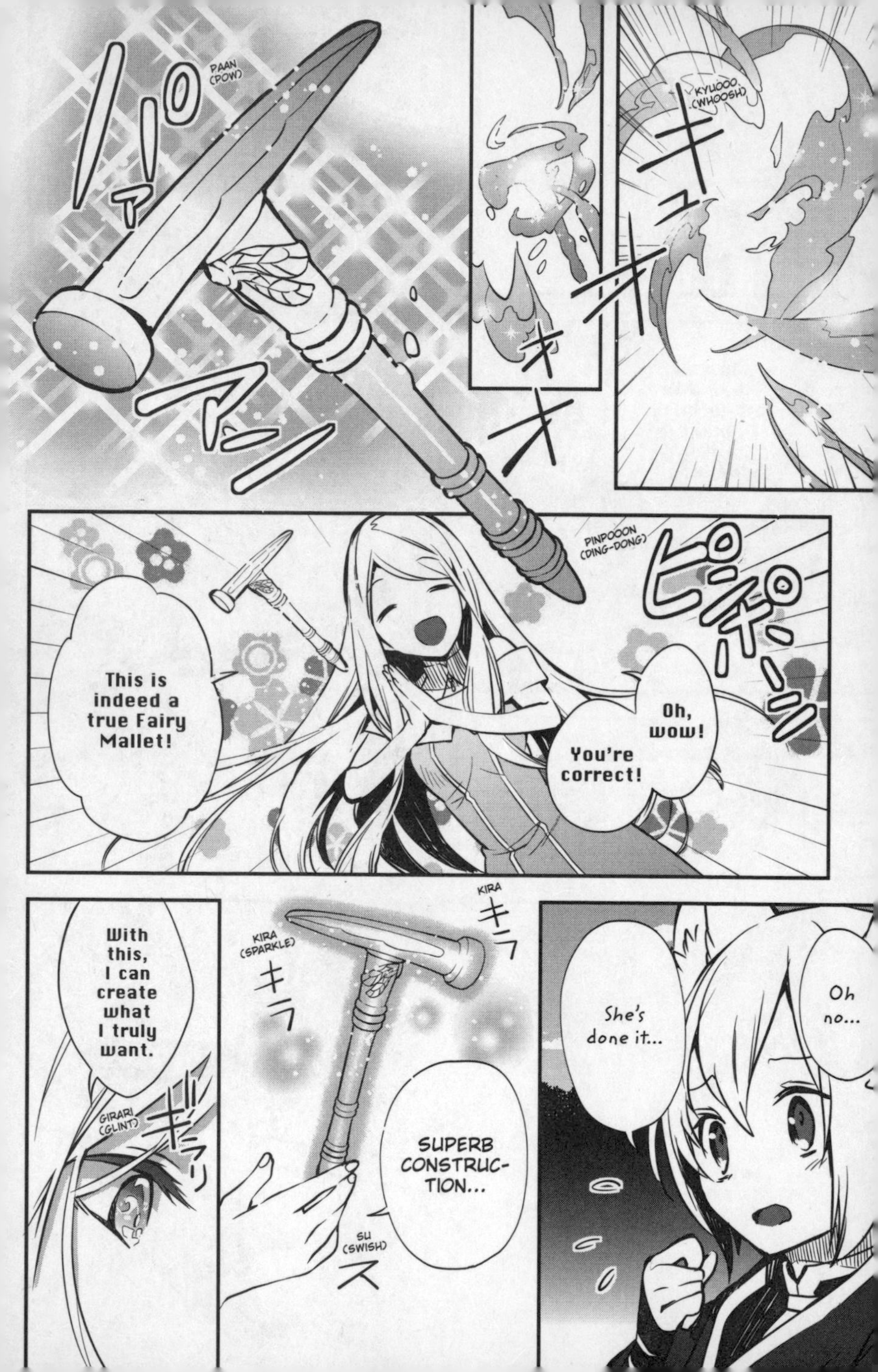
KYUOOO (WHOOSH)
PAAN (POW)
PINPOOON (DING-DONG)
Oh, wow! You're correct!
This is indeed a true Fairy Mallet!
Oh no...
She's done it...
KIRA
KIRA (SPARKLE)
SUPERB CONSTRUC-TION...
SU (SWISH)
With this, I can create what I truly want.
GIRARI (GLINT)

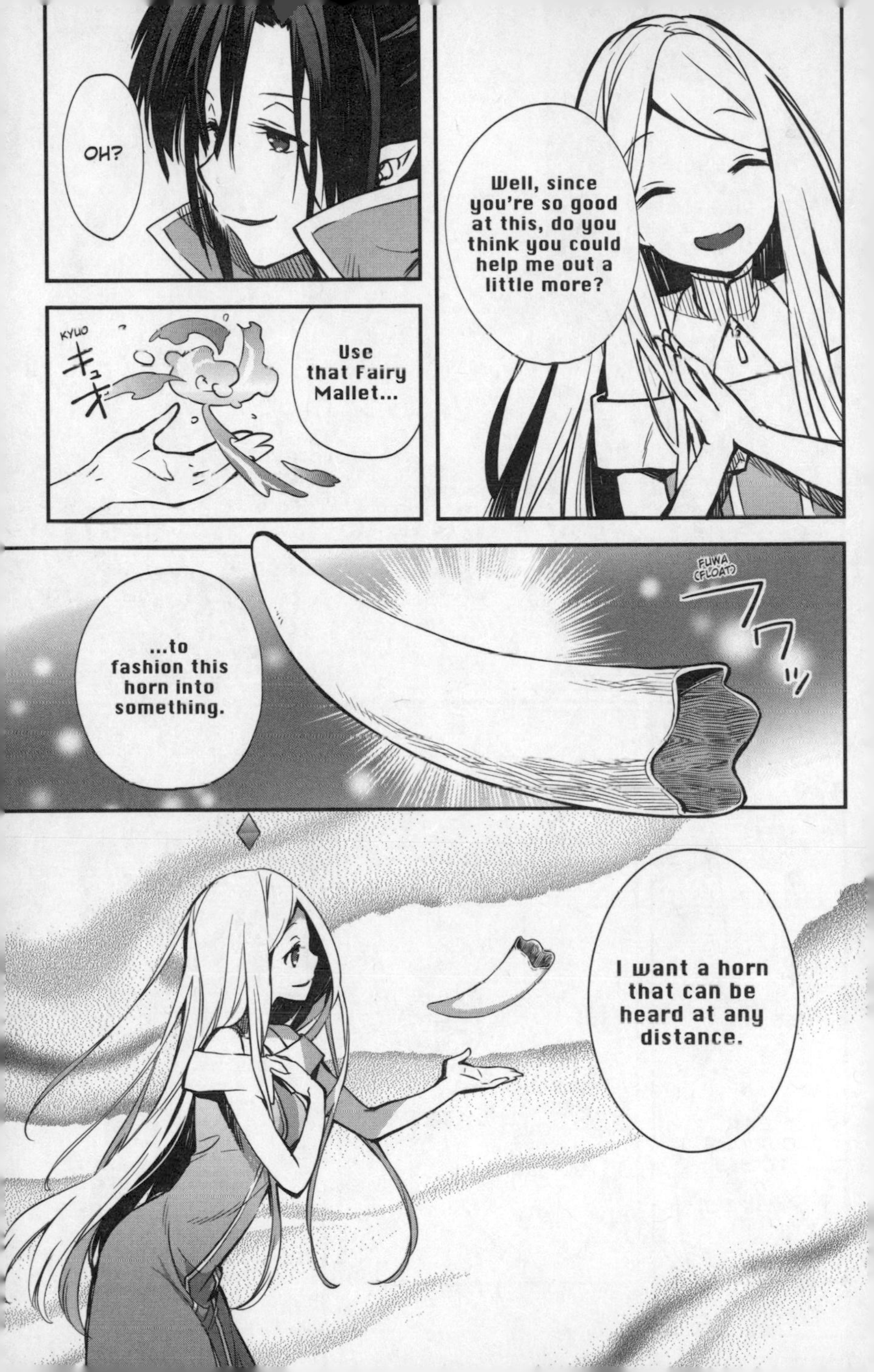
Well, since you're so good at this, do you think you could help me out a little more?
OH?
Use that Fairy Mallet...
KYUO
キュオ
FUWA (FLOAT)
フワッ
...to fashion this horn into something.
I want a horn that can be heard at any distance.

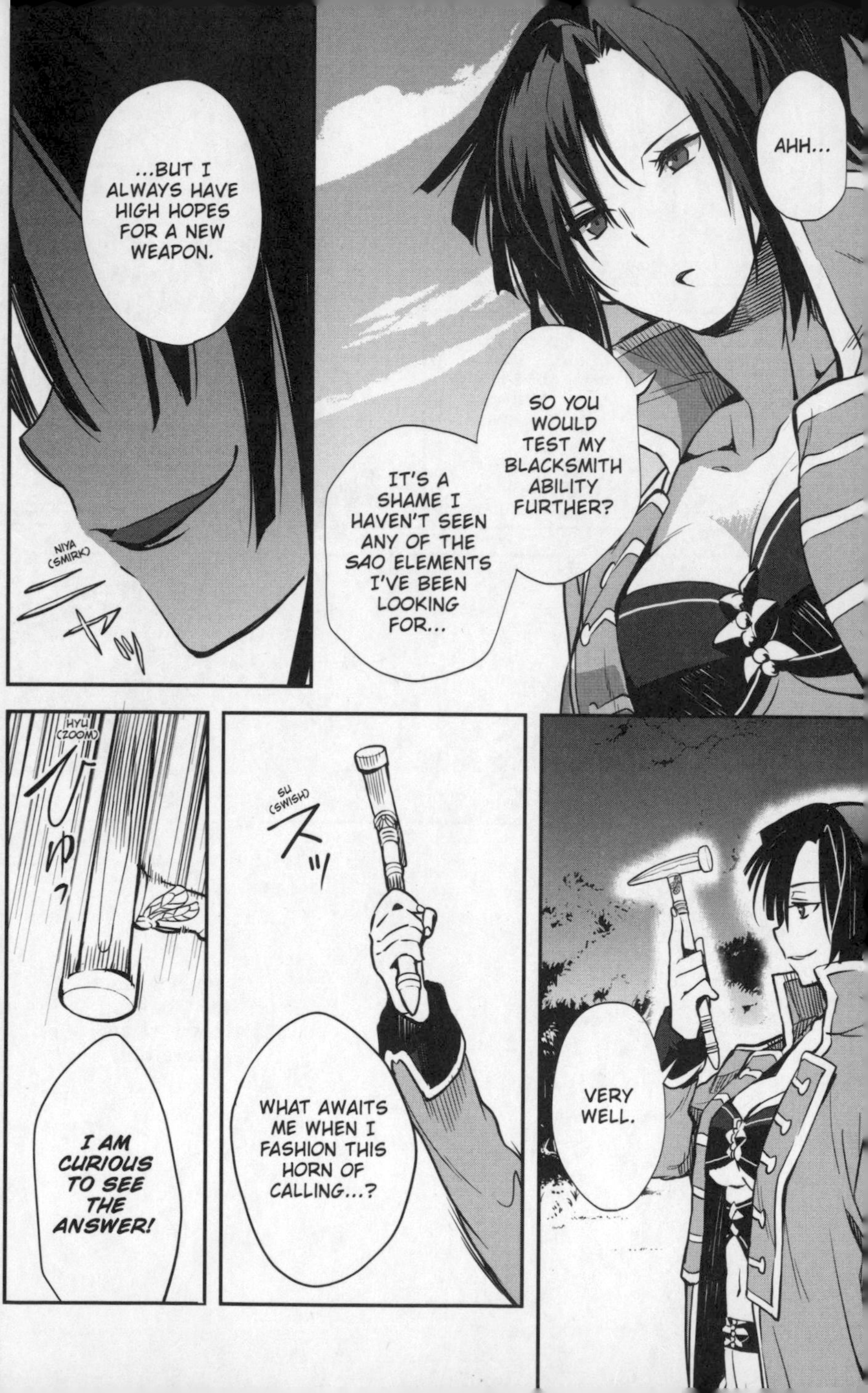
AHH...
SO YOU WOULD TEST MY BLACKSMITH ABILITY FURTHER?
IT'S A SHAME I HAVEN'T SEEN ANY OF THE SAO ELEMENTS I'VE BEEN LOOKING FOR...
...BUT I ALWAYS HAVE HIGH HOPES FOR A NEW WEAPON.
NIYA (SMIRK)
ニヤッ
VERY WELL.
SU (SWISH)
スッ
WHAT AWAITS ME WHEN I FASHION THIS HORN OF CALLING...?
HYU (ZOOM)
ひゅっ
I AM CURIOUS TO SEE THE ANSWER!

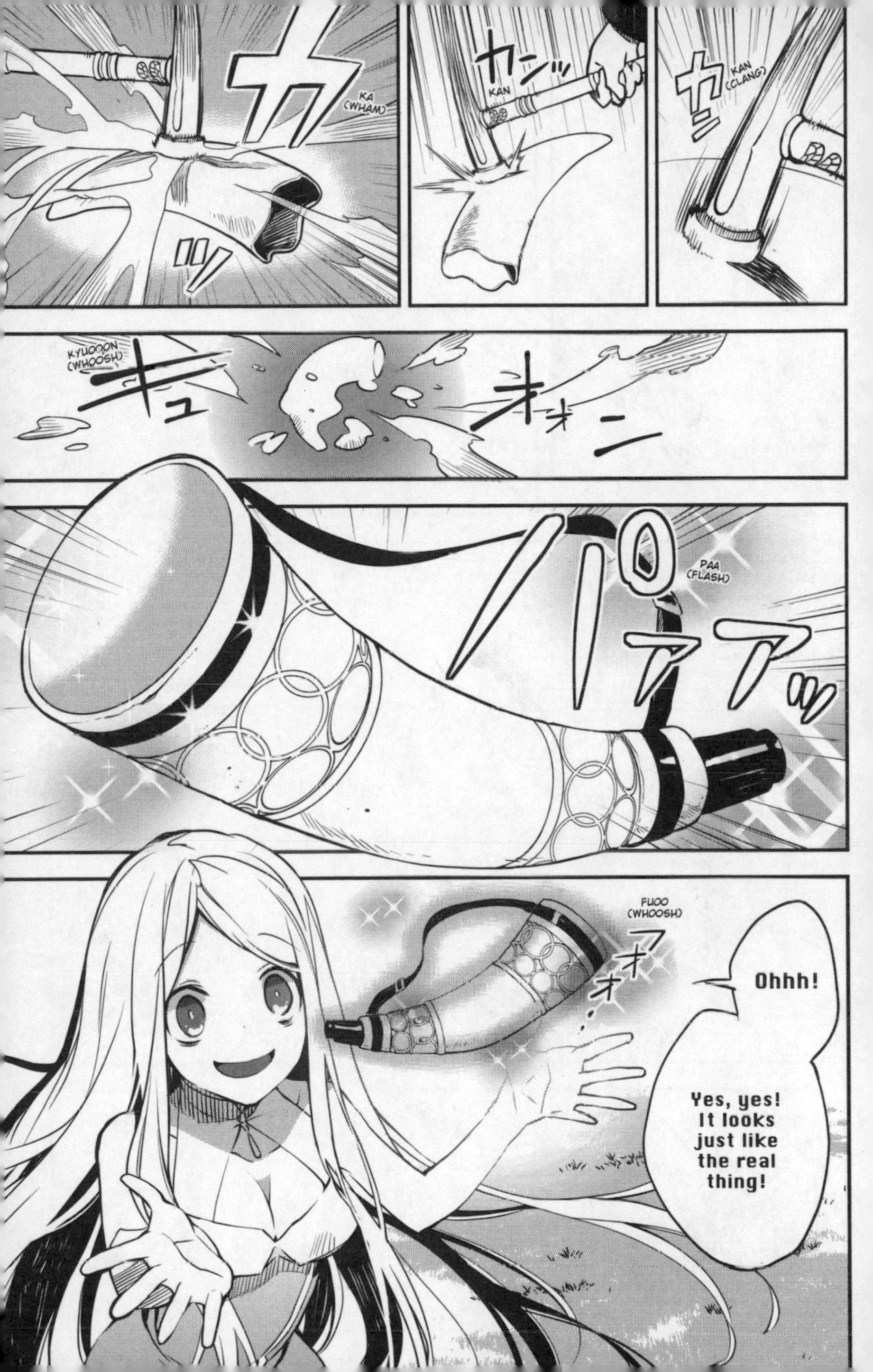

カンッ
KAN
カ〜ン
KAN (CLANG)
カ
KA (WHAM)
ゴッ
キュオオーン
KYUOOON (WHOOSH)
パアアッ
PAA (FLASH)
フオオ
FUOO (WHOOSH)
Ohhh!
Yes, yes! It looks just like the real thing!

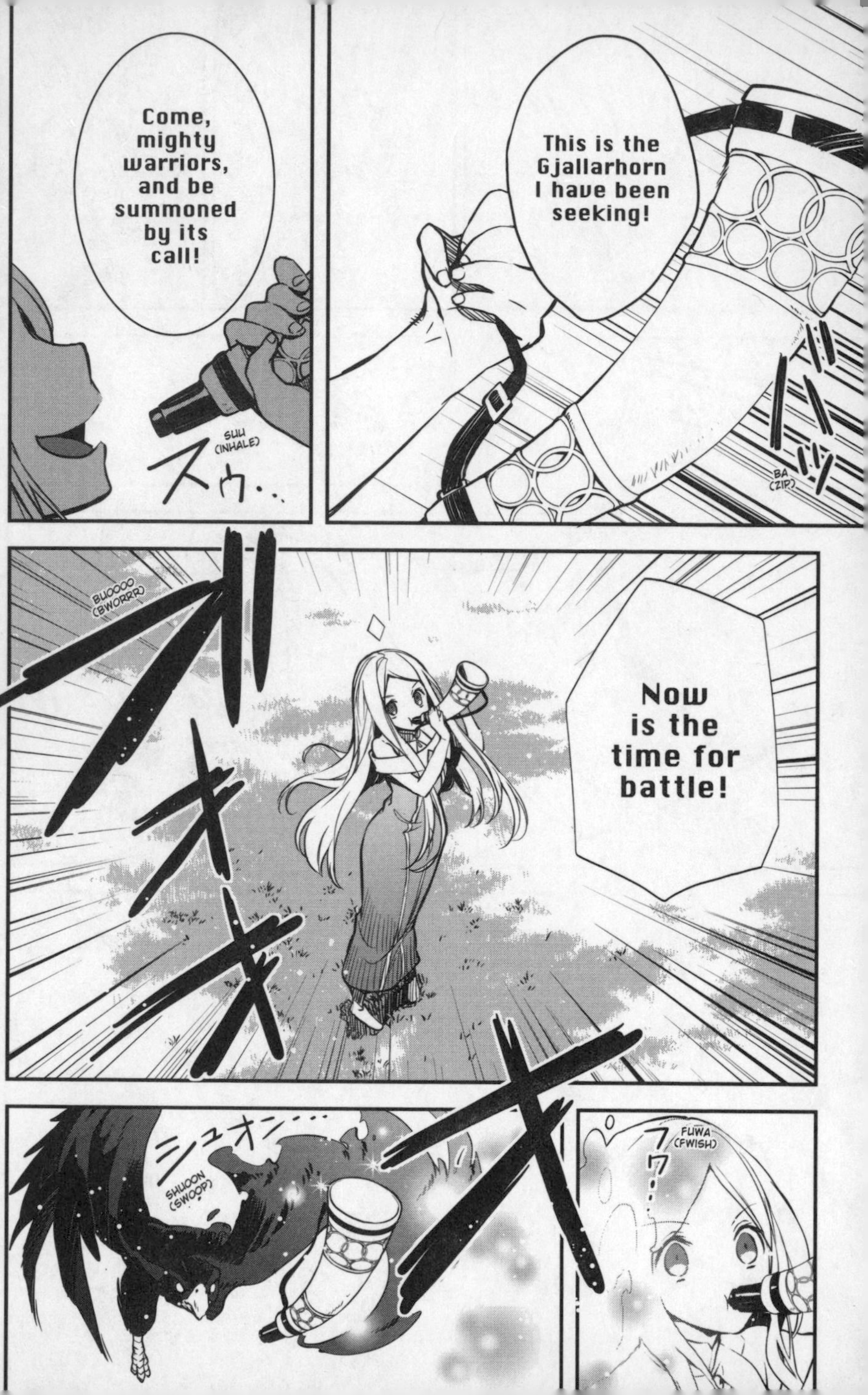
This is the Gjallarhorn I have been seeking!
BA (ZIP)
Come, mighty warriors, and be summoned by its call!
SUU (INHALE)
スゥ…
BUOOOO (BWORRR)
Now is the time for battle!
FUWA (FWISH)
フワ…
SHUOON (SWOOP)
シュオン…

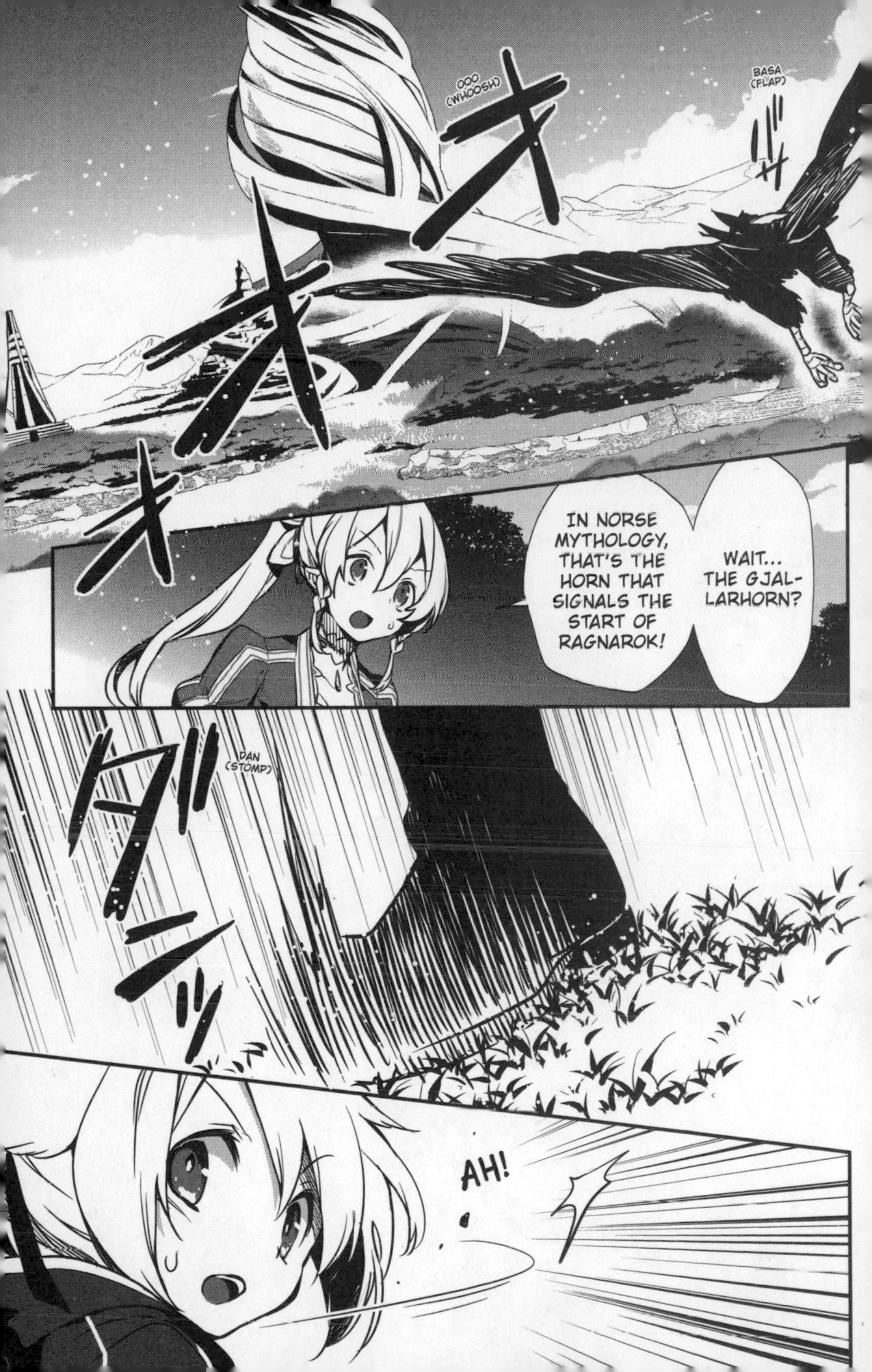
BASA
(FLAP)
OOO
(WHOOSH)
WAIT... THE GJAL-LARHORN?
IN NORSE MYTHOLOGY, THAT'S THE HORN THAT SIGNALS THE START OF RAGNAROK!
DAN
(STOMP)
AH!

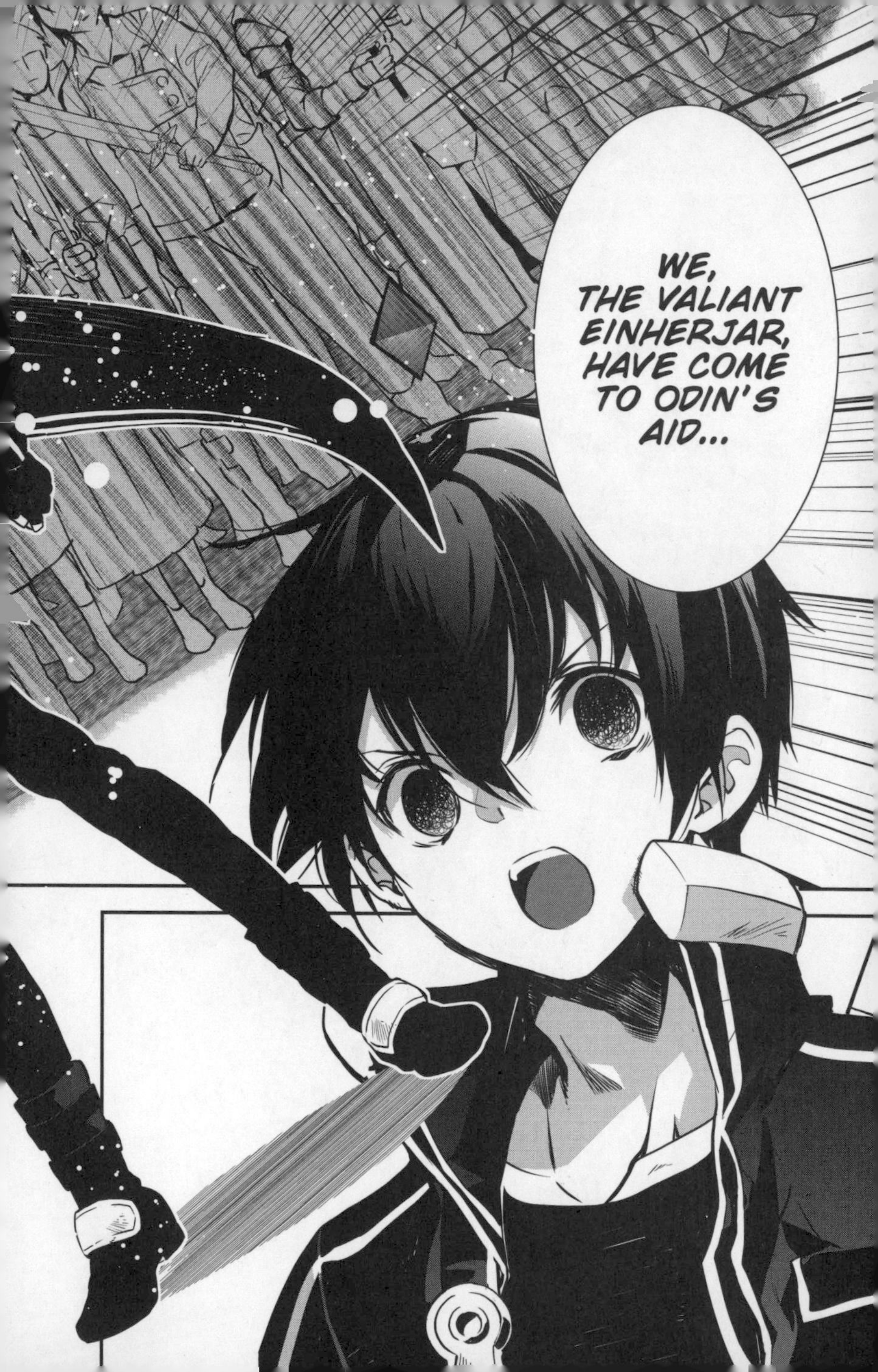
WE, THE VALIANT EINHERJAR, HAVE COME TO ODIN'S AID...

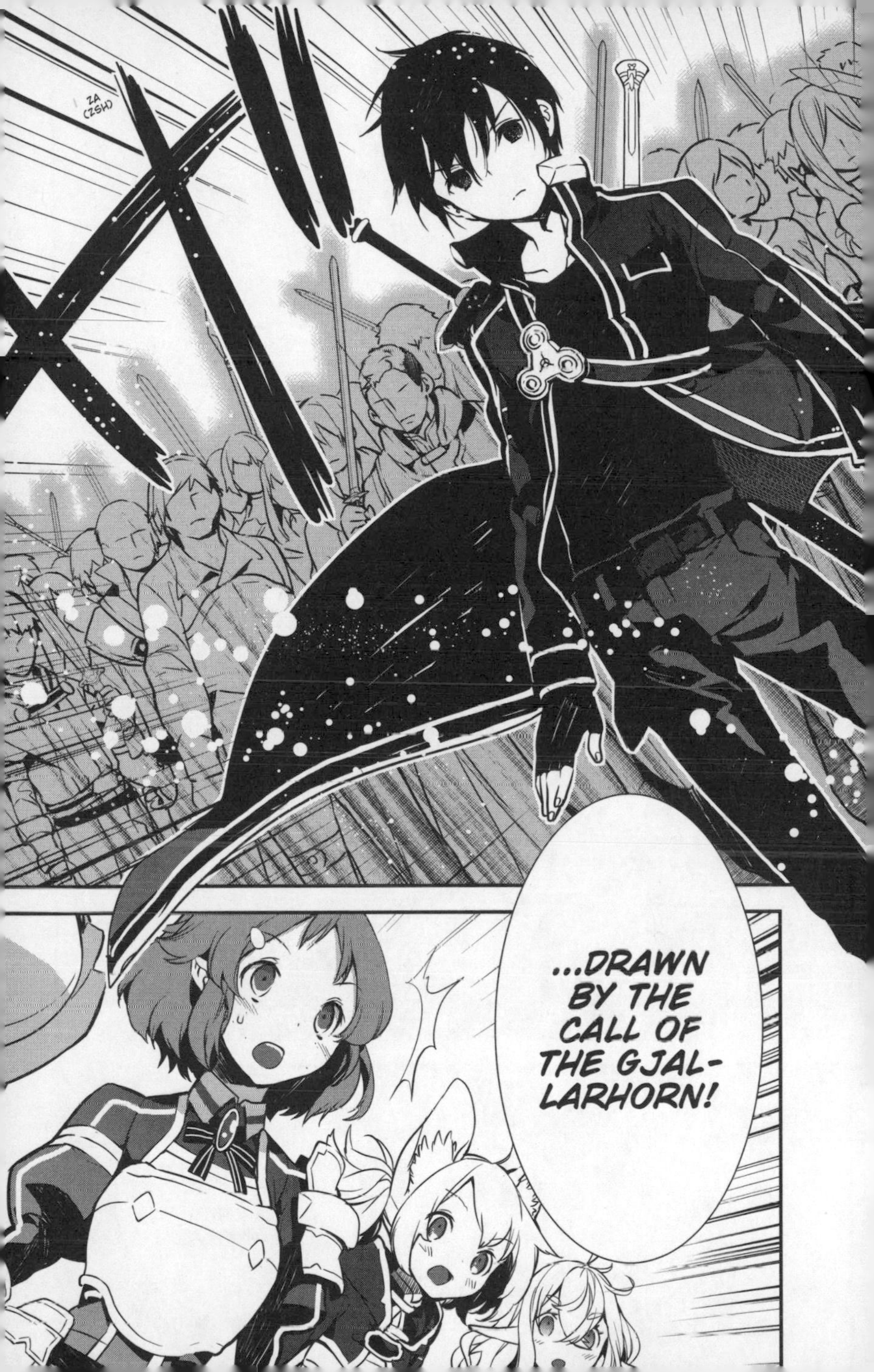
ZA (ZSH)
...DRAWN BY THE CALL OF THE GJAL-LARHORN!

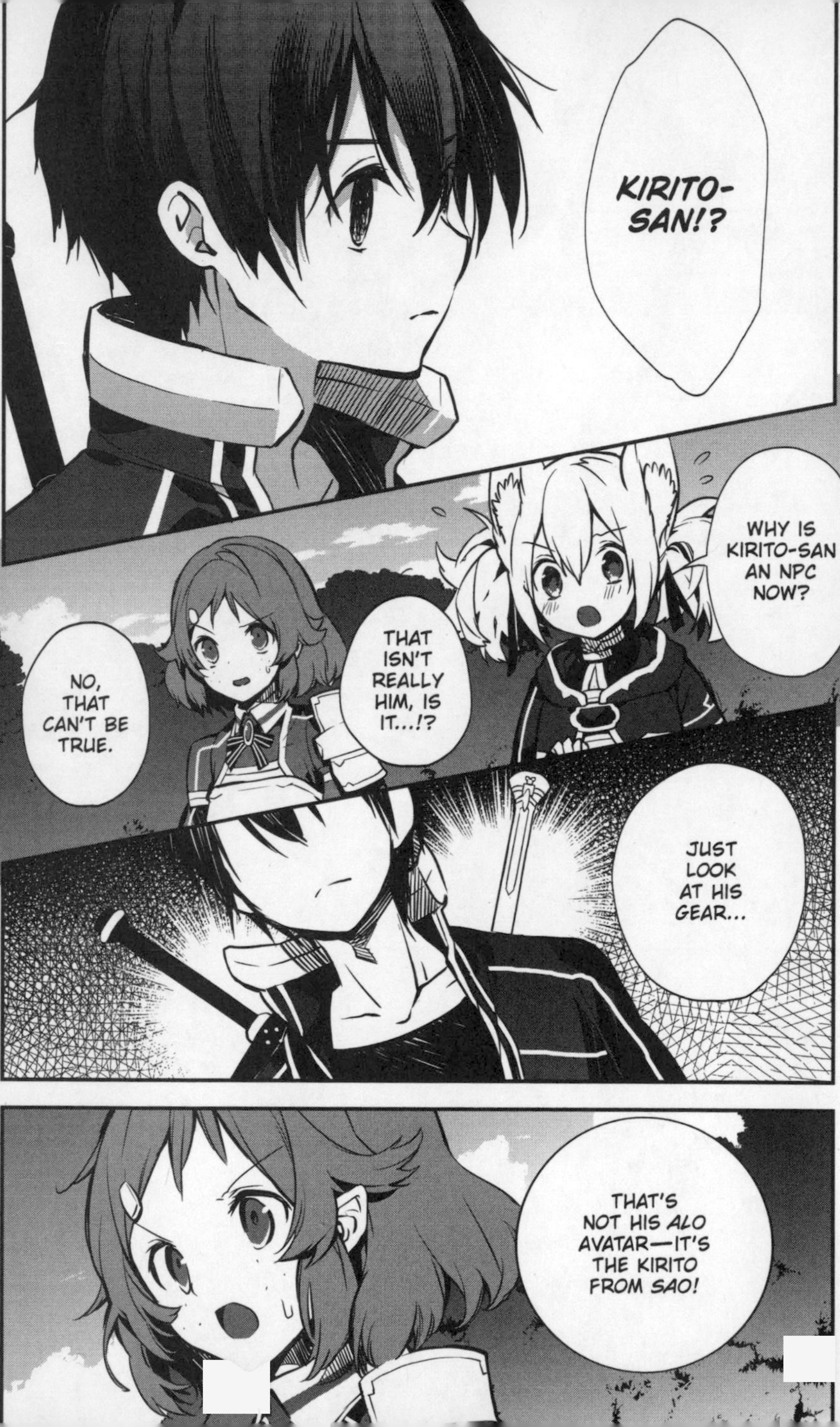
KIRITO-SAN!?
WHY IS KIRITO-SAN AN NPC NOW?
THAT ISN'T REALLY HIM, IS IT...!?
NO, THAT CAN'T BE TRUE.
JUST LOOK AT HIS GEAR...
THAT'S NOT HIS *ALO* AVATAR—IT'S THE KIRITO FROM *SAO*!

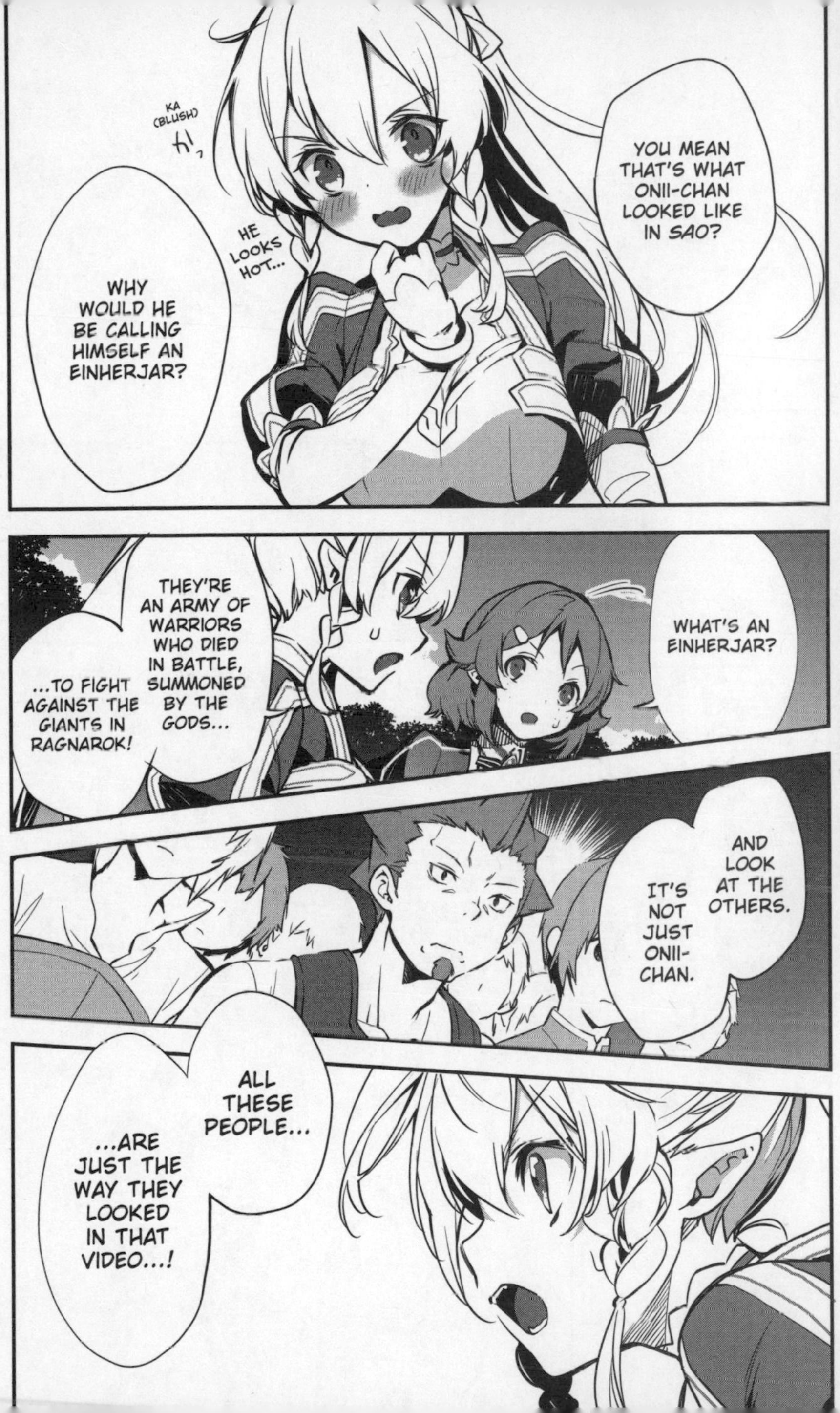
YOU MEAN THAT'S WHAT ONII-CHAN LOOKED LIKE IN SAO?
KA (BLUSH)
HE LOOKS HOT...
WHY WOULD HE BE CALLING HIMSELF AN EINHERJAR?
WHAT'S AN EINHERJAR?
THEY'RE AN ARMY OF WARRIORS WHO DIED IN BATTLE, SUMMONED BY THE GODS...
...TO FIGHT AGAINST THE GIANTS IN RAGNAROK!
AND LOOK AT THE OTHERS.
IT'S NOT JUST ONII-CHAN.
ALL THESE PEOPLE...
...ARE JUST THE WAY THEY LOOKED IN THAT VIDEO...!

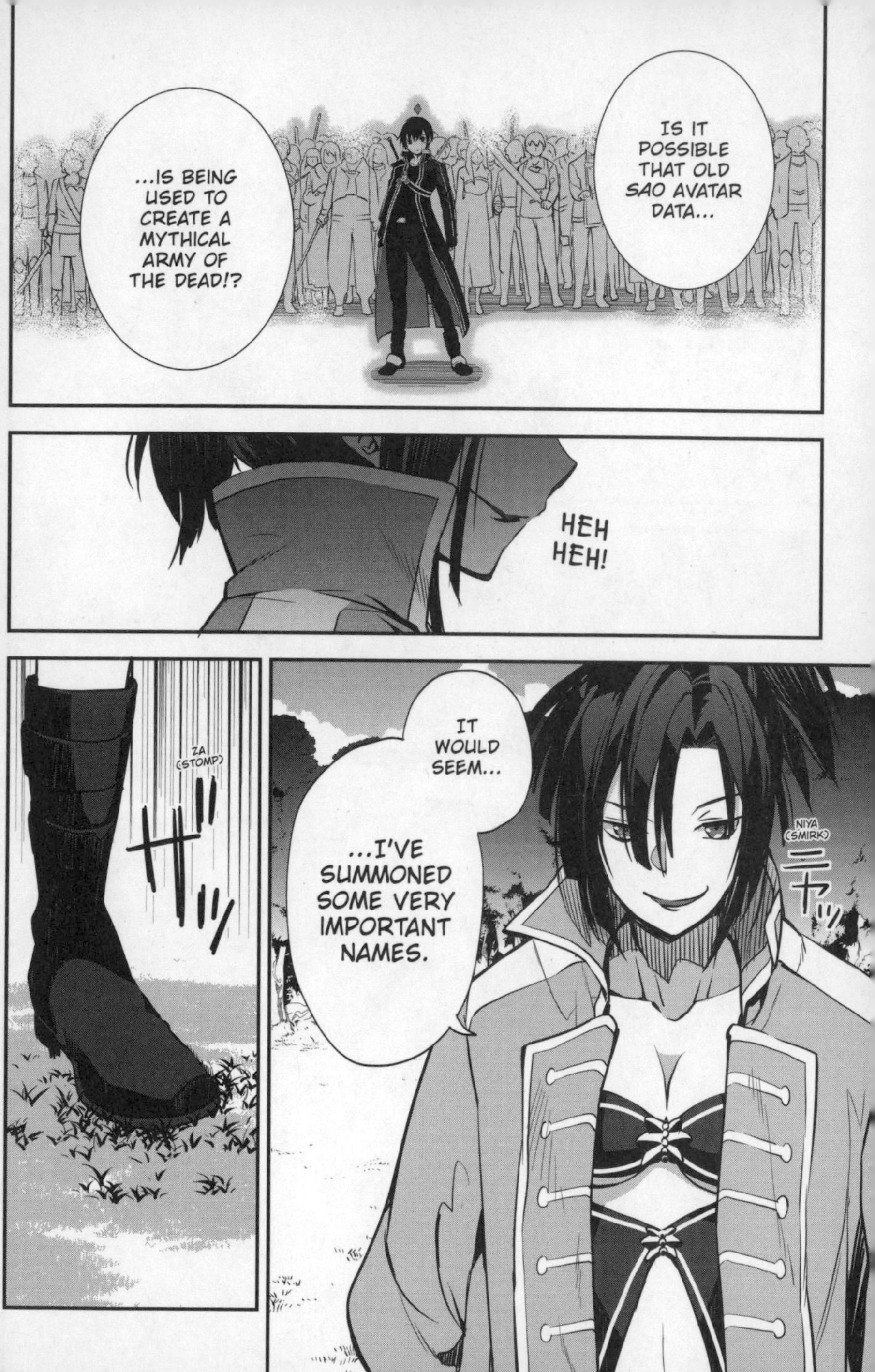
IS IT POSSIBLE THAT OLD SAO AVATAR DATA...
...IS BEING USED TO CREATE A MYTHICAL ARMY OF THE DEAD!?
HEH HEH!
IT WOULD SEEM...
...I'VE SUMMONED SOME VERY IMPORTANT NAMES.
NIYA (SMIRK)
ニヤッ
ZA (STOMP)
ザッ

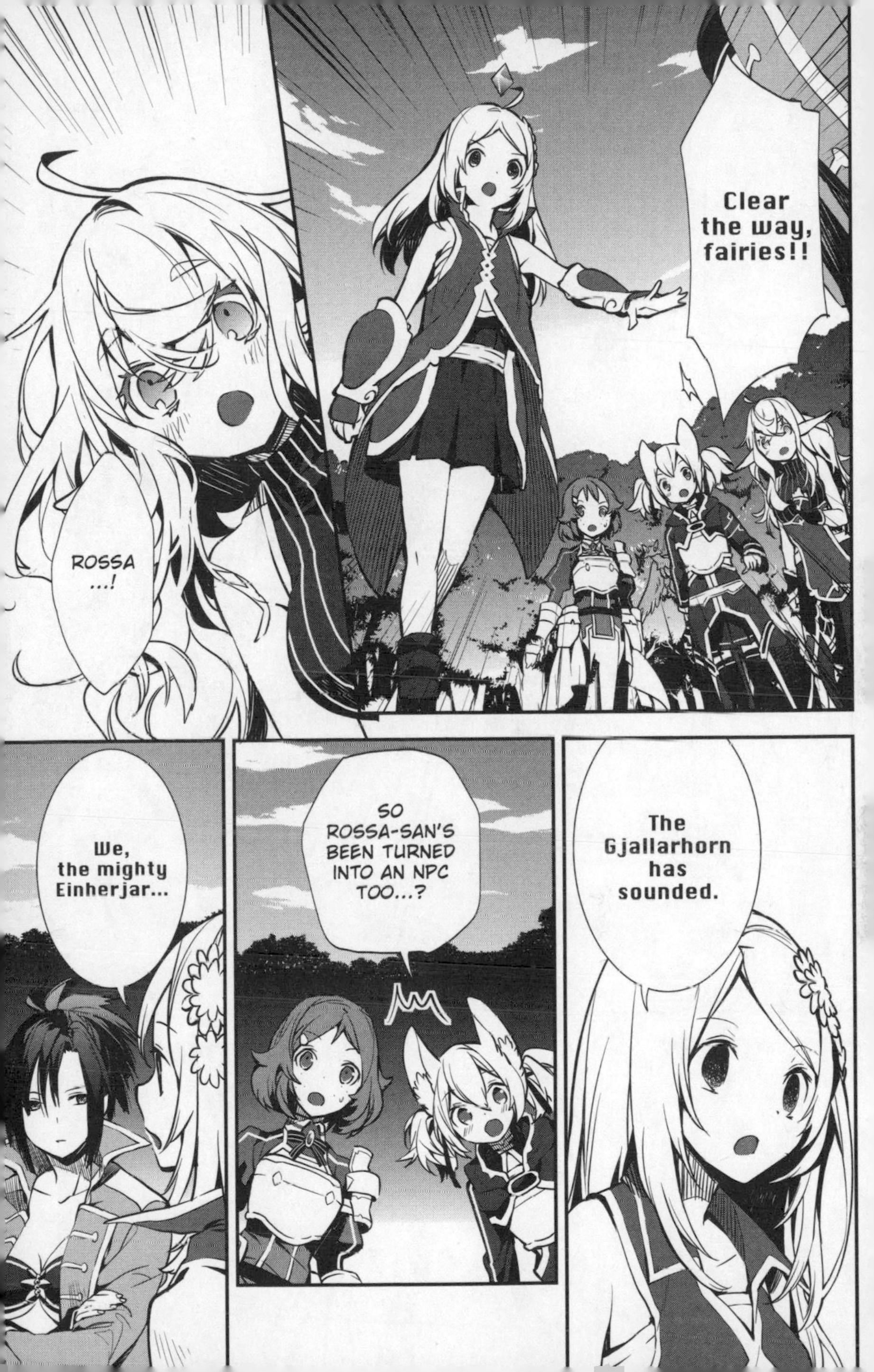
Clear the way, fairies!!
ROSSA ...!
The Gjallarhorn has sounded.
SO ROSSA-SAN'S BEEN TURNED INTO AN NPC TOO...?
We, the mighty Einherjar...

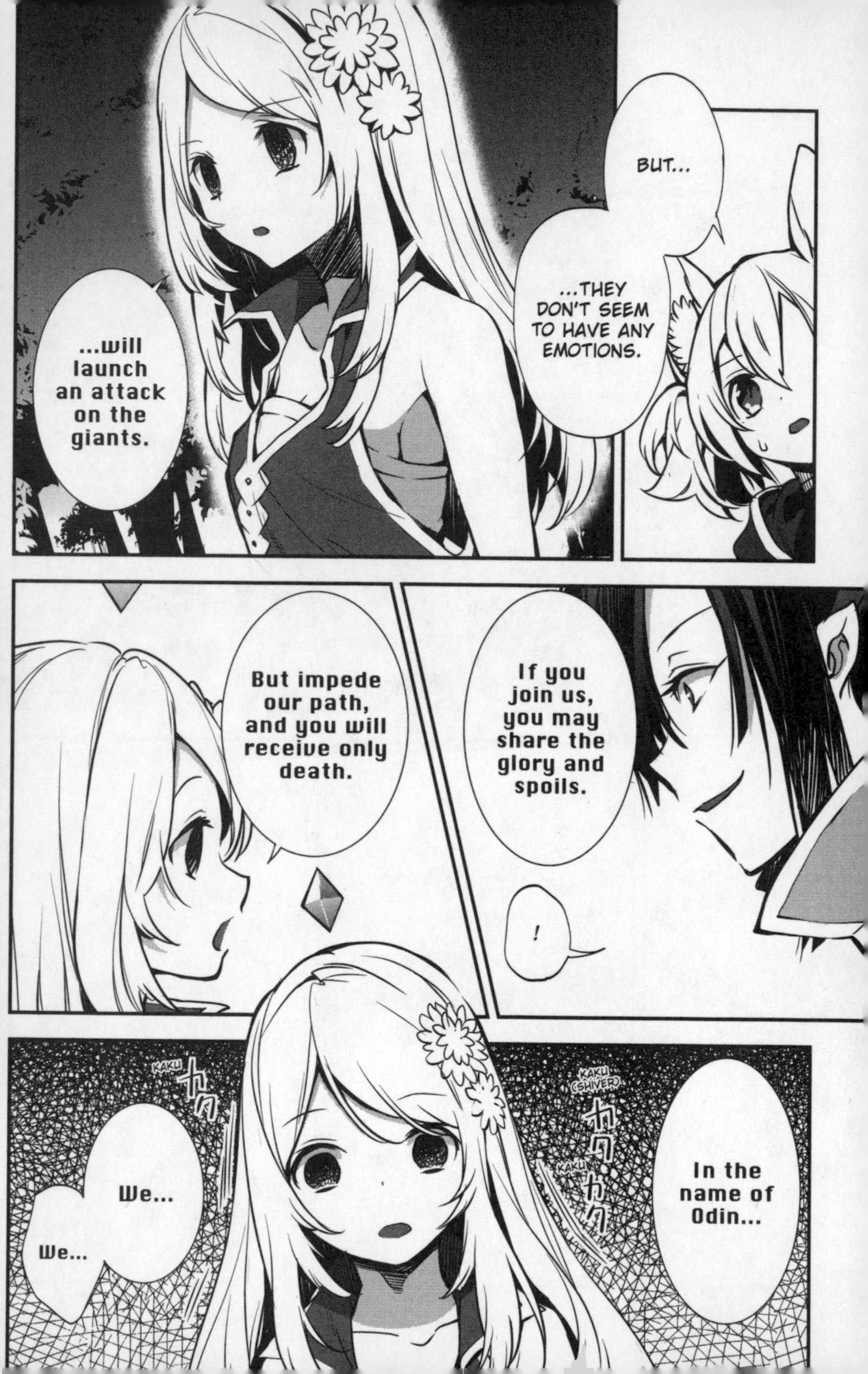
BUT...
...THEY DON'T SEEM TO HAVE ANY EMOTIONS.
...will launch an attack on the giants.
If you join us, you may share the glory and spoils.
!
But impede our path, and you will receive only death.
In the name of Odin...
KAKU (SHIVER)
KAKU
KAKU
We...
We...

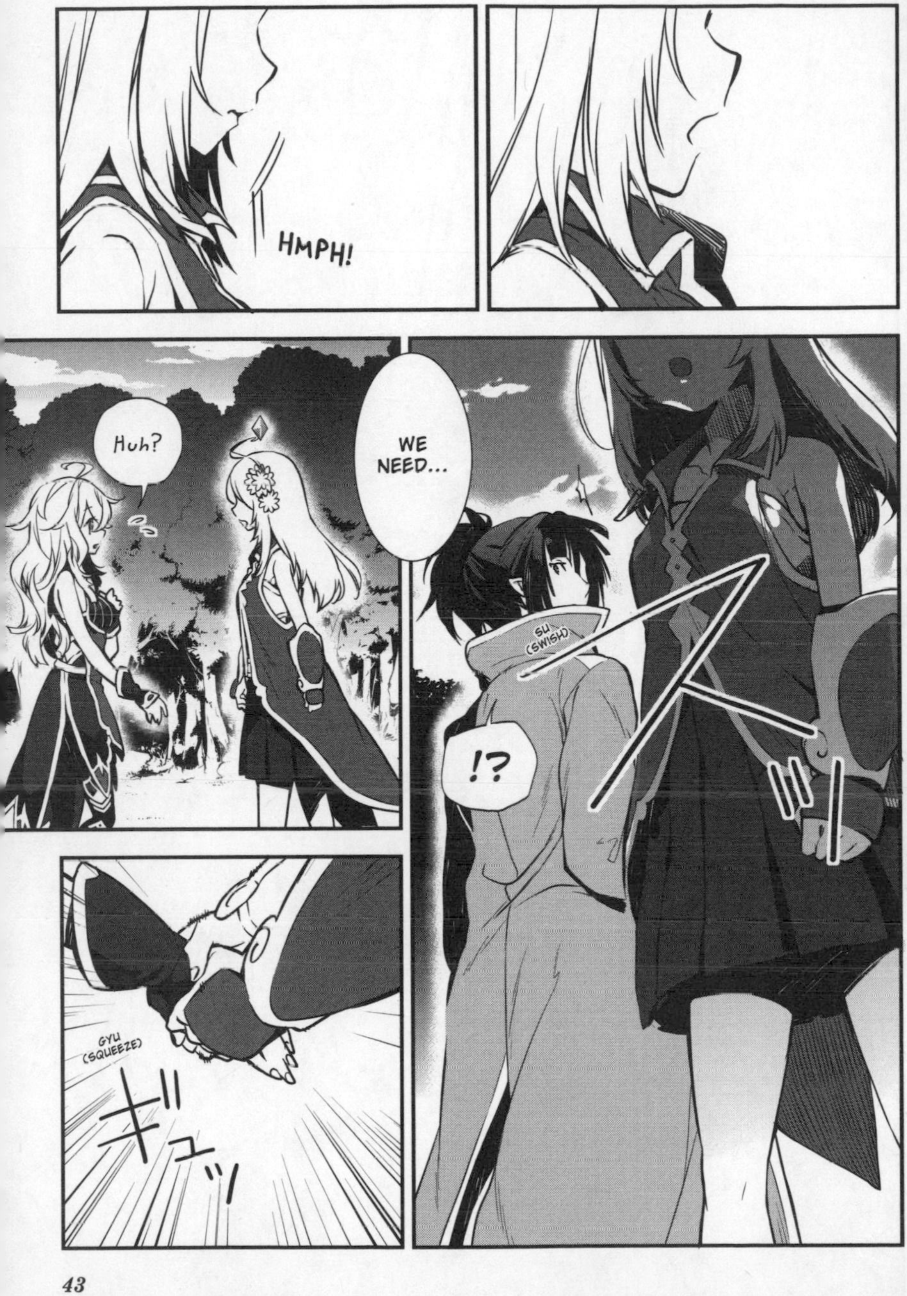
HMPH!
WE NEED...
Huh?
SU (SWISH)
!?
GYU (SQUEEZE)
ギュッ

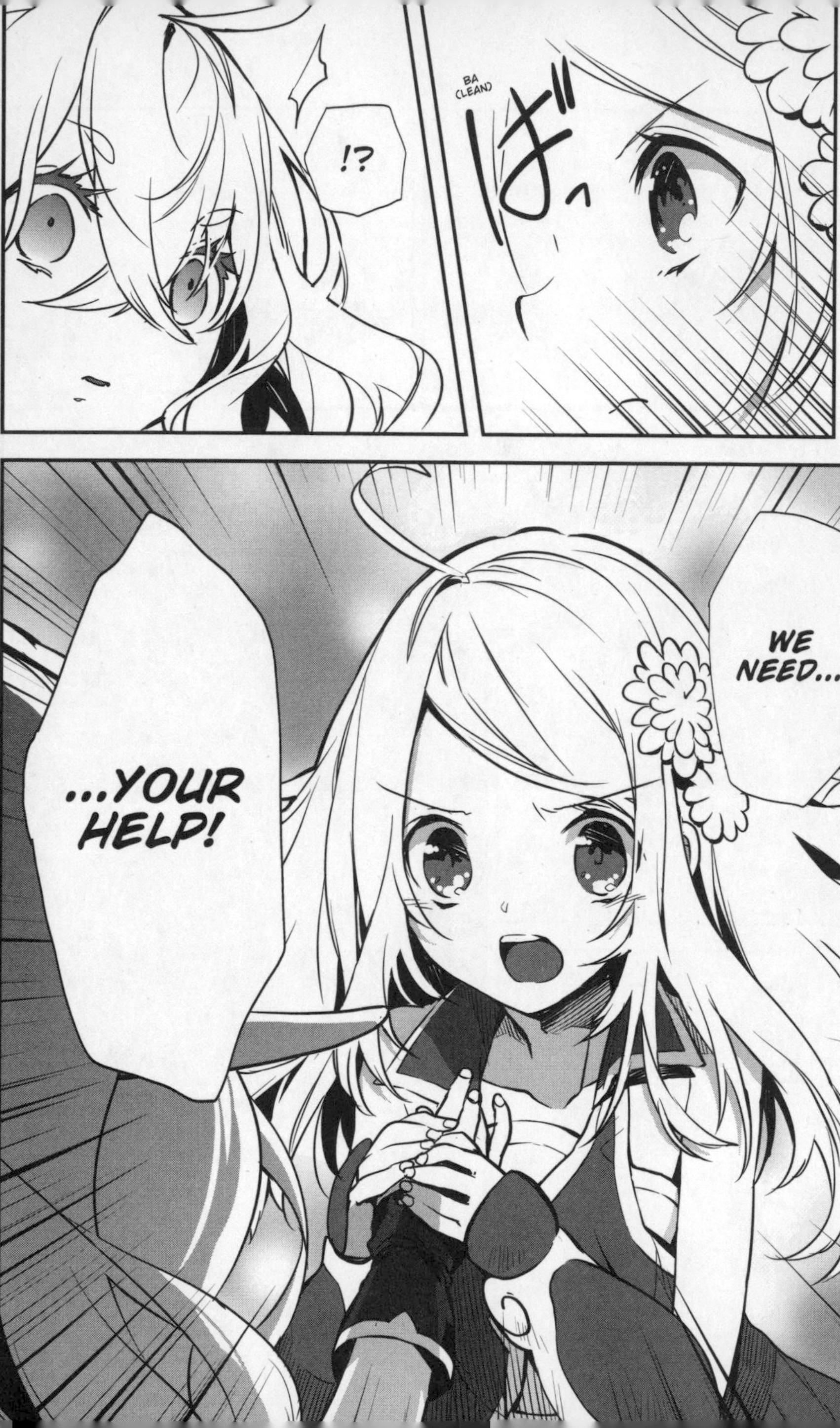
BA (CLEAN)
ば
!?
WE NEED...
...YOUR HELP!

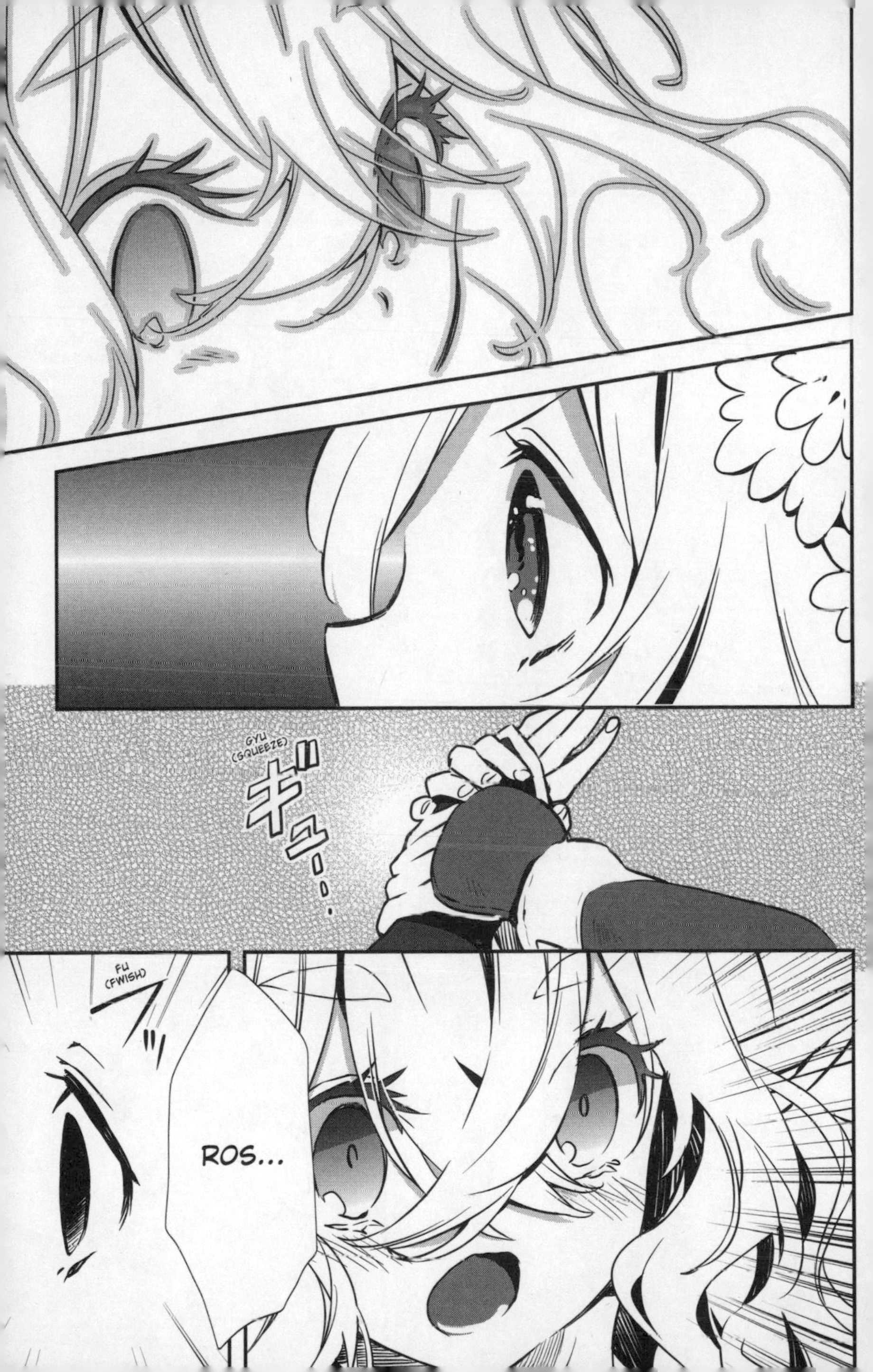
GYU (SQUEEZE)
ギュー…
FU (FWISH)
ROS...

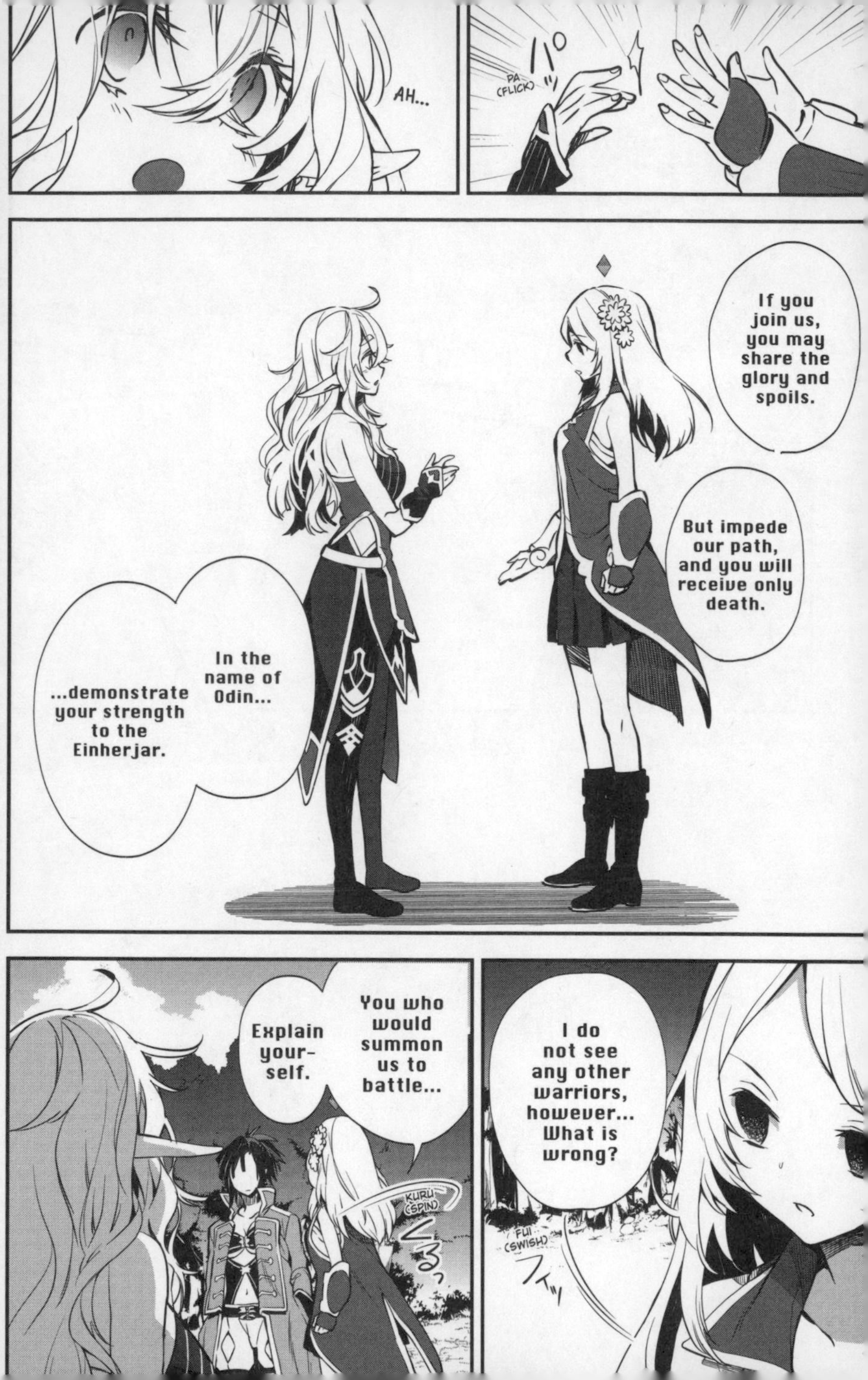

パ
PA (FLICK)
AH...
If you join us, you may share the glory and spoils.
But impede our path, and you will receive only death.
In the name of Odin...
...demonstrate your strength to the Einherjar.
I do not see any other warriors, however... What is wrong?
FUI (SWISH)
フイッ
You who would summon us to battle...
Explain your-self.
KURU (SPIN)
くるっ

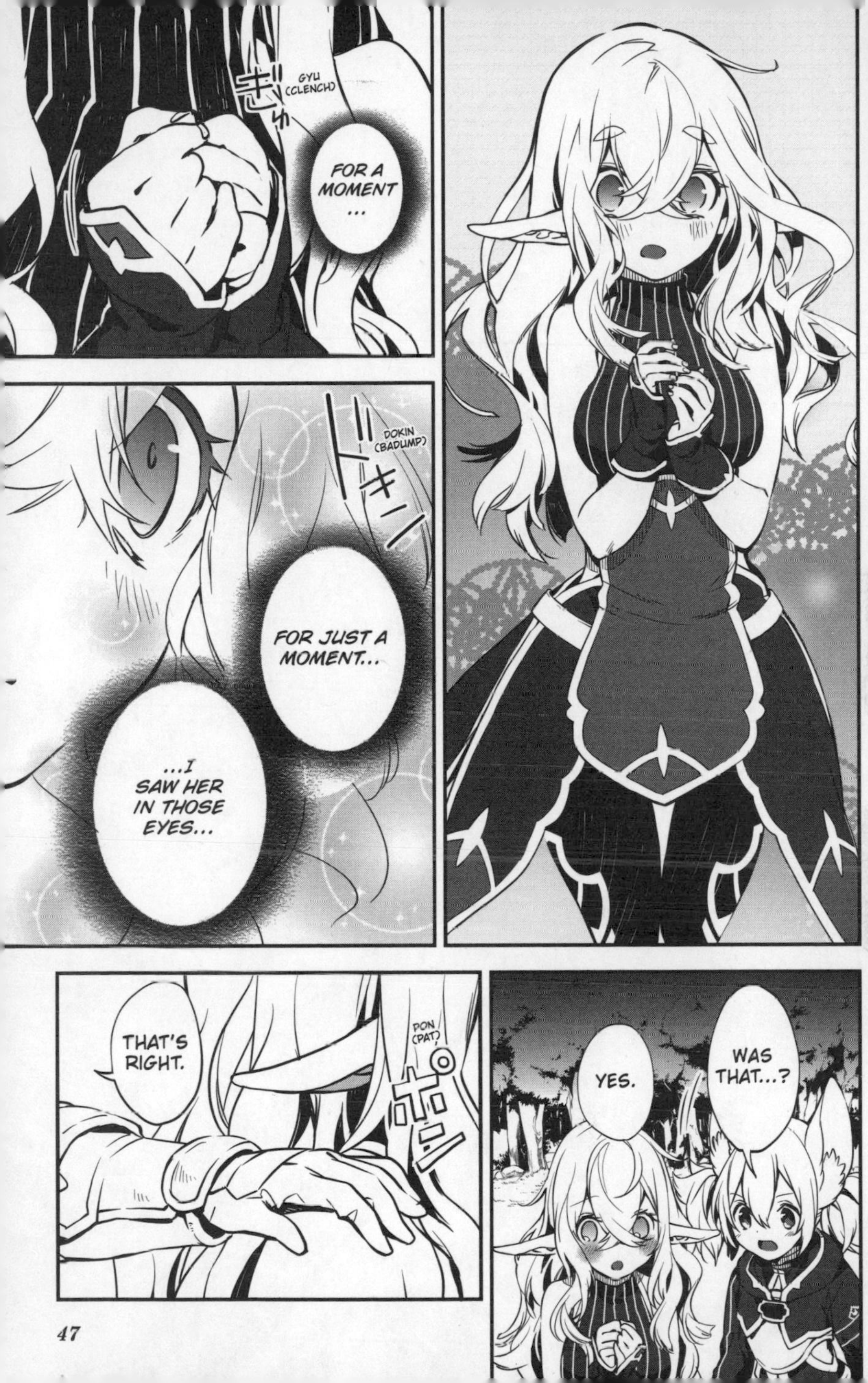
GYU (CLENCH)
FOR A MOMENT ...
DOKIN (BADUMP)
FOR JUST A MOMENT...
...I SAW HER IN THOSE EYES...
WAS THAT...?
YES.
PON (PAT)
THAT'S RIGHT.

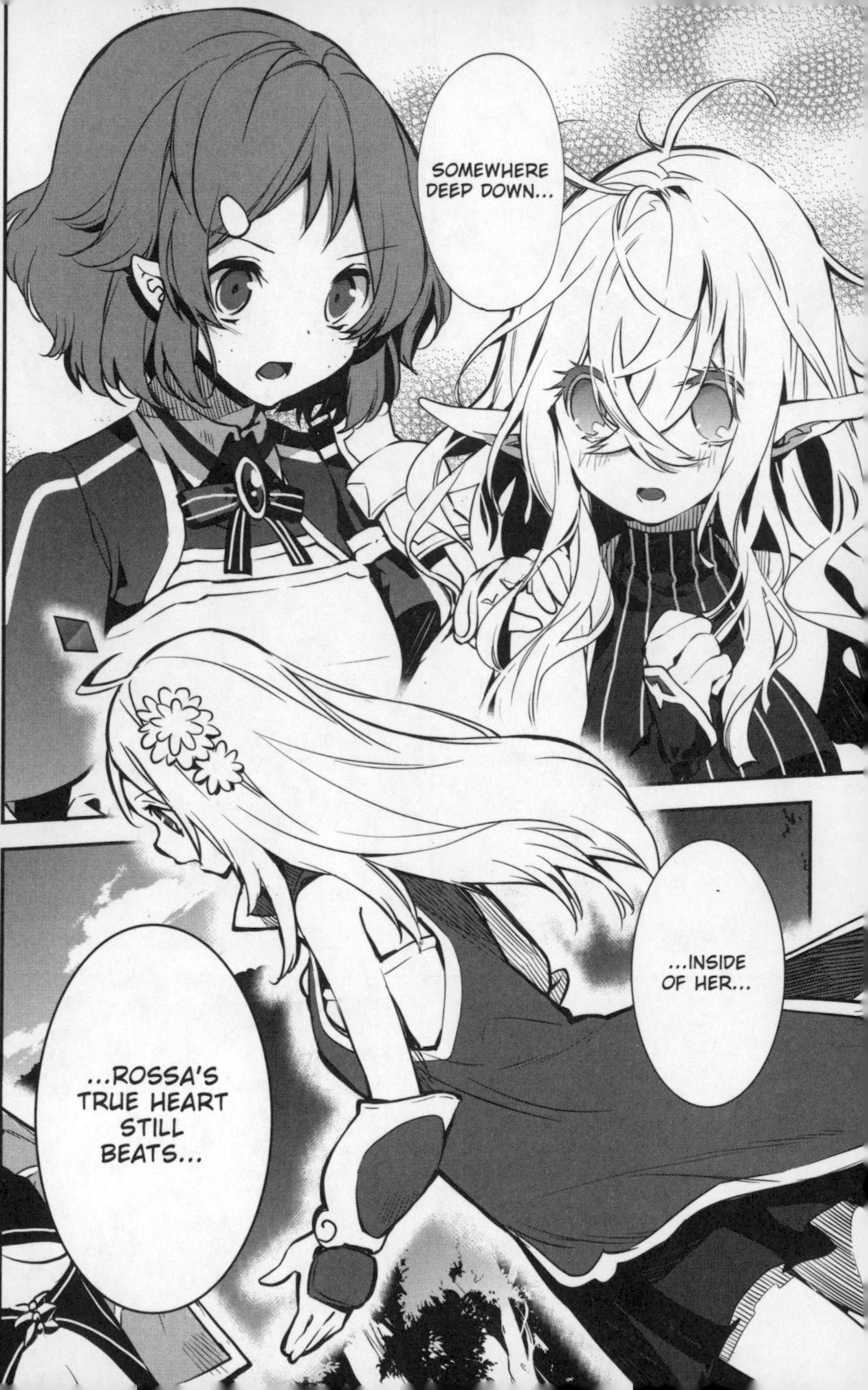
SOMEWHERE DEEP DOWN...
...INSIDE OF HER...
...ROSSA'S TRUE HEART STILL BEATS...

SWORD ART ONLINE
GIRLS' OPS

OCTOBER 4TH

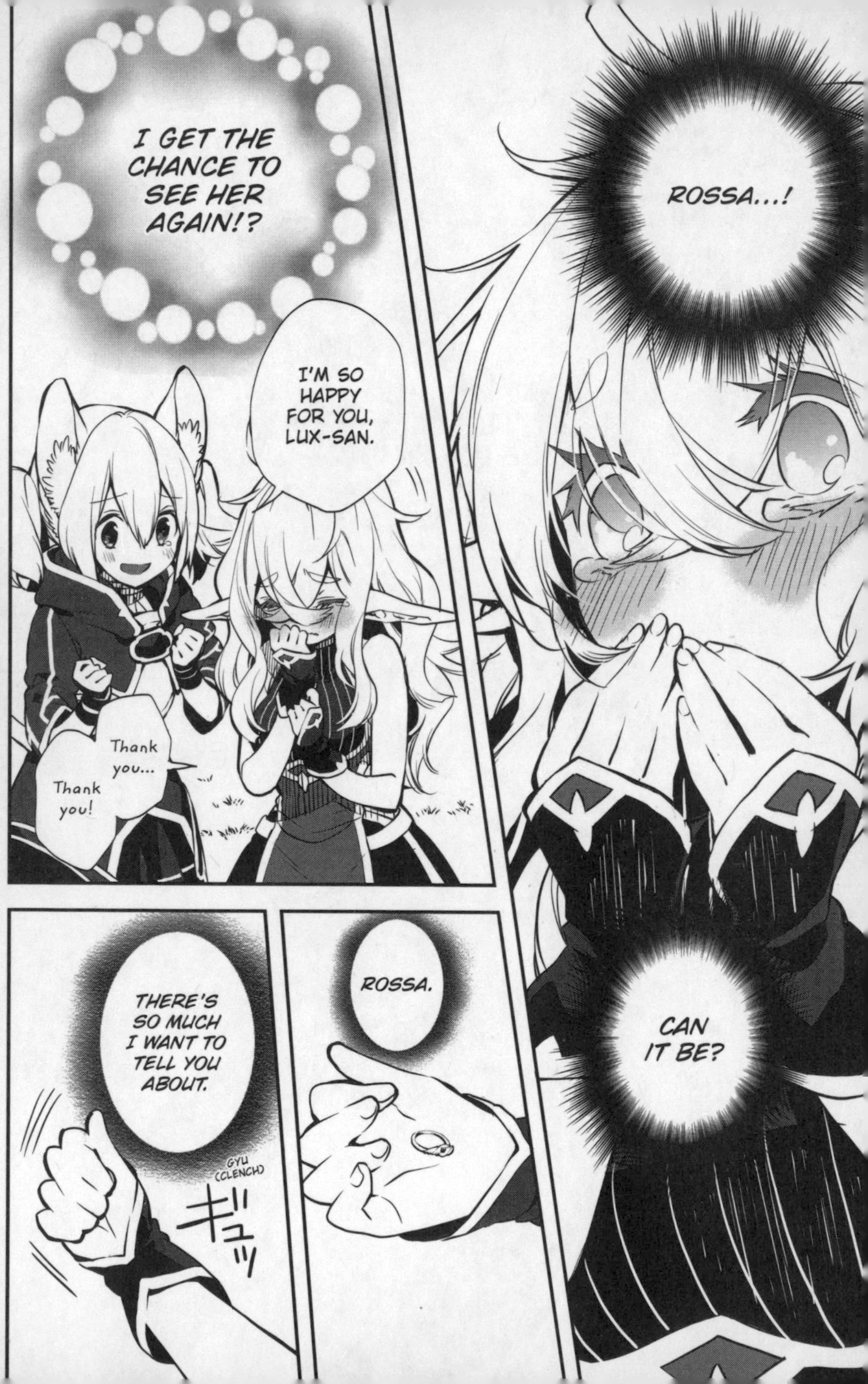
ROSSA...!
I GET THE CHANCE TO SEE HER AGAIN!?
I'M SO HAPPY FOR YOU, LUX-SAN.
Thank you... Thank you!
CAN IT BE?
ROSSA.
THERE'S SO MUCH I WANT TO TELL YOU ABOUT.
GYU (CLENCH)
ギュッ

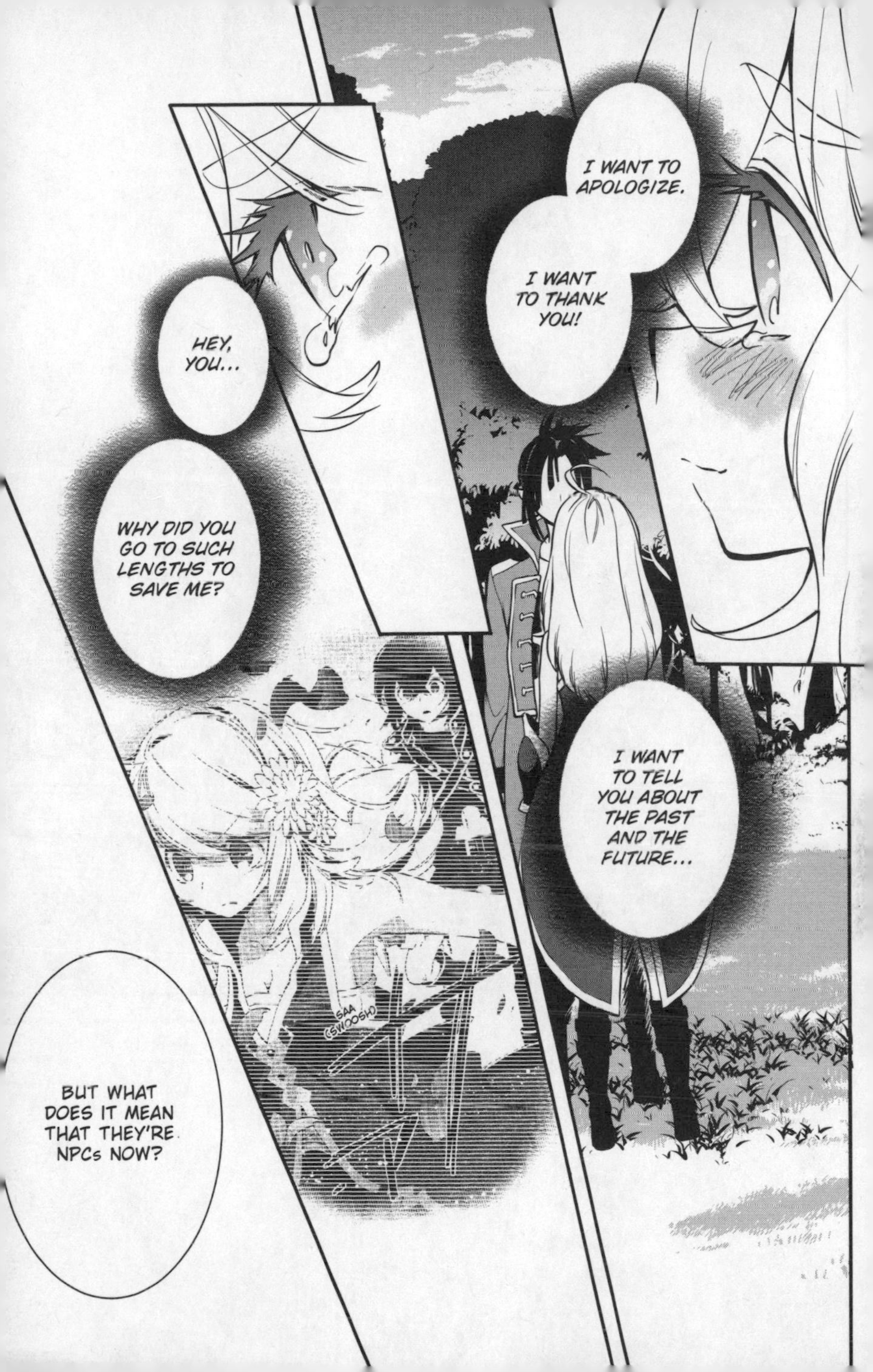
I WANT TO APOLOGIZE.
I WANT TO THANK YOU!
HEY, YOU...
WHY DID YOU GO TO SUCH LENGTHS TO SAVE ME?
I WANT TO TELL YOU ABOUT THE PAST AND THE FUTURE...
SAA (SWOOSH)
BUT WHAT DOES IT MEAN THAT THEY'RE NPCs NOW?

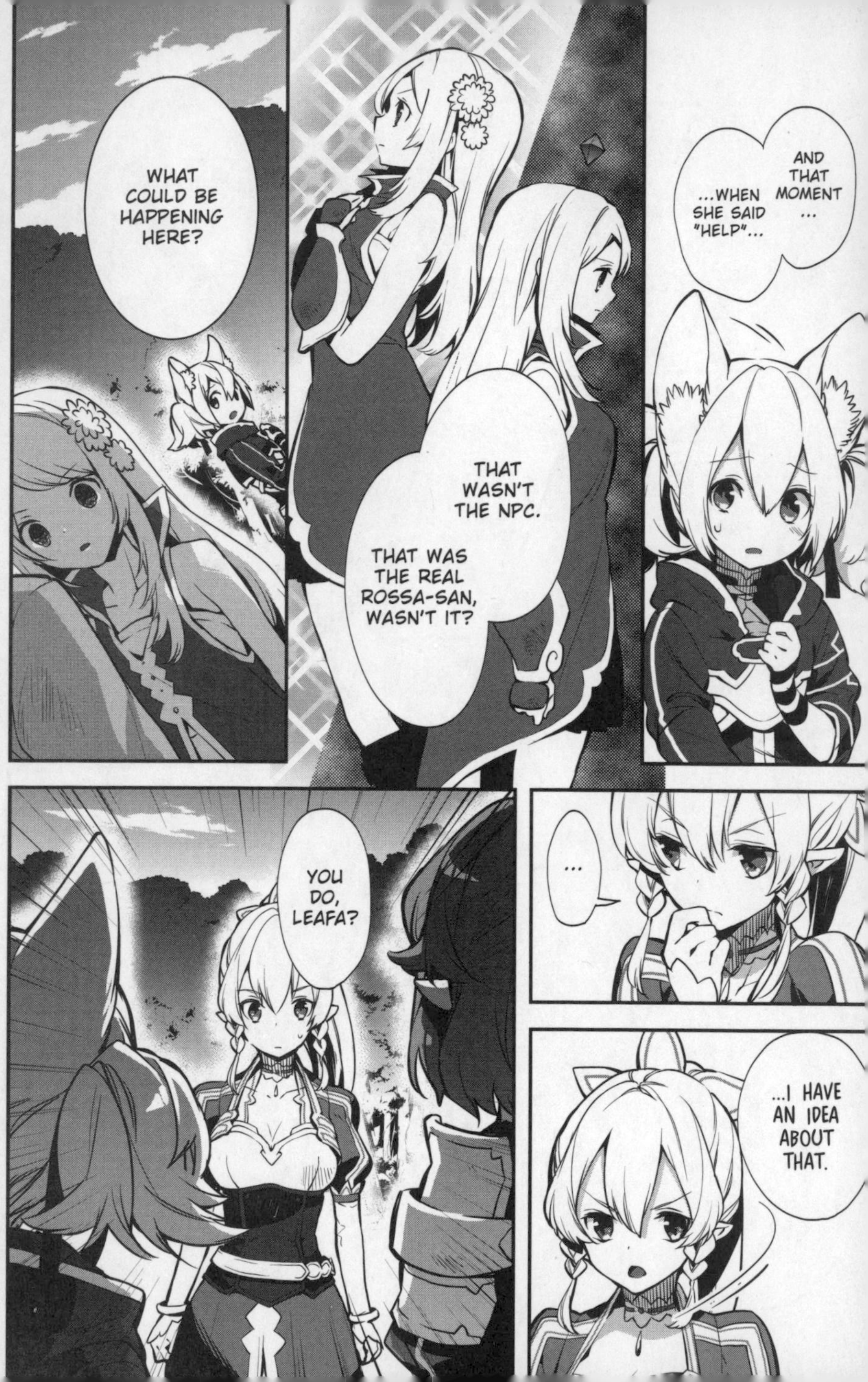
...WHEN SHE SAID "HELP"...
AND THAT MOMENT ...
THAT WASN'T THE NPC.
THAT WAS THE REAL ROSSA-SAN, WASN'T IT?
WHAT COULD BE HAPPENING HERE?
...
YOU DO, LEAFA?
...I HAVE AN IDEA ABOUT THAT.

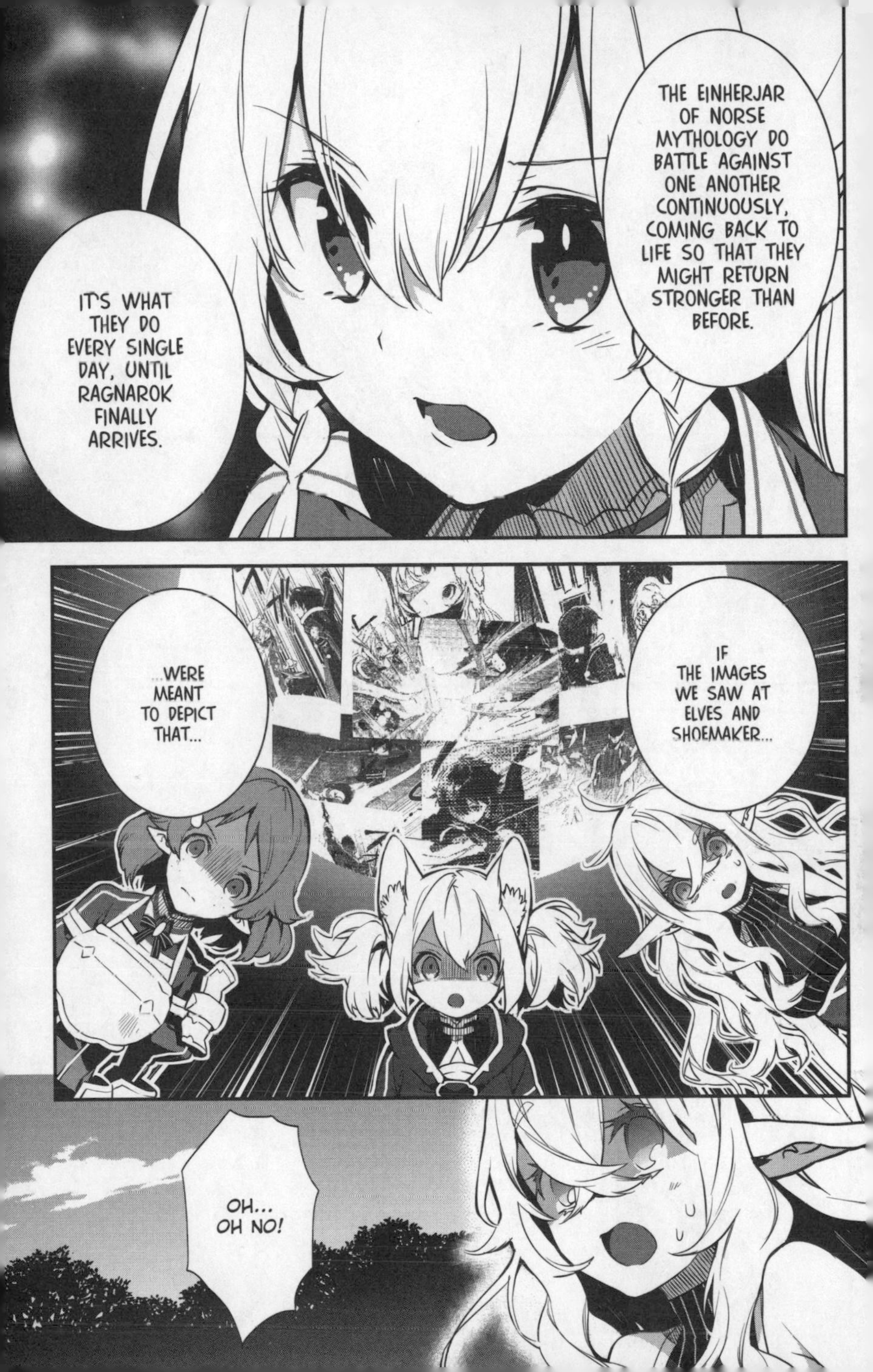
THE EINHERJAR OF NORSE MYTHOLOGY DO BATTLE AGAINST ONE ANOTHER CONTINUOUSLY, COMING BACK TO LIFE SO THAT THEY MIGHT RETURN STRONGER THAN BEFORE.
IT'S WHAT THEY DO EVERY SINGLE DAY, UNTIL RAGNAROK FINALLY ARRIVES.
IF THE IMAGES WE SAW AT ELVES AND SHOEMAKER...
...WERE MEANT TO DEPICT THAT...
OH... OH NO!

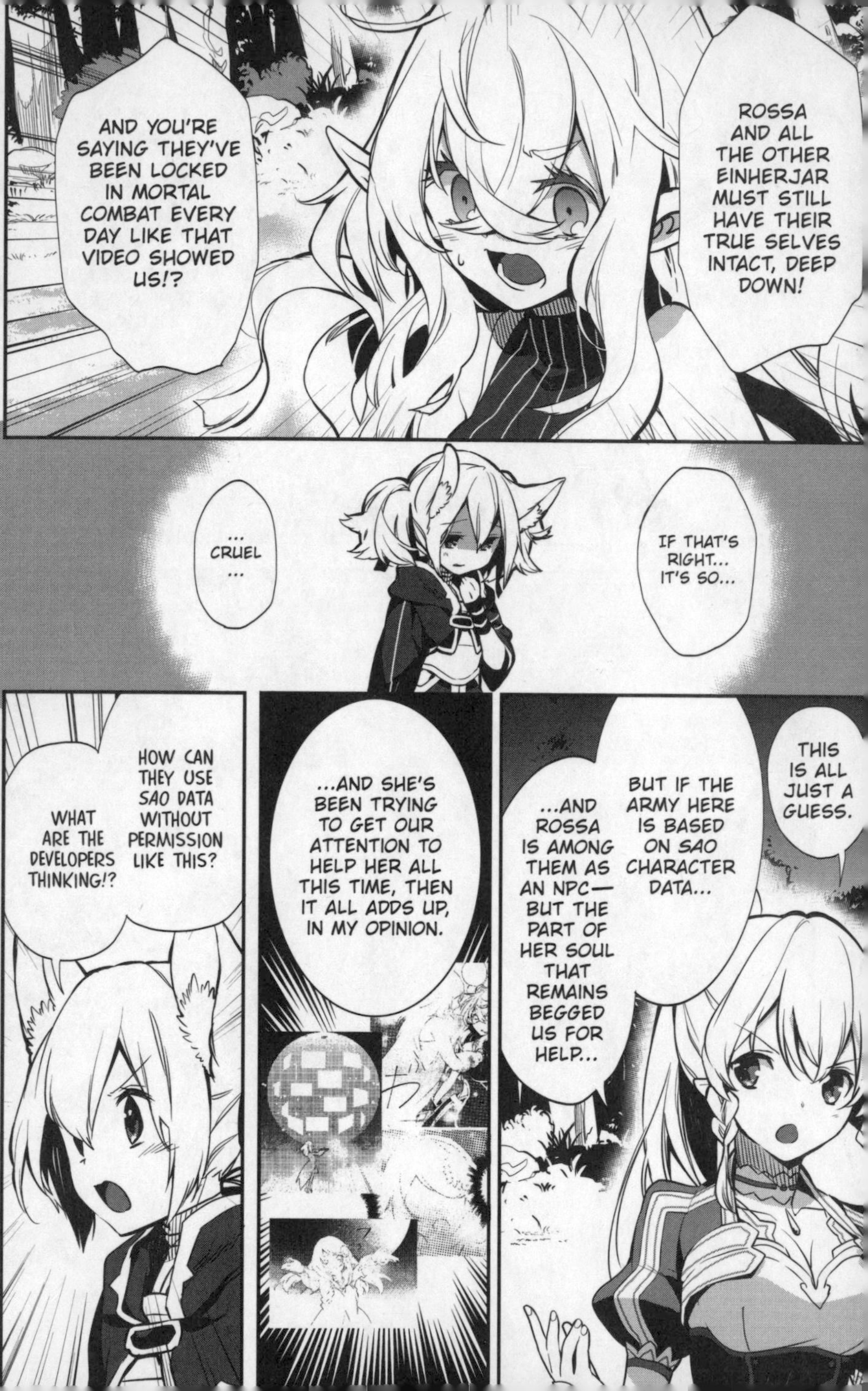
ROSSA AND ALL THE OTHER EINHERJAR MUST STILL HAVE THEIR TRUE SELVES INTACT, DEEP DOWN!
AND YOU'RE SAYING THEY'VE BEEN LOCKED IN MORTAL COMBAT EVERY DAY LIKE THAT VIDEO SHOWED US!?
IF THAT'S RIGHT... IT'S SO...
...CRUEL...
THIS IS ALL JUST A GUESS.
BUT IF THE ARMY HERE IS BASED ON SAO CHARACTER DATA...
...AND ROSSA IS AMONG THEM AS AN NPC—BUT THE PART OF HER SOUL THAT REMAINS BEGGED US FOR HELP...
...AND SHE'S BEEN TRYING TO GET OUR ATTENTION TO HELP HER ALL THIS TIME, THEN IT ALL ADDS UP, IN MY OPINION.
HOW CAN THEY USE SAO DATA WITHOUT PERMISSION LIKE THIS?
WHAT ARE THE DEVELOPERS THINKING!?

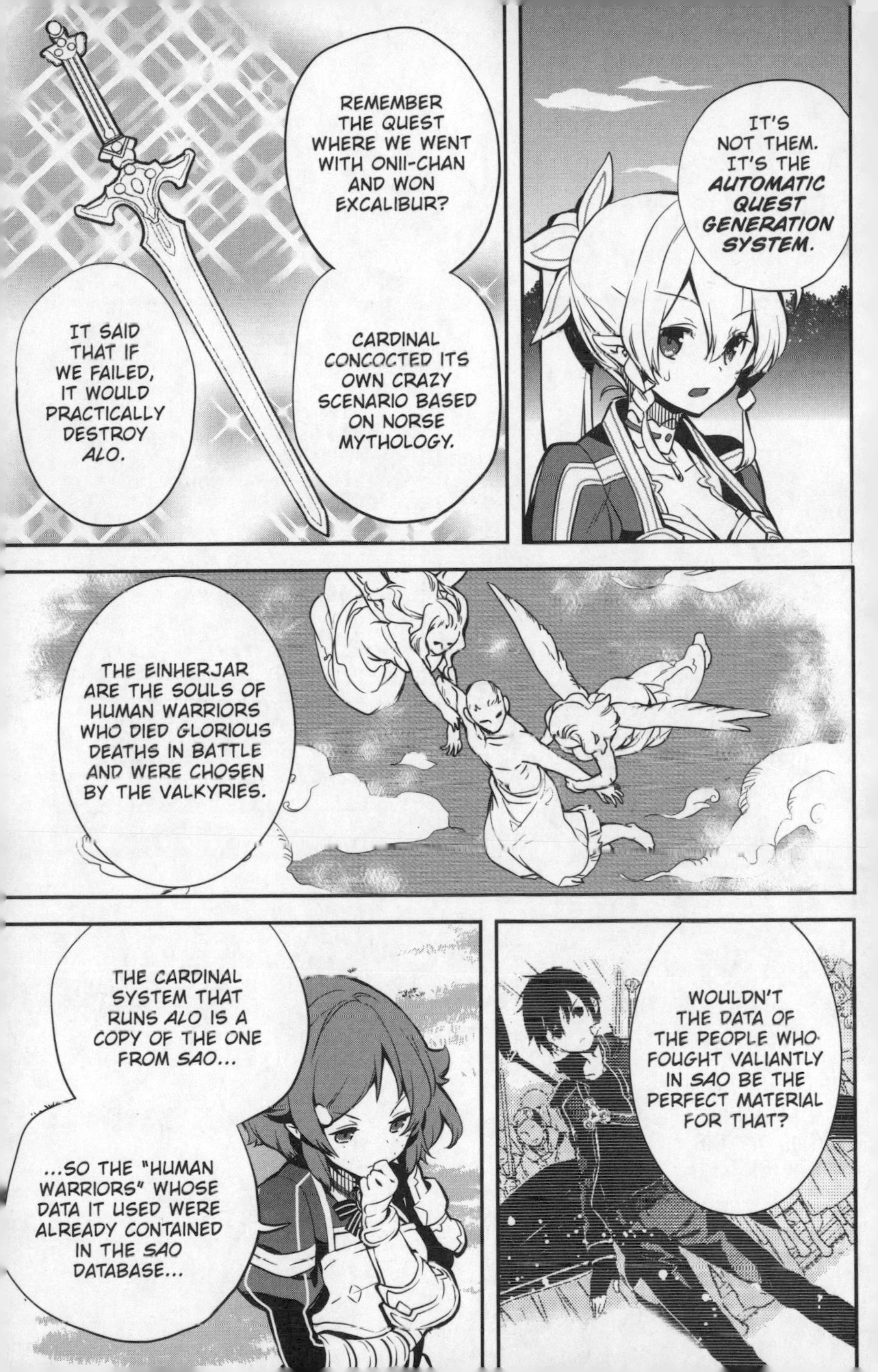
IT'S NOT THEM. IT'S THE *AUTOMATIC QUEST GENERATION SYSTEM*.
REMEMBER THE QUEST WHERE WE WENT WITH ONII-CHAN AND WON EXCALIBUR?
CARDINAL CONCOCTED ITS OWN CRAZY SCENARIO BASED ON NORSE MYTHOLOGY.
IT SAID THAT IF WE FAILED, IT WOULD PRACTICALLY DESTROY *ALO*.
THE EINHERJAR ARE THE SOULS OF HUMAN WARRIORS WHO DIED GLORIOUS DEATHS IN BATTLE AND WERE CHOSEN BY THE VALKYRIES.
WOULDN'T THE DATA OF THE PEOPLE WHO FOUGHT VALIANTLY IN *SAO* BE THE PERFECT MATERIAL FOR THAT?
THE CARDINAL SYSTEM THAT RUNS *ALO* IS A COPY OF THE ONE FROM *SAO*...
...SO THE "HUMAN WARRIORS" WHOSE DATA IT USED WERE ALREADY CONTAINED IN THE *SAO* DATABASE...

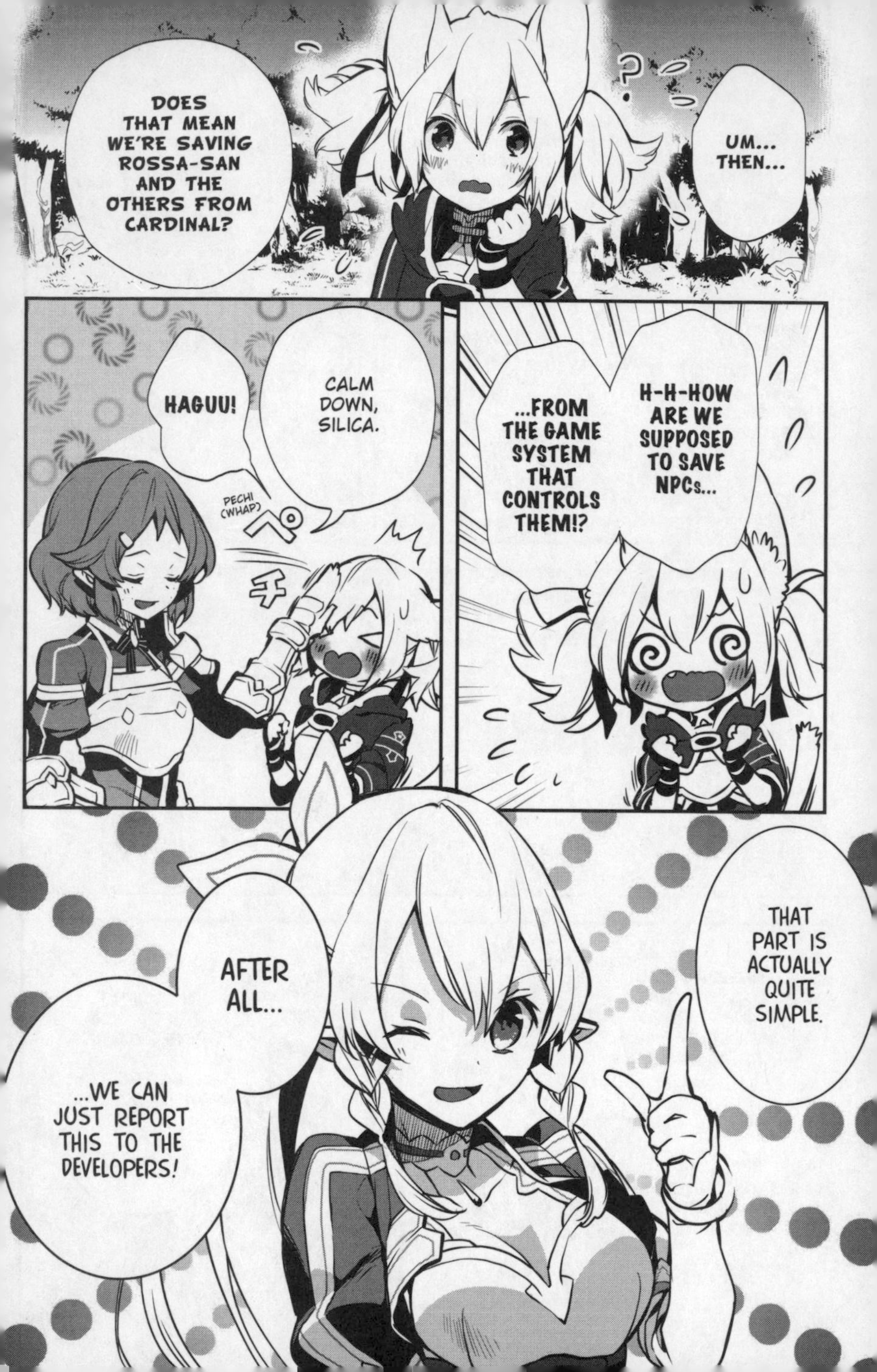
UM... THEN...
DOES THAT MEAN WE'RE SAVING ROSSA-SAN AND THE OTHERS FROM CARDINAL?
H-H-HOW ARE WE SUPPOSED TO SAVE NPCs...
...FROM THE GAME SYSTEM THAT CONTROLS THEM!?
CALM DOWN, SILICA.
PECHI (WHAP)
HAGUU!
THAT PART IS ACTUALLY QUITE SIMPLE.
AFTER ALL...
...WE CAN JUST REPORT THIS TO THE DEVELOPERS!

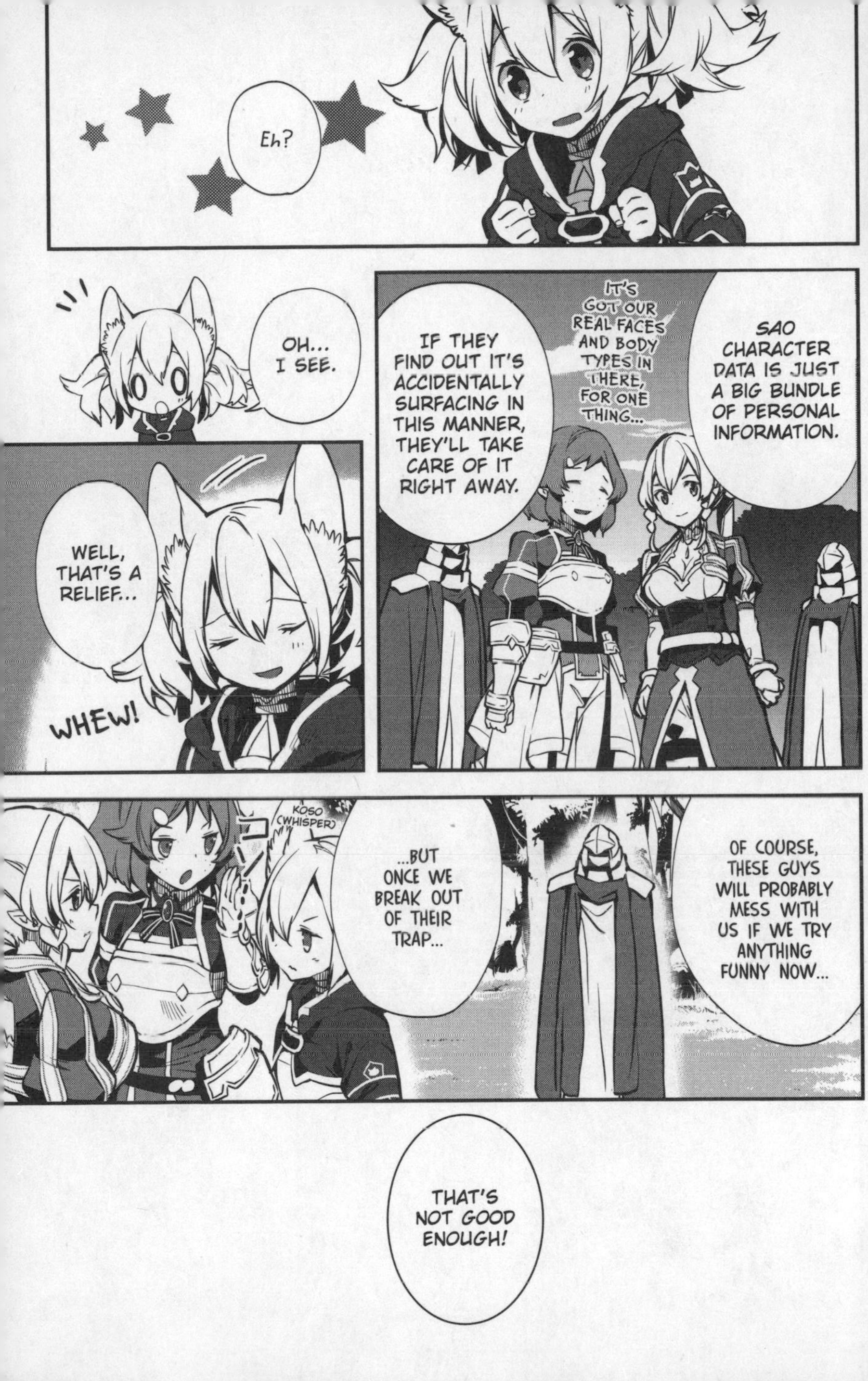
Eh?
SAO CHARACTER DATA IS JUST A BIG BUNDLE OF PERSONAL INFORMATION.
IT'S GOT OUR REAL FACES AND BODY TYPES IN THERE, FOR ONE THING...
IF THEY FIND OUT IT'S ACCIDENTALLY SURFACING IN THIS MANNER, THEY'LL TAKE CARE OF IT RIGHT AWAY.
OH... I SEE.
WELL, THAT'S A RELIEF...
WHEW!
OF COURSE, THESE GUYS WILL PROBABLY MESS WITH US IF WE TRY ANYTHING FUNNY NOW...
KOSO (WHISPER)
...BUT ONCE WE BREAK OUT OF THEIR TRAP...
THAT'S NOT GOOD ENOUGH!

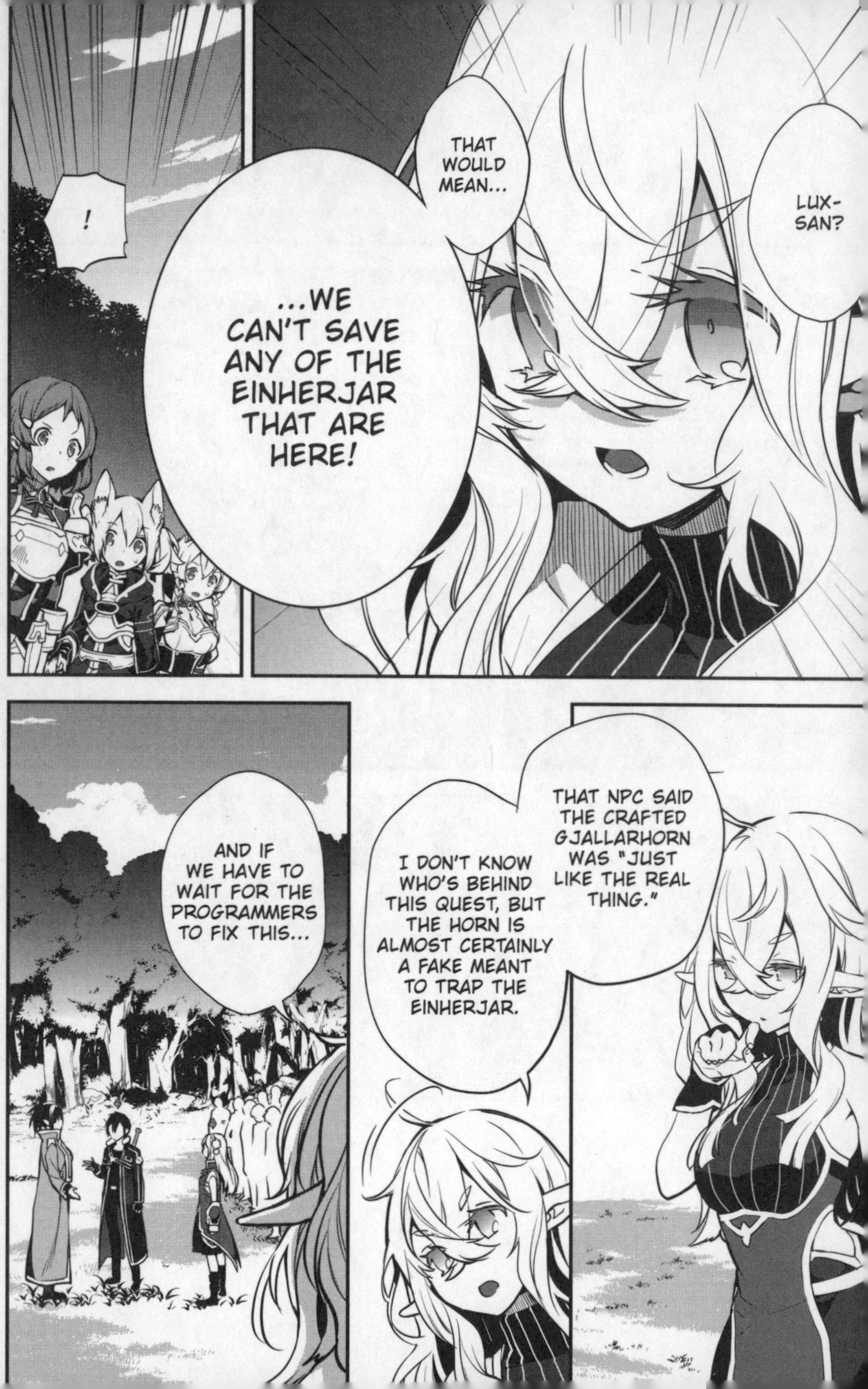
LUX-SAN?
THAT WOULD MEAN...
...WE CAN'T SAVE ANY OF THE EINHERJAR THAT ARE HERE!
!
THAT NPC SAID THE CRAFTED GJALLARHORN WAS "JUST LIKE THE REAL THING."
I DON'T KNOW WHO'S BEHIND THIS QUEST, BUT THE HORN IS ALMOST CERTAINLY A FAKE MEANT TO TRAP THE EINHERJAR.
AND IF WE HAVE TO WAIT FOR THE PROGRAMMERS TO FIX THIS...

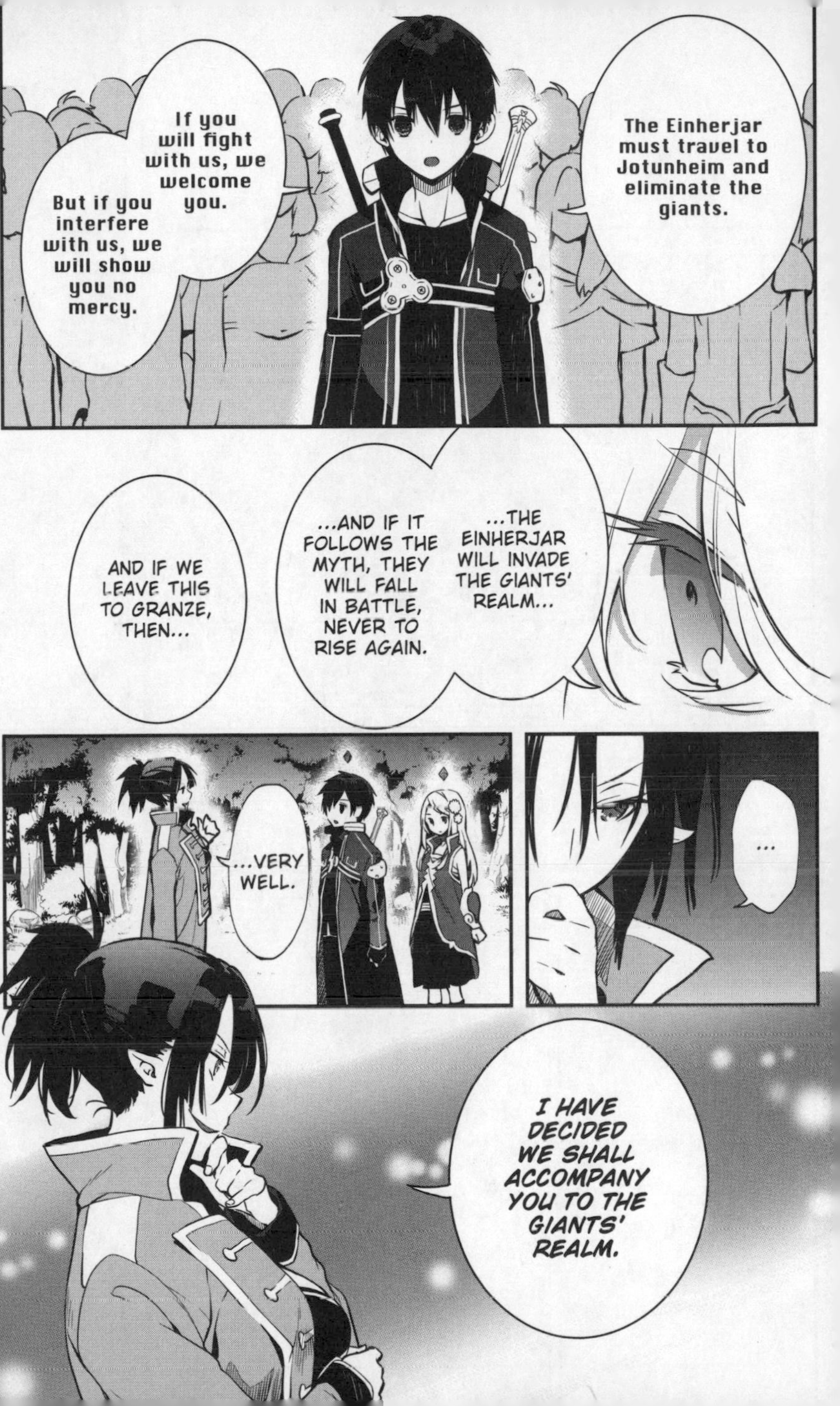
The Einherjar must travel to Jotunheim and eliminate the giants.
If you will fight with us, we welcome you.
But if you interfere with us, we will show you no mercy.
...THE EINHERJAR WILL INVADE THE GIANTS' REALM...
...AND IF IT FOLLOWS THE MYTH, THEY WILL FALL IN BATTLE, NEVER TO RISE AGAIN.
AND IF WE LEAVE THIS TO GRANZE, THEN...
...
...VERY WELL.
I HAVE DECIDED WE SHALL ACCOMPANY YOU TO THE GIANTS' REALM.

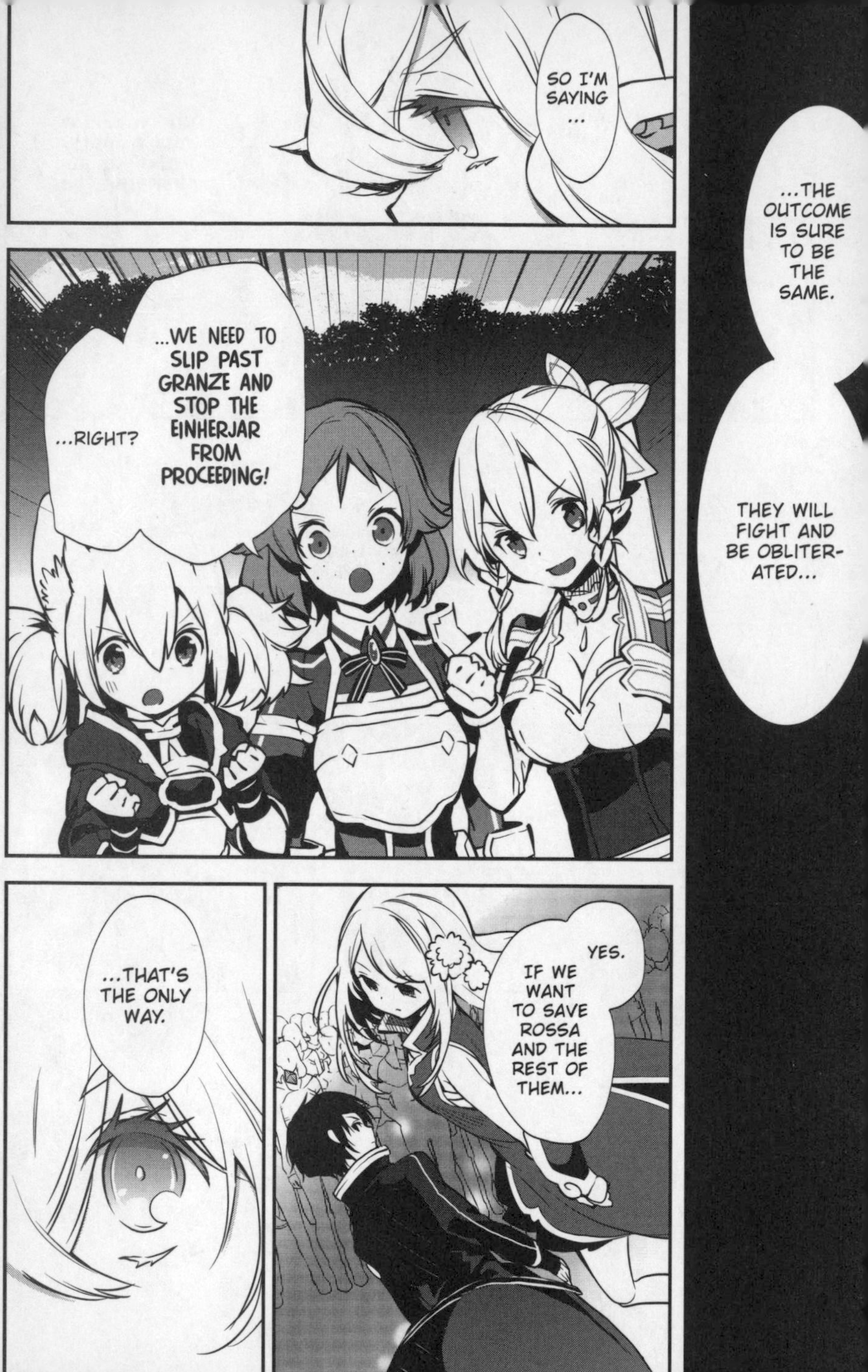
SO I'M SAYING ...
...THE OUTCOME IS SURE TO BE THE SAME.
THEY WILL FIGHT AND BE OBLITER-ATED...
...WE NEED TO SLIP PAST GRANZE AND STOP THE EINHERJAR FROM PROCEEDING!
...RIGHT?
YES. IF WE WANT TO SAVE ROSSA AND THE REST OF THEM...
...THAT'S THE ONLY WAY.

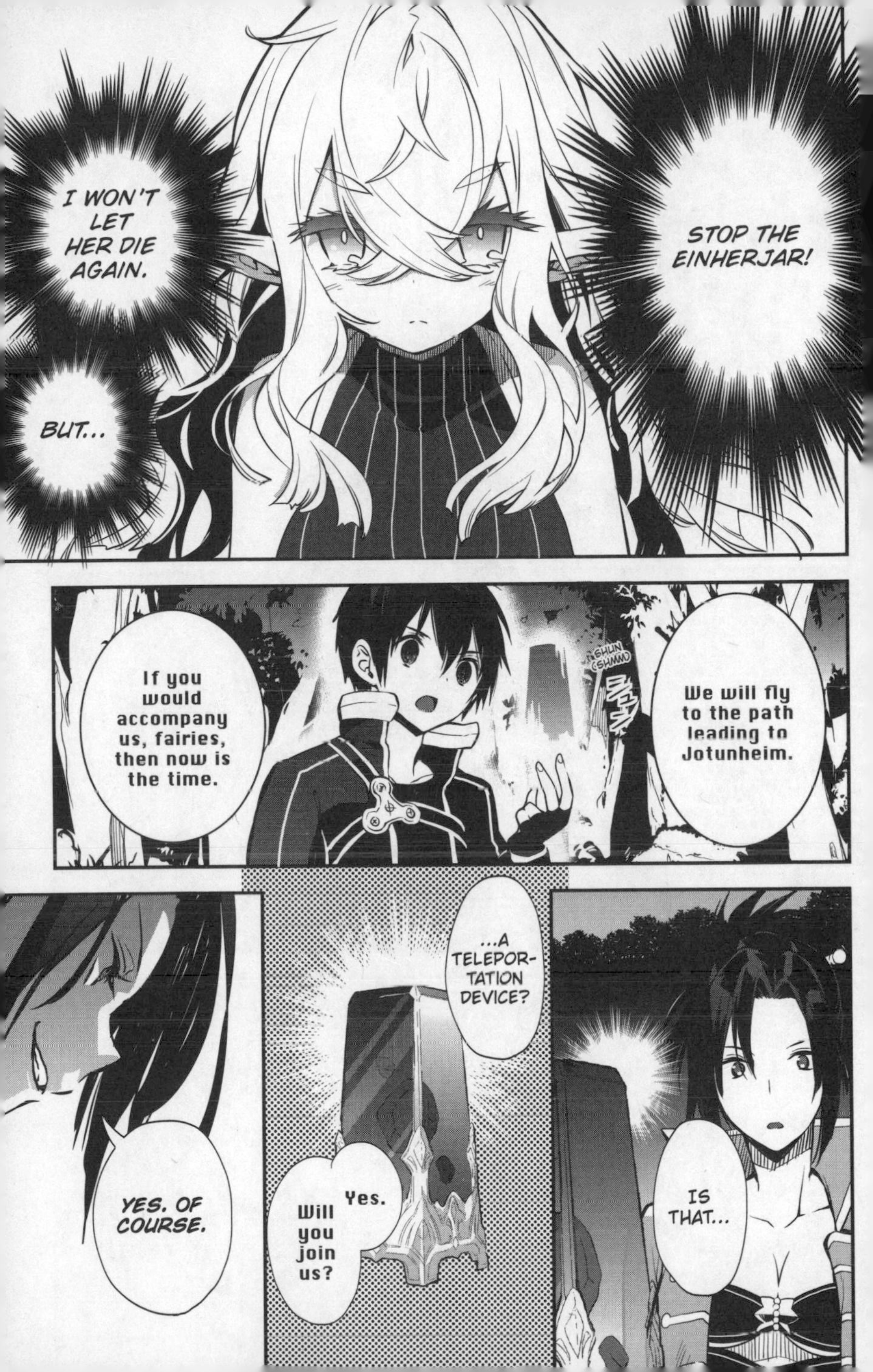
STOP THE EINHERJAR!
I WON'T LET HER DIE AGAIN.
BUT...
We will fly to the path leading to Jotunheim.
SHUN (SHWM)
If you would accompany us, fairies, then now is the time.
IS THAT...
...A TELEPORTATION DEVICE?
Yes. Will you join us?
YES. OF COURSE.

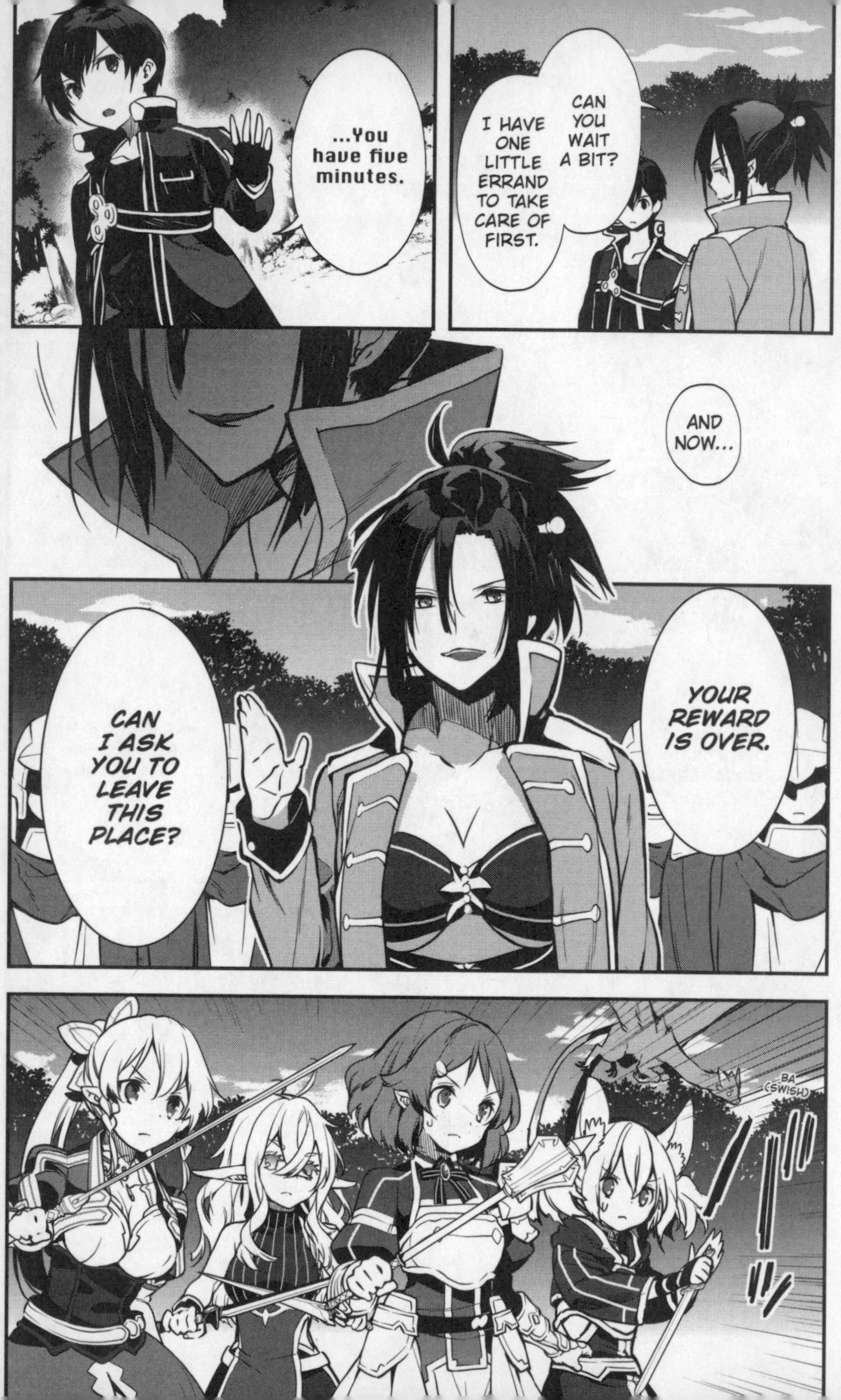
CAN YOU WAIT A BIT?
I HAVE ONE LITTLE ERRAND TO TAKE CARE OF FIRST.
...You have five minutes.
AND NOW...
YOUR REWARD IS OVER.
CAN I ASK YOU TO LEAVE THIS PLACE?
BA (SWISH)

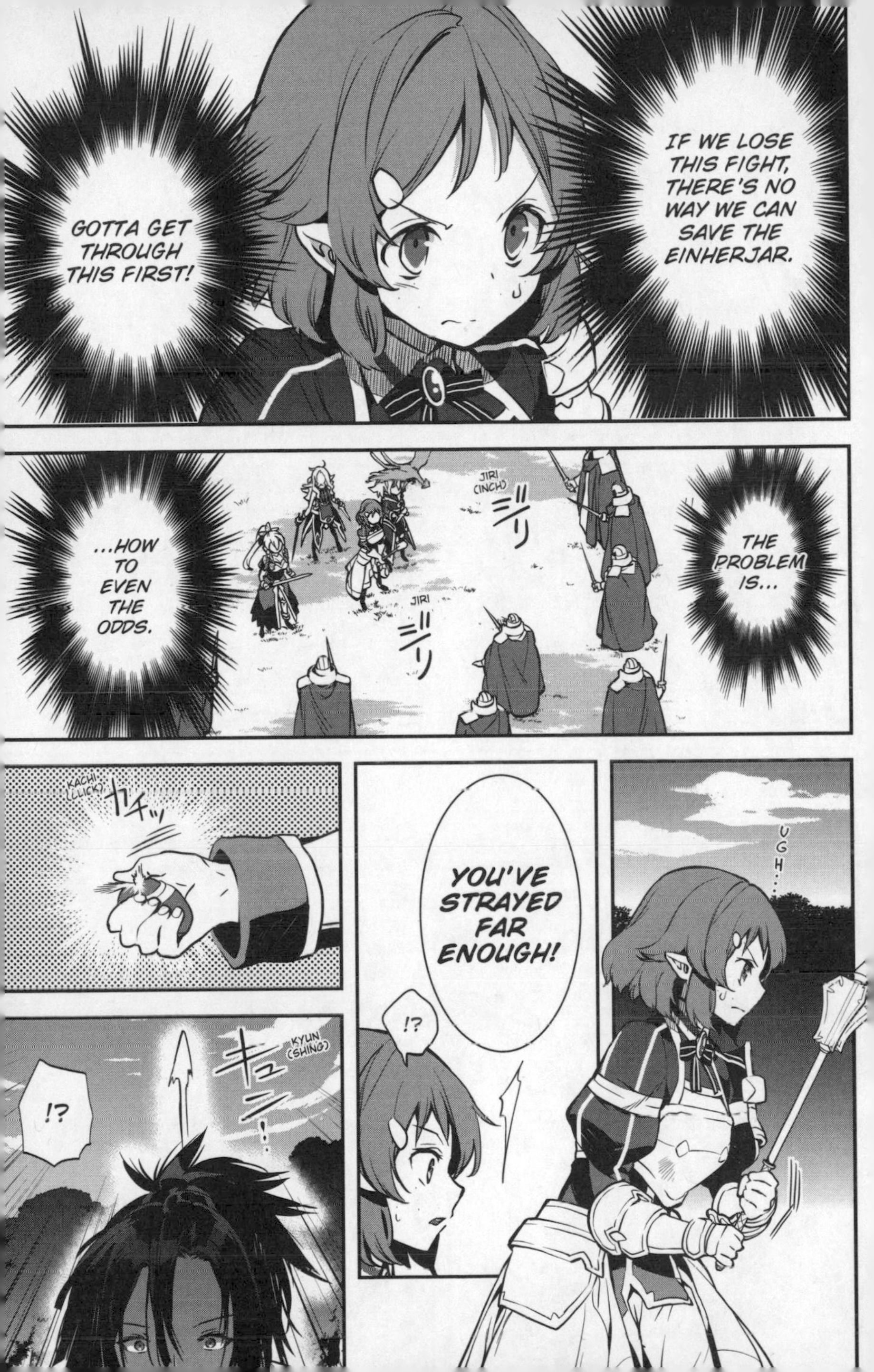
IF WE LOSE THIS FIGHT, THERE'S NO WAY WE CAN SAVE THE EINHERJAR.
GOTTA GET THROUGH THIS FIRST!
THE PROBLEM IS...
JIRI (INCH)
ジリ
JIRI
ジリ
...HOW TO EVEN THE ODDS.
UGH...
YOU'VE STRAYED FAR ENOUGH!
KACHI (CLICK)
カチッ
!?
KYUN (SHING)
キュン
!?

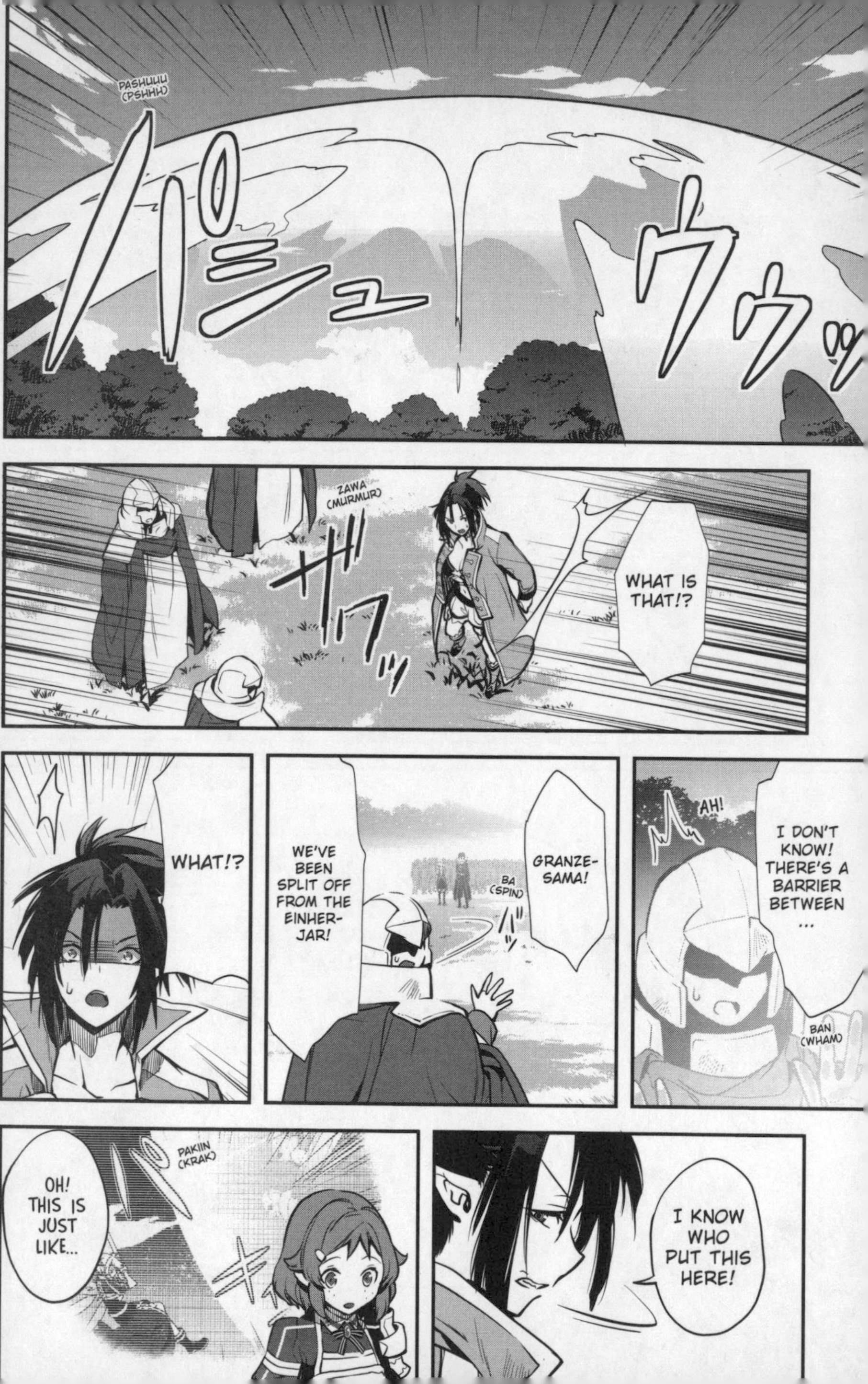
PASHUUU (PSHHH)
パシュウウウッ
ZAWA (MURMUR)
ザワッ
WHAT IS THAT!?
WHAT!?
GRANZE-SAMA!
BA (SPIN)
バッ
WE'VE BEEN SPLIT OFF FROM THE EINHER-JAR!
AH!
I DON'T KNOW! THERE'S A BARRIER BETWEEN ...
BAN (WHAM)
PAKIIN (KRAK)
OH! THIS IS JUST LIKE...
I KNOW WHO PUT THIS HERE!

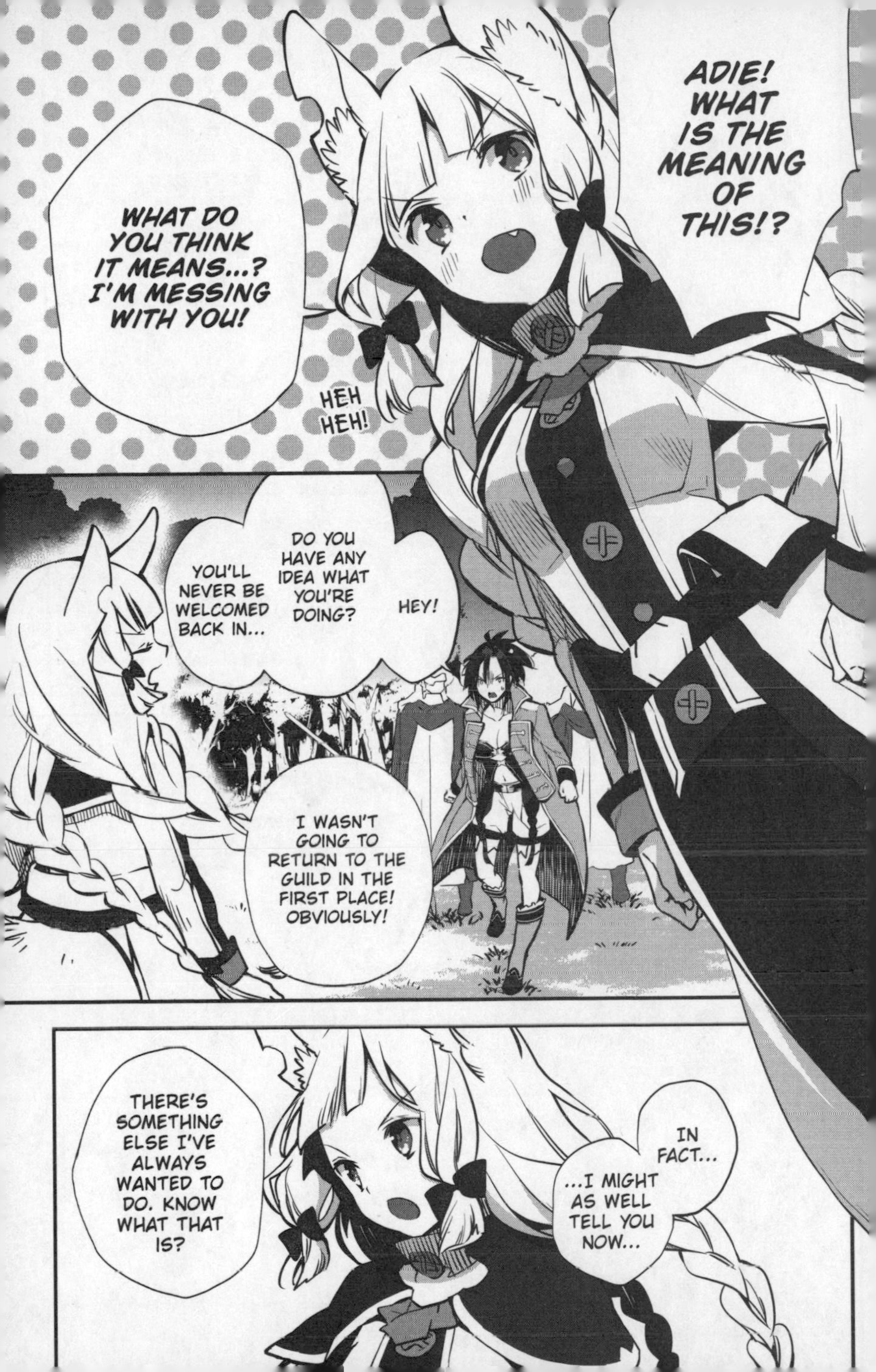
ADIE! WHAT IS THE MEANING OF THIS!?
WHAT DO YOU THINK IT MEANS...? I'M MESSING WITH YOU!
HEH HEH!
HEY!
DO YOU HAVE ANY IDEA WHAT YOU'RE DOING?
YOU'LL NEVER BE WELCOMED BACK IN...
I WASN'T GOING TO RETURN TO THE GUILD IN THE FIRST PLACE! OBVIOUSLY!
IN FACT...
...I MIGHT AS WELL TELL YOU NOW...
THERE'S SOMETHING ELSE I'VE ALWAYS WANTED TO DO. KNOW WHAT THAT IS?

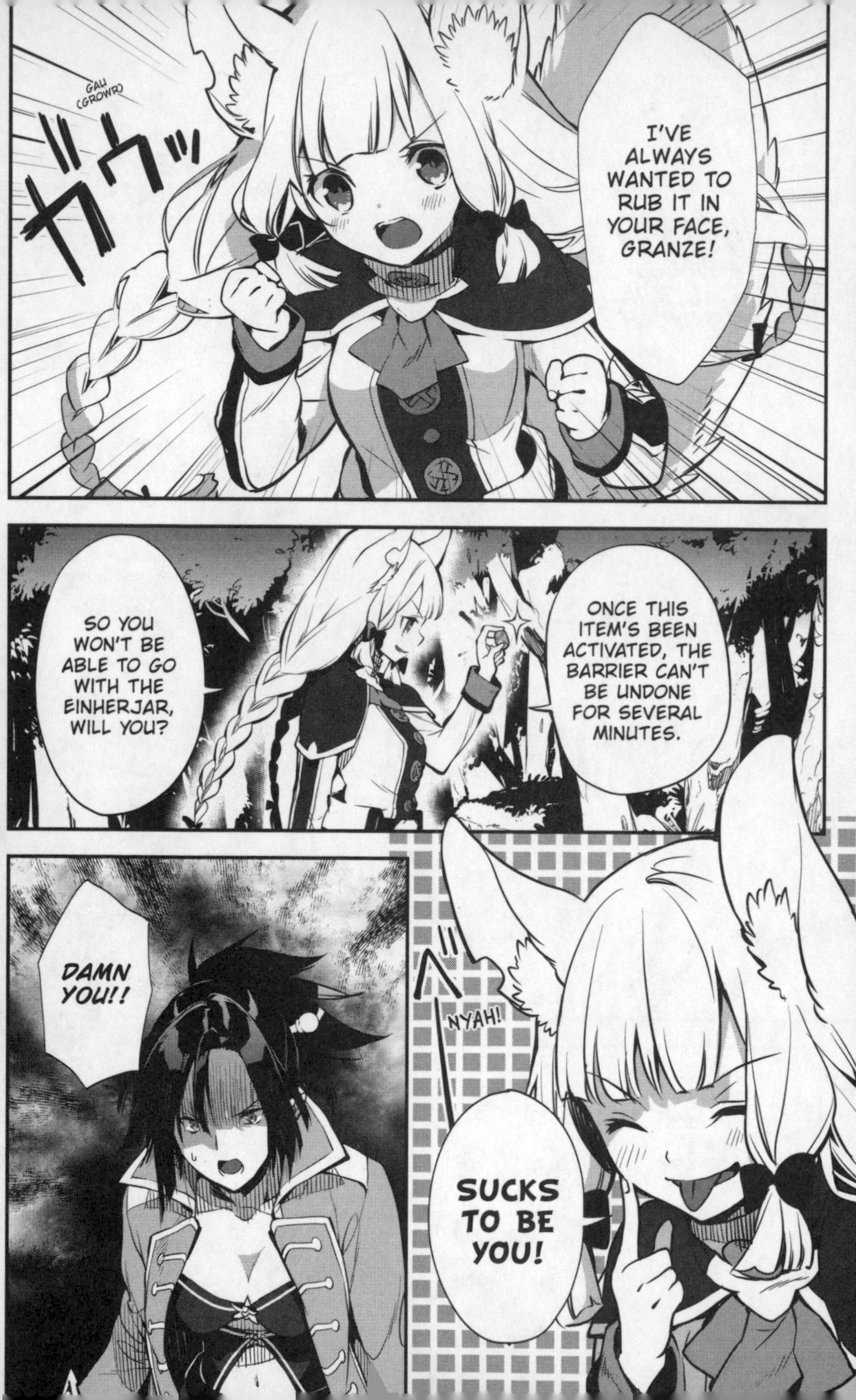
I'VE ALWAYS WANTED TO RUB IT IN YOUR FACE, GRANZE!
ガウッ
GAU (GROWR)
ONCE THIS ITEM'S BEEN ACTIVATED, THE BARRIER CAN'T BE UNDONE FOR SEVERAL MINUTES.
SO YOU WON'T BE ABLE TO GO WITH THE EINHERJAR, WILL YOU?
SUCKS TO BE YOU!
NYAH!
DAMN YOU!!

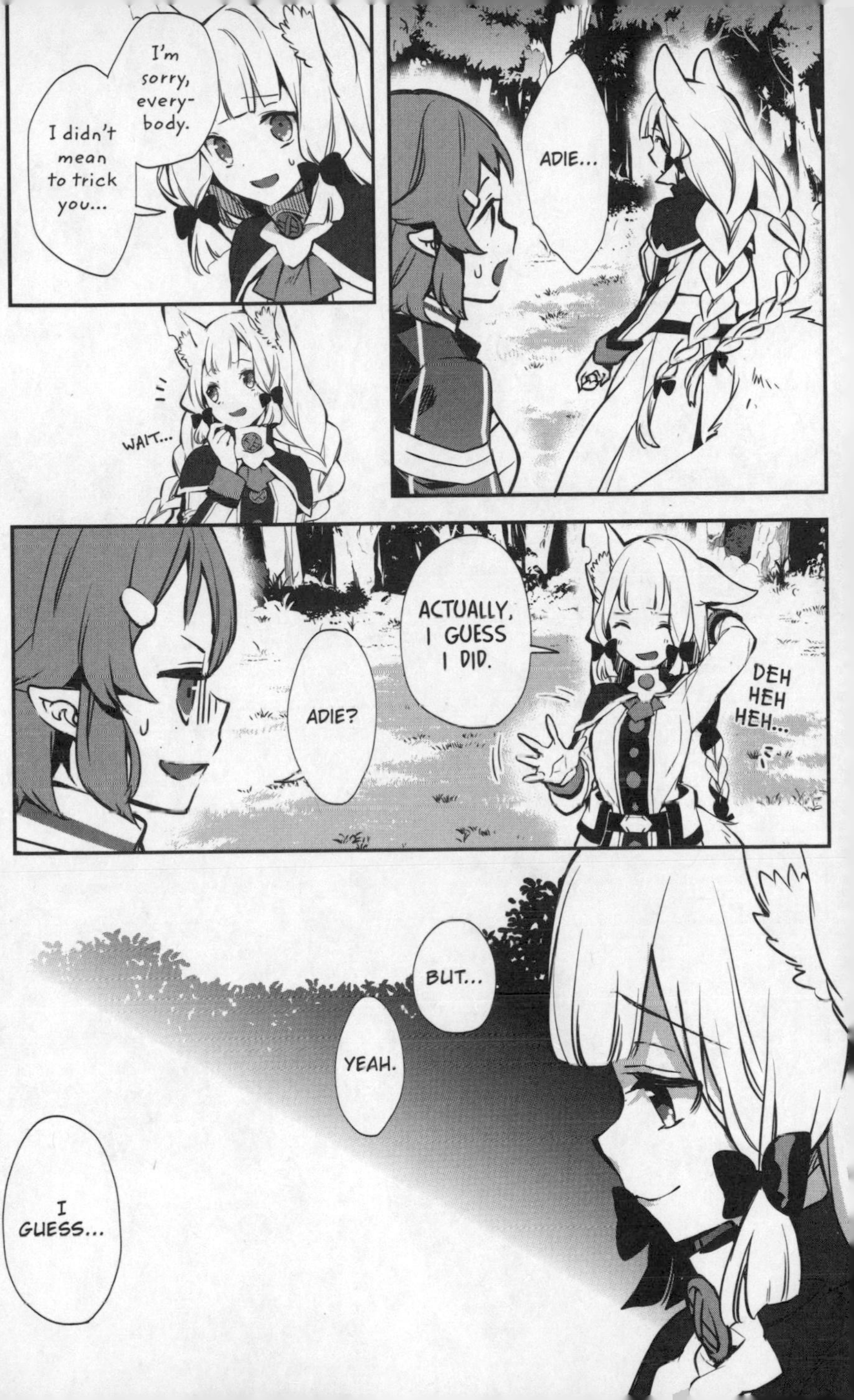
ADIE...
I'm sorry, everybody.
I didn't mean to trick you...
WAIT...
ACTUALLY, I GUESS I DID.
DEH HEH HEH...
ADIE?
BUT...
YEAH.
I GUESS...

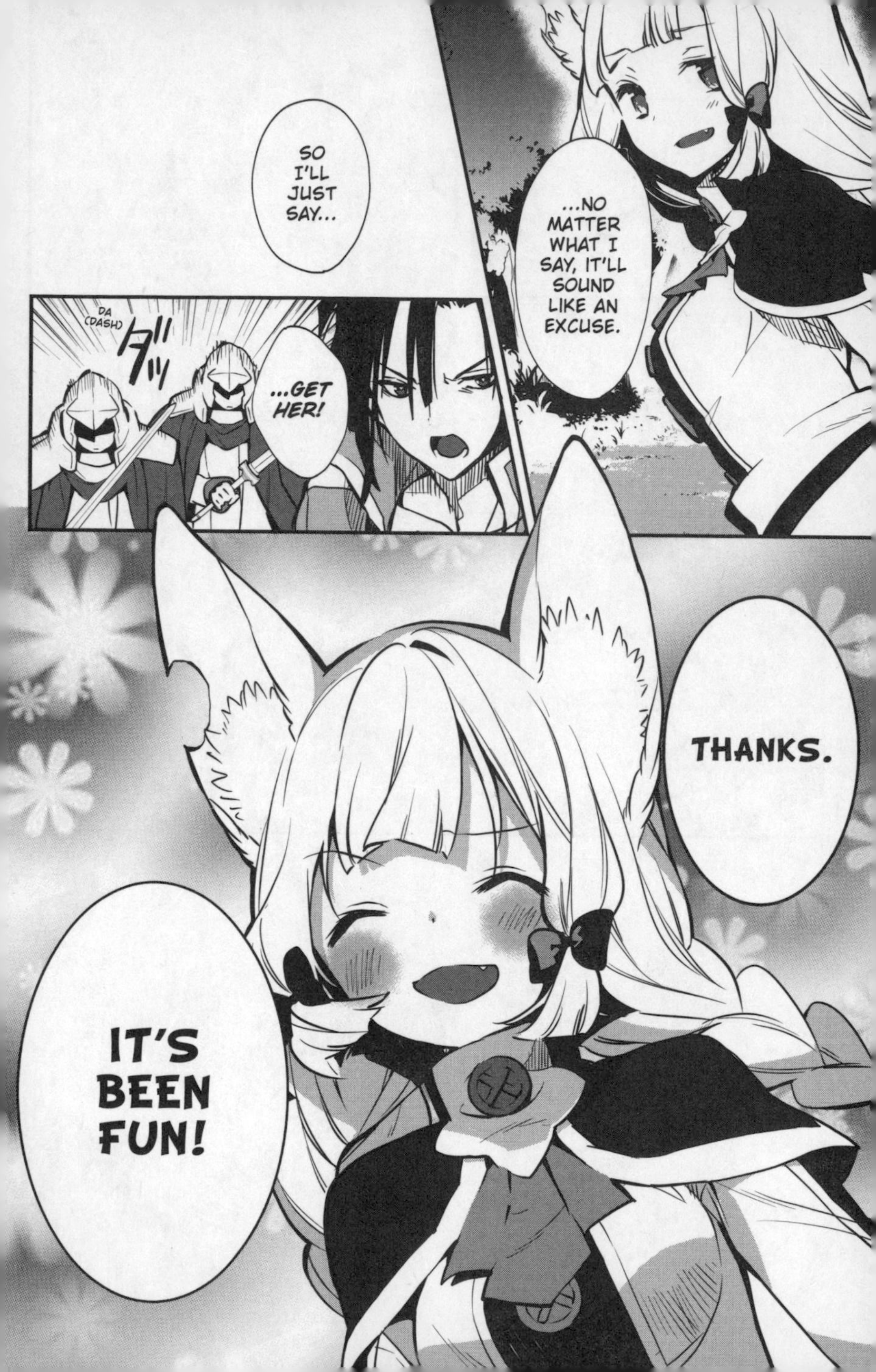
...NO MATTER WHAT I SAY, IT'LL SOUND LIKE AN EXCUSE.
SO I'LL JUST SAY...
...GET HER!
DA (DASH) ダッ
THANKS.
IT'S BEEN FUN!

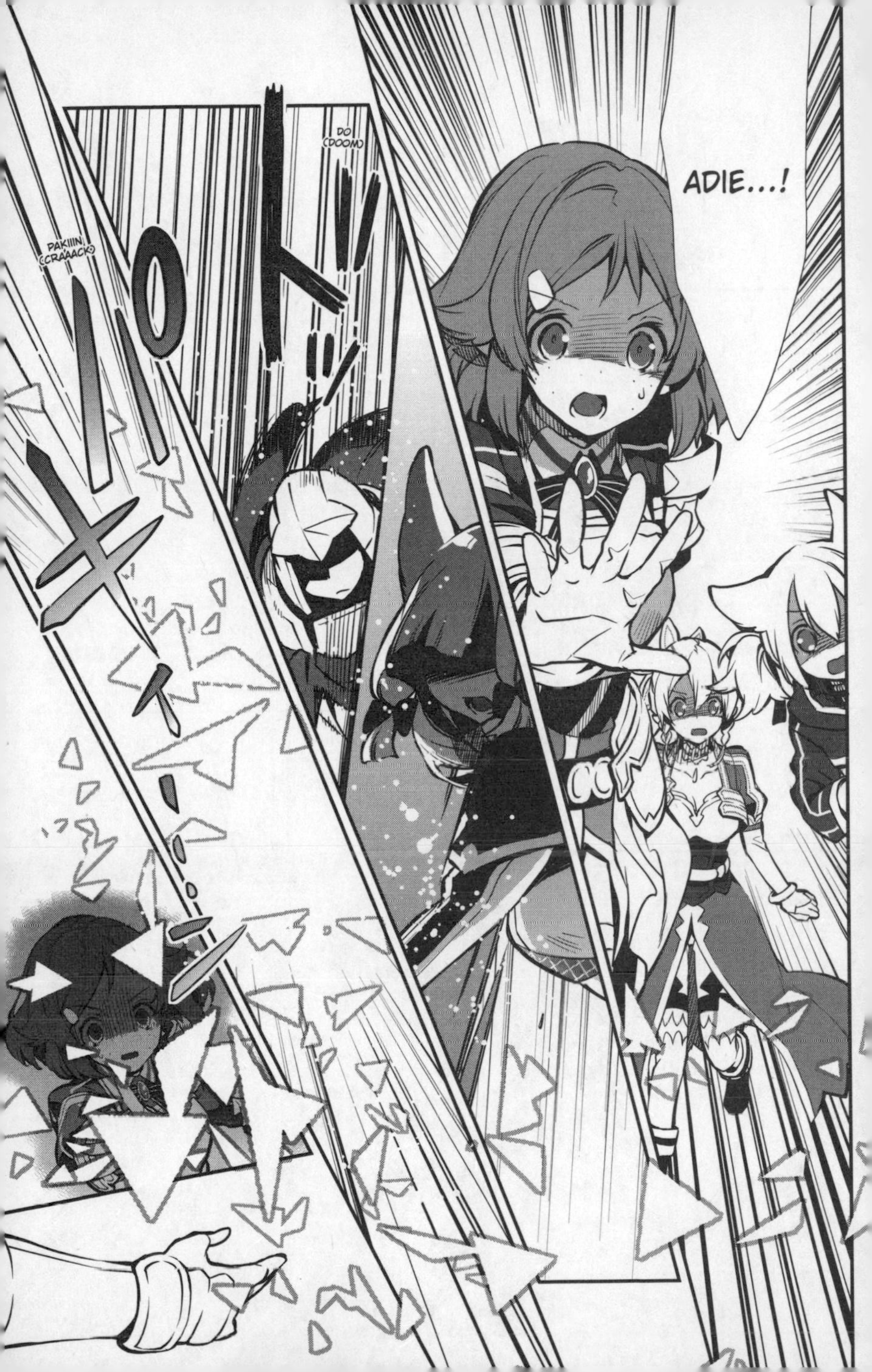
ADIE...!
DO
(DOOM)
PAKIIIN
(CRAAACK)

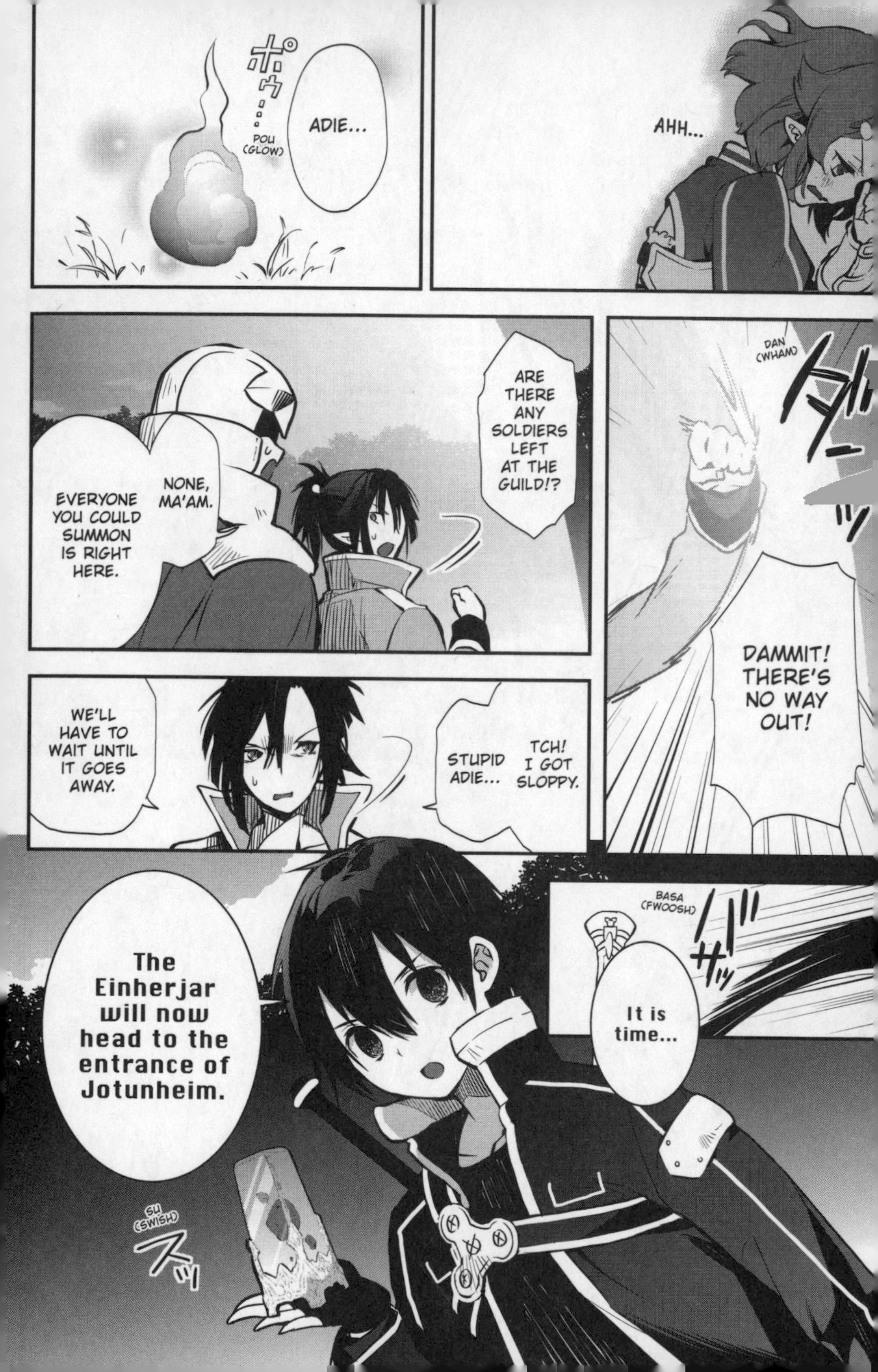
AHH...
ポウ...
POU (GLOW)
ADIE...
DAN (WHAM)
DAMMIT! THERE'S NO WAY OUT!
ARE THERE ANY SOLDIERS LEFT AT THE GUILD!?
NONE, MA'AM.
EVERYONE YOU COULD SUMMON IS RIGHT HERE.
TCH! I GOT SLOPPY.
STUPID ADIE...
WE'LL HAVE TO WAIT UNTIL IT GOES AWAY.
BASA (FWOOSH)
It is time...
The Einherjar will now head to the entrance of Jotunheim.
SU (SWISH)

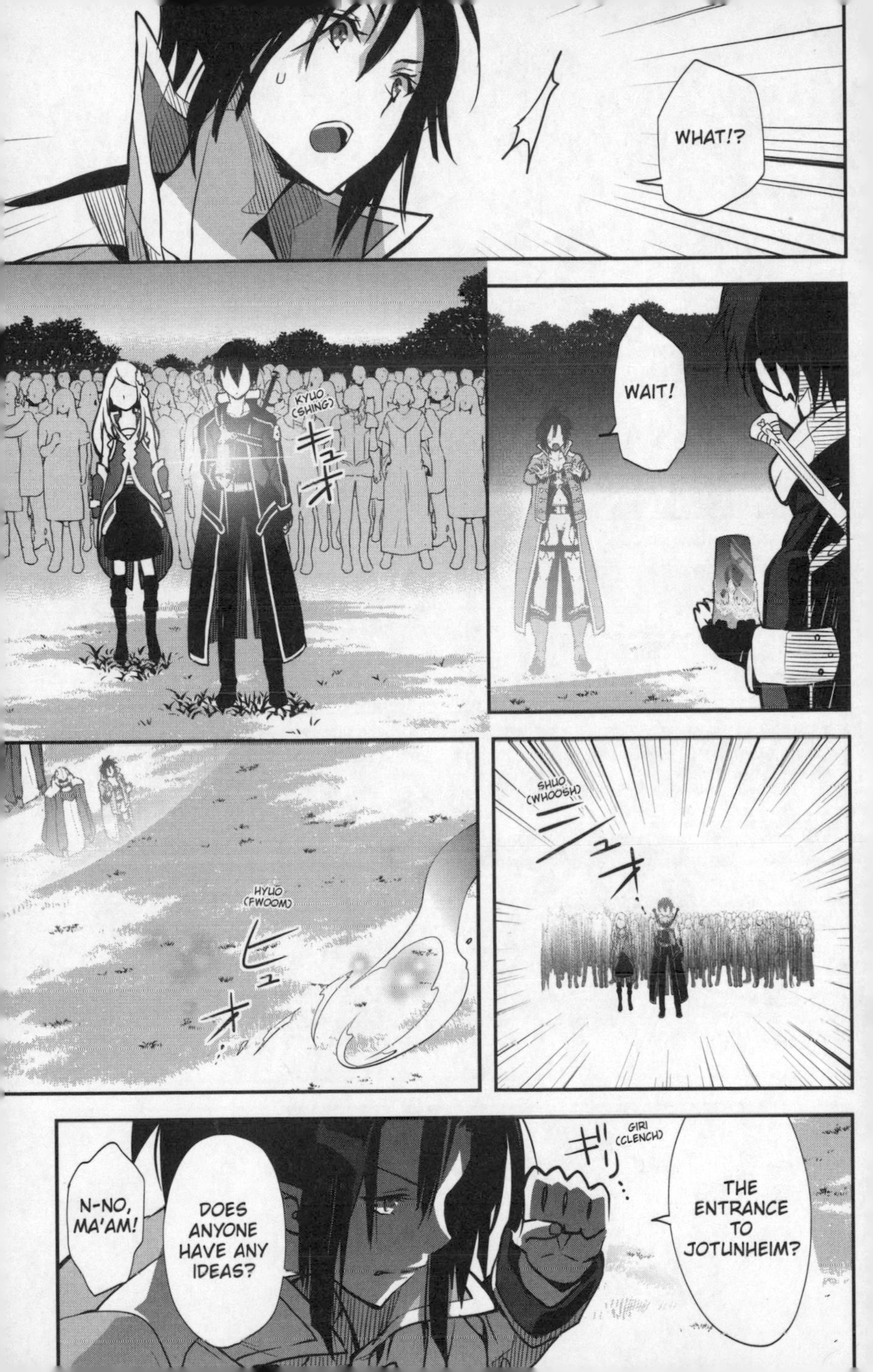
WHAT!?
WAIT!
KYUO (SHING)
キュオ
SHUO (WHOOSH)
シュオ
HYUO (FWOOM)
ヒュオ
THE ENTRANCE TO JOTUNHEIM?
GIRI (CLENCH)
ギリ…
DOES ANYONE HAVE ANY IDEAS?
N-NO, MA'AM!

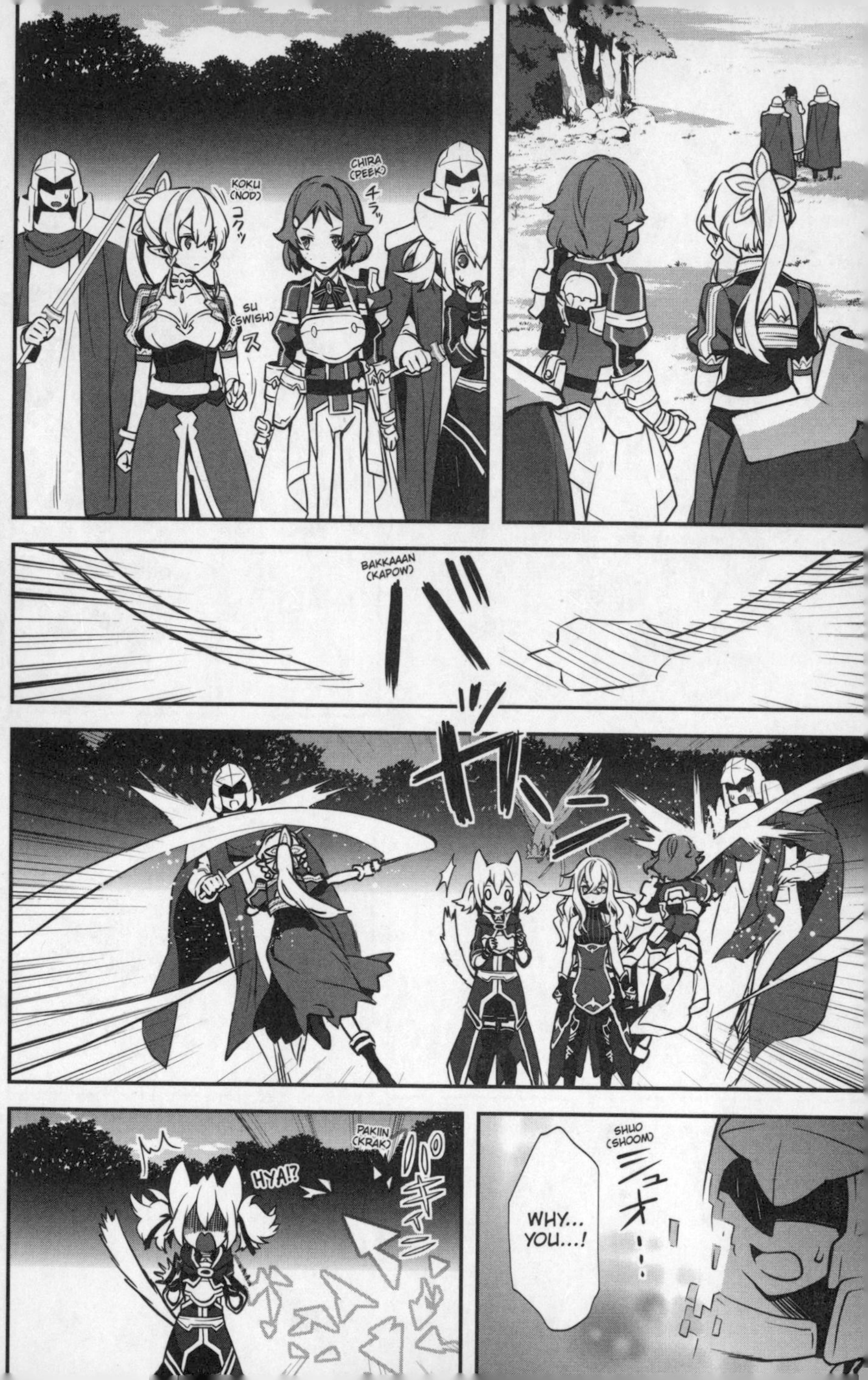
CHIRA (PEEK)
チラッ
KOKU (NOD)
コクッ
SU (SWISH)
ス
BAKKAAAN (KAPOW)
SHUO (SHOOM)
シュオ・・・
WHY... YOU...!
PAKIIN (KRAK)
パキィン
HYA!?

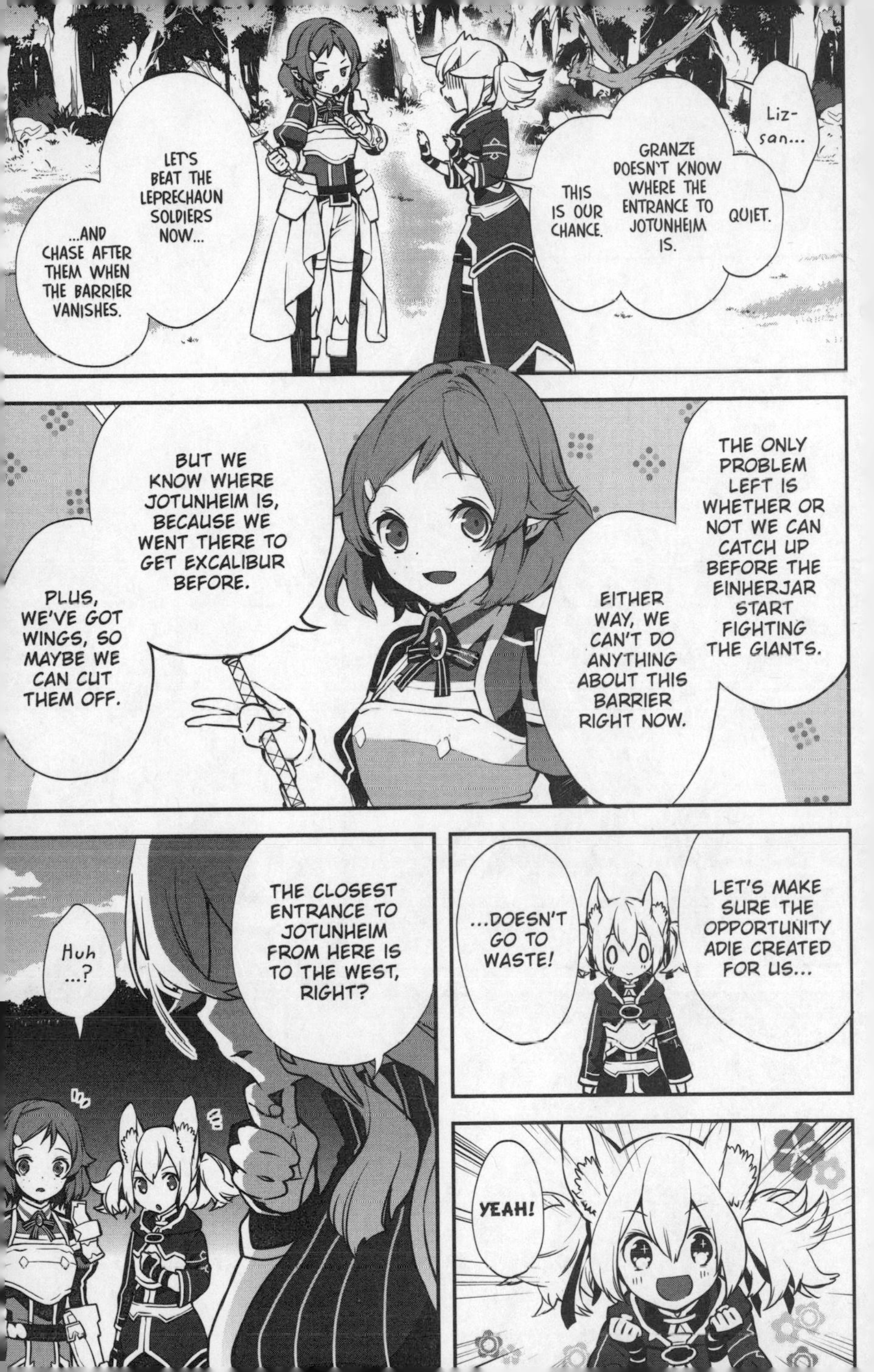
Liz-san...
QUIET.
GRANZE DOESN'T KNOW WHERE THE ENTRANCE TO JOTUNHEIM IS.
THIS IS OUR CHANCE.
LET'S BEAT THE LEPRECHAUN SOLDIERS NOW...
...AND CHASE AFTER THEM WHEN THE BARRIER VANISHES.
THE ONLY PROBLEM LEFT IS WHETHER OR NOT WE CAN CATCH UP BEFORE THE EINHERJAR START FIGHTING THE GIANTS.
EITHER WAY, WE CAN'T DO ANYTHING ABOUT THIS BARRIER RIGHT NOW.
BUT WE KNOW WHERE JOTUNHEIM IS, BECAUSE WE WENT THERE TO GET EXCALIBUR BEFORE.
PLUS, WE'VE GOT WINGS, SO MAYBE WE CAN CUT THEM OFF.
LET'S MAKE SURE THE OPPORTUNITY ADIE CREATED FOR US...
...DOESN'T GO TO WASTE!
YEAH!
THE CLOSEST ENTRANCE TO JOTUNHEIM FROM HERE IS TO THE WEST, RIGHT?
Huh ...?

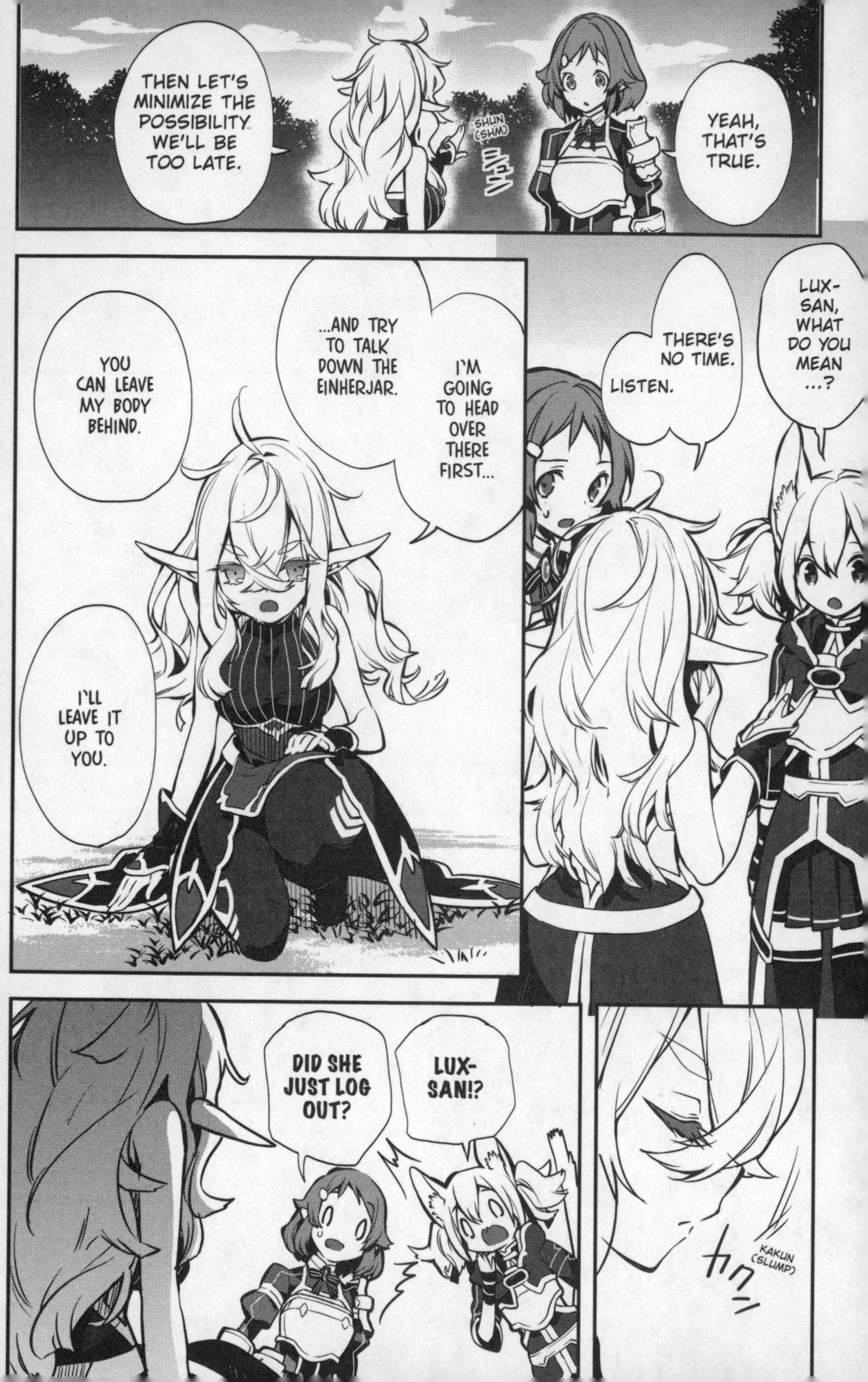
YEAH, THAT'S TRUE.
SHUN (SHM)
THEN LET'S MINIMIZE THE POSSIBILITY WE'LL BE TOO LATE.
LUX-SAN, WHAT DO YOU MEAN ...?
THERE'S NO TIME. LISTEN.
I'M GOING TO HEAD OVER THERE FIRST...
...AND TRY TO TALK DOWN THE EINHERJAR.
YOU CAN LEAVE MY BODY BEHIND.
I'LL LEAVE IT UP TO YOU.
KAKUN (SLUMP)
LUX-SAN!?
DID SHE JUST LOG OUT?

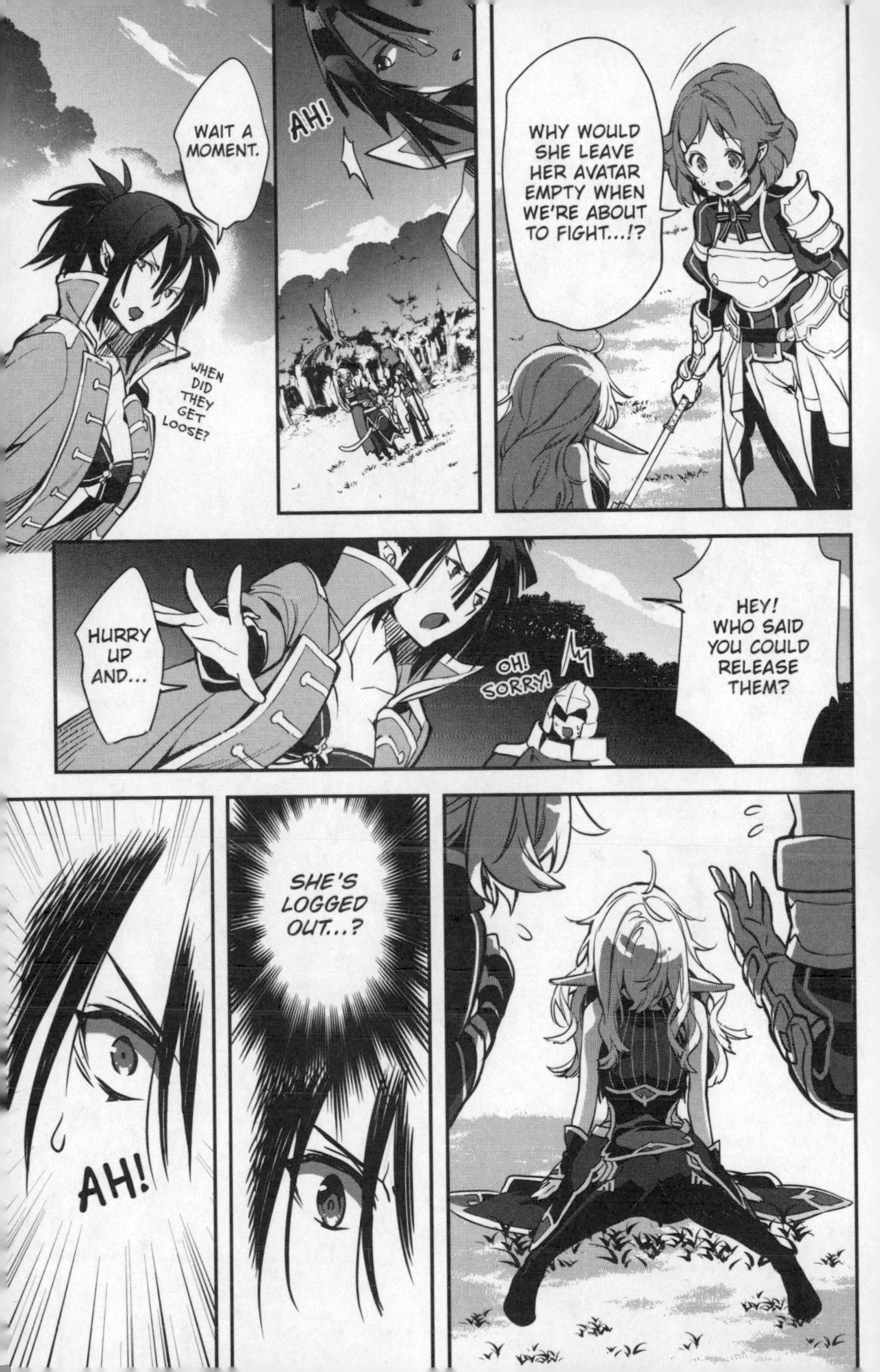
WHY WOULD SHE LEAVE HER AVATAR EMPTY WHEN WE'RE ABOUT TO FIGHT...!?
AH!
WAIT A MOMENT.
WHEN DID THEY GET LOOSE?
HEY! WHO SAID YOU COULD RELEASE THEM?
OH! SORRY!
HURRY UP AND...
SHE'S LOGGED OUT...?
AH!

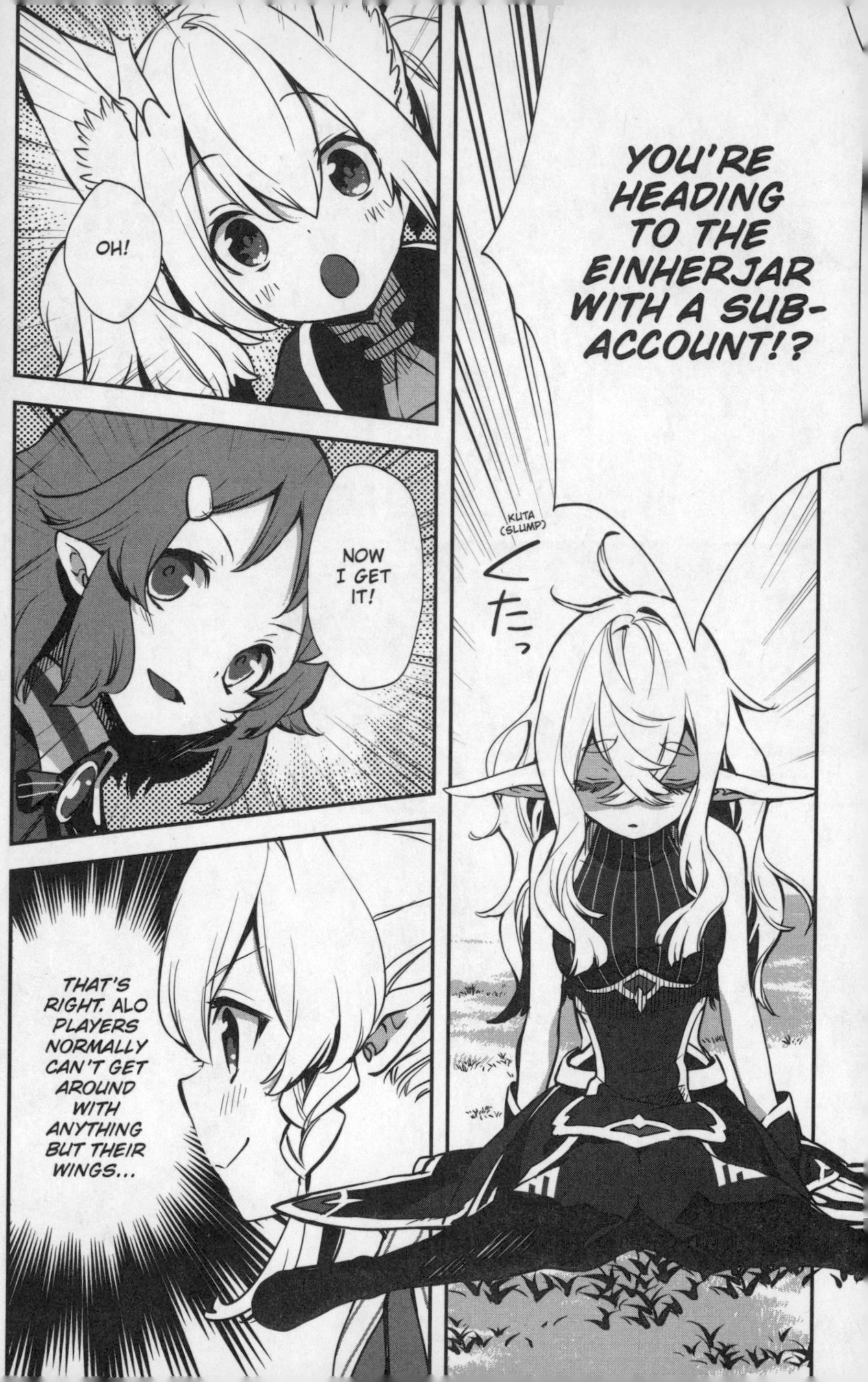
YOU'RE HEADING TO THE EINHERJAR WITH A SUB-ACCOUNT!?
OH!
NOW I GET IT!
KUTA (SLUMP)
くたっ
THAT'S RIGHT. ALO PLAYERS NORMALLY CAN'T GET AROUND WITH ANYTHING BUT THEIR WINGS...

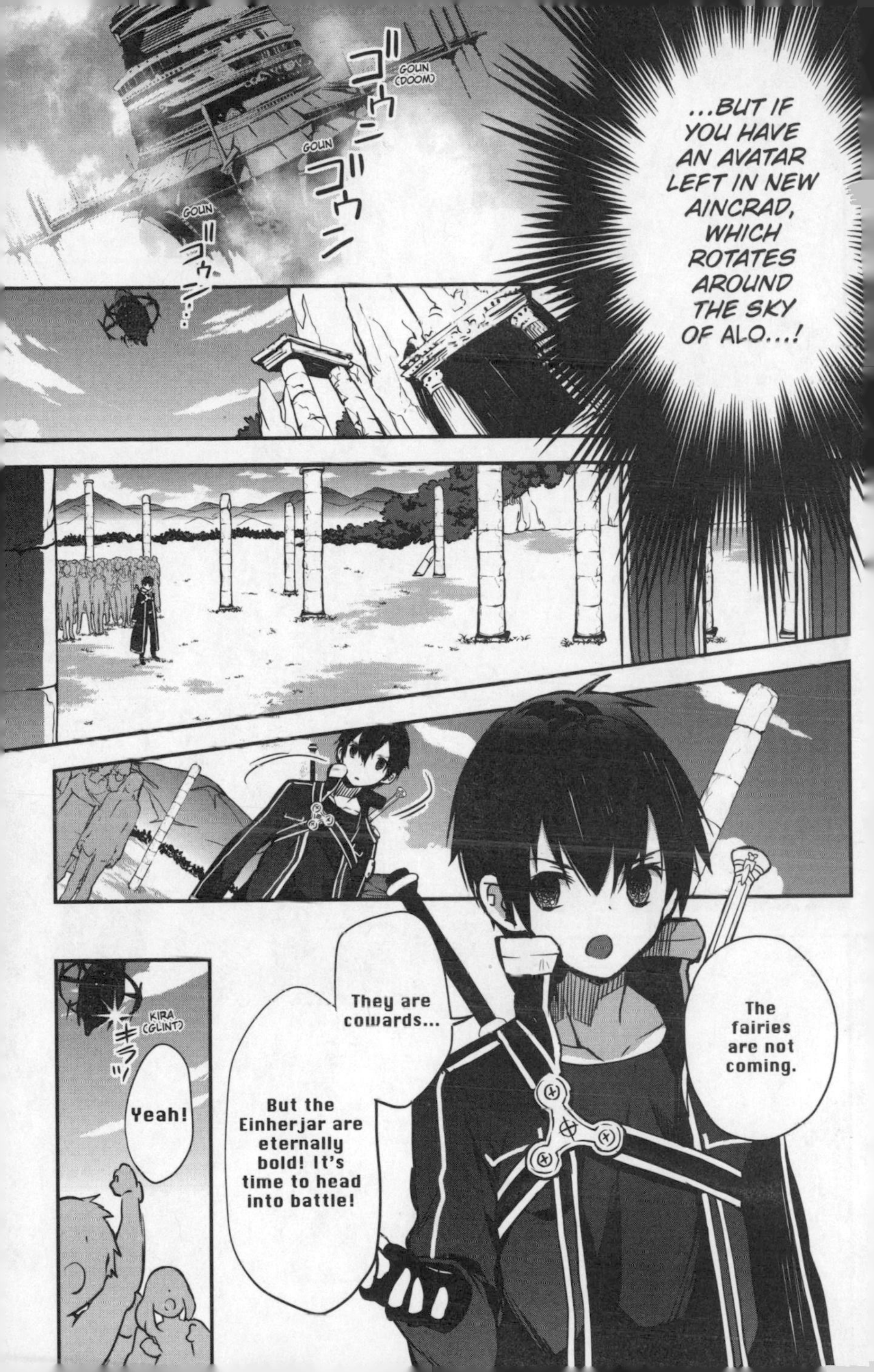
...BUT IF YOU HAVE AN AVATAR LEFT IN NEW AINCRAD, WHICH ROTATES AROUND THE SKY OF ALO...!
ゴウン
GOUN (DOOM)
ゴウン
GOUN
ゴウン...
GOUN
The fairies are not coming.
They are cowards...
But the Einherjar are eternally bold! It's time to head into battle!
キラッ
KIRA (GLINT)
Yeah!

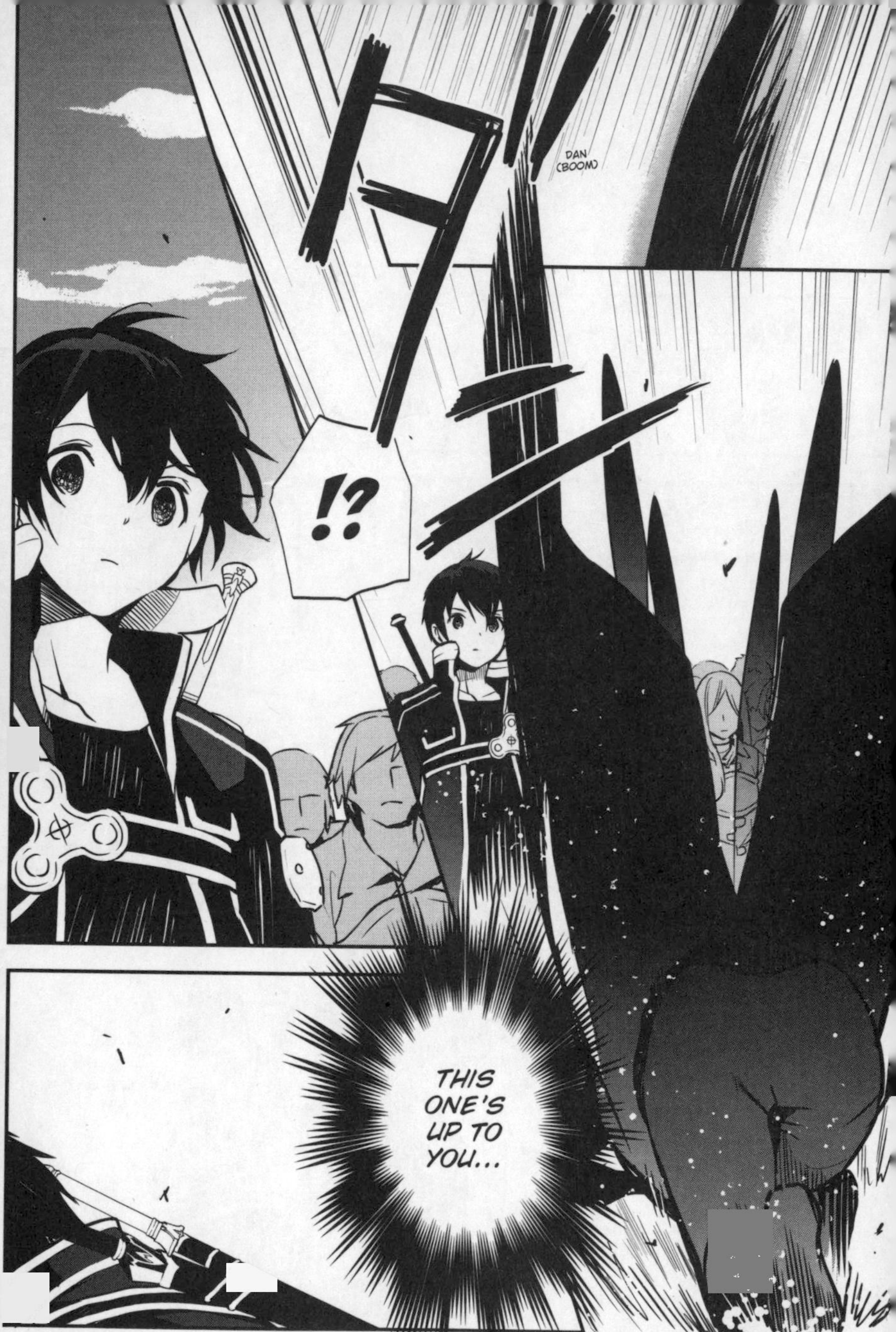
DAN
(BOOM)
!?
THIS ONE'S UP TO YOU...

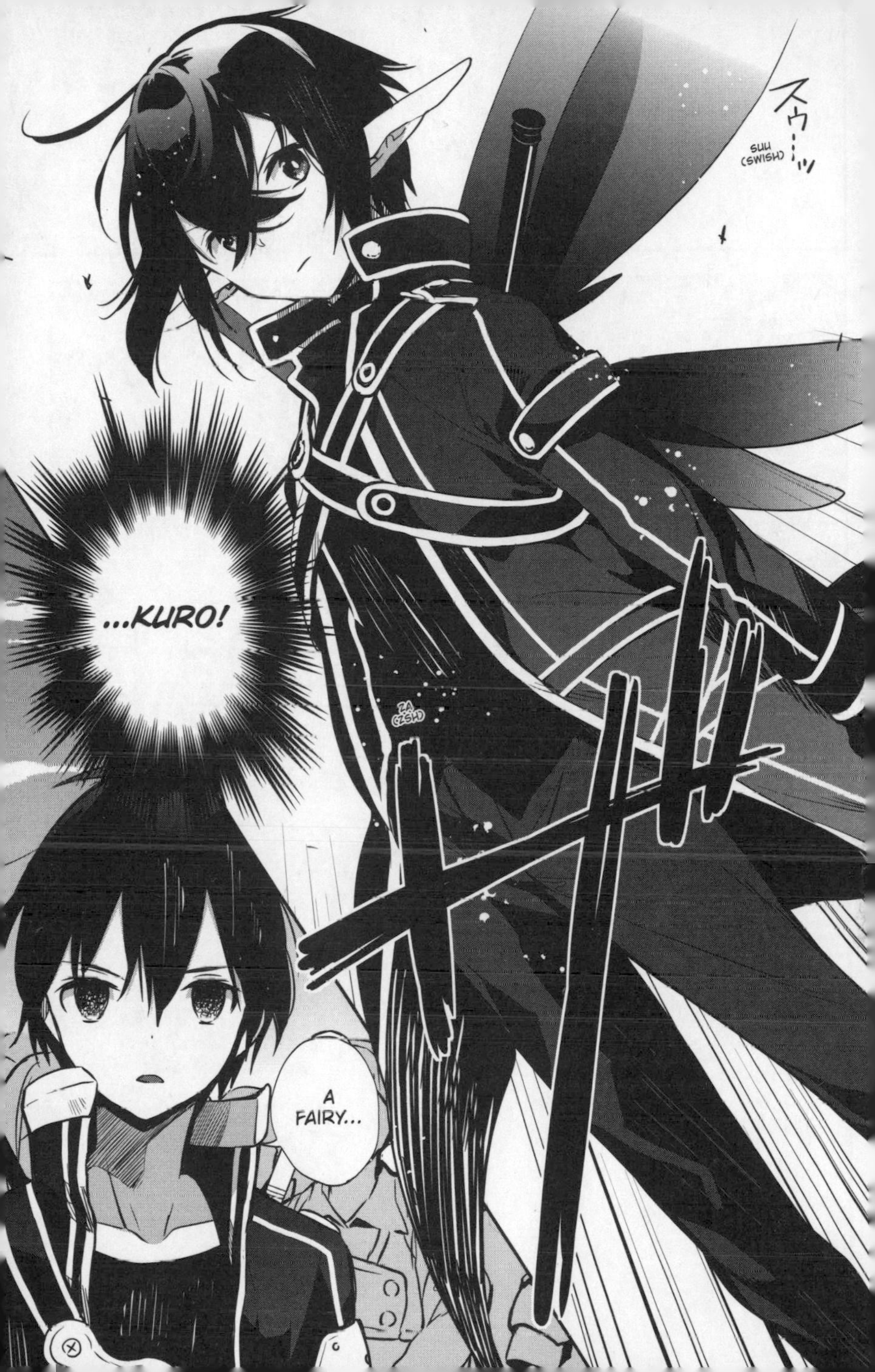
スウーッ
SUU (SWISH)
...KURO!
ZA (ZSHD)
A FAIRY...

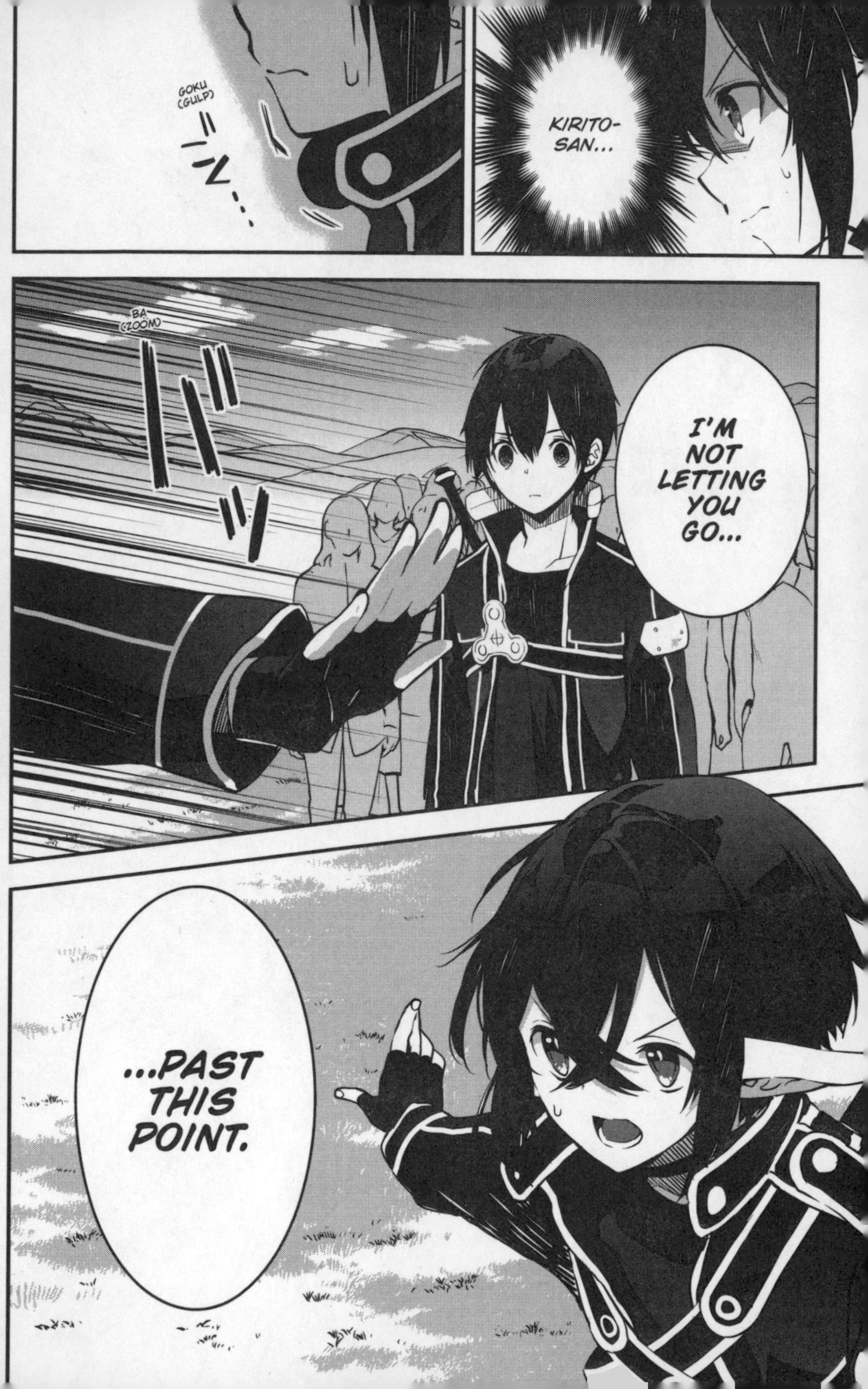
KIRITO-SAN...
GOKU (GULP)
I'M NOT LETTING YOU GO...
BA (ZOOM)
...PAST THIS POINT.

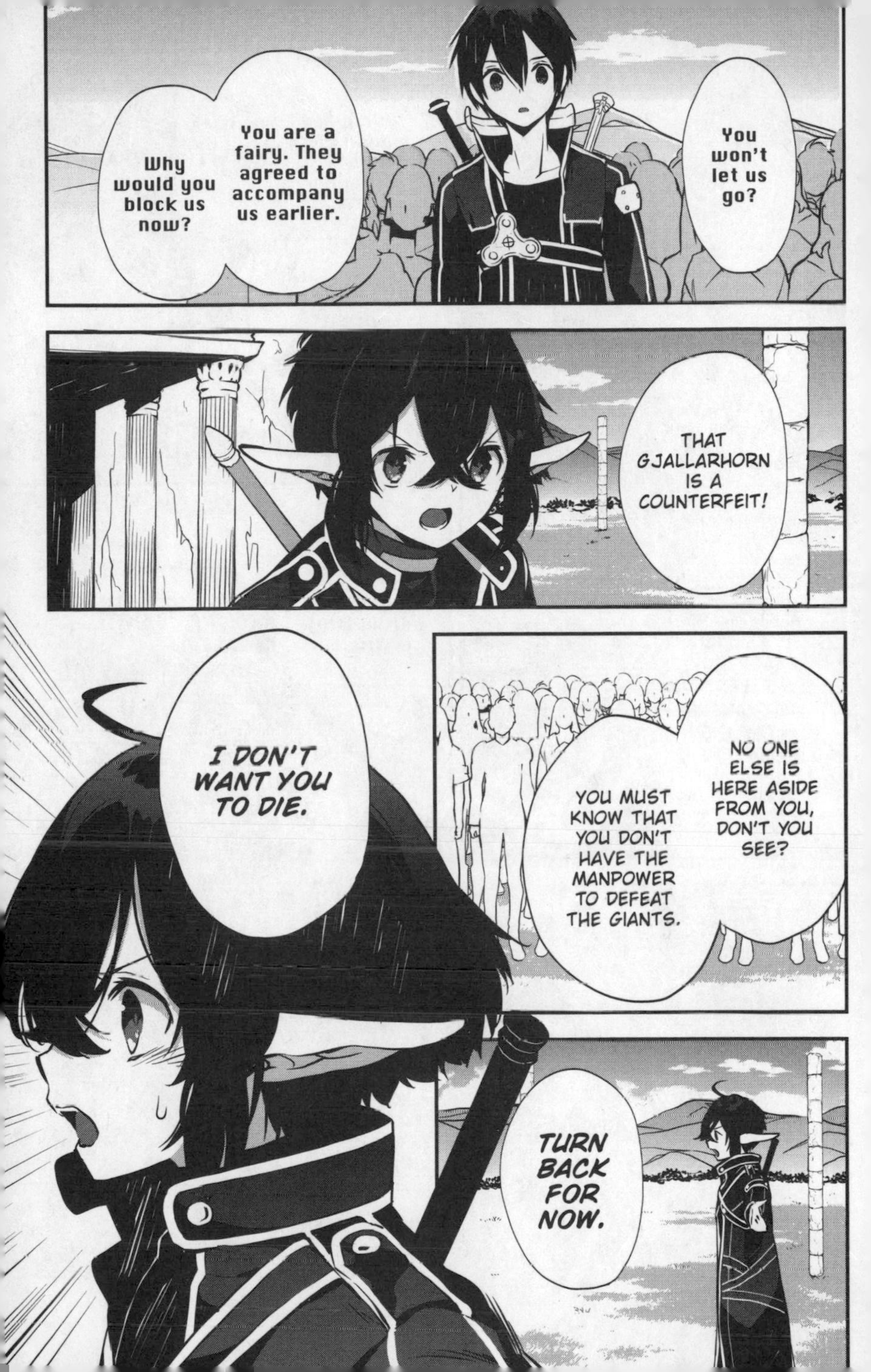
You won't let us go?
You are a fairy. They agreed to accompany us earlier.
Why would you block us now?
THAT GJALLARHORN IS A COUNTERFEIT!
NO ONE ELSE IS HERE ASIDE FROM YOU, DON'T YOU SEE?
YOU MUST KNOW THAT YOU DON'T HAVE THE MANPOWER TO DEFEAT THE GIANTS.
TURN BACK FOR NOW.
I DON'T WANT YOU TO DIE.

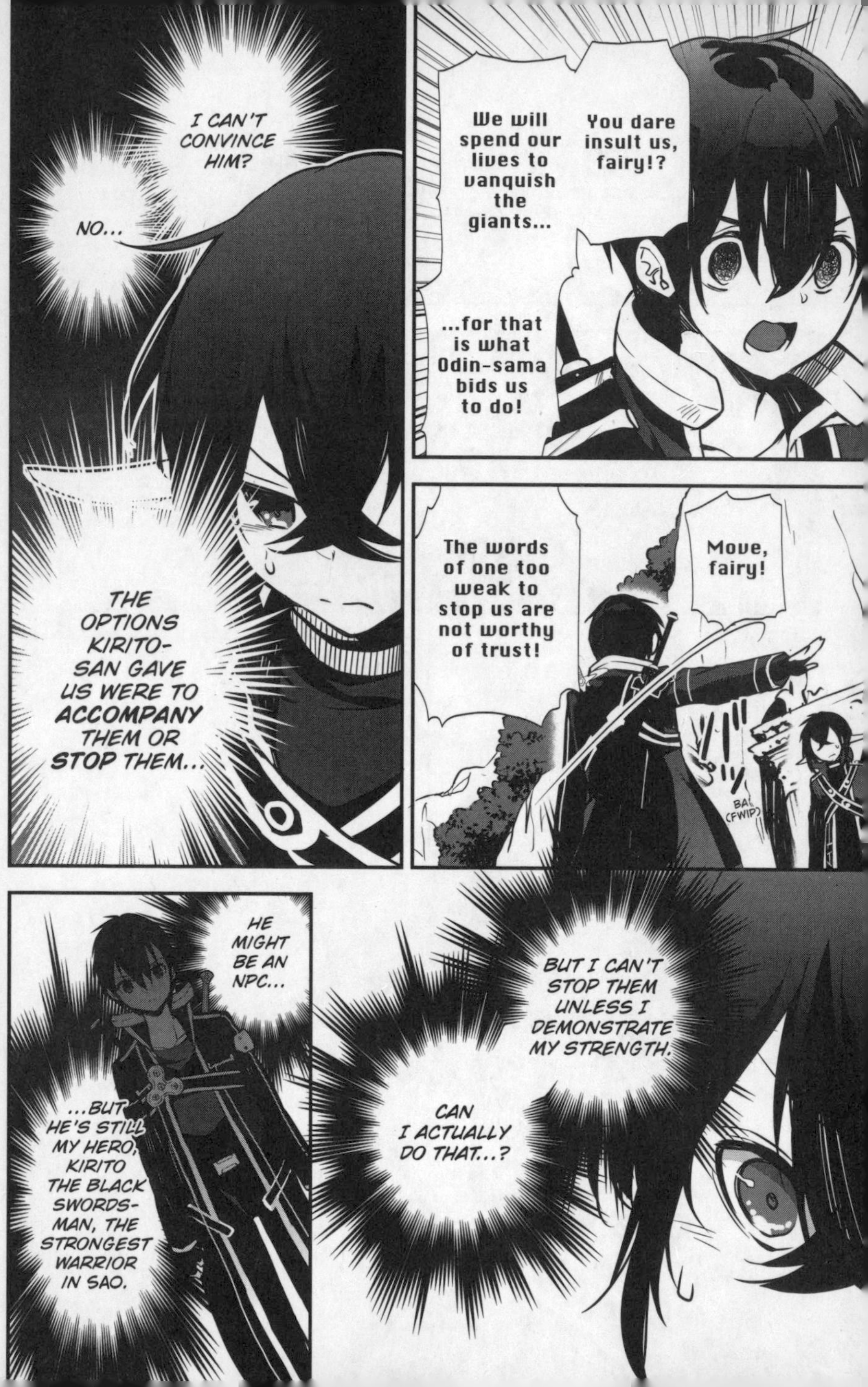

You dare insult us, fairy!?
We will spend our lives to vanquish the giants...
...for that is what Odin-sama bids us to do!
Move, fairy!
The words of one too weak to stop us are not worthy of trust!
BA (FWIP)
I CAN'T CONVINCE HIM?
NO...
THE OPTIONS KIRITO-SAN GAVE US WERE TO ACCOMPANY THEM OR STOP THEM...
BUT I CAN'T STOP THEM UNLESS I DEMONSTRATE MY STRENGTH.
CAN I ACTUALLY DO THAT...?
HE MIGHT BE AN NPC...
...BUT HE'S STILL MY HERO, KIRITO THE BLACK SWORDS-MAN, THE STRONGEST WARRIOR IN SAO.

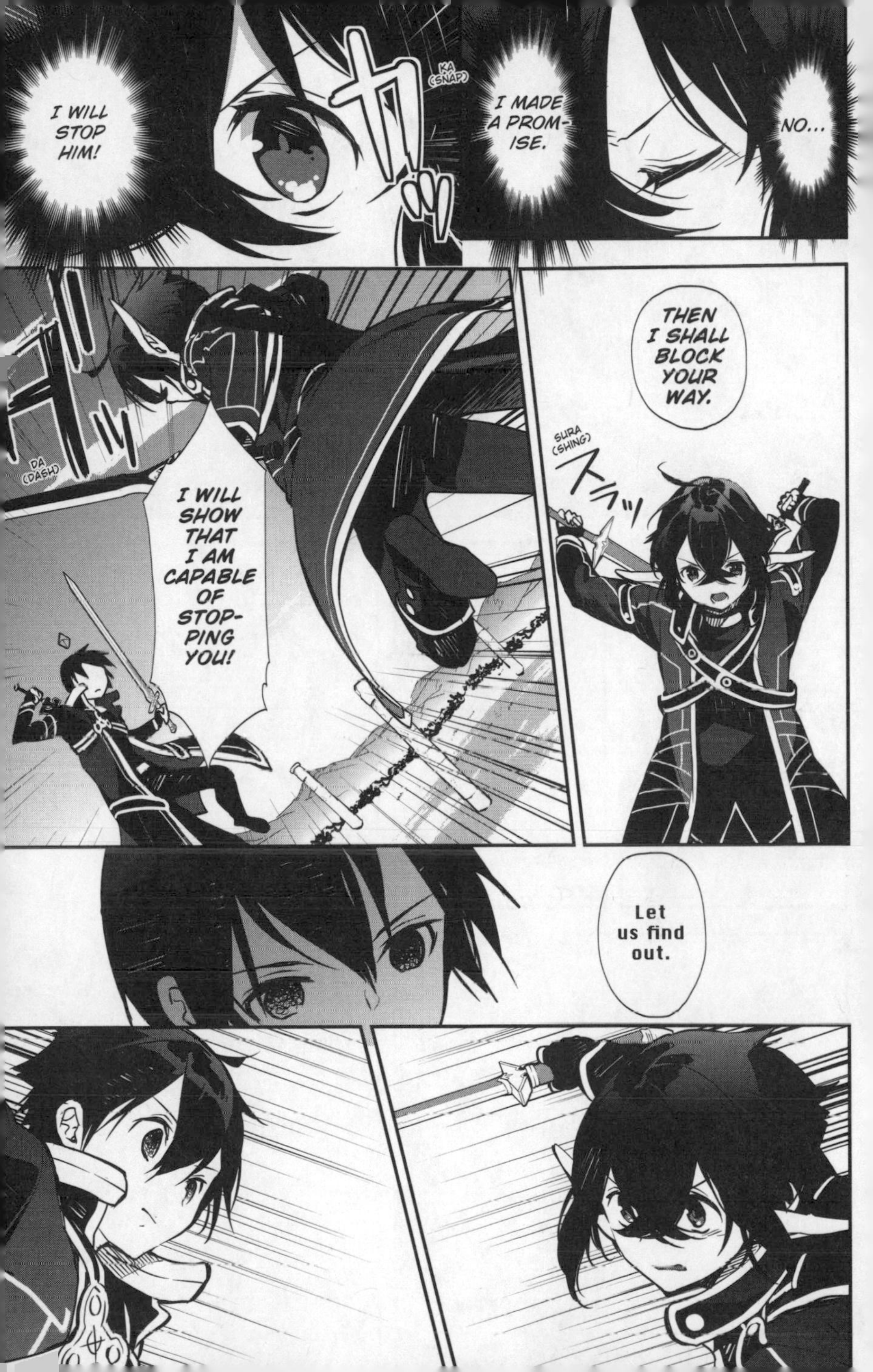
NO...
I MADE A PROMISE.
KA (SNAP)
I WILL STOP HIM!
THEN I SHALL BLOCK YOUR WAY.
SURA (SHING)
DA (DASH)
I WILL SHOW THAT I AM CAPABLE OF STOPPING YOU!
Let us find out.

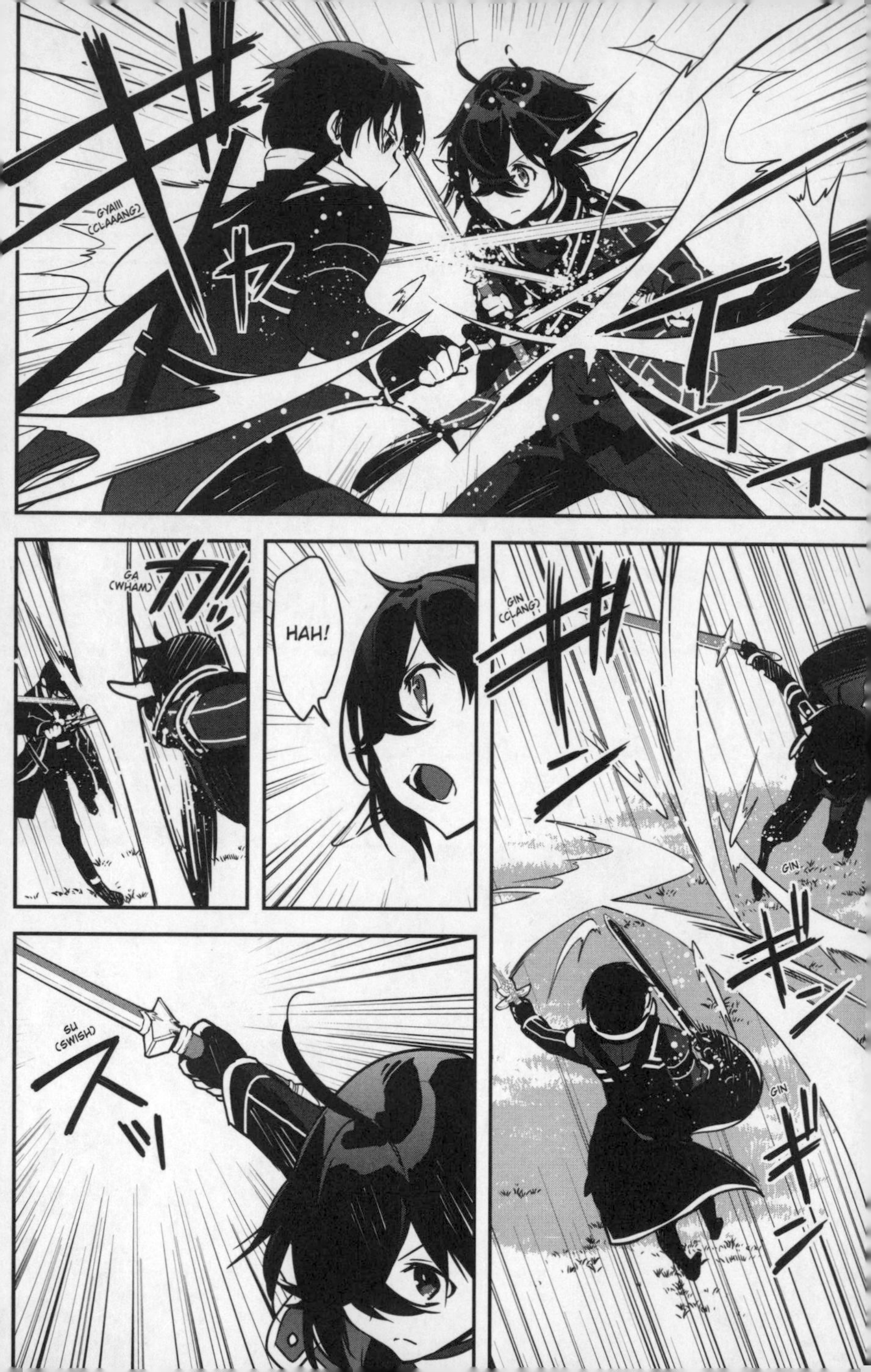
GYAIII (CLAAANG)
GIN (CLANG)
HAH!
GA (WHAM)
GIN
GIN
SU (SWISH)

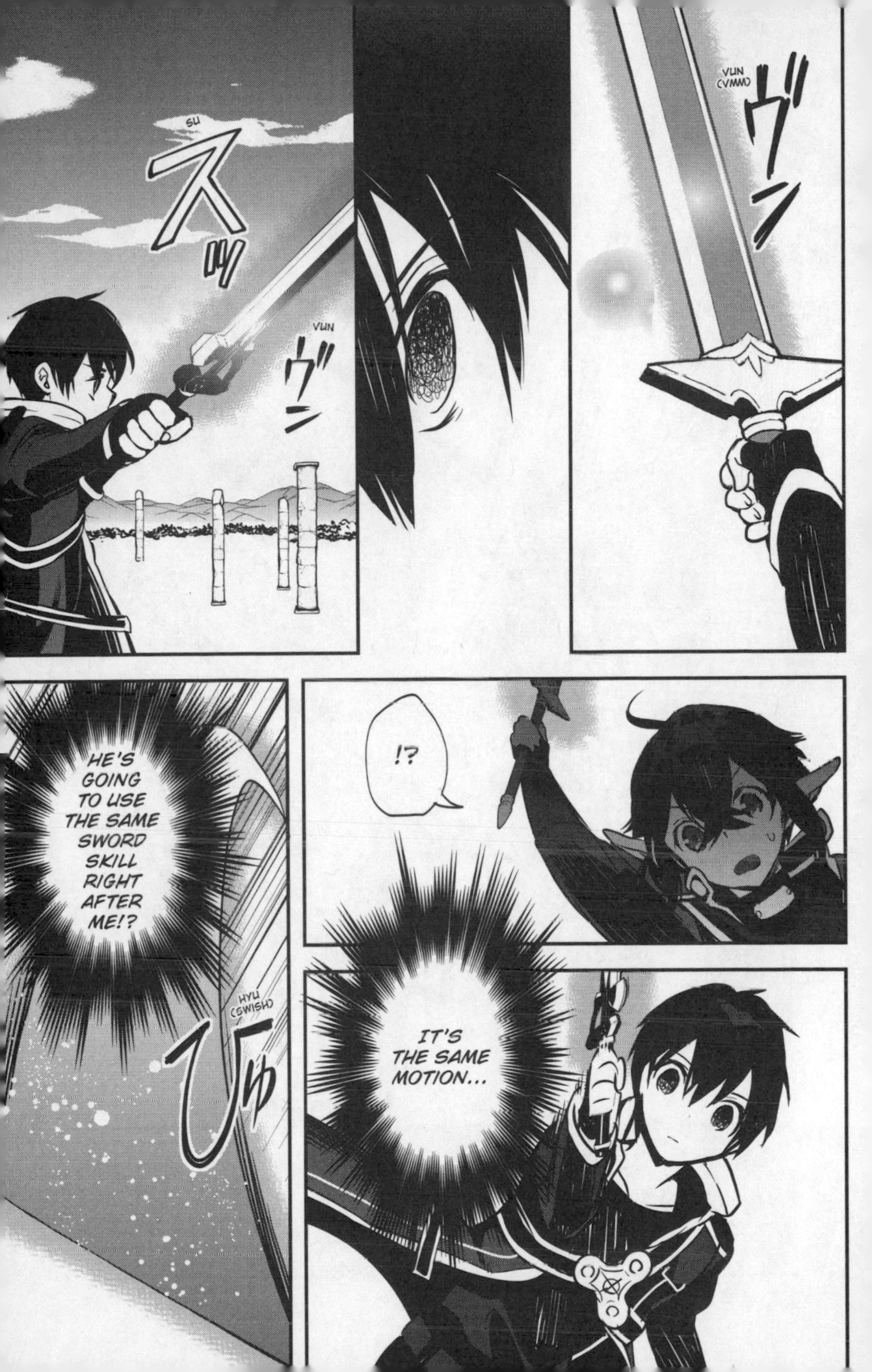
VUN (VMM)
ヴゥン
SU
スッ
VUN
ヴン
!?
HE'S GOING TO USE THE SAME SWORD SKILL RIGHT AFTER ME!?
IT'S THE SAME MOTION...
HYU (SWISH)
ひゅ

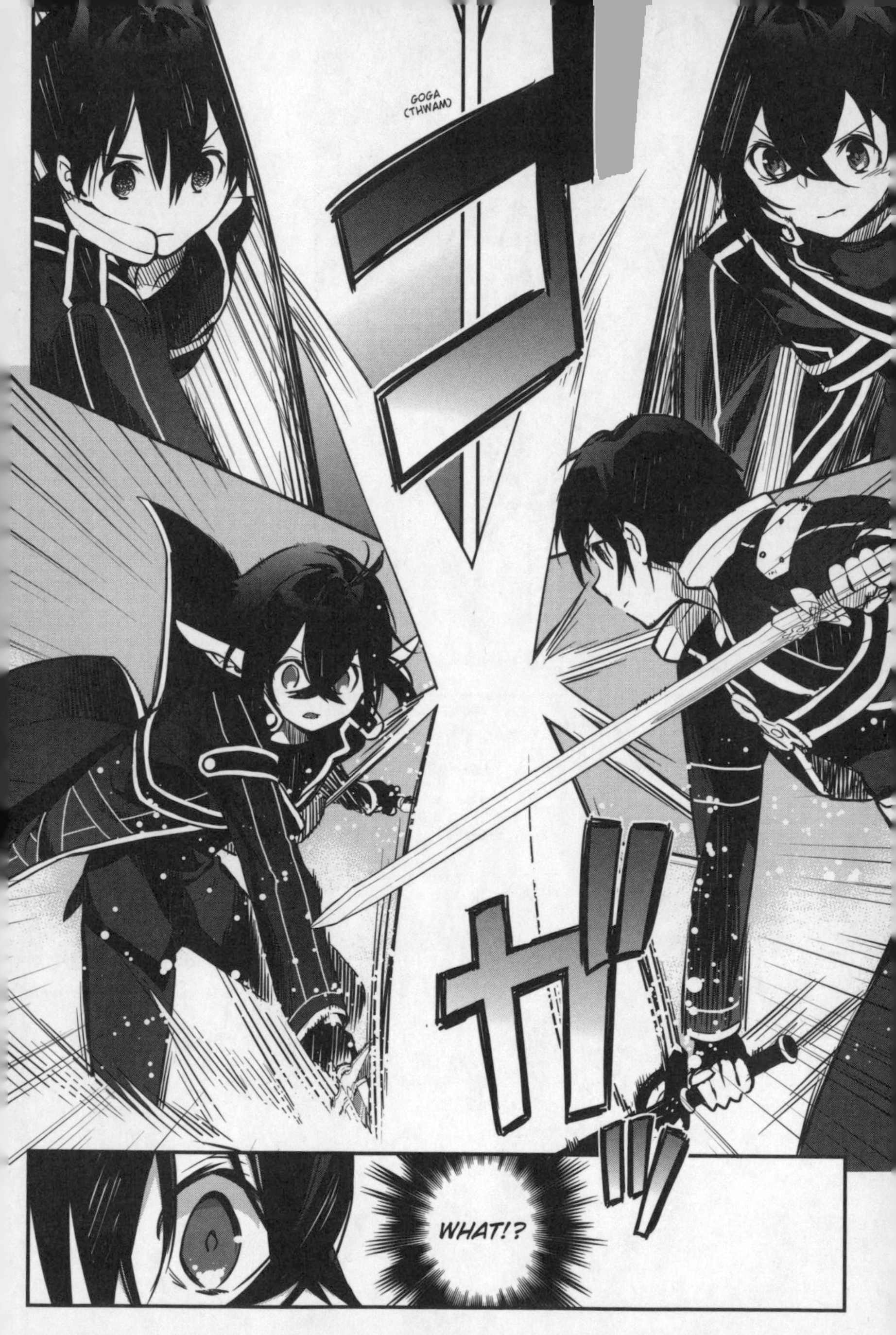
GOGA
(THWAM)
WHAT!?

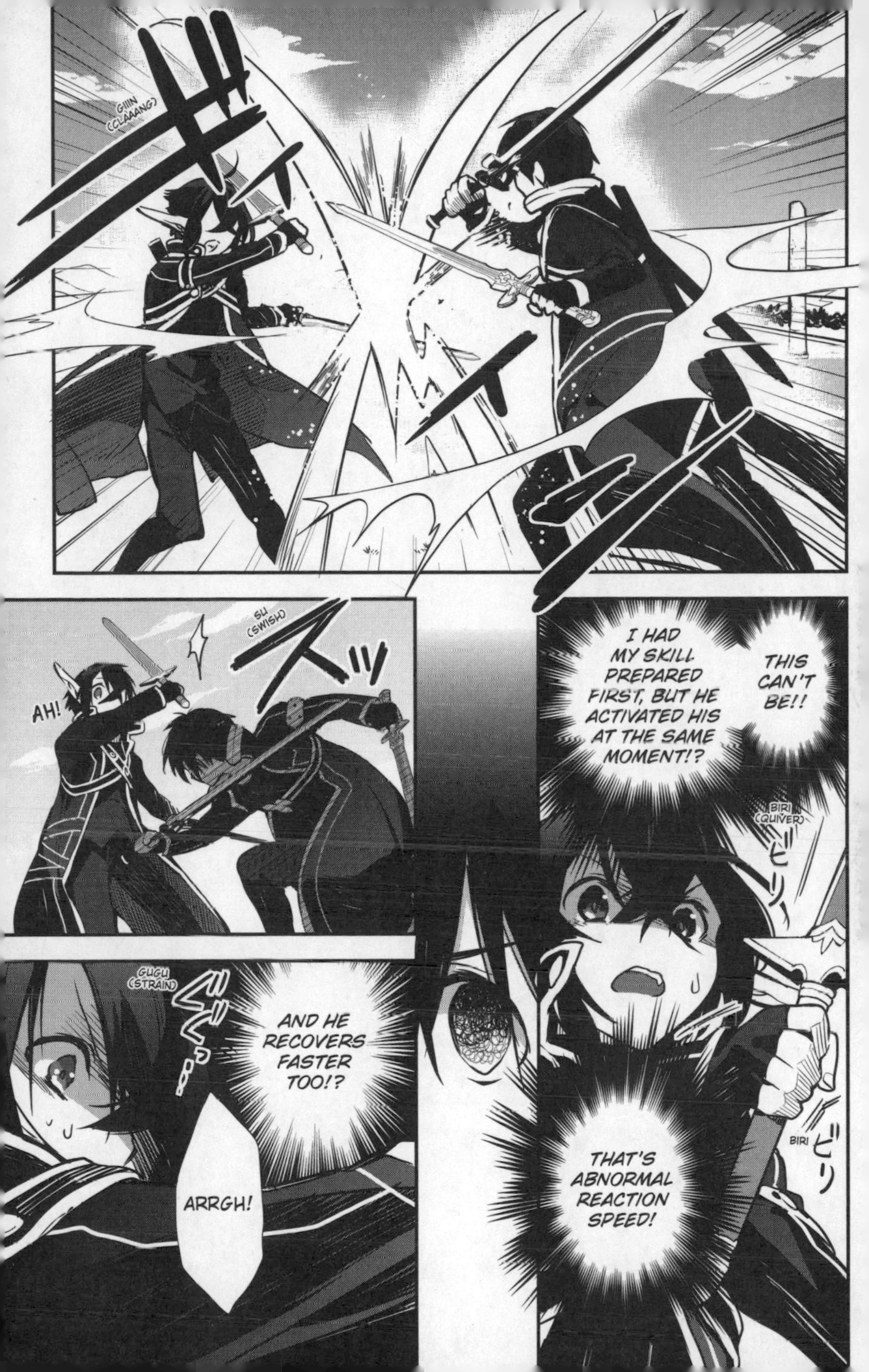

GIIIN (CLAAANG)
I HAD MY SKILL PREPARED FIRST, BUT HE ACTIVATED HIS AT THE SAME MOMENT!?
THIS CAN'T BE!!
SU (SWISH)
AH!
BIRI (QUIVER)
GUGU (STRAIN)
AND HE RECOVERS FASTER TOO!?
THAT'S ABNORMAL REACTION SPEED!
BIRI
ARRGH!

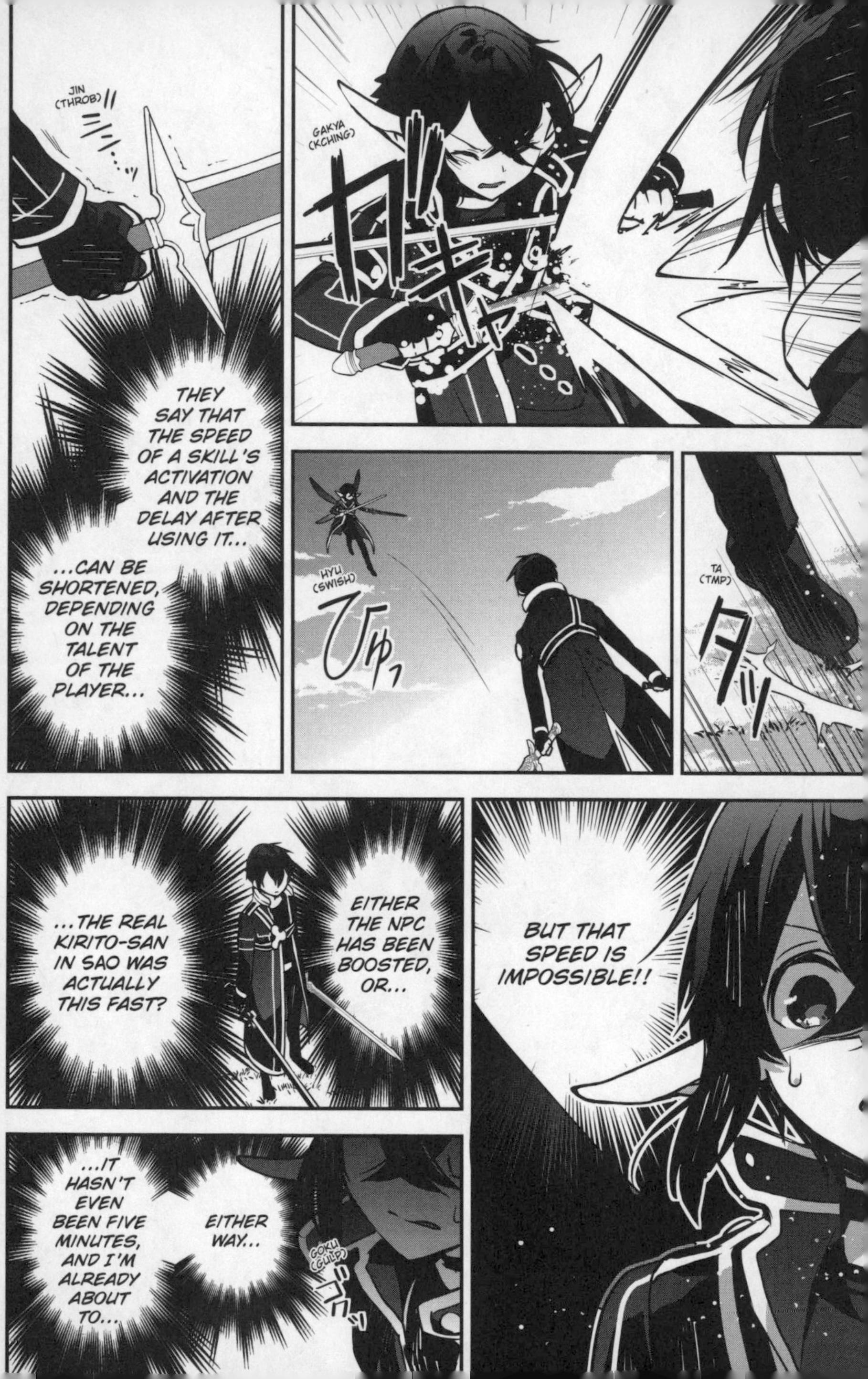

GAKYA (KCHING)
JIN (THROB)
THEY SAY THAT THE SPEED OF A SKILL'S ACTIVATION AND THE DELAY AFTER USING IT...
TA (TMP)
HYU (SWISH)
...CAN BE SHORTENED, DEPENDING ON THE TALENT OF THE PLAYER...
BUT THAT SPEED IS IMPOSSIBLE!!
EITHER THE NPC HAS BEEN BOOSTED, OR...
...THE REAL KIRITO-SAN IN SAO WAS ACTUALLY THIS FAST?
GOKU (GULP)
EITHER WAY...
...IT HASN'T EVEN BEEN FIVE MINUTES, AND I'M ALREADY ABOUT TO...

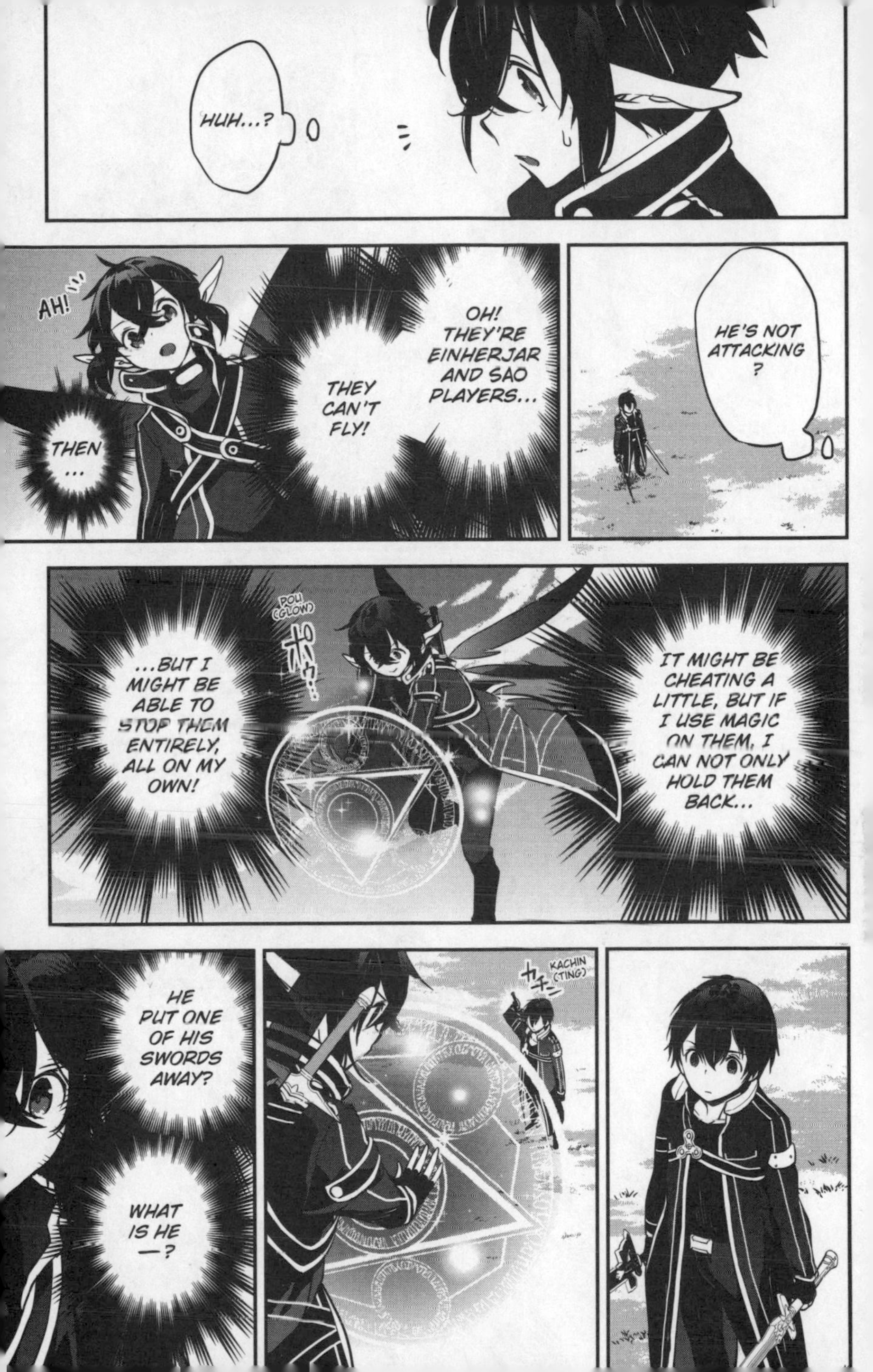
HUH...?
HE'S NOT ATTACKING?
OH! THEY'RE EINHERJAR AND SAO PLAYERS...
THEY CAN'T FLY!
AH!
THEN...
IT MIGHT BE CHEATING A LITTLE, BUT IF I USE MAGIC ON THEM, I CAN NOT ONLY HOLD THEM BACK...
POU (GLOW)
...BUT I MIGHT BE ABLE TO STOP THEM ENTIRELY, ALL ON MY OWN!
KACHIN (TING)
HE PUT ONE OF HIS SWORDS AWAY?
WHAT IS HE—?

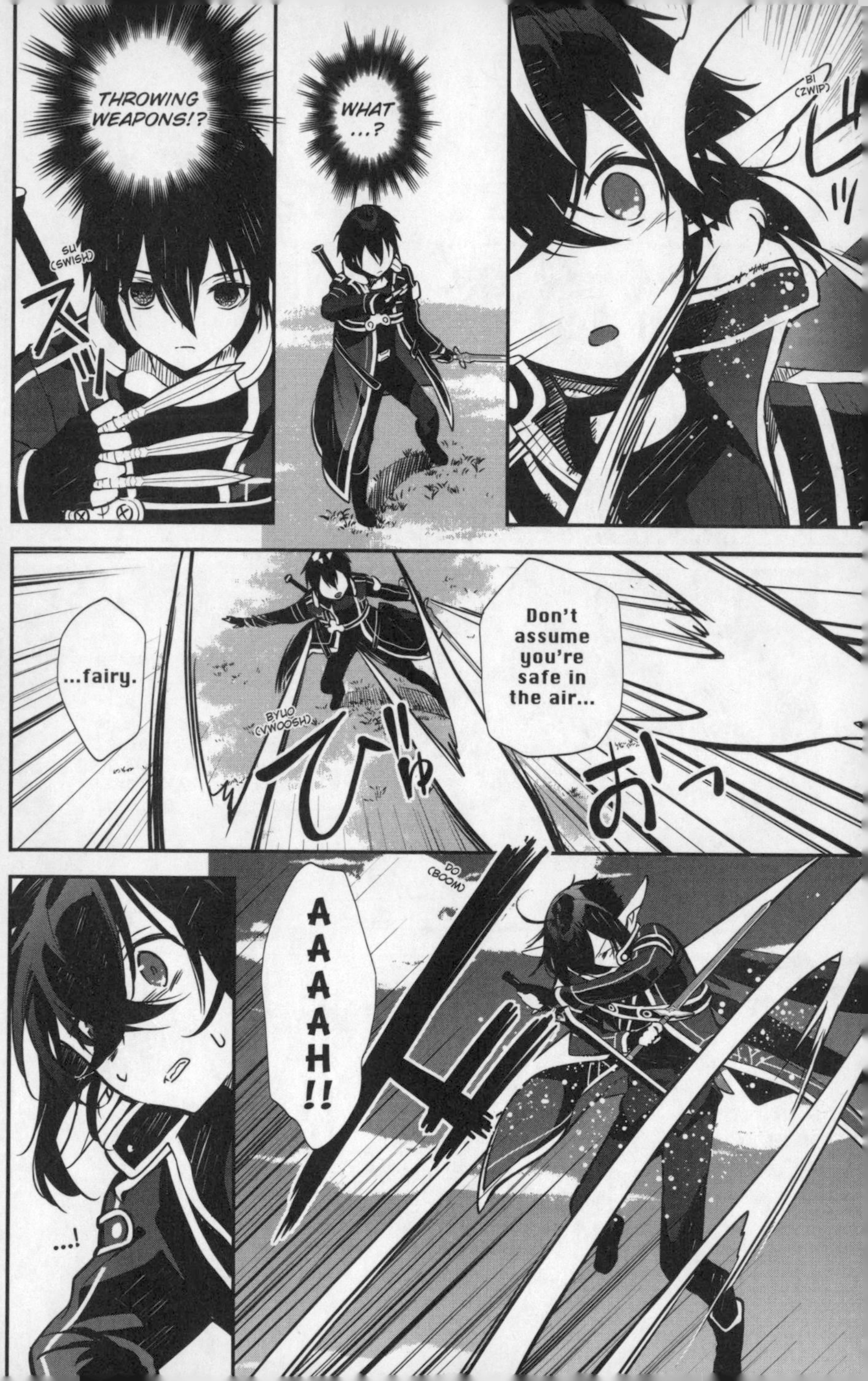
BI (ZWIP)
WHAT ...?
THROWING WEAPONS!?
SU (SWISH)
Don't assume you're safe in the air...
...fairy.
BYUO (VWOOSH)
DO (BOOM)
AAAAAH!!
...!

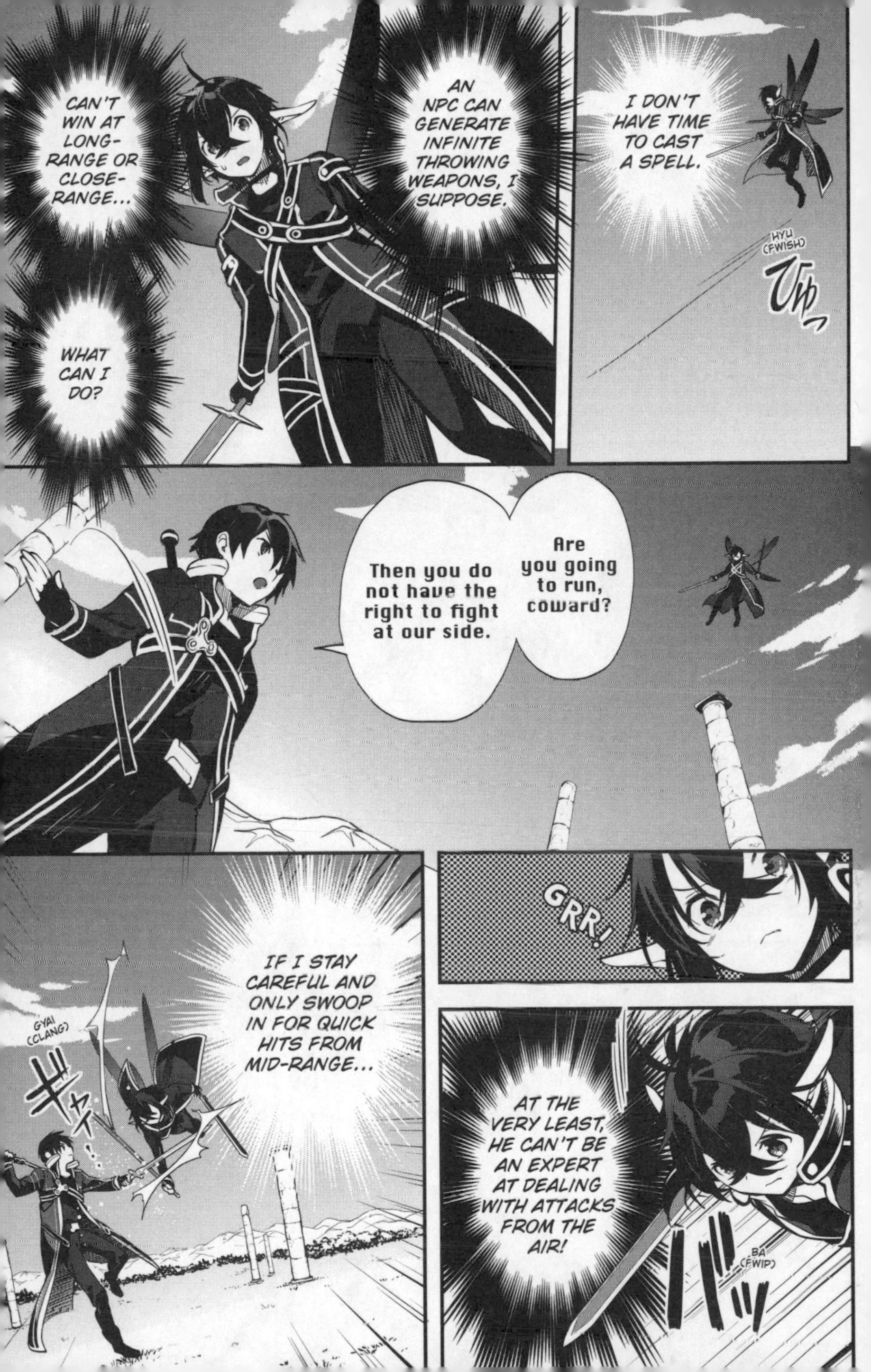
I DON'T HAVE TIME TO CAST A SPELL.
HYU (FWISH)
AN NPC CAN GENERATE INFINITE THROWING WEAPONS, I SUPPOSE.
CAN'T WIN AT LONG-RANGE OR CLOSE-RANGE...
WHAT CAN I DO?
Are you going to run, coward?
Then you do not have the right to fight at our side.
GRR!
IF I STAY CAREFUL AND ONLY SWOOP IN FOR QUICK HITS FROM MID-RANGE...
GYA! (CLANG)
AT THE VERY LEAST, HE CAN'T BE AN EXPERT AT DEALING WITH ATTACKS FROM THE AIR!
BA (FWIP)

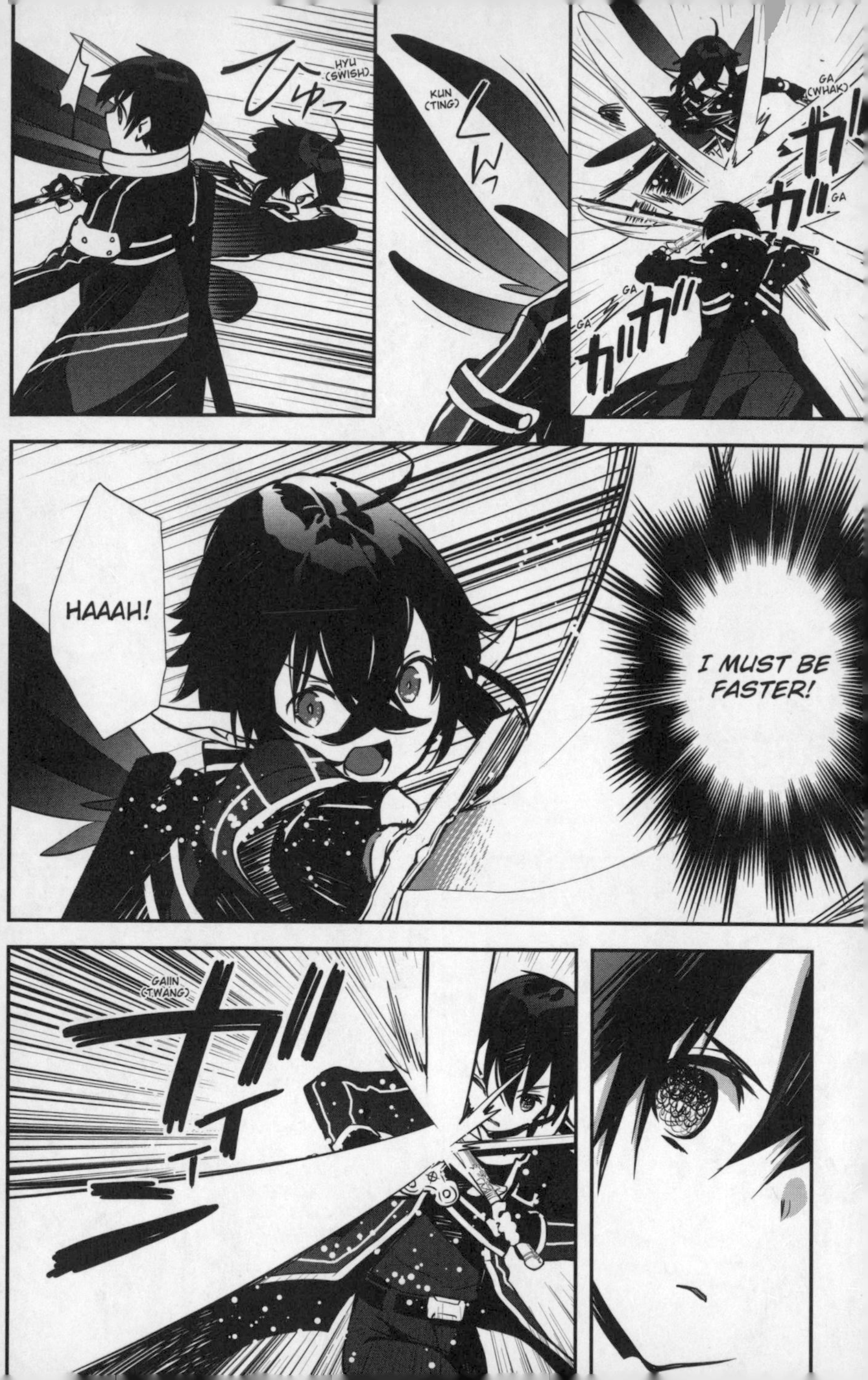

GA (WHAK)
GA
GA
GA
KUN (TING)
HYU (SWISH)
I MUST BE FASTER!
HAAAH!
GAIIN (T.WANG)

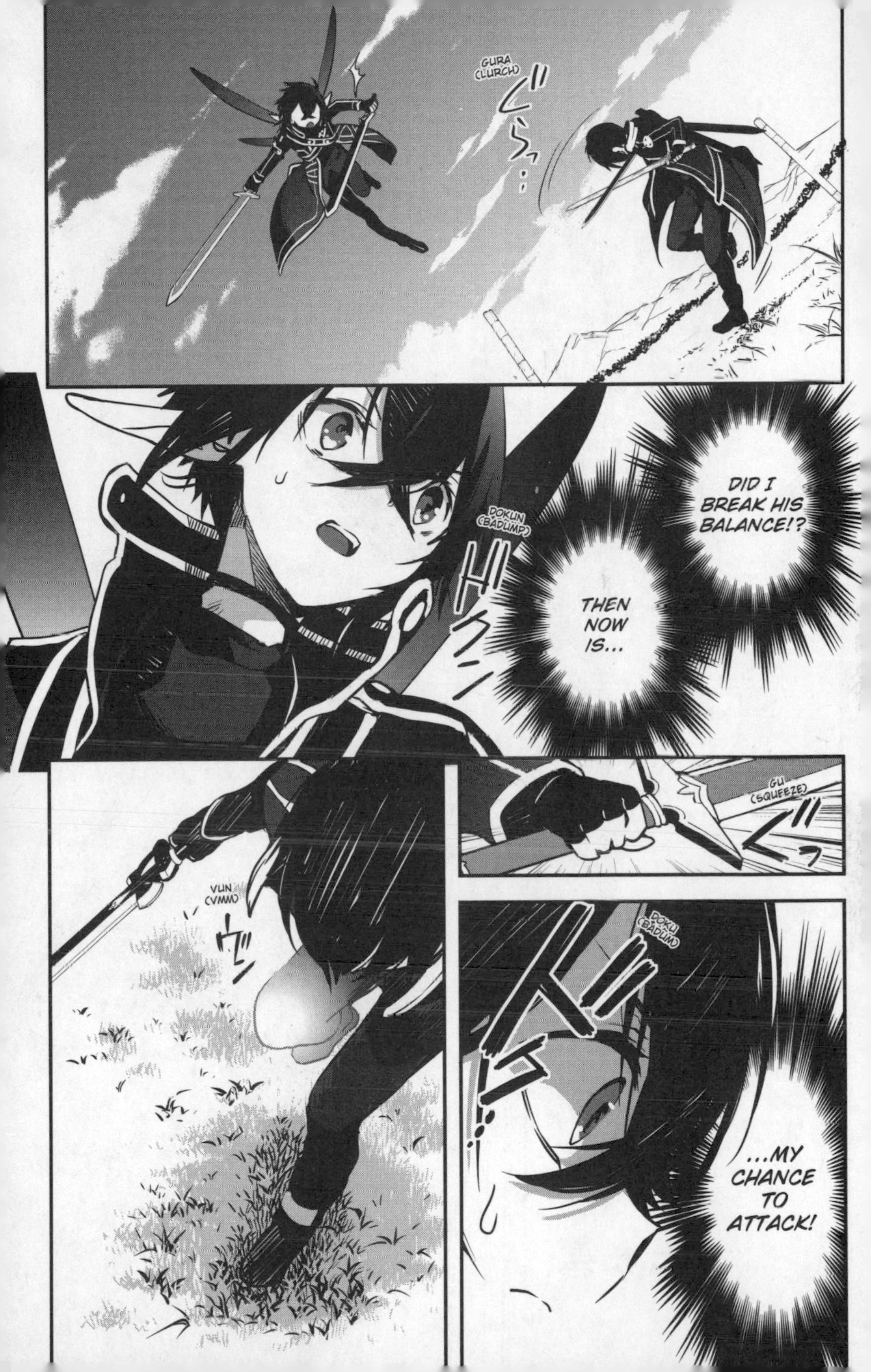
GURA (LURCH)
DOKUN (BADUMP)
DID I BREAK HIS BALANCE!?
THEN NOW IS...
GU (SQUEEZE)
VUN (VMM)
DOKU (BADUM)
...MY CHANCE TO ATTACK!

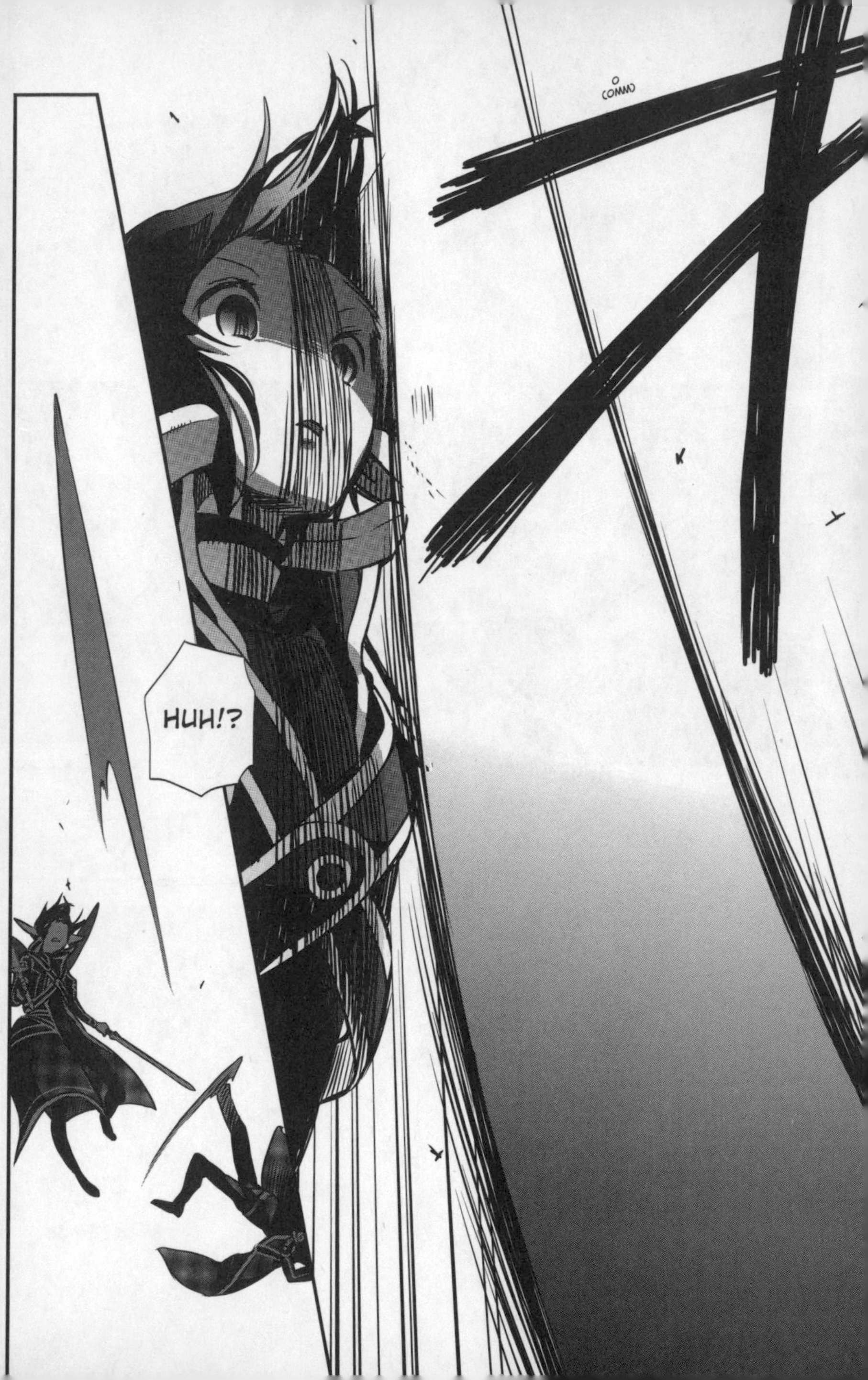
HUH!?

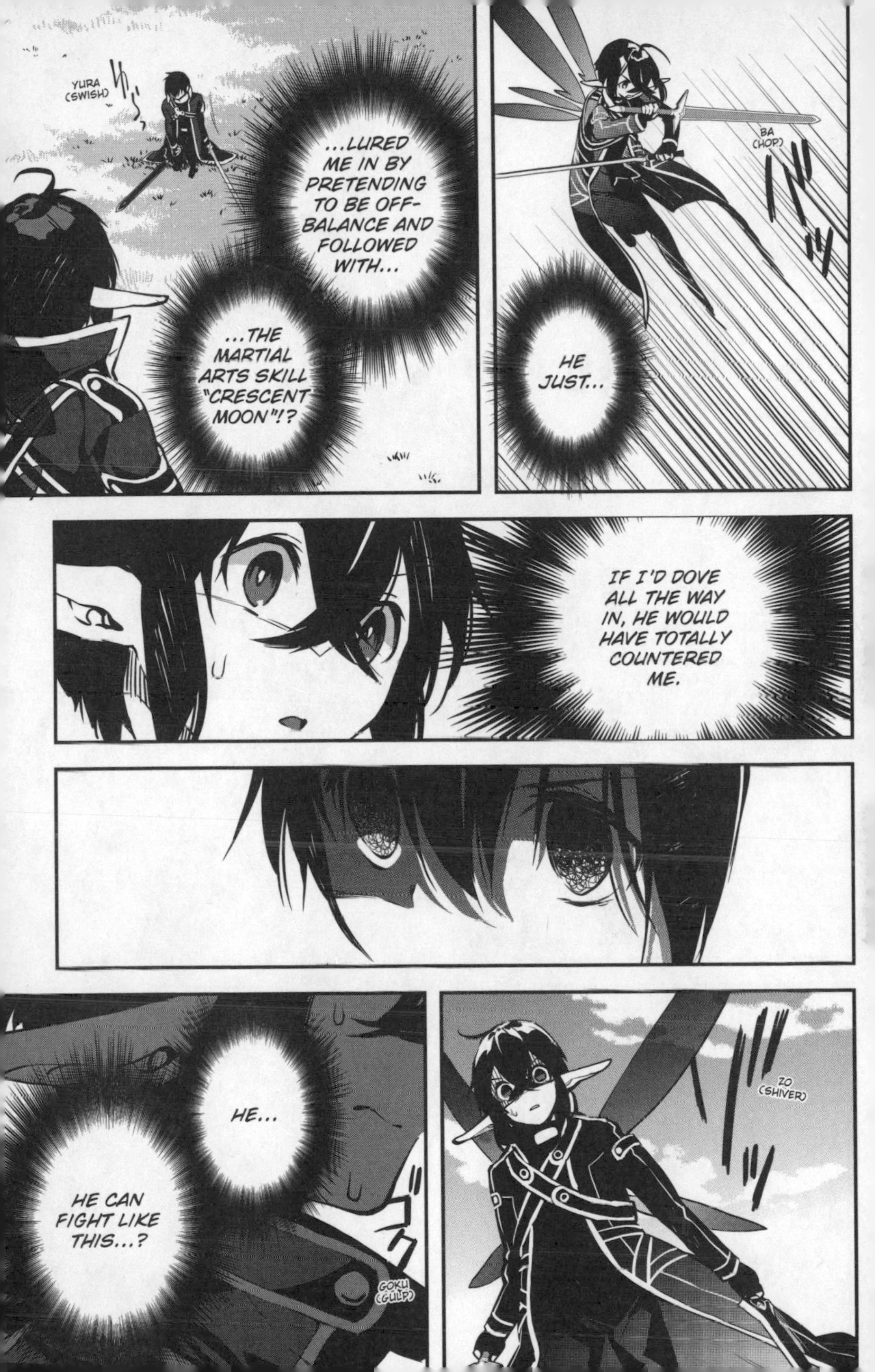
BA (HOP)
HE JUST...
YURA (SWISH)
...LURED ME IN BY PRETENDING TO BE OFF-BALANCE AND FOLLOWED WITH...
...THE MARTIAL ARTS SKILL "CRESCENT MOON"!?
IF I'D DOVE ALL THE WAY IN, HE WOULD HAVE TOTALLY COUNTERED ME.
ZO (SHIVER)
HE...
HE CAN FIGHT LIKE THIS...?
GOKU (GULP)

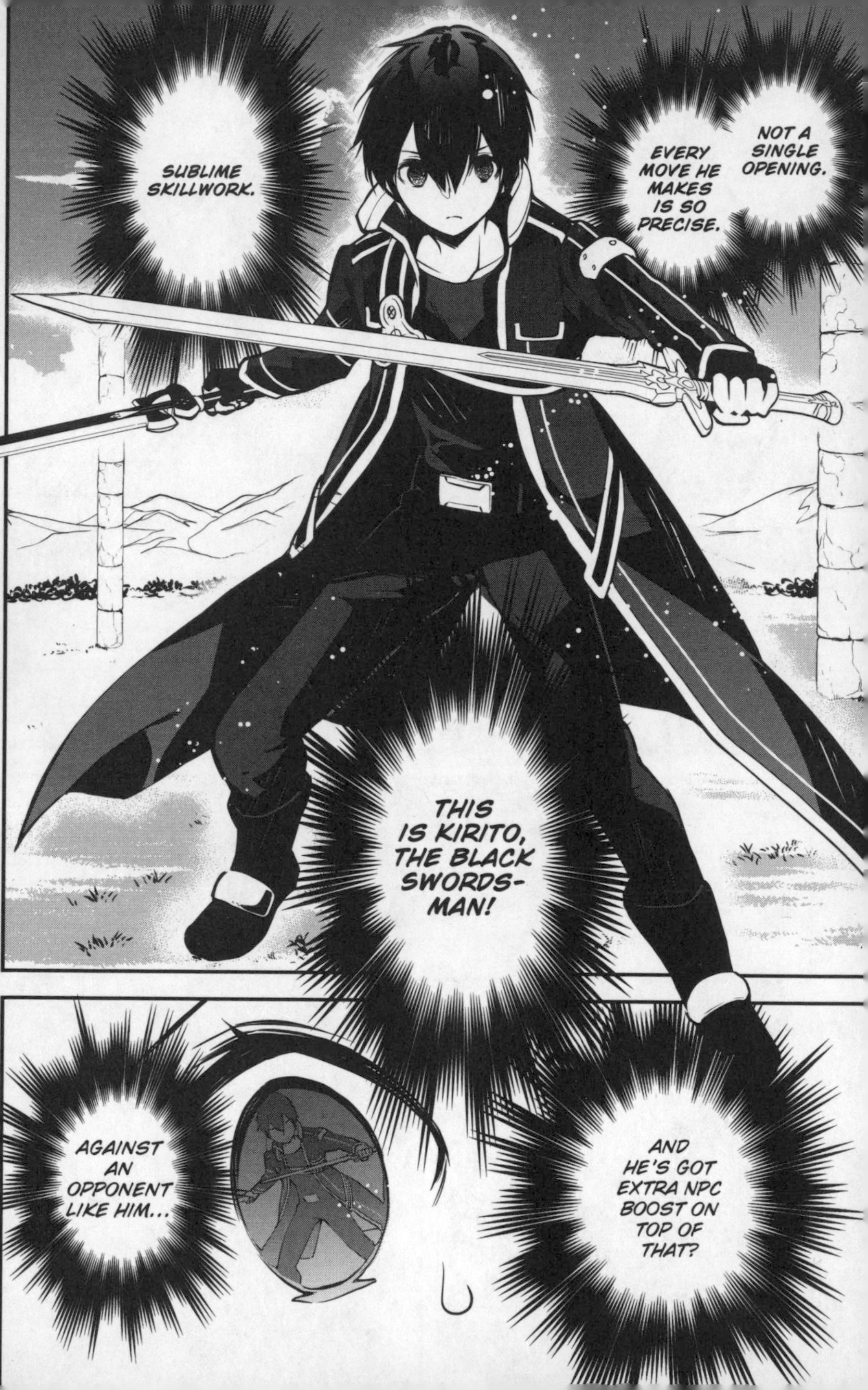
NOT A SINGLE OPENING.
EVERY MOVE HE MAKES IS SO PRECISE.
SUBLIME SKILLWORK.
THIS IS KIRITO, THE BLACK SWORDS-MAN!
AND HE'S GOT EXTRA NPC BOOST ON TOP OF THAT?
AGAINST AN OPPONENT LIKE HIM...

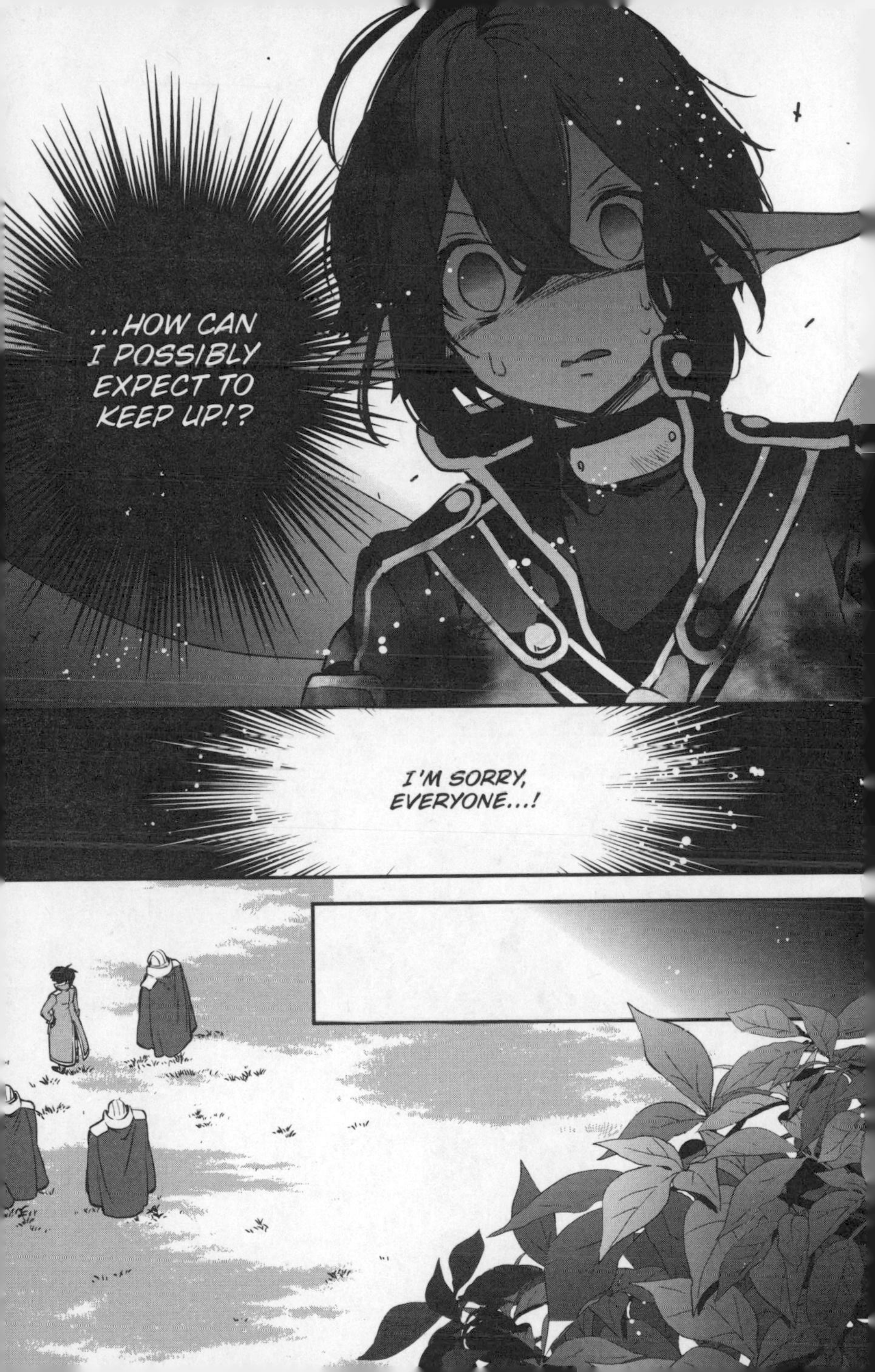
...HOW CAN I POSSIBLY EXPECT TO KEEP UP!?
I'M SORRY, EVERYONE...!

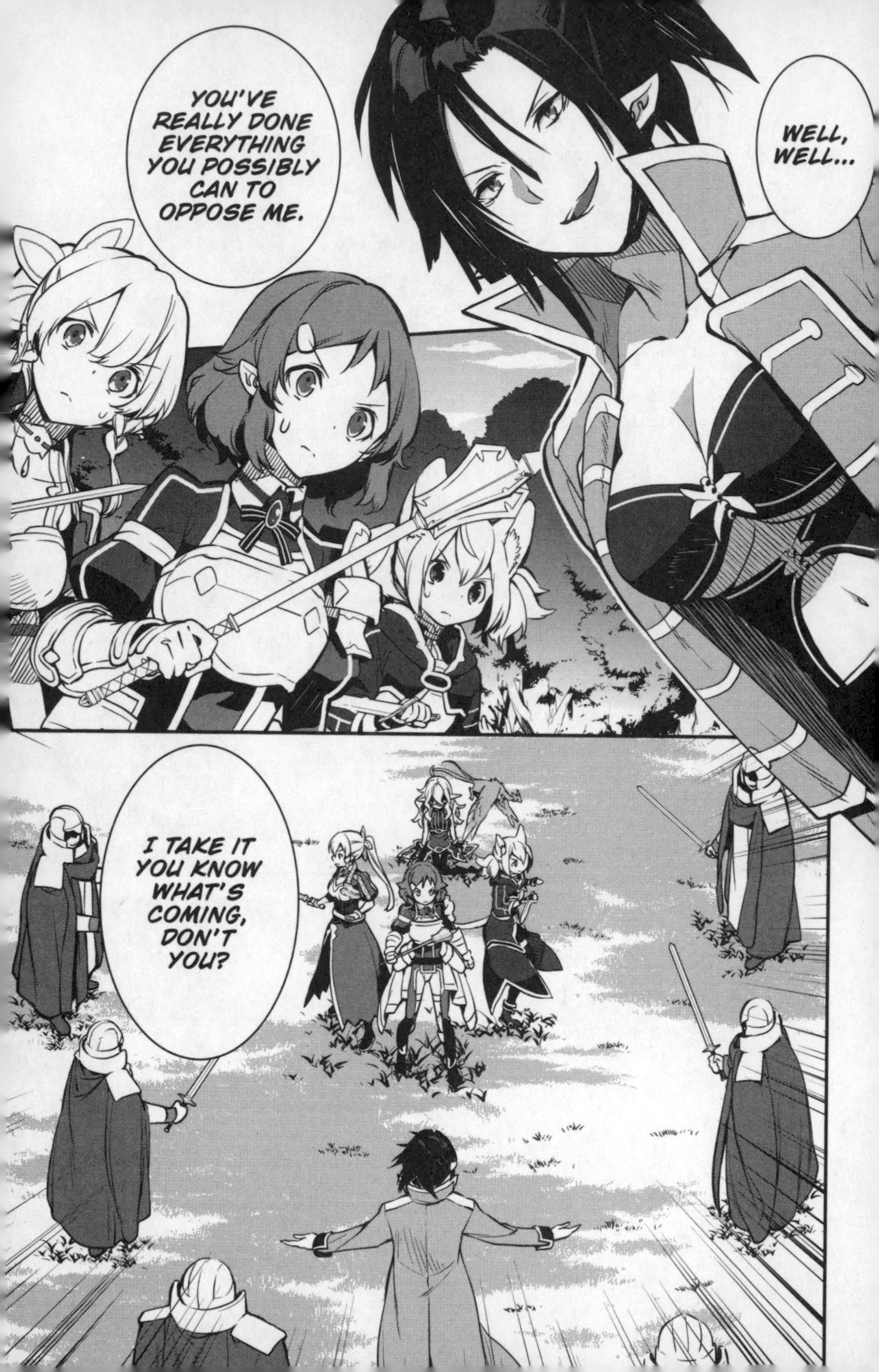
WELL, WELL...
YOU'VE REALLY DONE EVERYTHING YOU POSSIBLY CAN TO OPPOSE ME.
I TAKE IT YOU KNOW WHAT'S COMING, DON'T YOU?

SWORD ART ONLINE
GIRLS' OPS

MAY 18TH

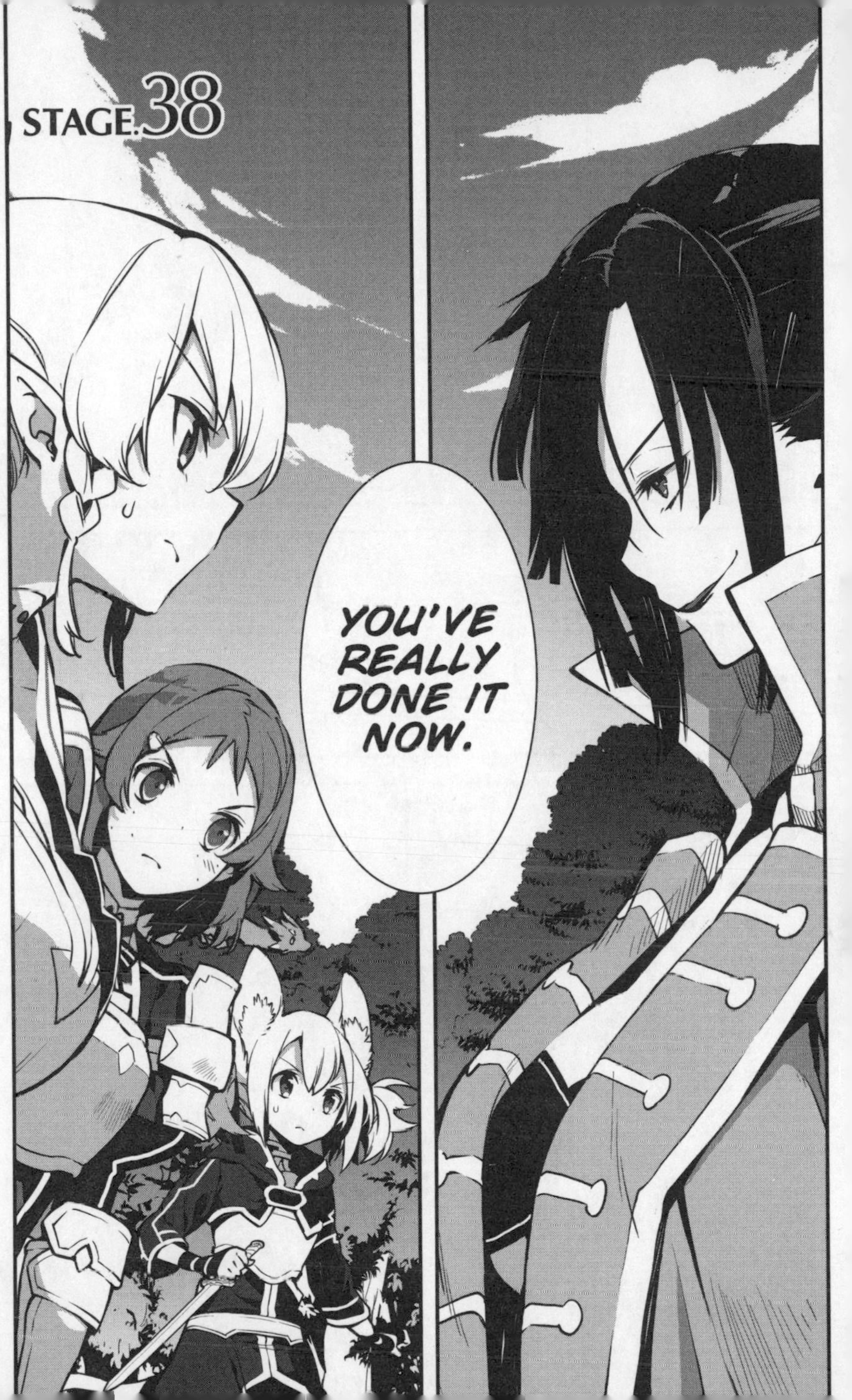
STAGE.38
YOU'VE REALLY DONE IT NOW.

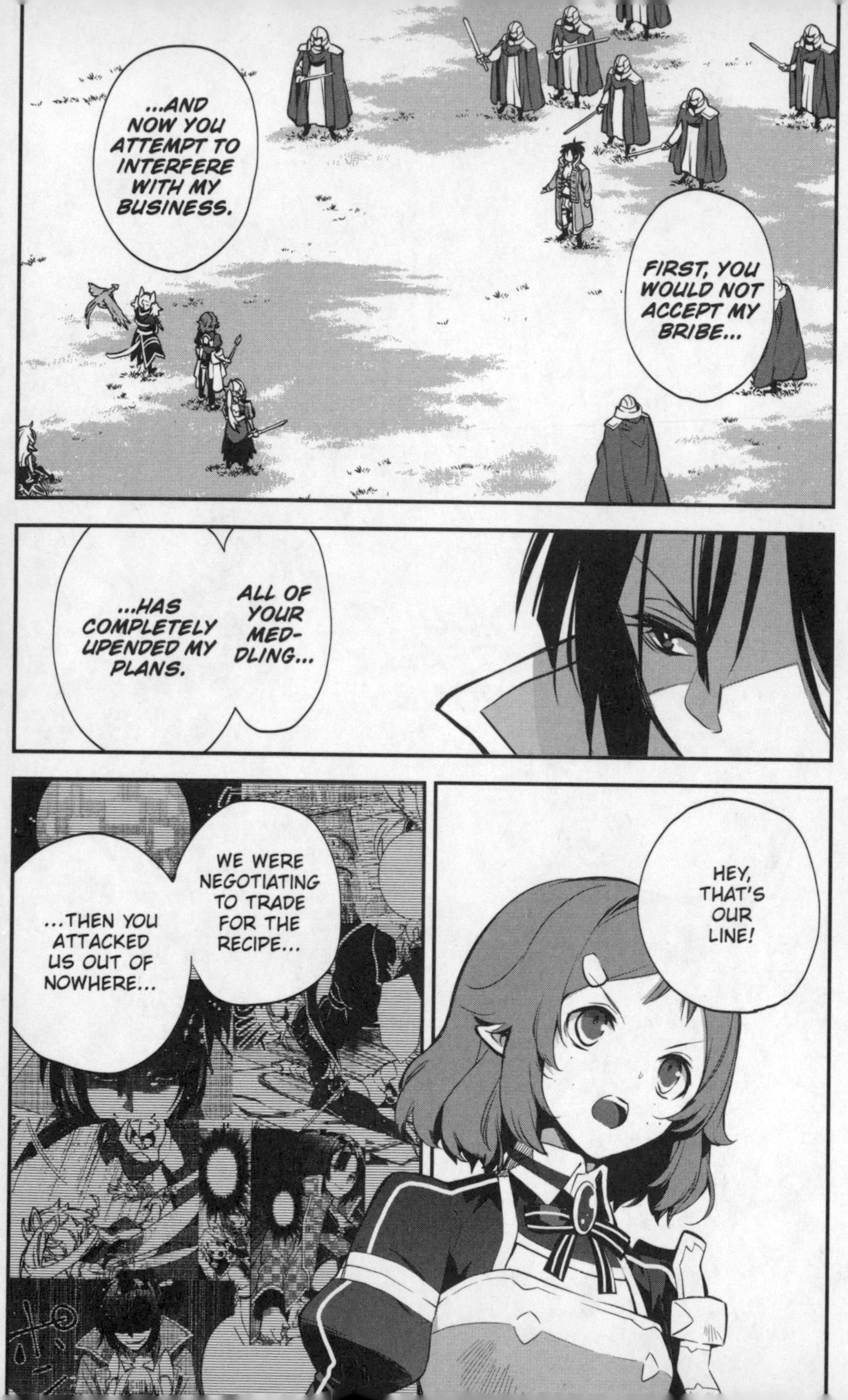
FIRST, YOU WOULD NOT ACCEPT MY BRIBE...
...AND NOW YOU ATTEMPT TO INTERFERE WITH MY BUSINESS.
ALL OF YOUR MED-DLING...
...HAS COMPLETELY UPENDED MY PLANS.
HEY, THAT'S OUR LINE!
WE WERE NEGOTIATING TO TRADE FOR THE RECIPE...
...THEN YOU ATTACKED US OUT OF NOWHERE...

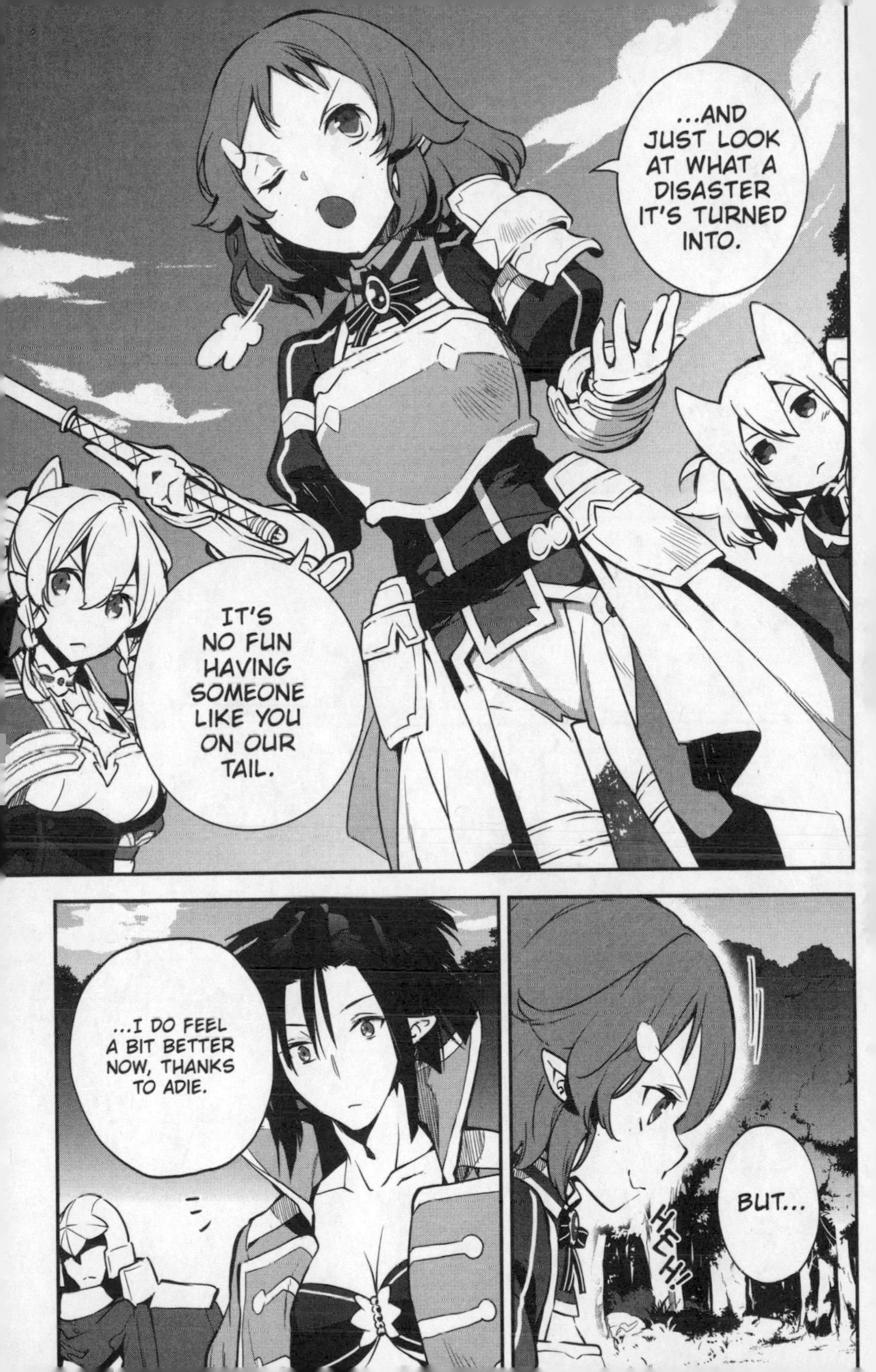
...AND JUST LOOK AT WHAT A DISASTER IT'S TURNED INTO.
IT'S NO FUN HAVING SOMEONE LIKE YOU ON OUR TAIL.
...I DO FEEL A BIT BETTER NOW, THANKS TO ADIE.
HEH!
BUT...

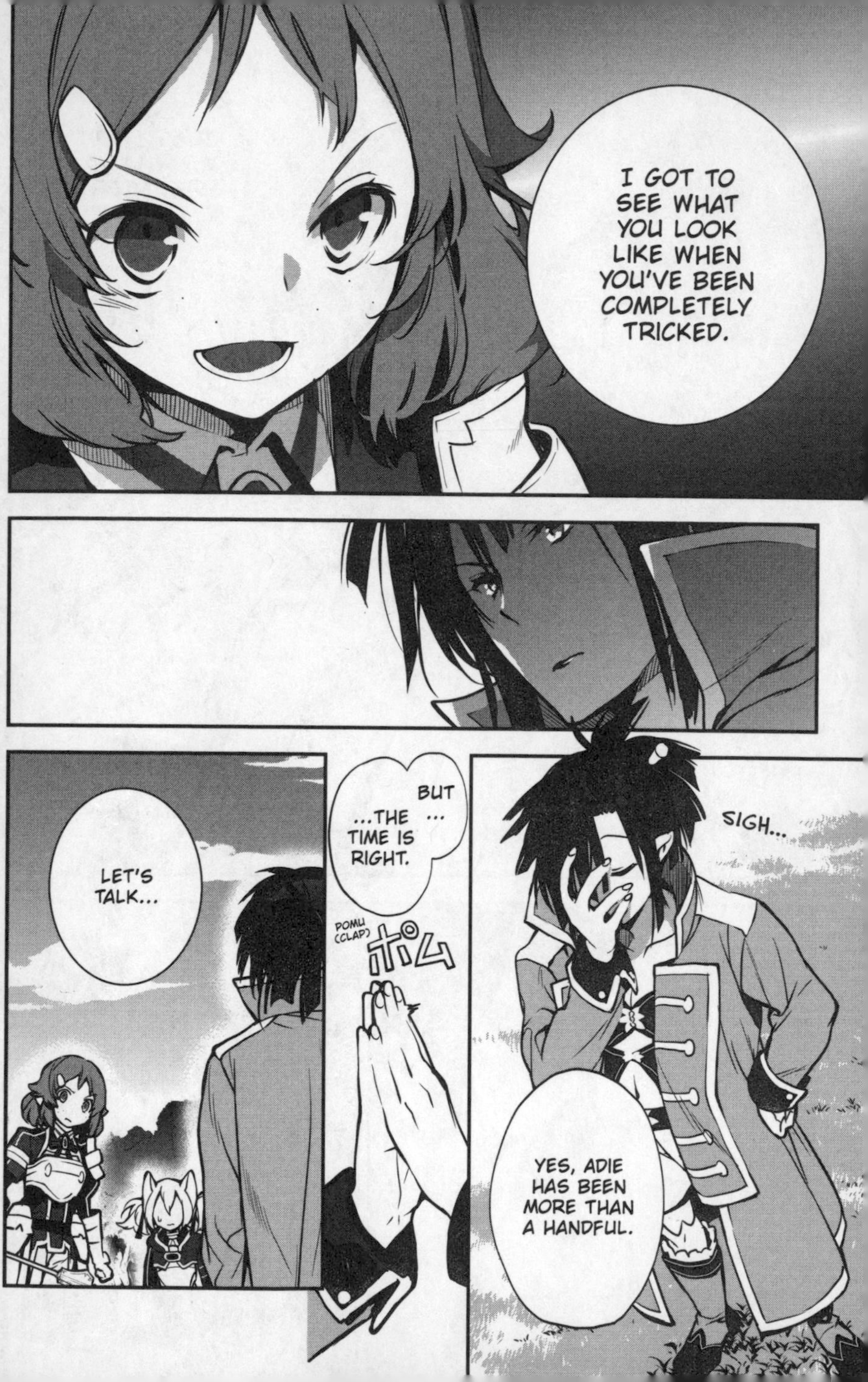
I GOT TO SEE WHAT YOU LOOK LIKE WHEN YOU'VE BEEN COMPLETELY TRICKED.
SIGH...
YES, ADIE HAS BEEN MORE THAN A HANDFUL.
BUT ...
...THE TIME IS RIGHT.
POMU (CLAP)
ポム
LET'S TALK...

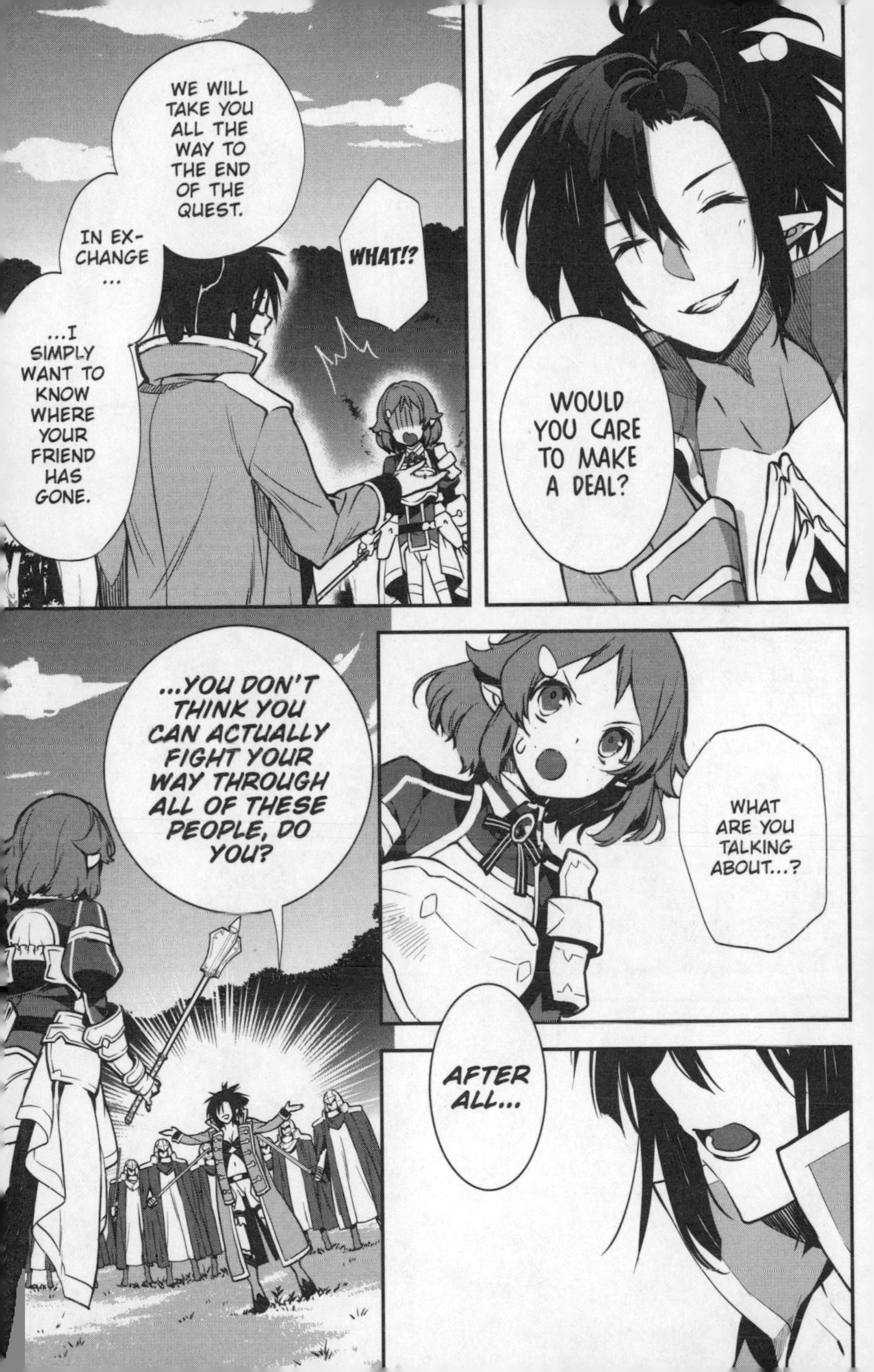
WOULD YOU CARE TO MAKE A DEAL?
WHAT!?
WE WILL TAKE YOU ALL THE WAY TO THE END OF THE QUEST.
IN EX-CHANGE ...
...I SIMPLY WANT TO KNOW WHERE YOUR FRIEND HAS GONE.
WHAT ARE YOU TALKING ABOUT...?
AFTER ALL...
...YOU DON'T THINK YOU CAN ACTUALLY FIGHT YOUR WAY THROUGH ALL OF THESE PEOPLE, DO YOU?

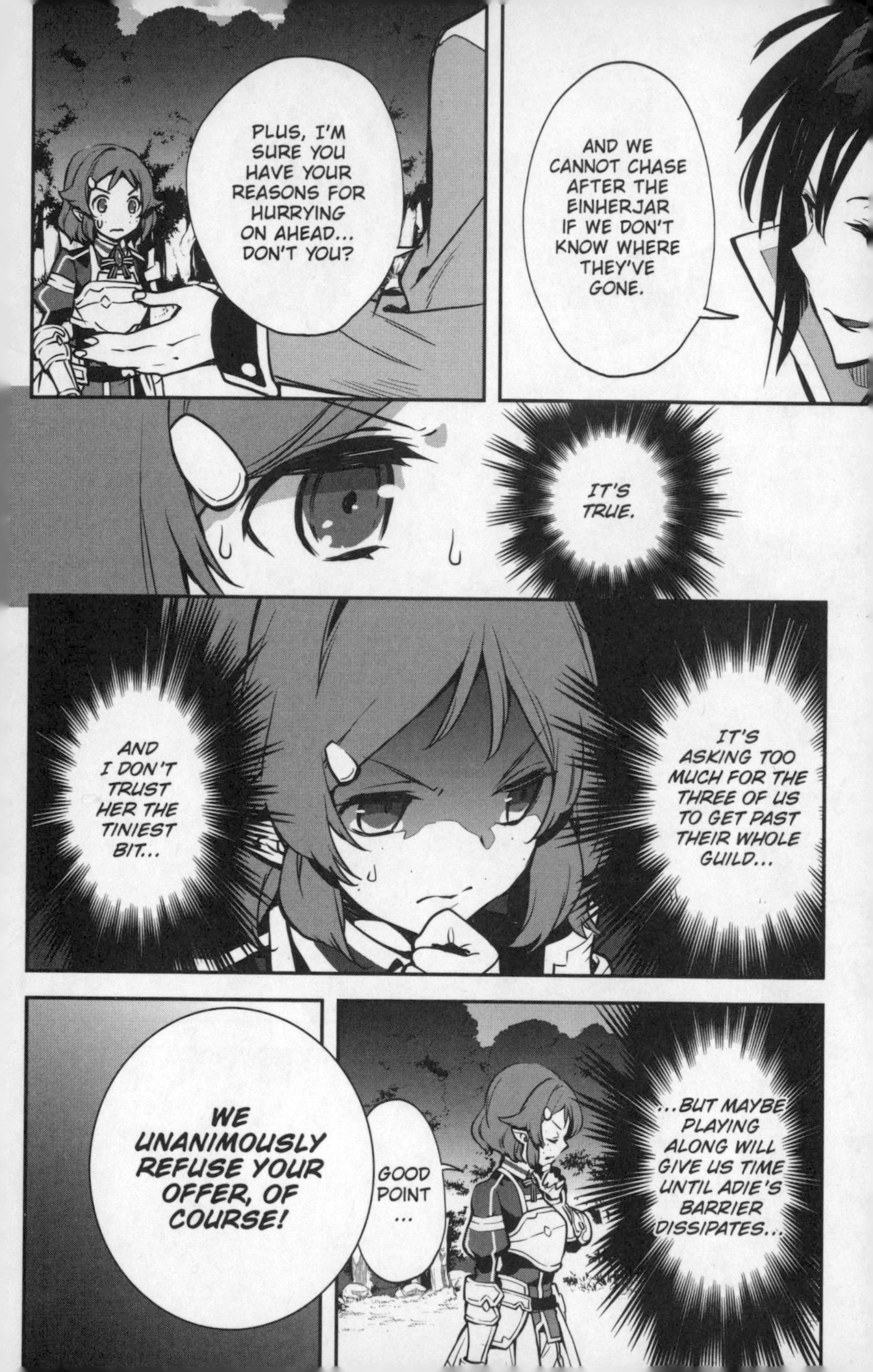
AND WE CANNOT CHASE AFTER THE EINHERJAR IF WE DON'T KNOW WHERE THEY'VE GONE.
PLUS, I'M SURE YOU HAVE YOUR REASONS FOR HURRYING ON AHEAD... DON'T YOU?
IT'S TRUE.
IT'S ASKING TOO MUCH FOR THE THREE OF US TO GET PAST THEIR WHOLE GUILD...
AND I DON'T TRUST HER THE TINIEST BIT...
...BUT MAYBE PLAYING ALONG WILL GIVE US TIME UNTIL ADIE'S BARRIER DISSIPATES...
GOOD POINT ...
WE UNANIMOUSLY REFUSE YOUR OFFER, OF COURSE!

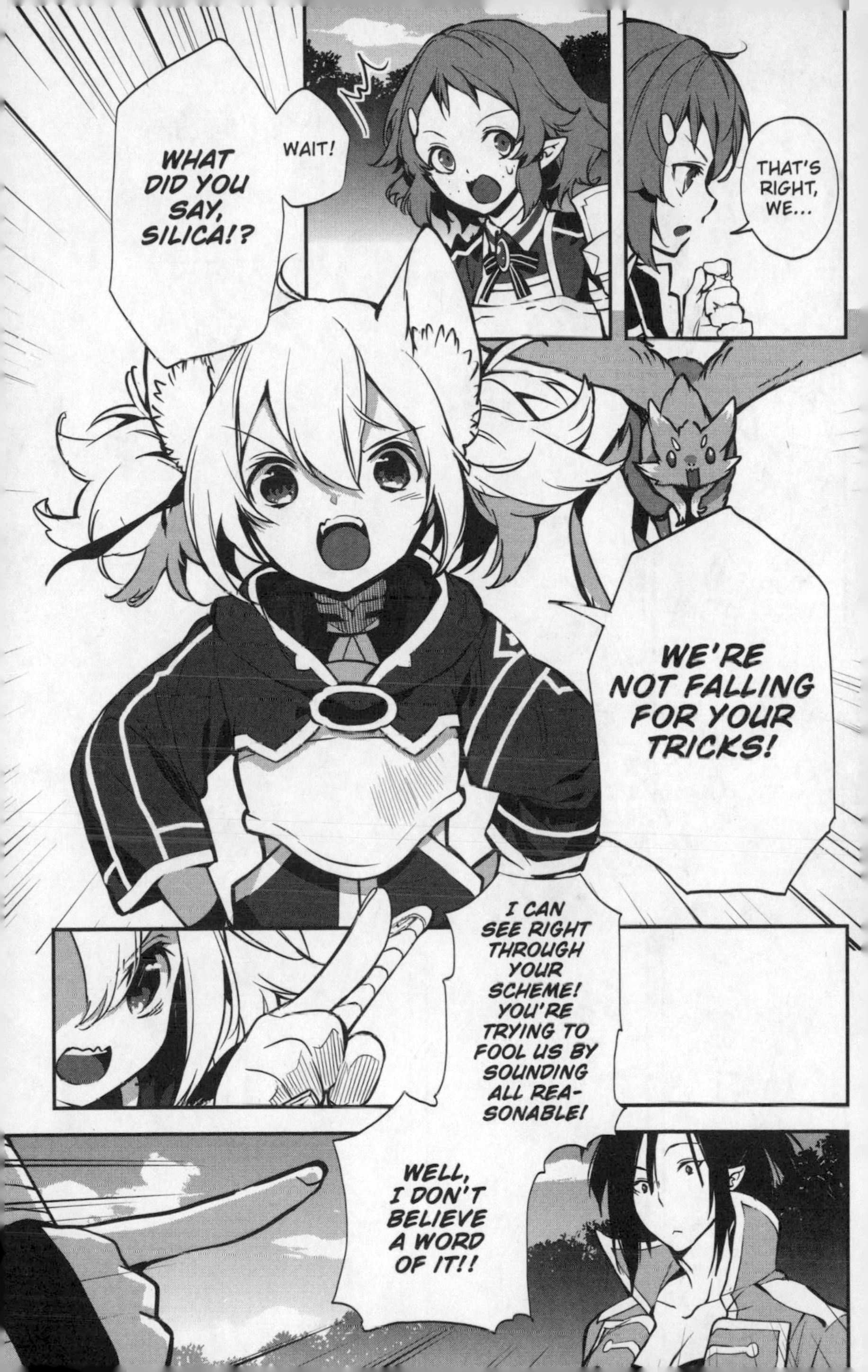
THAT'S RIGHT, WE...
WAIT!
WHAT DID YOU SAY, SILICA!?
WE'RE NOT FALLING FOR YOUR TRICKS!
I CAN SEE RIGHT THROUGH YOUR SCHEME! YOU'RE TRYING TO FOOL US BY SOUNDING ALL REA-SONABLE!
WELL, I DON'T BELIEVE A WORD OF IT!!

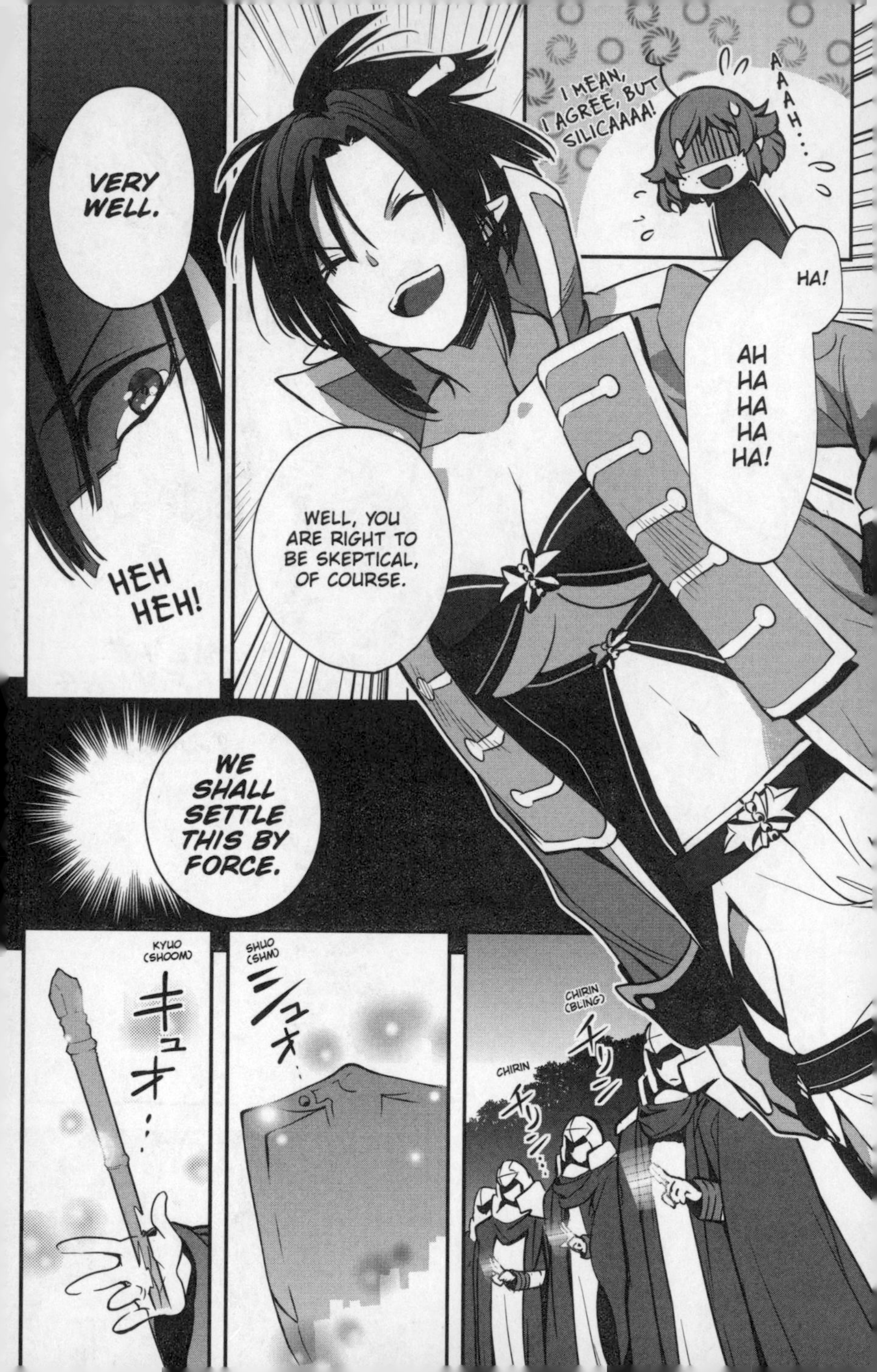
AAAH...
I MEAN, I AGREE, BUT SILICAAAA!
HA!
AH HA HA HA HA HA!
WELL, YOU ARE RIGHT TO BE SKEPTICAL, OF COURSE.
VERY WELL.
HEH HEH!
WE SHALL SETTLE THIS BY FORCE.
CHIRIN (BLING)
チリン
CHIRIN
チリン…
SHUO (SHM)
シュオ…
KYUO (SHOOM)
キュオ…

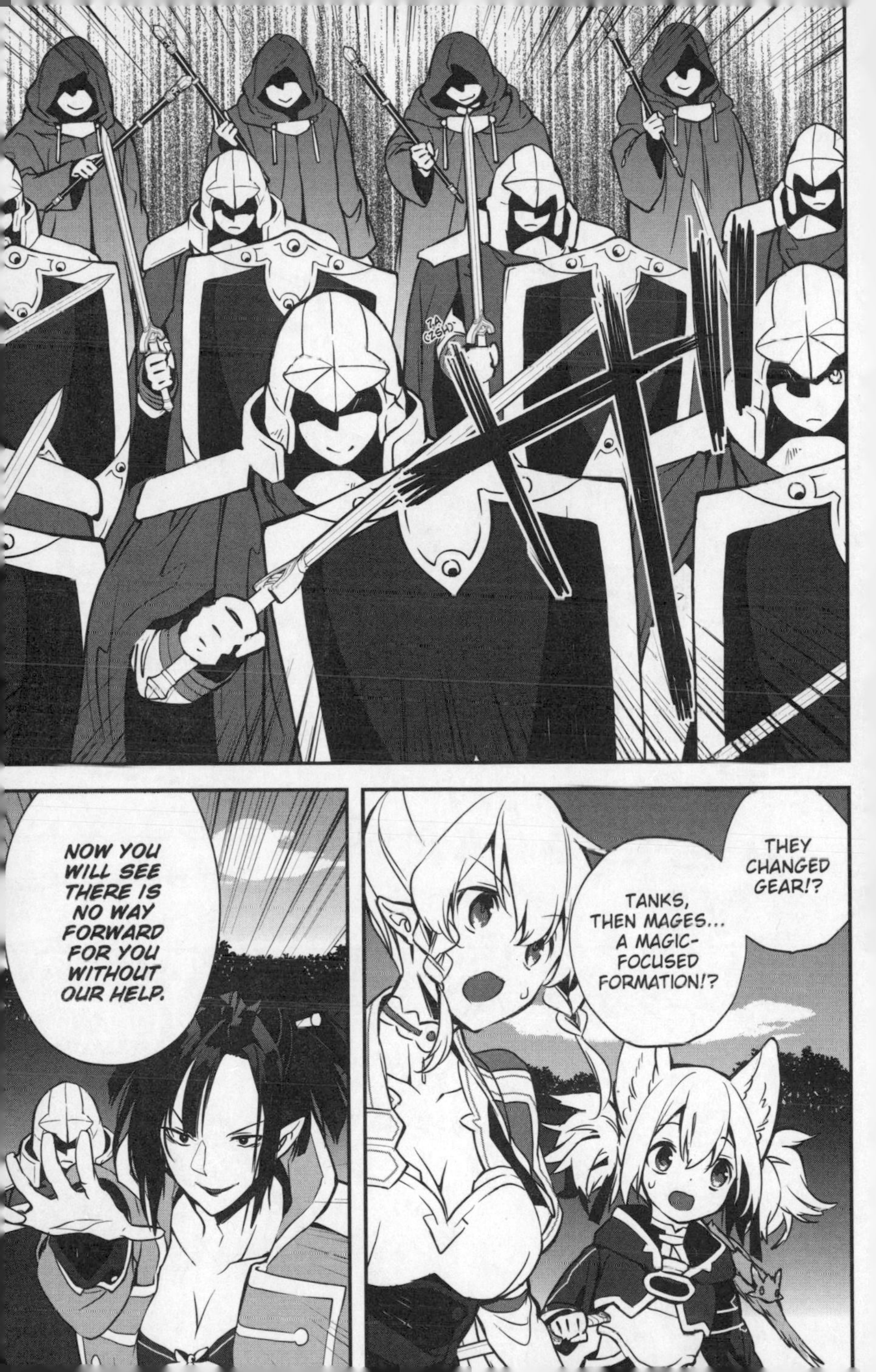
ZA (ZSH)
THEY CHANGED GEAR!?
TANKS, THEN MAGES... A MAGIC-FOCUSED FORMATION!?
NOW YOU WILL SEE THERE IS NO WAY FORWARD FOR YOU WITHOUT OUR HELP.

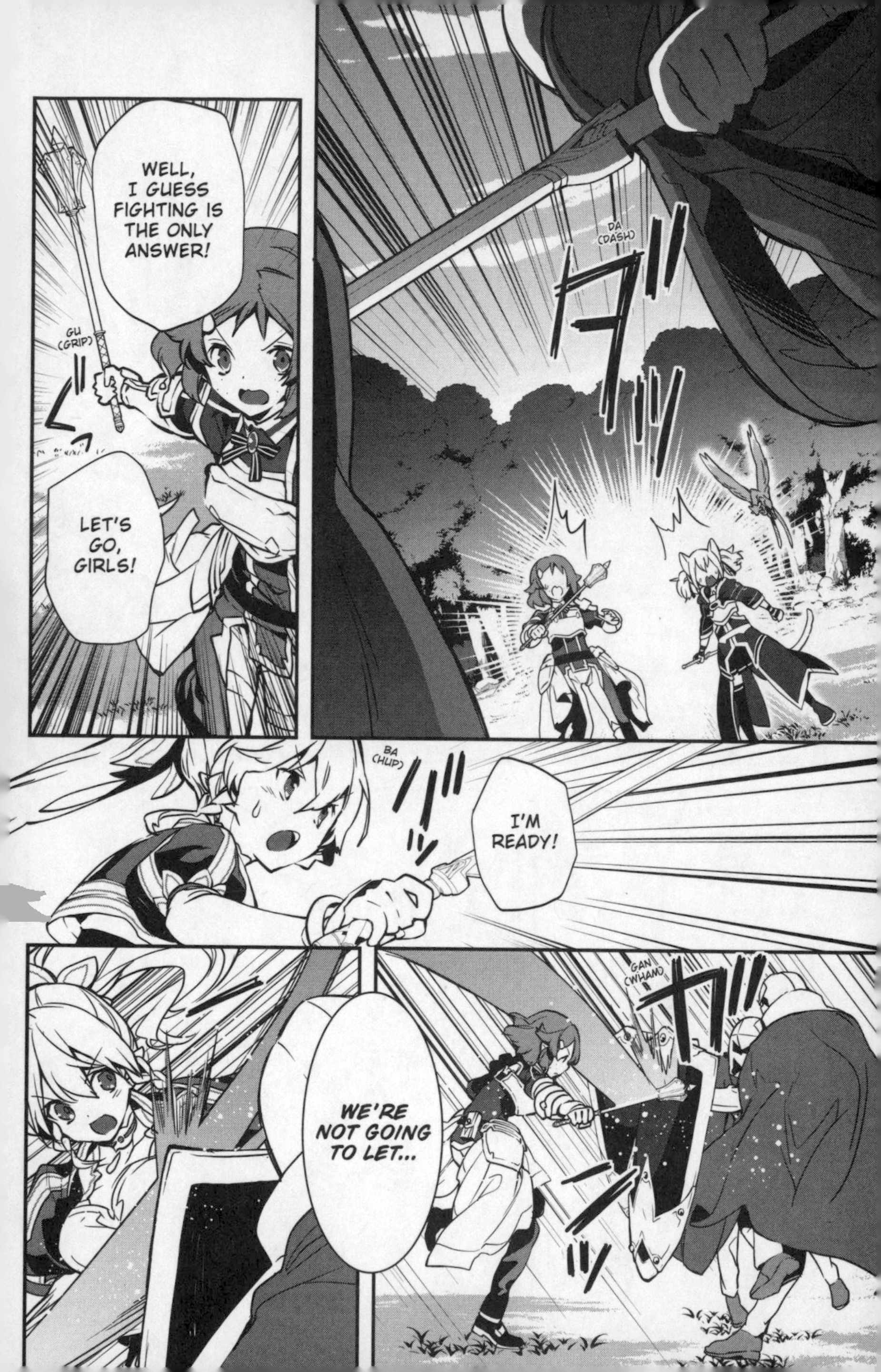
DA (DASH)
WELL, I GUESS FIGHTING IS THE ONLY ANSWER!
GU (GRIP)
LET'S GO, GIRLS!
BA (HUP)
I'M READY!
GAN (WHAM)
WE'RE NOT GOING TO LET...

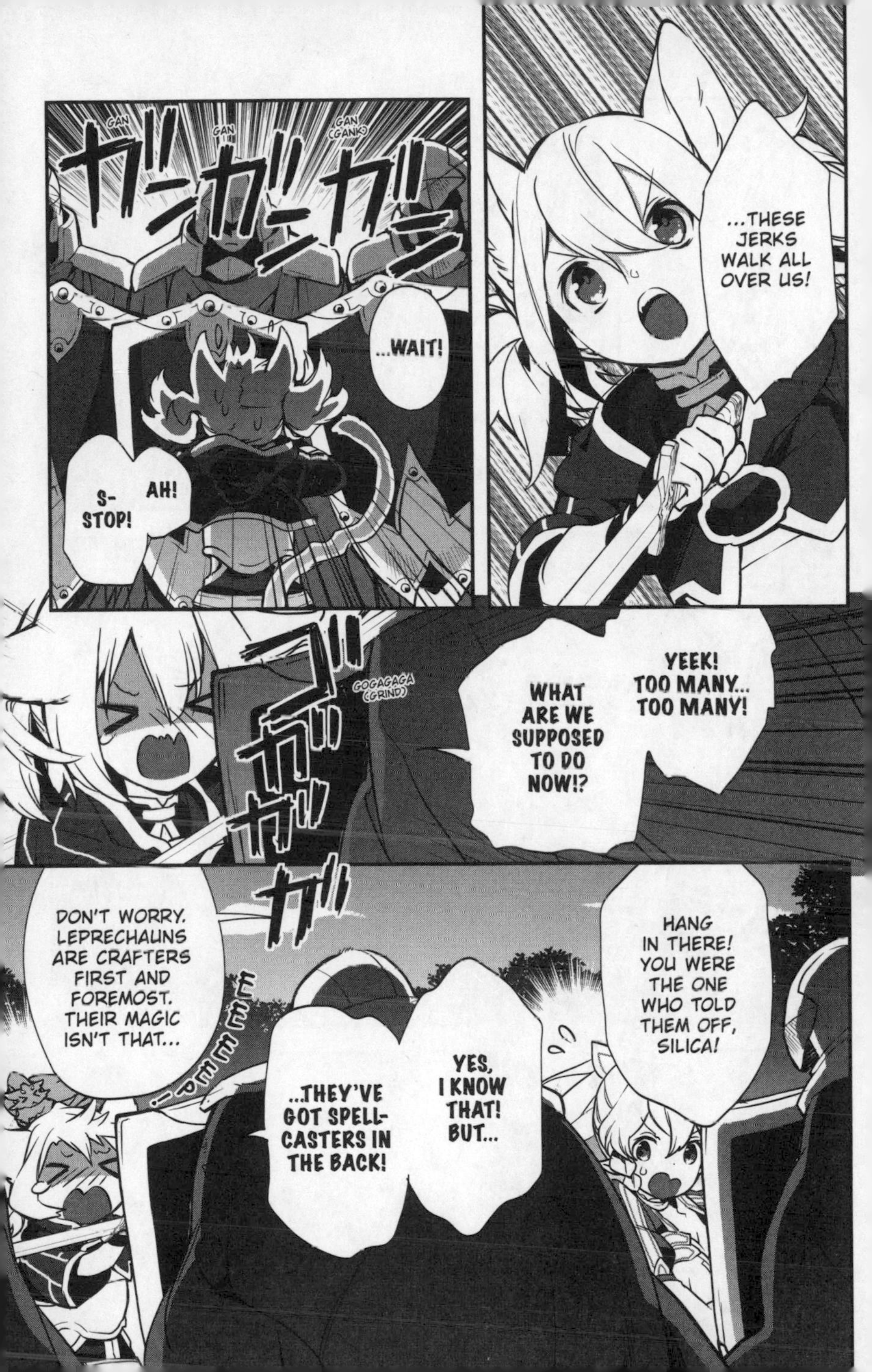
...THESE JERKS WALK ALL OVER US!
GAN GAN GAN (GANK)
...WAIT!
AH!
S-STOP!
YEEK! TOO MANY... TOO MANY!
WHAT ARE WE SUPPOSED TO DO NOW!?
GOGAGAGA (GRIND)
HANG IN THERE! YOU WERE THE ONE WHO TOLD THEM OFF, SILICA!
YES, I KNOW THAT! BUT...
...THEY'VE GOT SPELL-CASTERS IN THE BACK!
DON'T WORRY. LEPRECHAUNS ARE CRAFTERS FIRST AND FOREMOST. THEIR MAGIC ISN'T THAT...

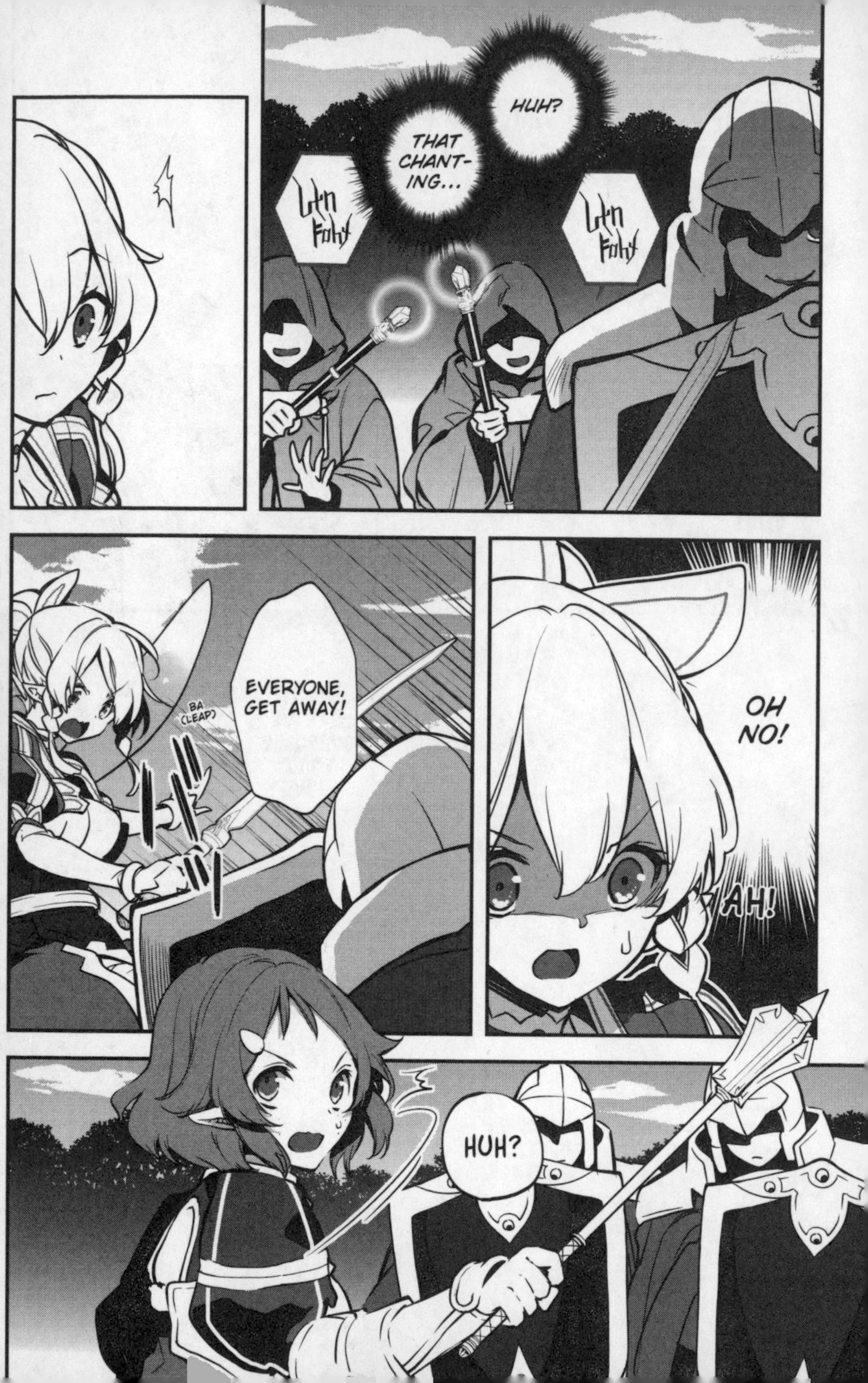
HUH?
THAT CHANT-ING...
OH NO!
AH!
EVERYONE, GET AWAY!
BA (LEAP)
HUH?

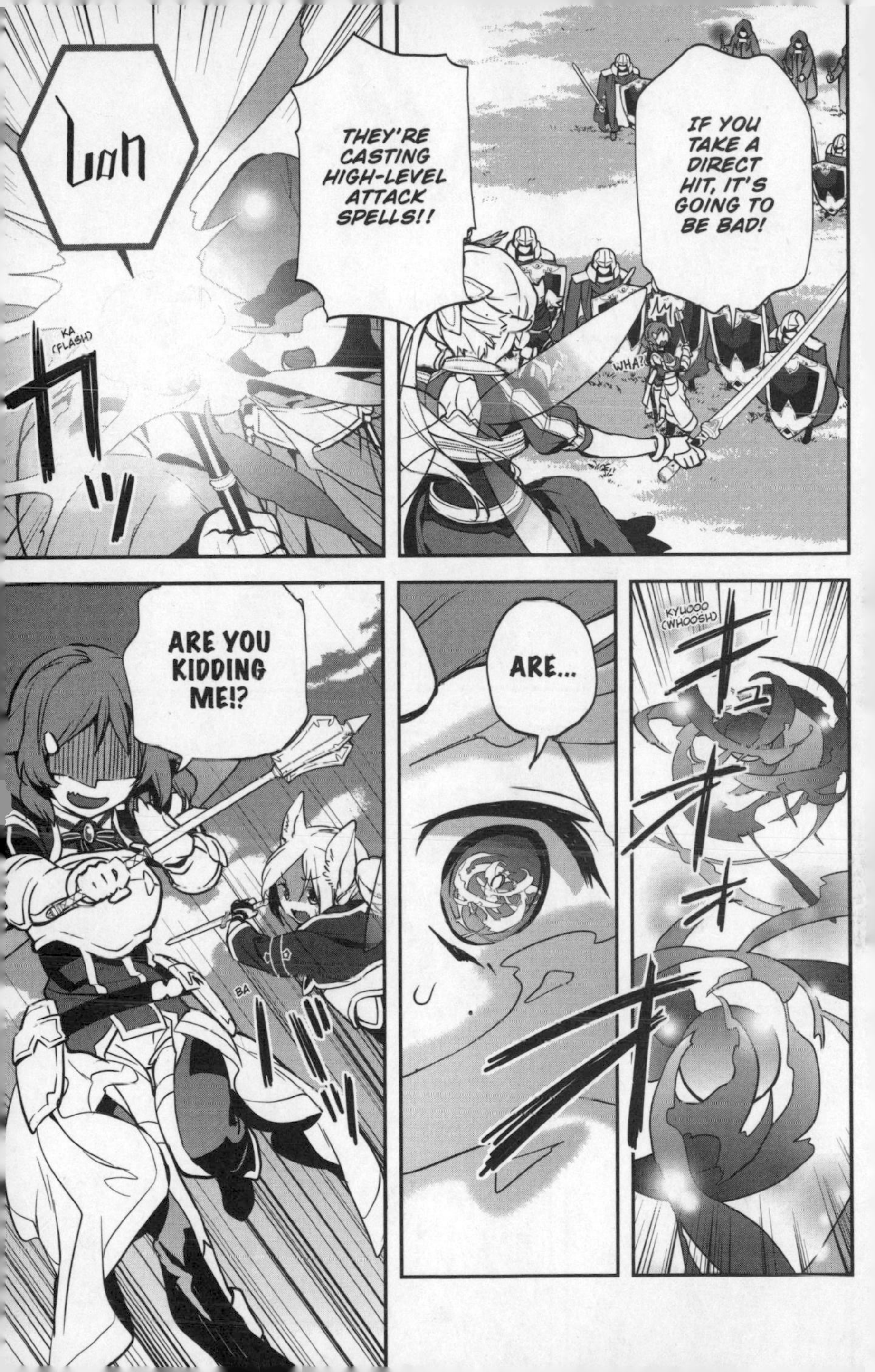
IF YOU TAKE A DIRECT HIT, IT'S GOING TO BE BAD!
WHA?
THEY'RE CASTING HIGH-LEVEL ATTACK SPELLS!!
KA (FLASH)
KYUOOO (WHOOSH)
ARE...
ARE YOU KIDDING ME!?
BA

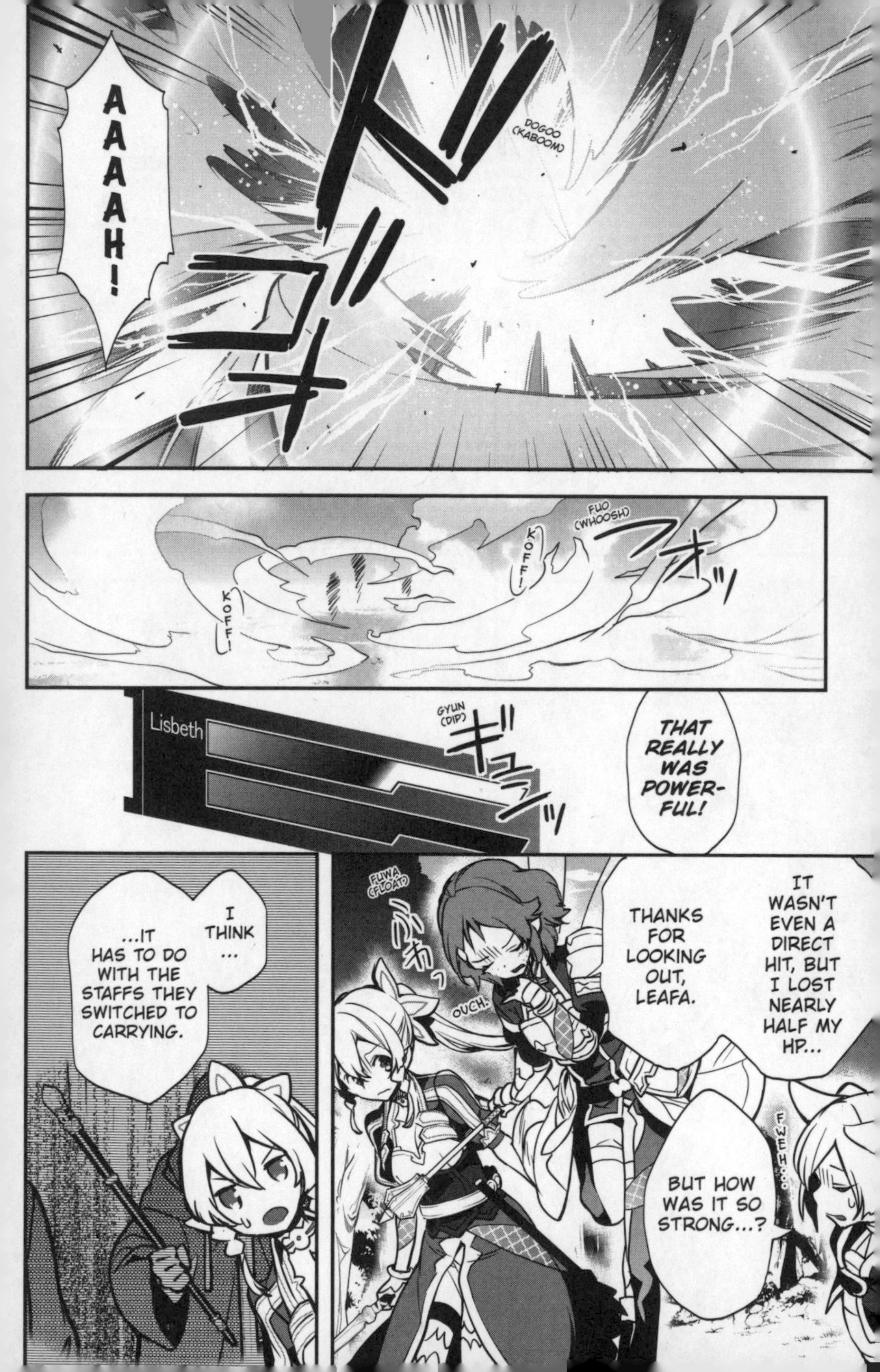
DOGOO (KABOOM)
AAAAAH!
FUO (WHOOSH)
KOFF!
KOFF!
GYUN (DIP)
THAT REALLY WAS POWER-FUL!
Lisbeth
IT WASN'T EVEN A DIRECT HIT, BUT I LOST NEARLY HALF MY HP...
THANKS FOR LOOKING OUT, LEAFA.
FUWA (FLOAT)
OUCH.
FWEH...
BUT HOW WAS IT SO STRONG...?
I THINK...
...IT HAS TO DO WITH THE STAFFS THEY SWITCHED TO CARRYING.

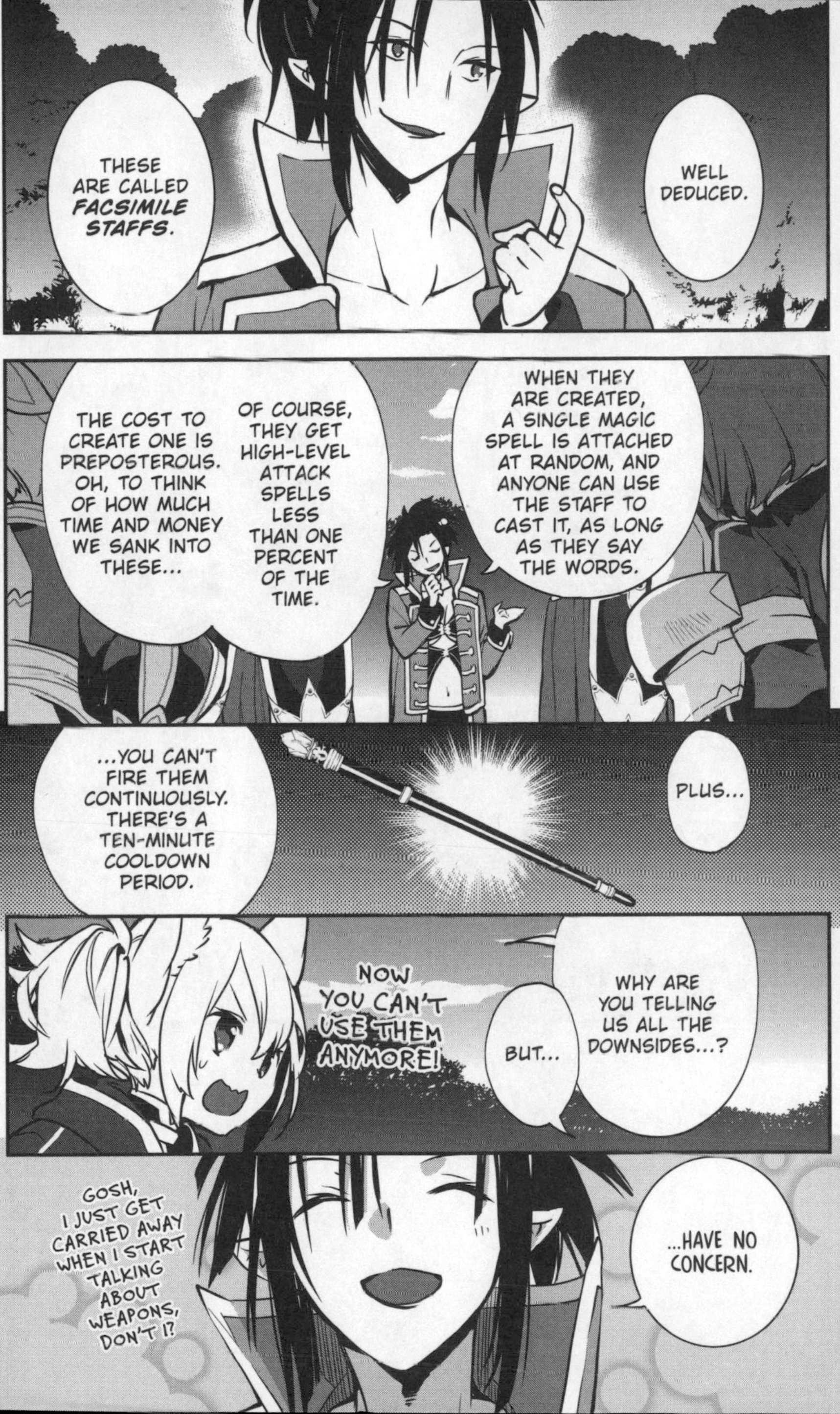
WELL DEDUCED.
THESE ARE CALLED *FACSIMILE STAFFS.*
WHEN THEY ARE CREATED, A SINGLE MAGIC SPELL IS ATTACHED AT RANDOM, AND ANYONE CAN USE THE STAFF TO CAST IT, AS LONG AS THEY SAY THE WORDS.
OF COURSE, THEY GET HIGH-LEVEL ATTACK SPELLS LESS THAN ONE PERCENT OF THE TIME.
THE COST TO CREATE ONE IS PREPOSTEROUS. OH, TO THINK OF HOW MUCH TIME AND MONEY WE SANK INTO THESE...
PLUS...
...YOU CAN'T FIRE THEM CONTINUOUSLY. THERE'S A TEN-MINUTE COOLDOWN PERIOD.
WHY ARE YOU TELLING US ALL THE DOWNSIDES...?
NOW YOU CAN'T USE THEM ANYMORE!
BUT...
...HAVE NO CONCERN.
GOSH, I JUST GET CARRIED AWAY WHEN I START TALKING ABOUT WEAPONS, DON'T I?

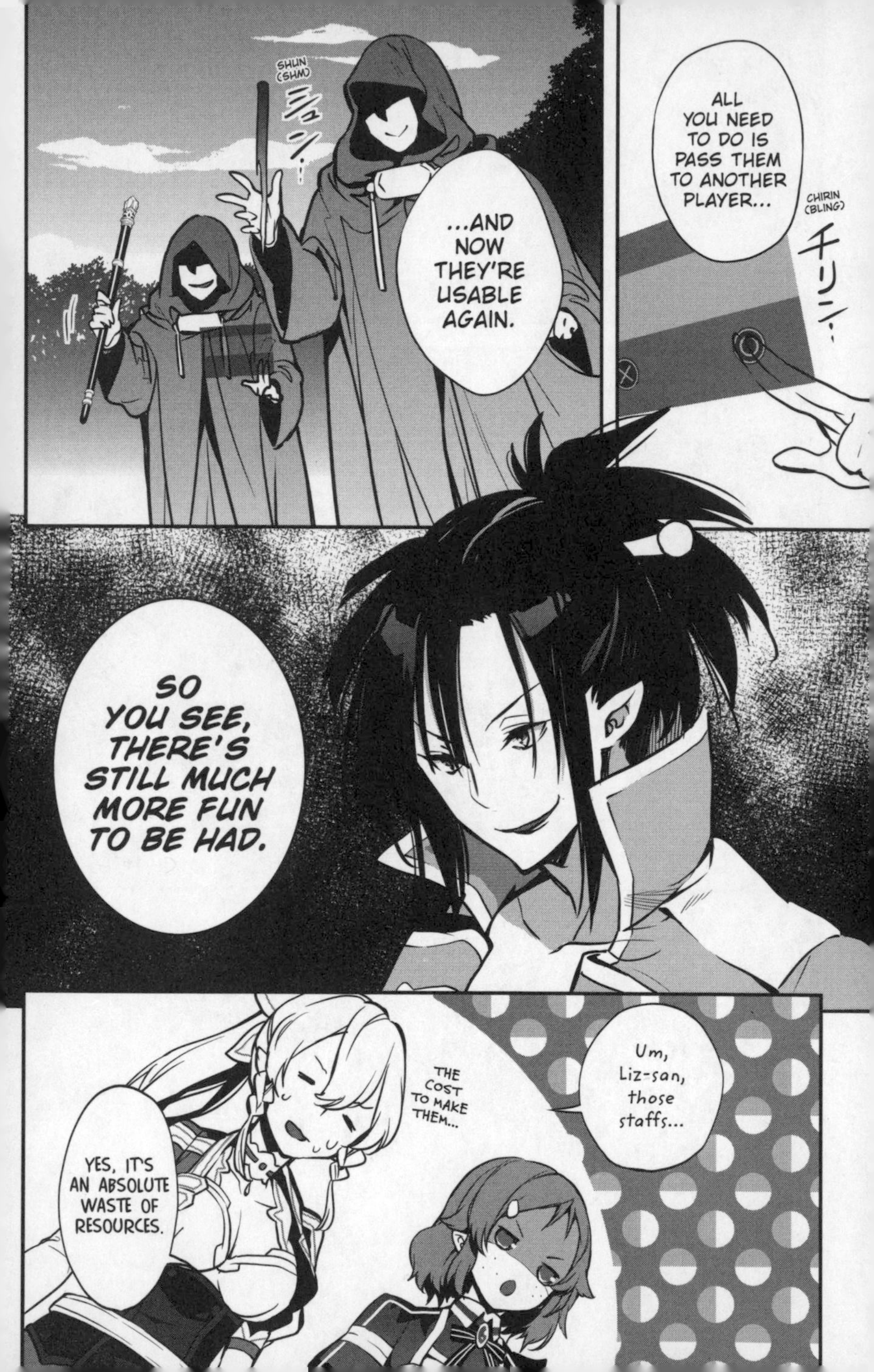
ALL YOU NEED TO DO IS PASS THEM TO ANOTHER PLAYER...
CHIRIN (BLING)
チリン
SHUN (SHM)
シュン
...AND NOW THEY'RE USABLE AGAIN.
SO YOU SEE, THERE'S STILL MUCH MORE FUN TO BE HAD.
Um, Liz-san, those staffs...
THE COST TO MAKE THEM...
YES, IT'S AN ABSOLUTE WASTE OF RESOURCES.

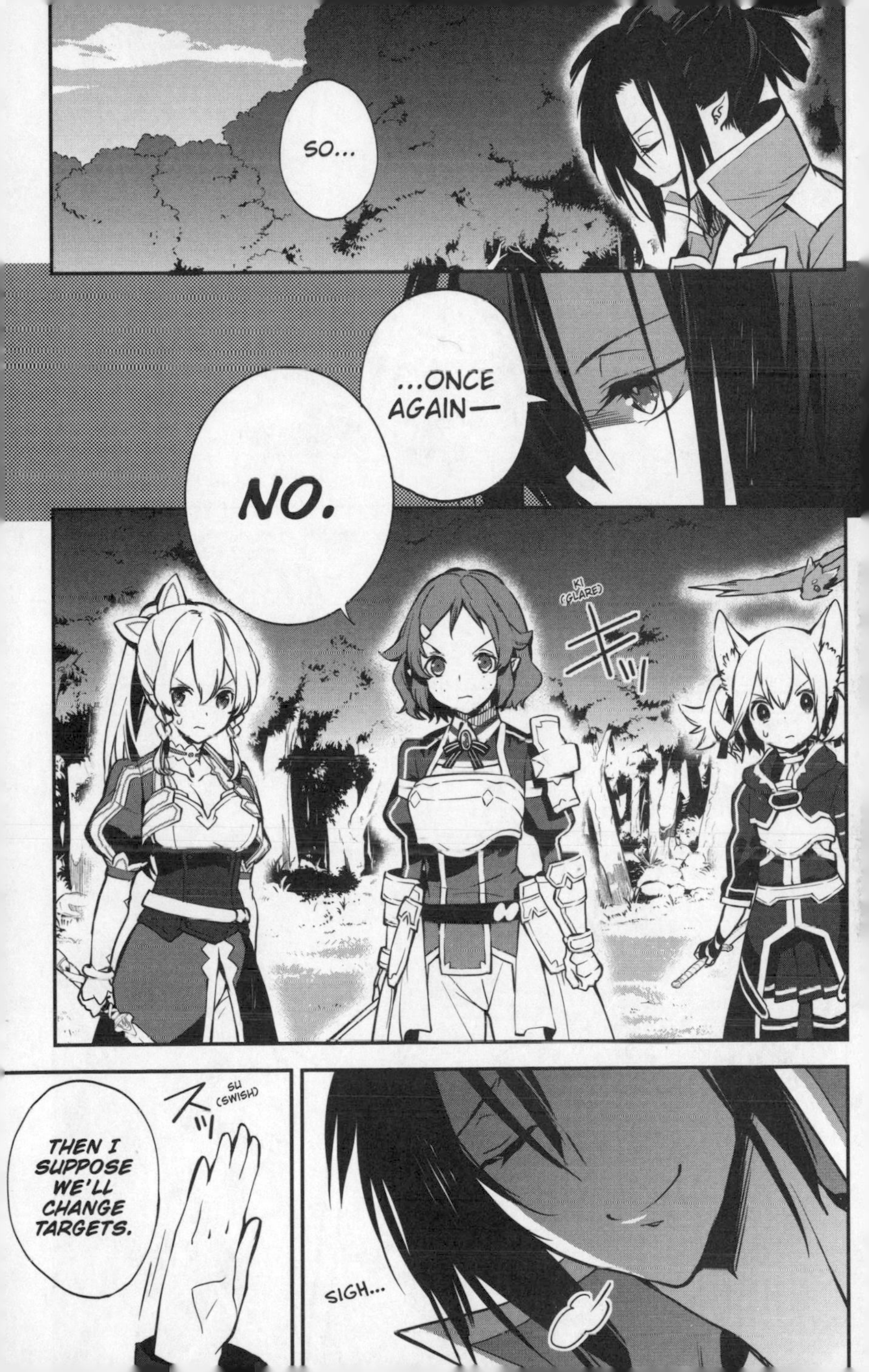
SO...
...ONCE AGAIN—
NO.
KI (GLARE)
THEN I SUPPOSE WE'LL CHANGE TARGETS.
SU (SWISH)
SIGH...

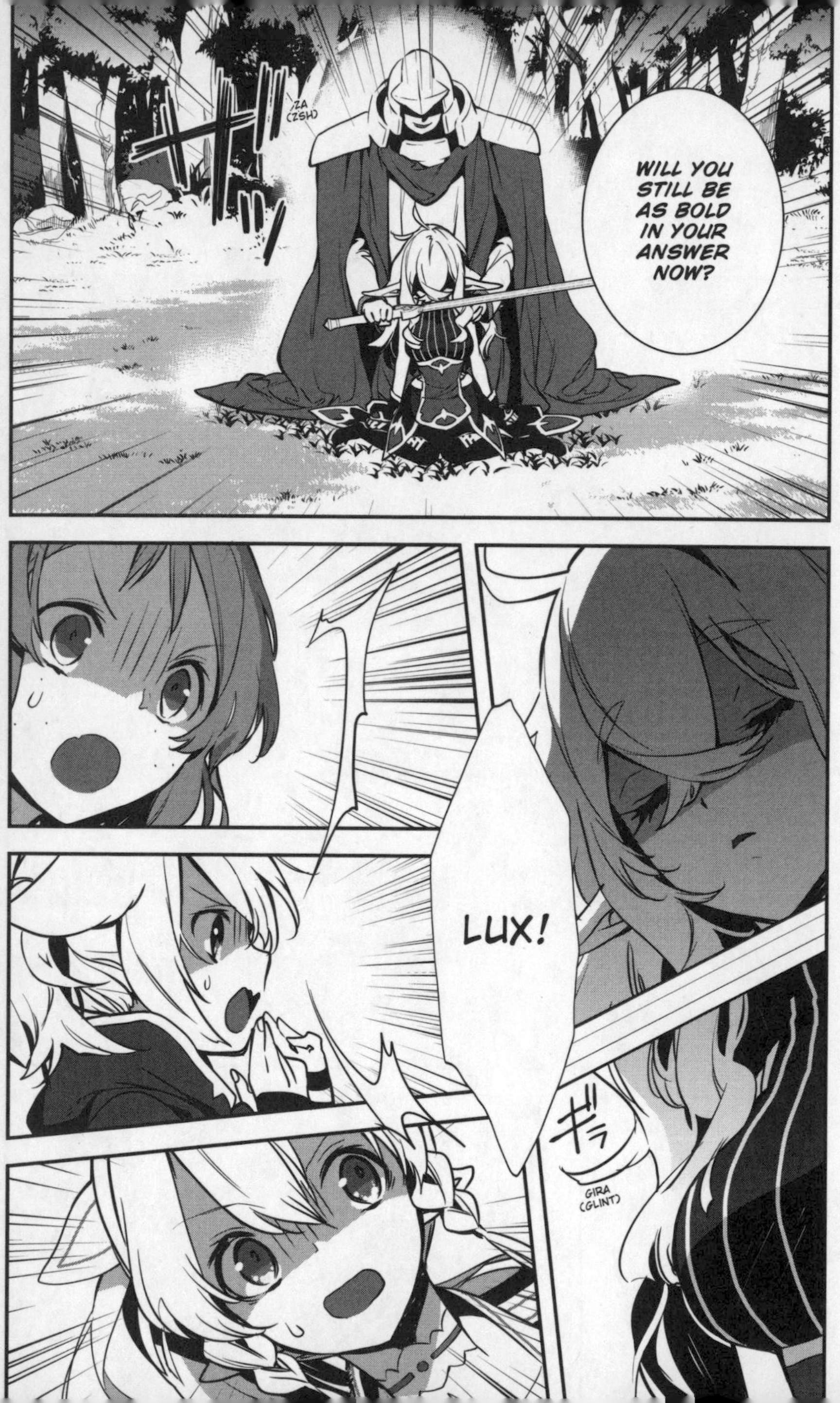
WILL YOU STILL BE AS BOLD IN YOUR ANSWER NOW?
ZA (ZSH)
LUX!
GIRA (GLINT)

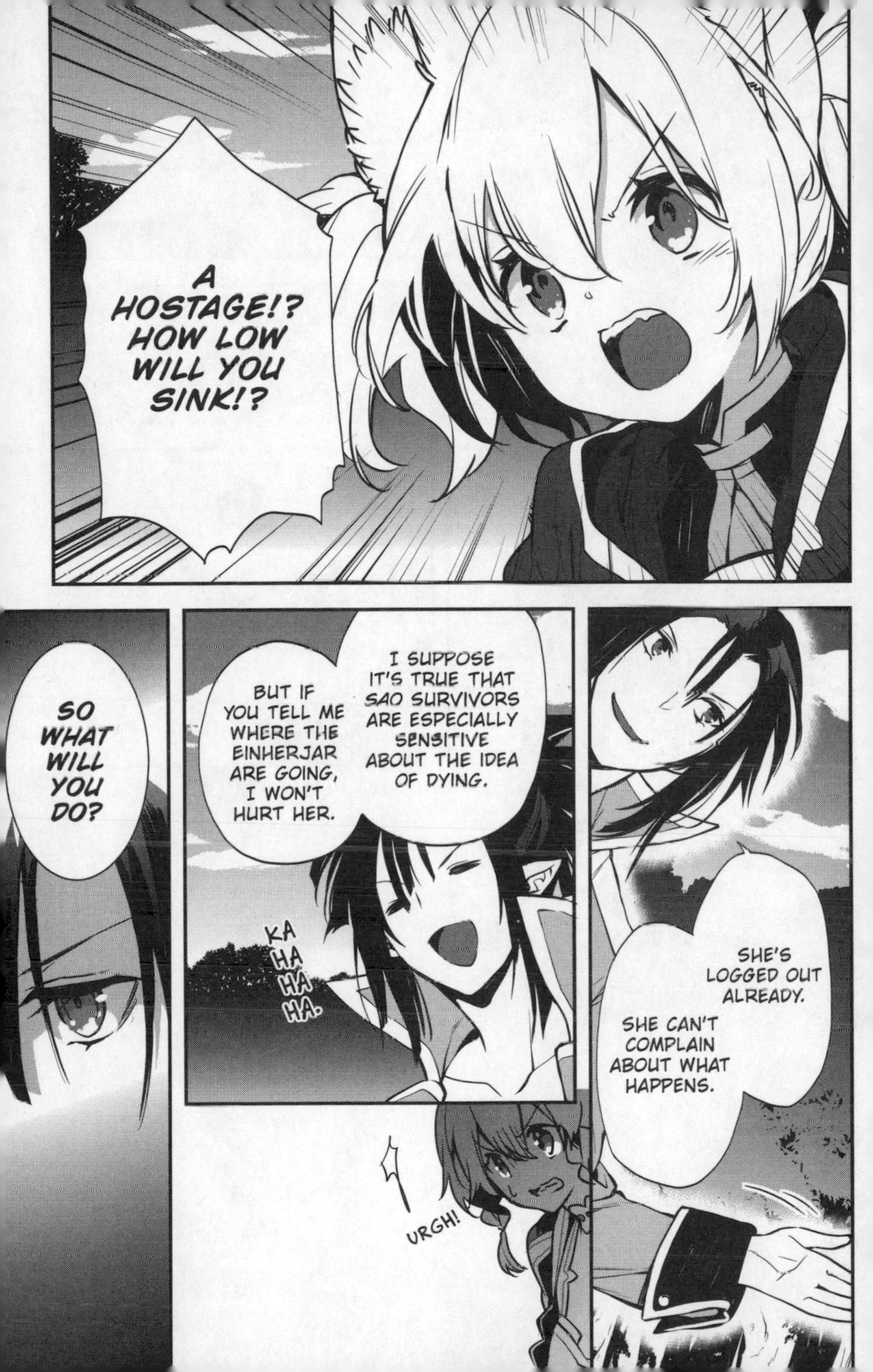
A HOSTAGE!? HOW LOW WILL YOU SINK!?
I SUPPOSE IT'S TRUE THAT SAO SURVIVORS ARE ESPECIALLY SENSITIVE ABOUT THE IDEA OF DYING.
BUT IF YOU TELL ME WHERE THE EINHERJAR ARE GOING, I WON'T HURT HER.
KA HA HA HA.
SO WHAT WILL YOU DO?
SHE'S LOGGED OUT ALREADY.
SHE CAN'T COMPLAIN ABOUT WHAT HAPPENS.
URGH!

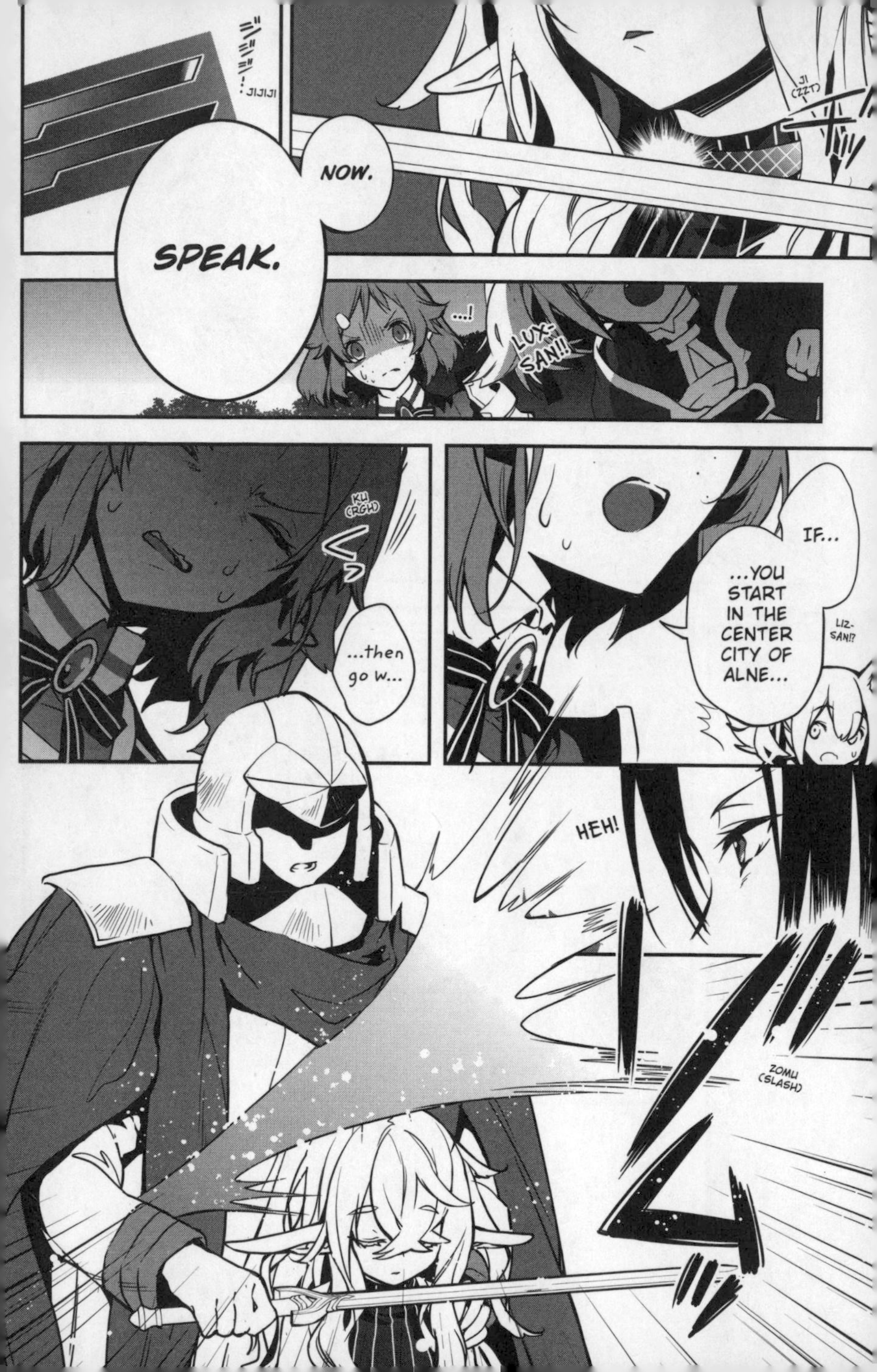
JI (ZZZT)
NOW.
SPEAK.
ジジジ…
JIJIJI
LUX-SAN!!
...!
IF...
...YOU START IN THE CENTER CITY OF ALNE...
LIZ-SAN!?
KU (RGH)
...then go w...
HEH!
ZOMU (SLASH)

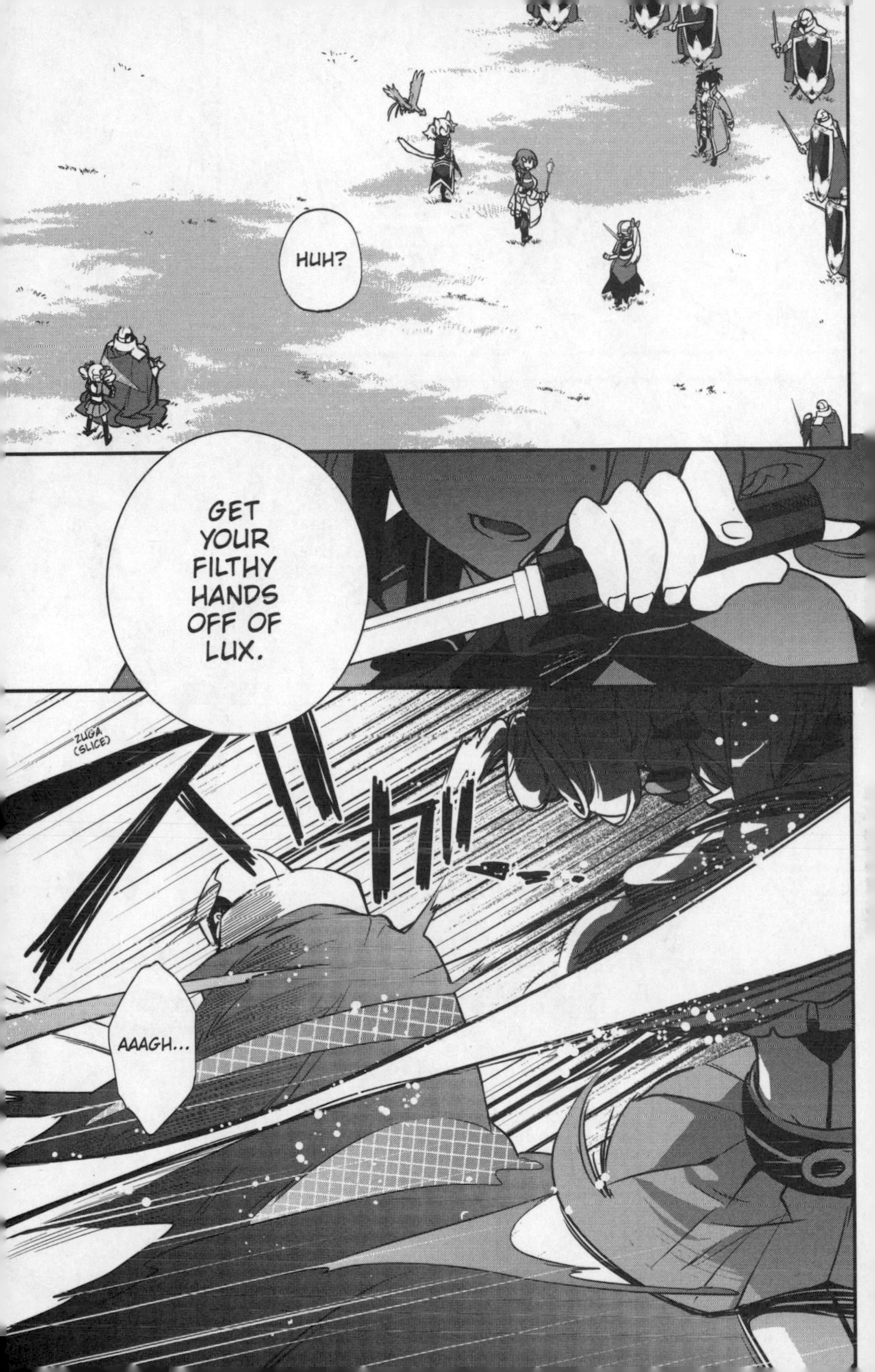
HUH?
GET YOUR FILTHY HANDS OFF OF LUX.
ZUGA (SLICE)
AAAGH...

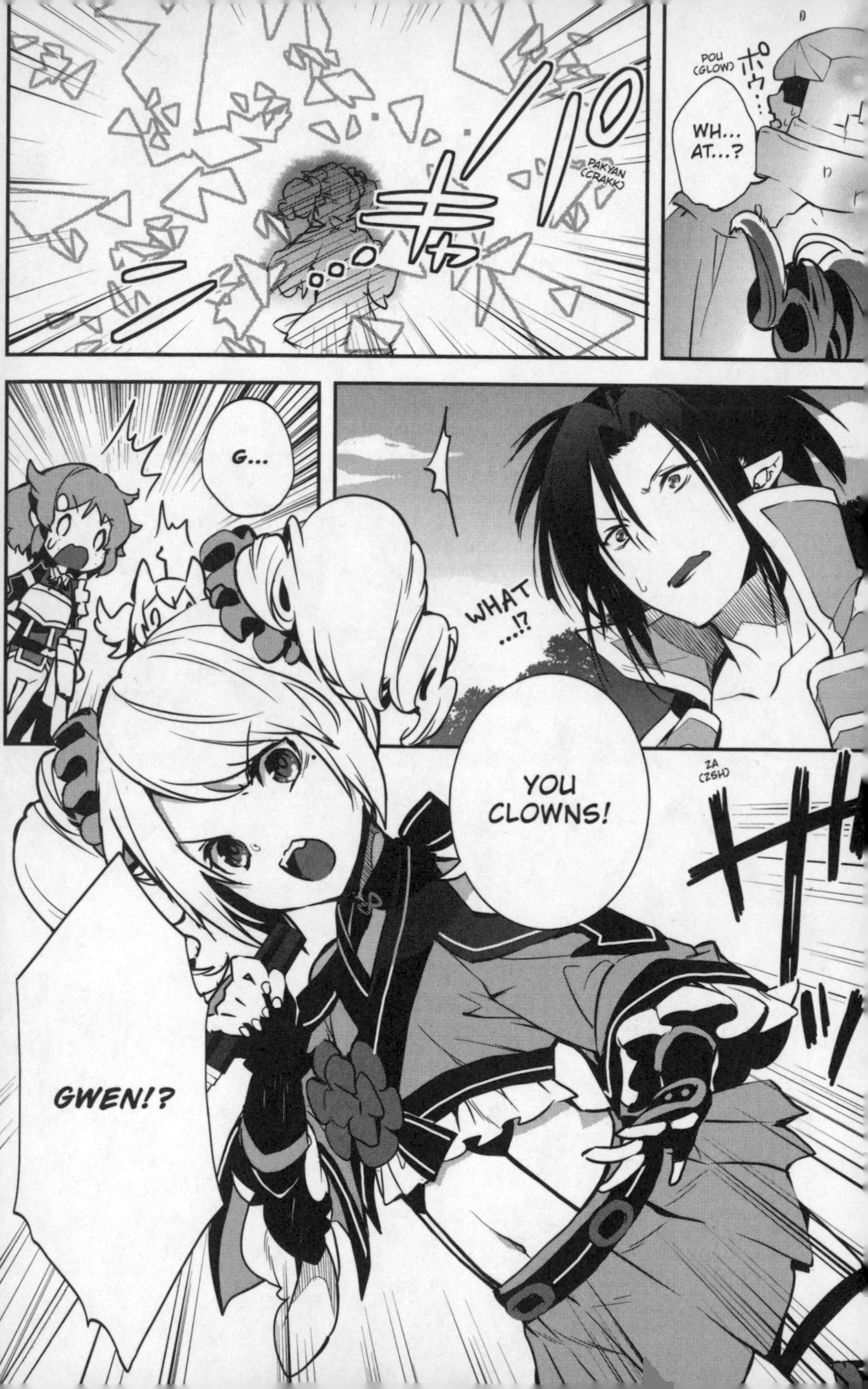
POU (GLOW)
WH... AT...?
PAKYAN (CRAKK)
WHAT ...!?
G...
ZA (ZSH)
YOU CLOWNS!
GWEN!?

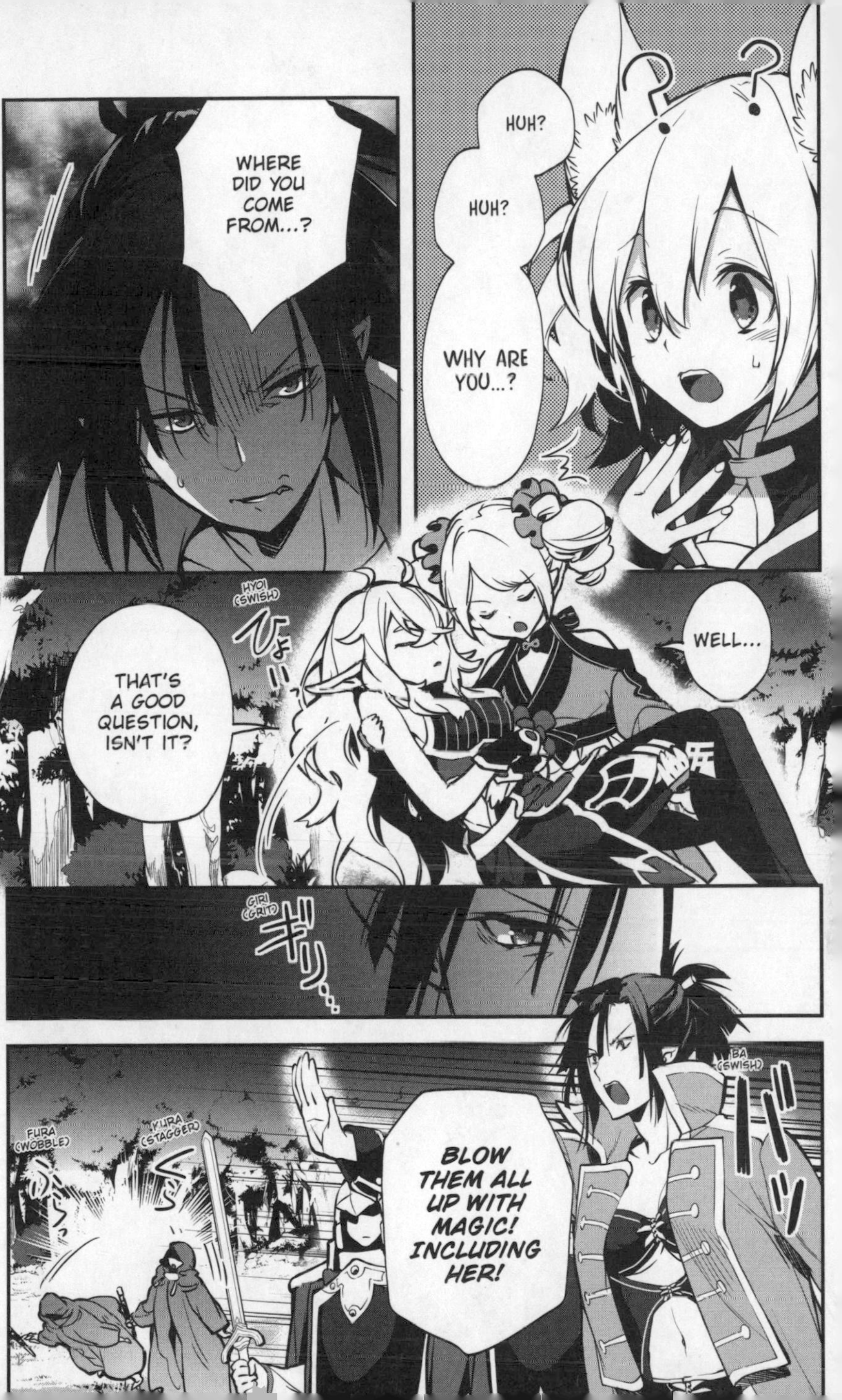
HUH?
HUH?
WHY ARE YOU...?
WHERE DID YOU COME FROM...?
WELL...
HYOI (SWISH)
THAT'S A GOOD QUESTION, ISN'T IT?
GIRI (GRIT)
BA (SWISH)
BLOW THEM ALL UP WITH MAGIC! INCLUDING HER!
KURA (STAGGER)
FURA (WOBBLE)

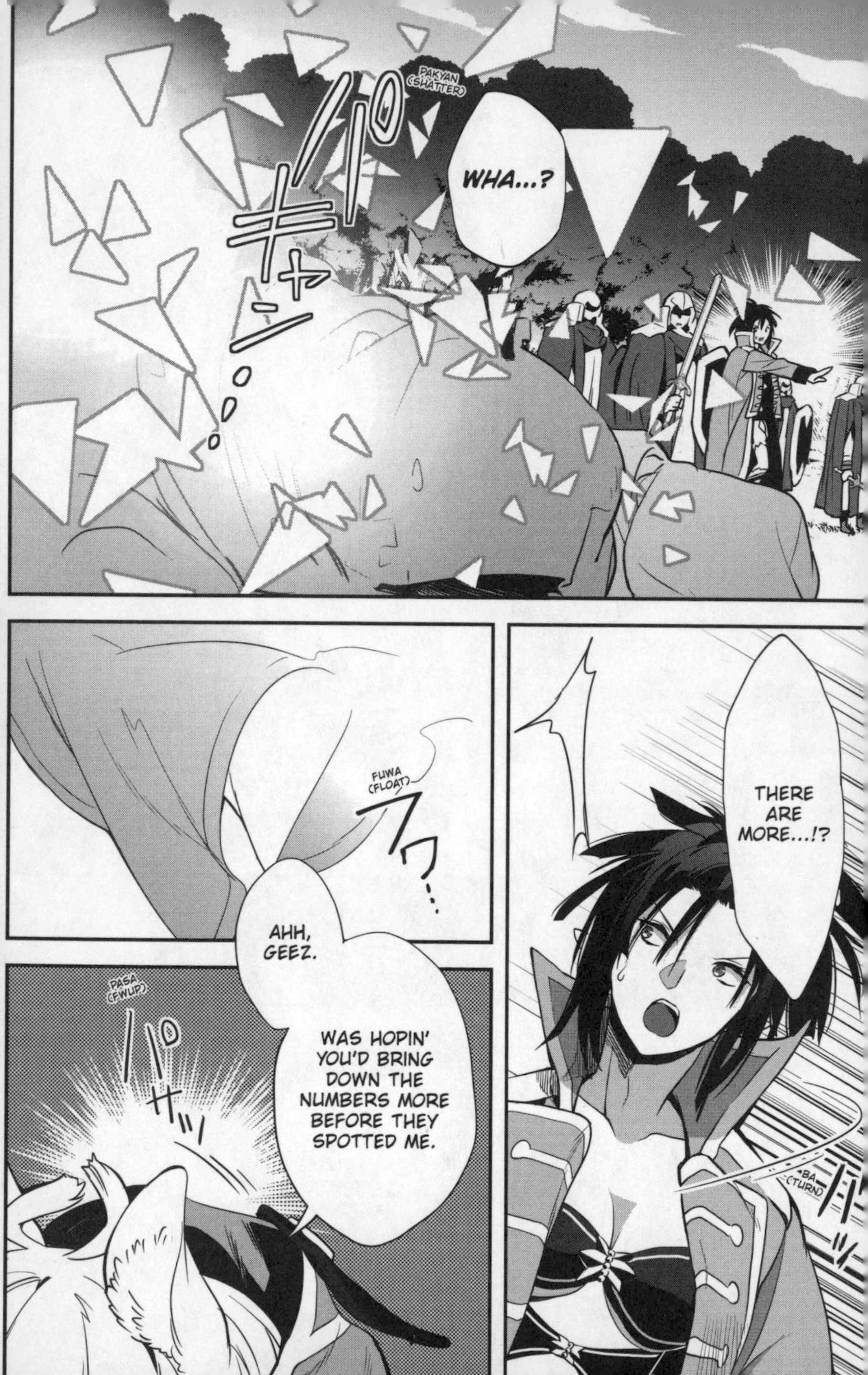
PAKYAN (SHATTER)
WHA...?
THERE ARE MORE...!?
BA (TURN)
FUWA (FLOAT)
AHH, GEEZ.
PASA (FWUP)
WAS HOPIN' YOU'D BRING DOWN THE NUMBERS MORE BEFORE THEY SPOTTED ME.

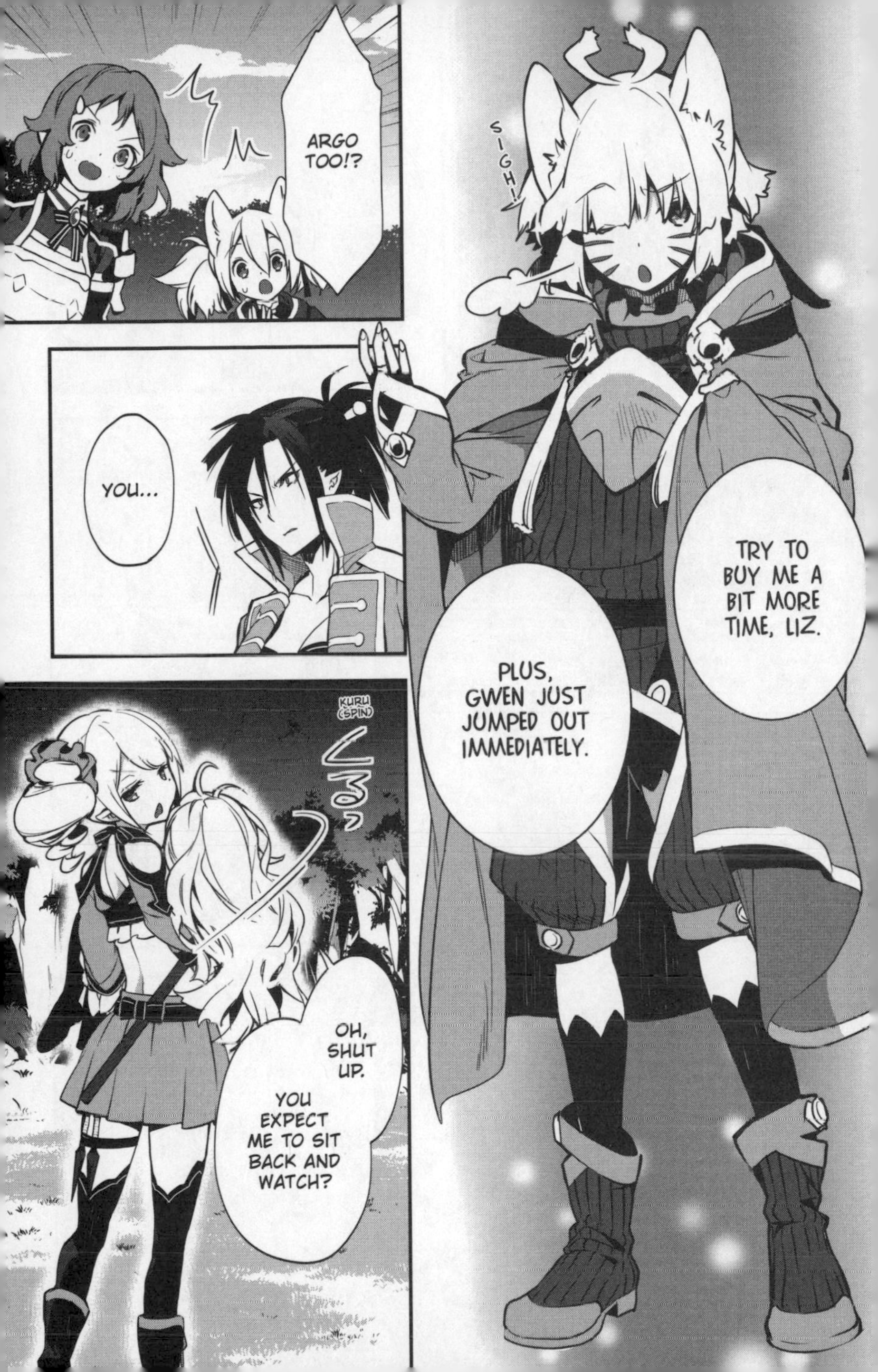

ARGO TOO!?
SIGH!
TRY TO BUY ME A BIT MORE TIME, LIZ.
PLUS, GWEN JUST JUMPED OUT IMMEDIATELY.
YOU...
KURU (SPIN)
OH, SHUT UP.
YOU EXPECT ME TO SIT BACK AND WATCH?

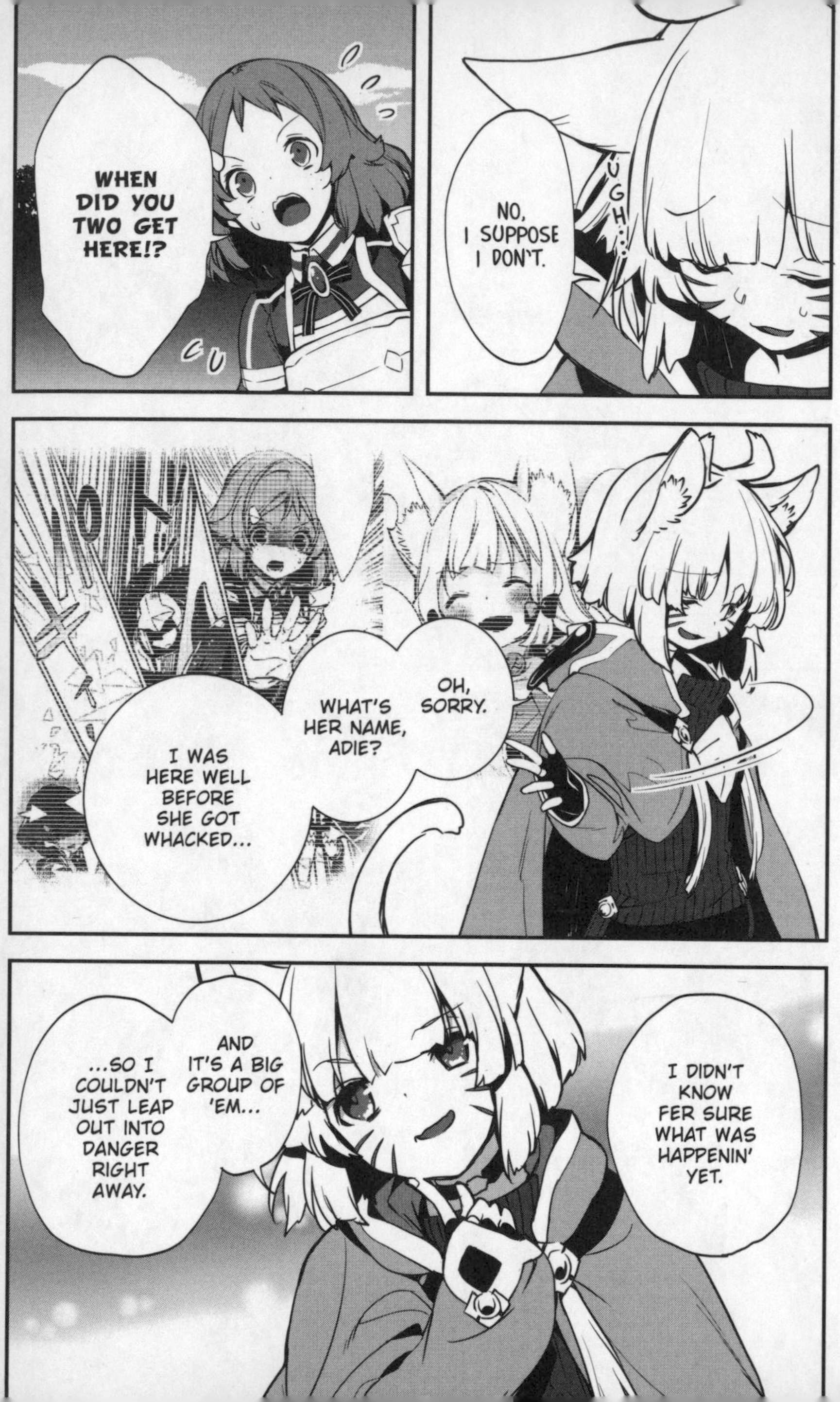

UGH...
NO, I SUPPOSE I DON'T.
WHEN DID YOU TWO GET HERE!?
OH, SORRY.
WHAT'S HER NAME, ADIE?
I WAS HERE WELL BEFORE SHE GOT WHACKED...
I DIDN'T KNOW FER SURE WHAT WAS HAPPENIN' YET.
AND IT'S A BIG GROUP OF 'EM...
...SO I COULDN'T JUST LEAP OUT INTO DANGER RIGHT AWAY.

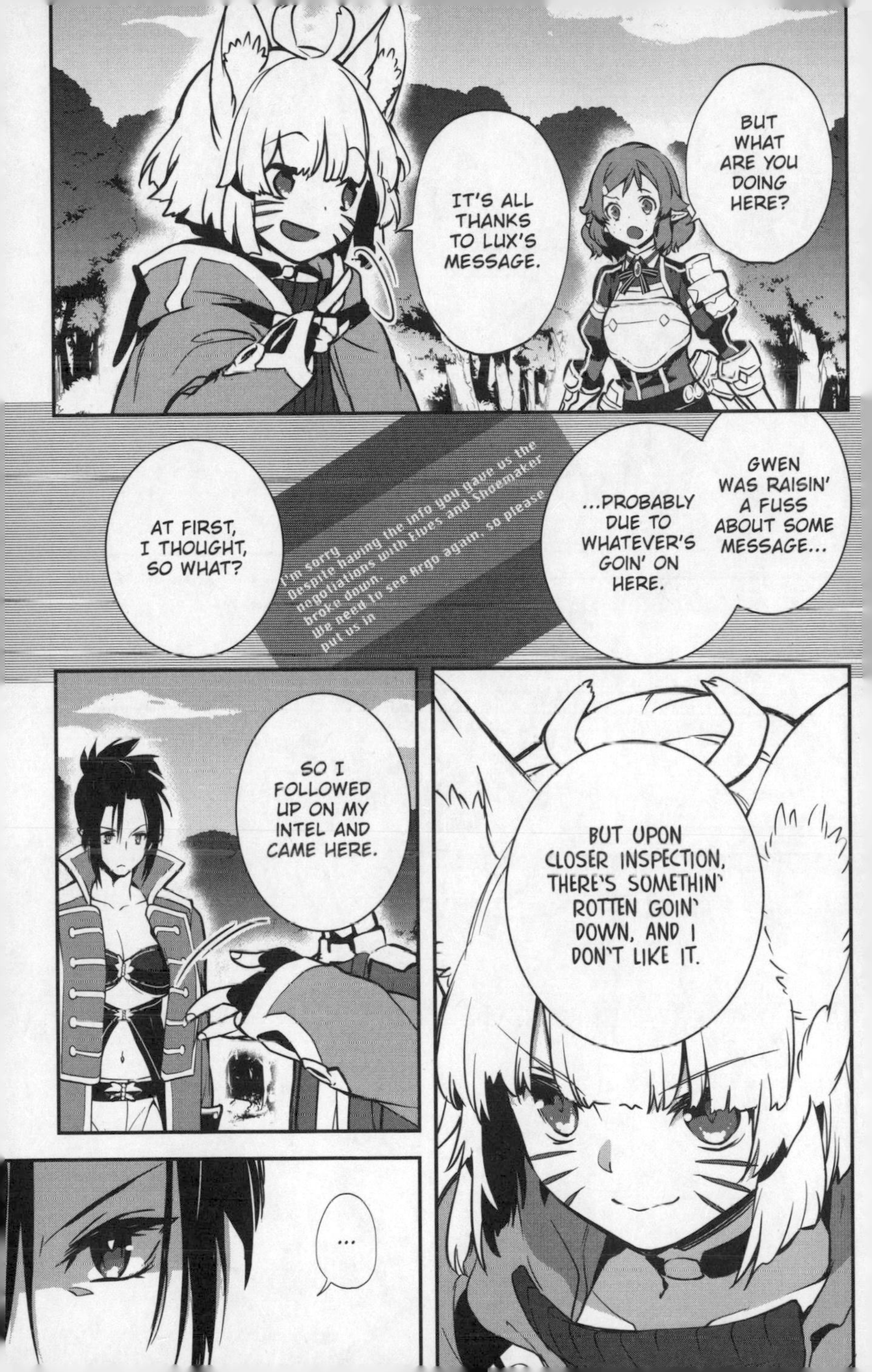
BUT WHAT ARE YOU DOING HERE?
IT'S ALL THANKS TO LUX'S MESSAGE.
GWEN WAS RAISIN' A FUSS ABOUT SOME MESSAGE...
...PROBABLY DUE TO WHATEVER'S GOIN' ON HERE.
I'm sorry
Despite having the info you gave us the
negotiations with Elves and Shoemaker
broke down.
We need to see Argo again, so please
put us in
AT FIRST, I THOUGHT, SO WHAT?
BUT UPON CLOSER INSPECTION, THERE'S SOMETHIN' ROTTEN GOIN' DOWN, AND I DON'T LIKE IT.
SO I FOLLOWED UP ON MY INTEL AND CAME HERE.
...

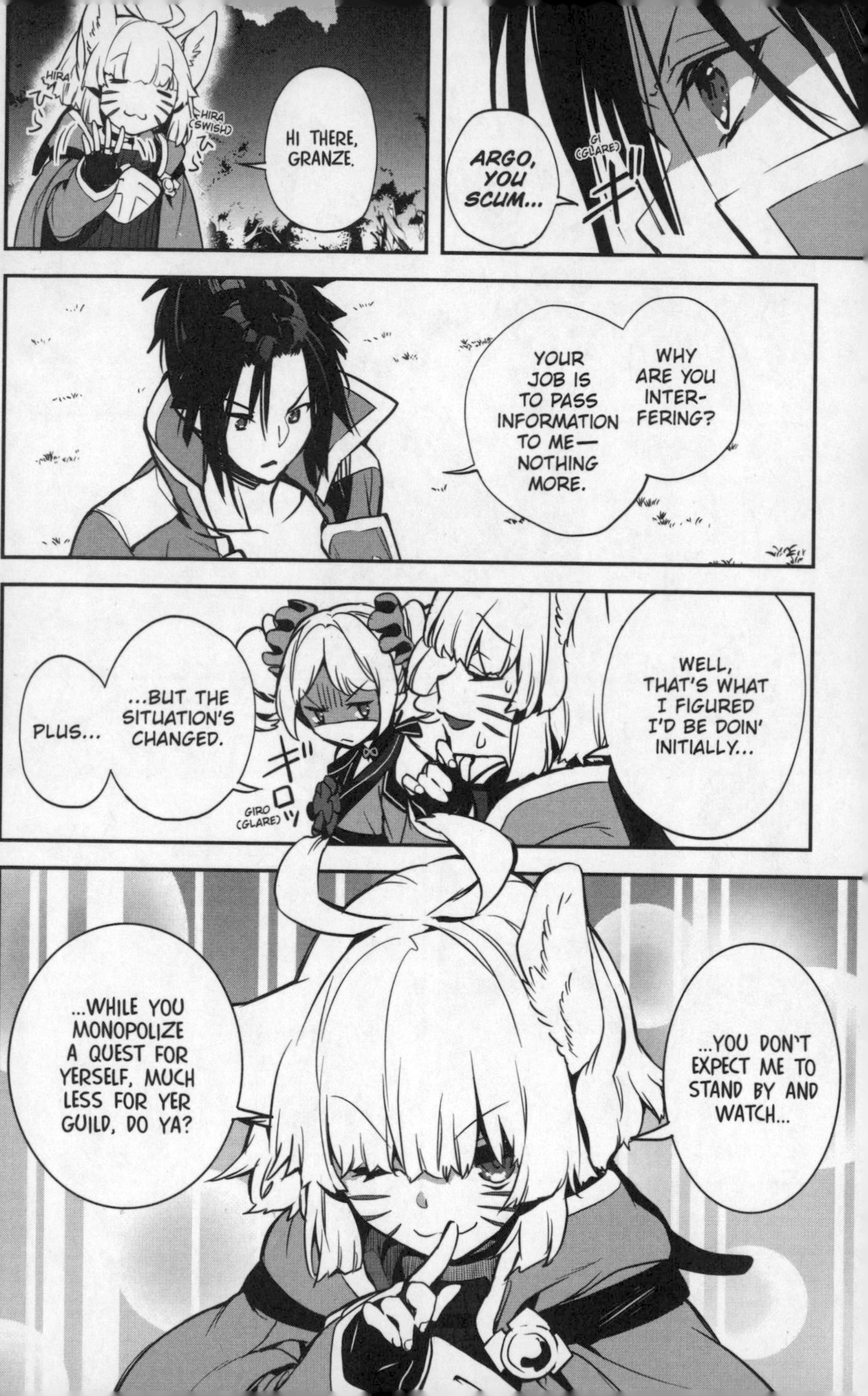
GI (GLARE)
ARGO, YOU SCUM...
HIRA
HIRA (SWISH)
HI THERE, GRANZE.
WHY ARE YOU INTERFERING?
YOUR JOB IS TO PASS INFORMATION TO ME—NOTHING MORE.
WELL, THAT'S WHAT I FIGURED I'D BE DOIN' INITIALLY...
...BUT THE SITUATION'S CHANGED.
PLUS...
GIRO (GLARE)
...YOU DON'T EXPECT ME TO STAND BY AND WATCH...
...WHILE YOU MONOPOLIZE A QUEST FOR YERSELF, MUCH LESS FOR YER GUILD, DO YA?

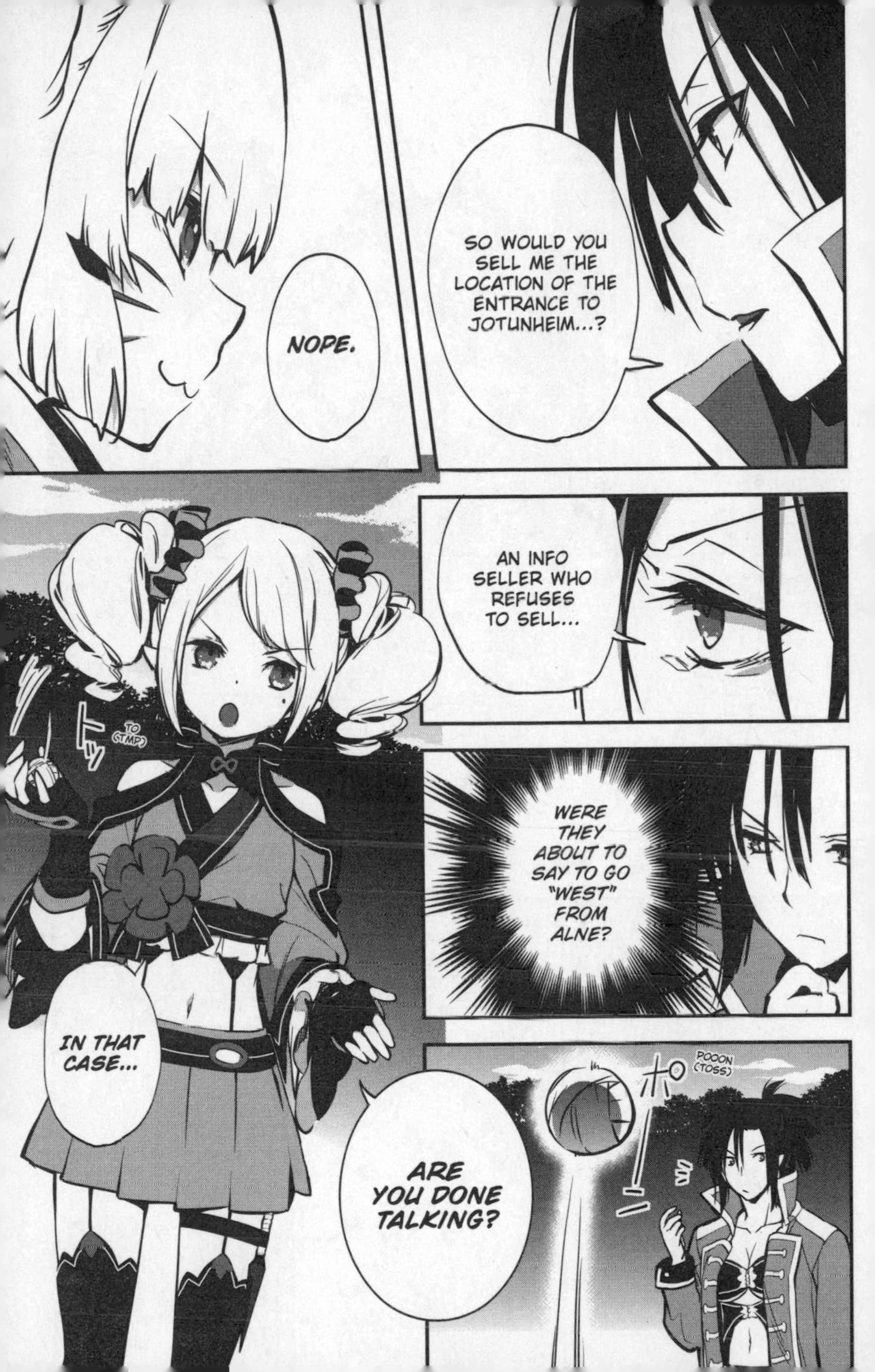
SO WOULD YOU SELL ME THE LOCATION OF THE ENTRANCE TO JOTUNHEIM...?
NOPE.
AN INFO SELLER WHO REFUSES TO SELL...
WERE THEY ABOUT TO SAY TO GO "WEST" FROM ALNE?
TO (TMP)
IN THAT CASE...
POOON (TOSS)
ARE YOU DONE TALKING?

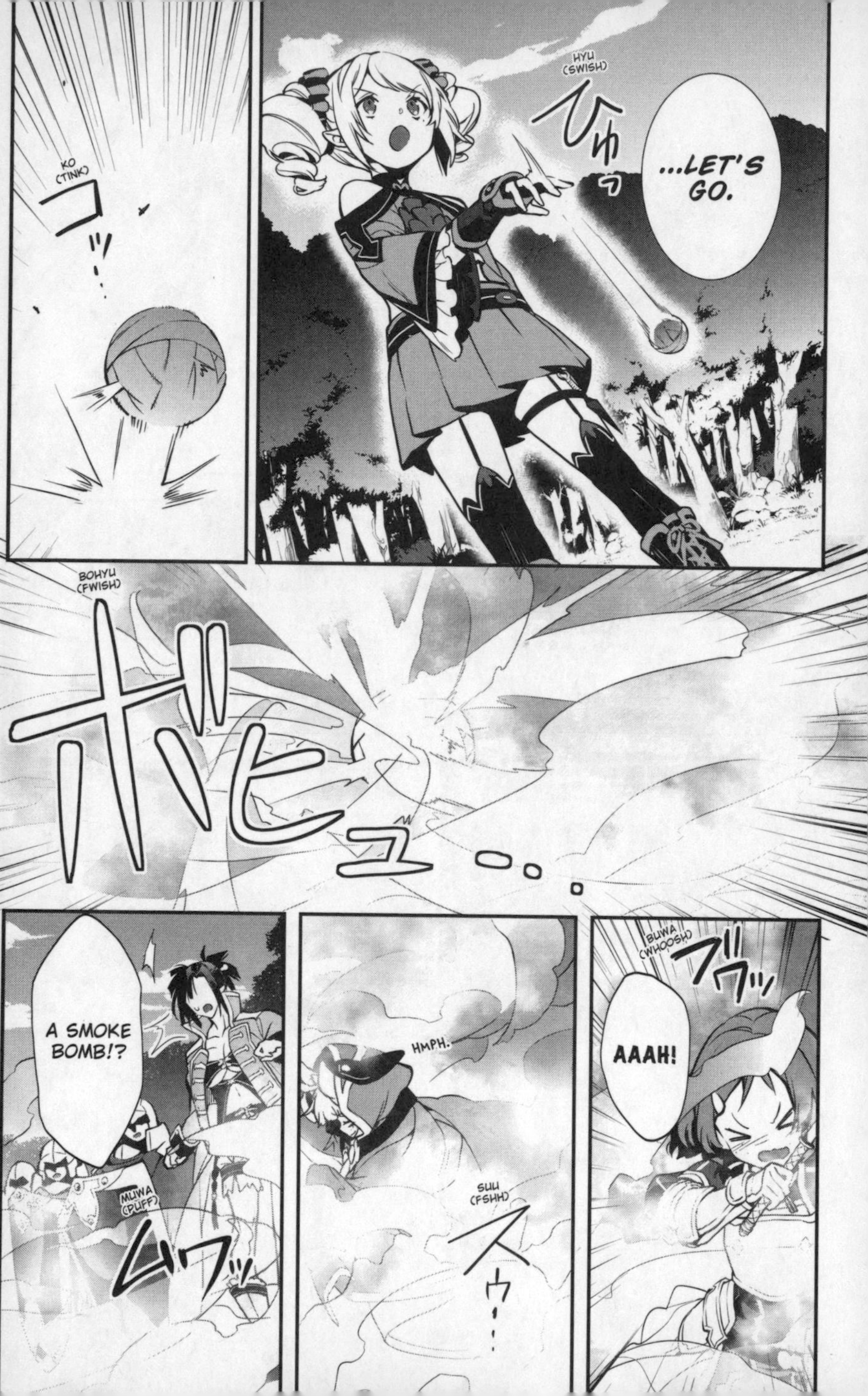
HYU (SWISH)
ひゅっ
...LET'S GO.
KO (TINK)
コッ
BOHYU (FWISH)
ボヒュ...
BUWA (WHOOSH)
ブワッ
AAAH!
HMPH.
SUU (FSHH)
スゥ...
A SMOKE BOMB!?
MUWA (PUFF)
ムワッ

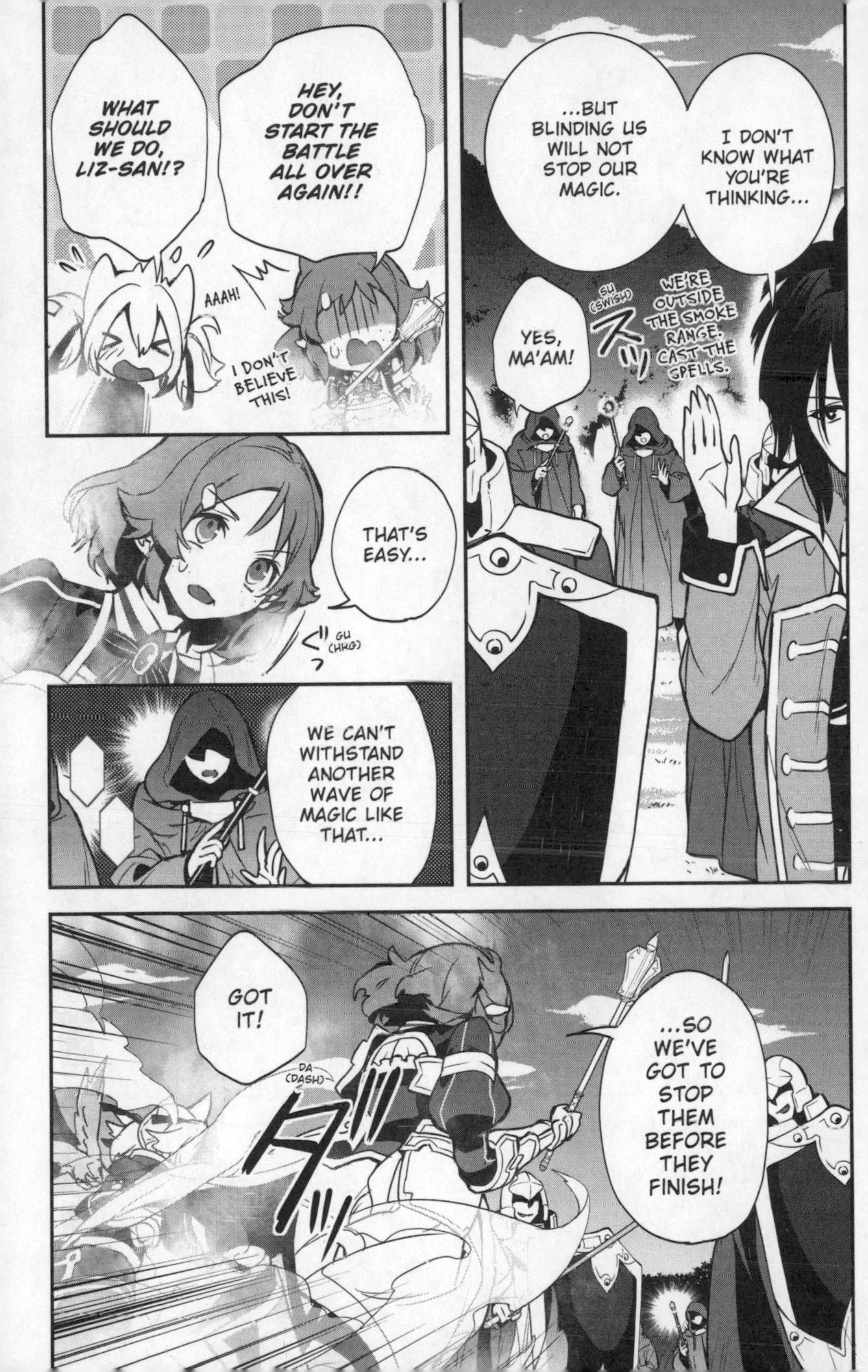

I DON'T KNOW WHAT YOU'RE THINKING...
...BUT BLINDING US WILL NOT STOP OUR MAGIC.
WE'RE OUTSIDE THE SMOKE RANGE. CAST THE SPELLS.
SU (SWISH)
YES, MA'AM!
HEY, DON'T START THE BATTLE ALL OVER AGAIN!!
WHAT SHOULD WE DO, LIZ-SAN!?
AAAH!
I DON'T BELIEVE THIS!
THAT'S EASY...
GU (HRG)
WE CAN'T WITHSTAND ANOTHER WAVE OF MAGIC LIKE THAT...
...SO WE'VE GOT TO STOP THEM BEFORE THEY FINISH!
GOT IT!
DA (DASH)

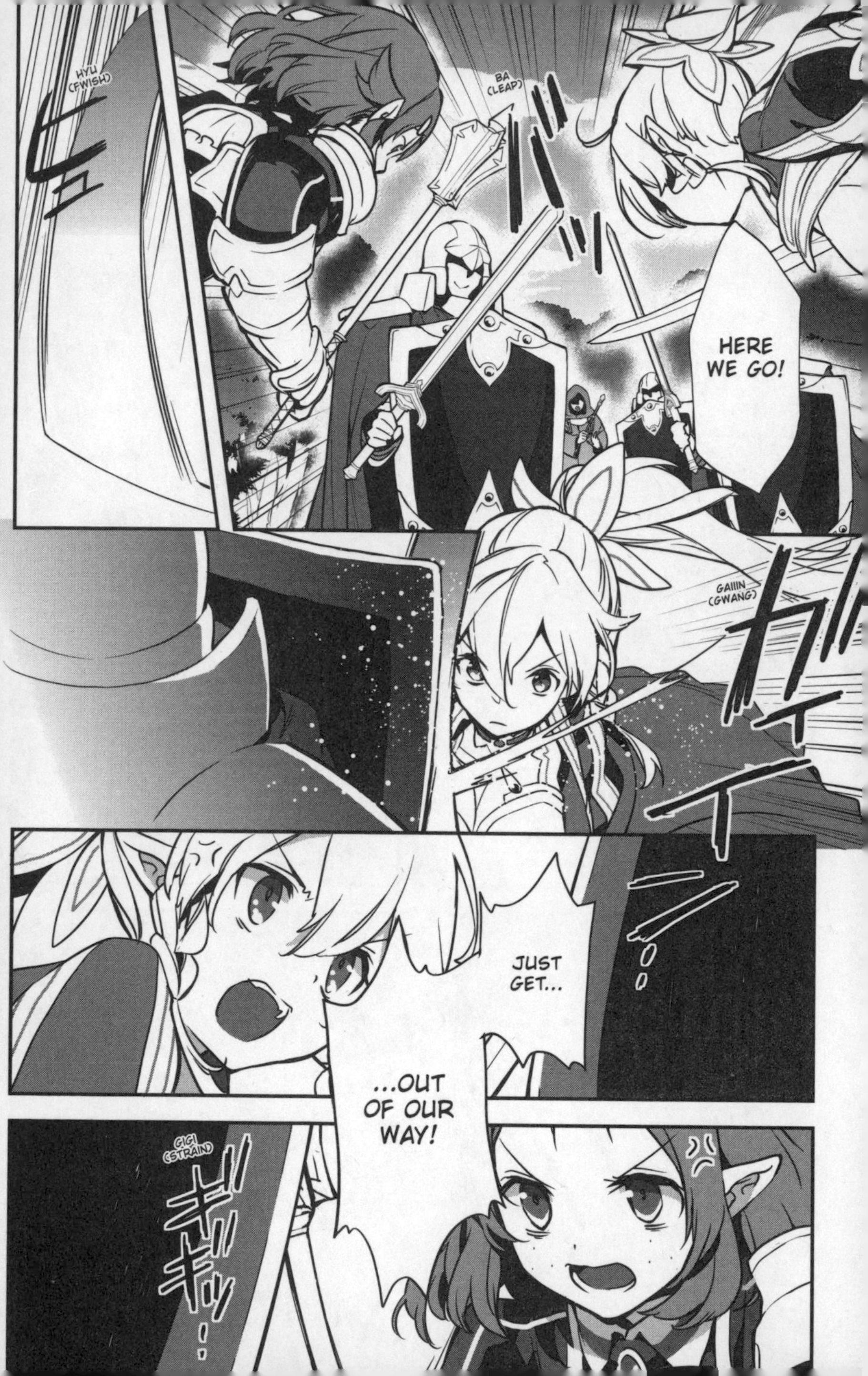
HERE WE GO!
BA (LEAP)
HYU (FWISH)
GAIIIN (GWANG)
JUST GET...
...OUT OF OUR WAY!
GIGI (STRAIN)

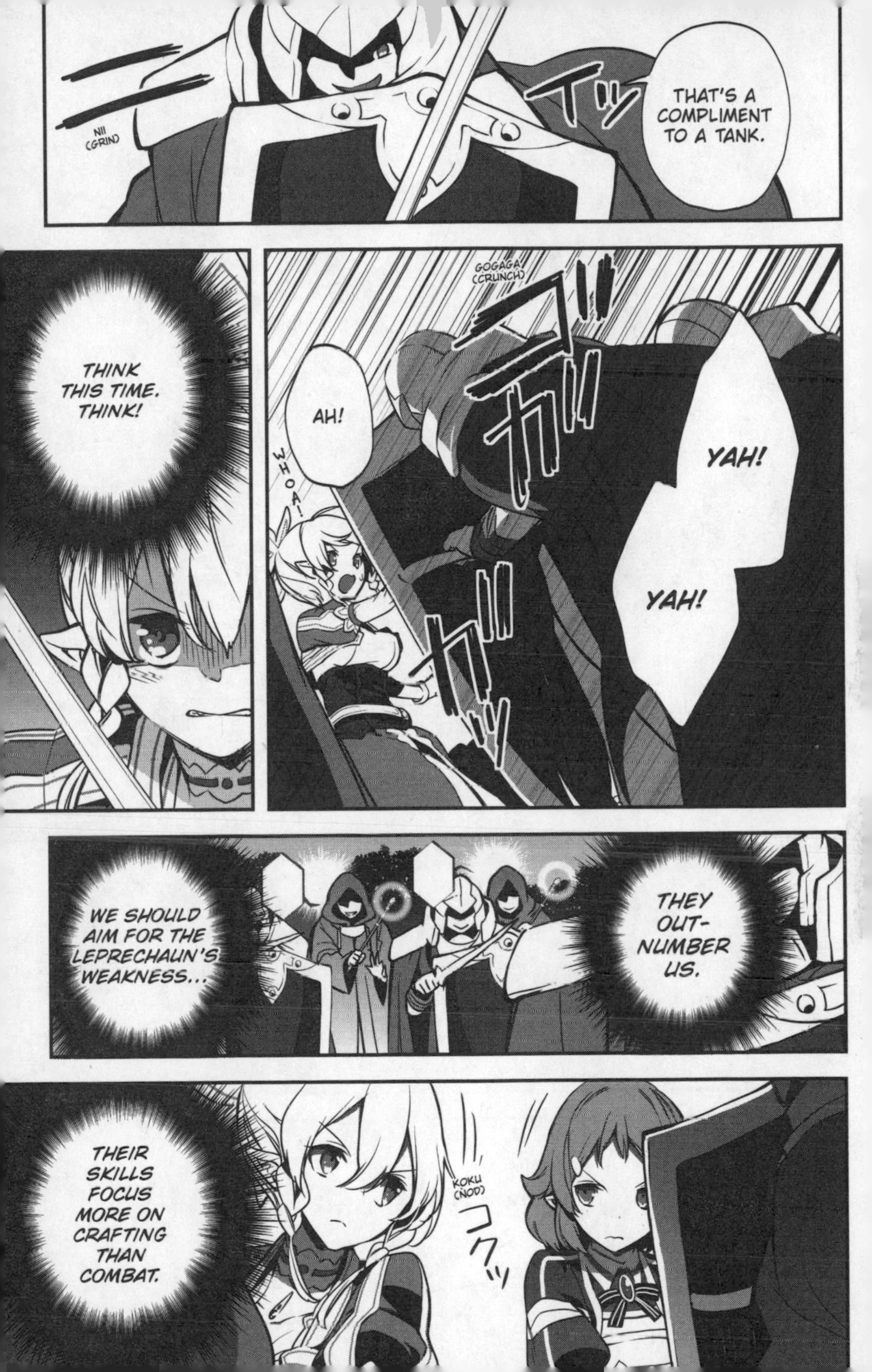
NII (GRIN)
THAT'S A COMPLIMENT TO A TANK.
GOGAGA (CRUNCH)
YAH!
YAH!
AH!
WHOA!
THINK THIS TIME. THINK!
THEY OUT-NUMBER US.
WE SHOULD AIM FOR THE LEPRECHAUN'S WEAKNESS...
KOKU (NOD)
THEIR SKILLS FOCUS MORE ON CRAFTING THAN COMBAT.

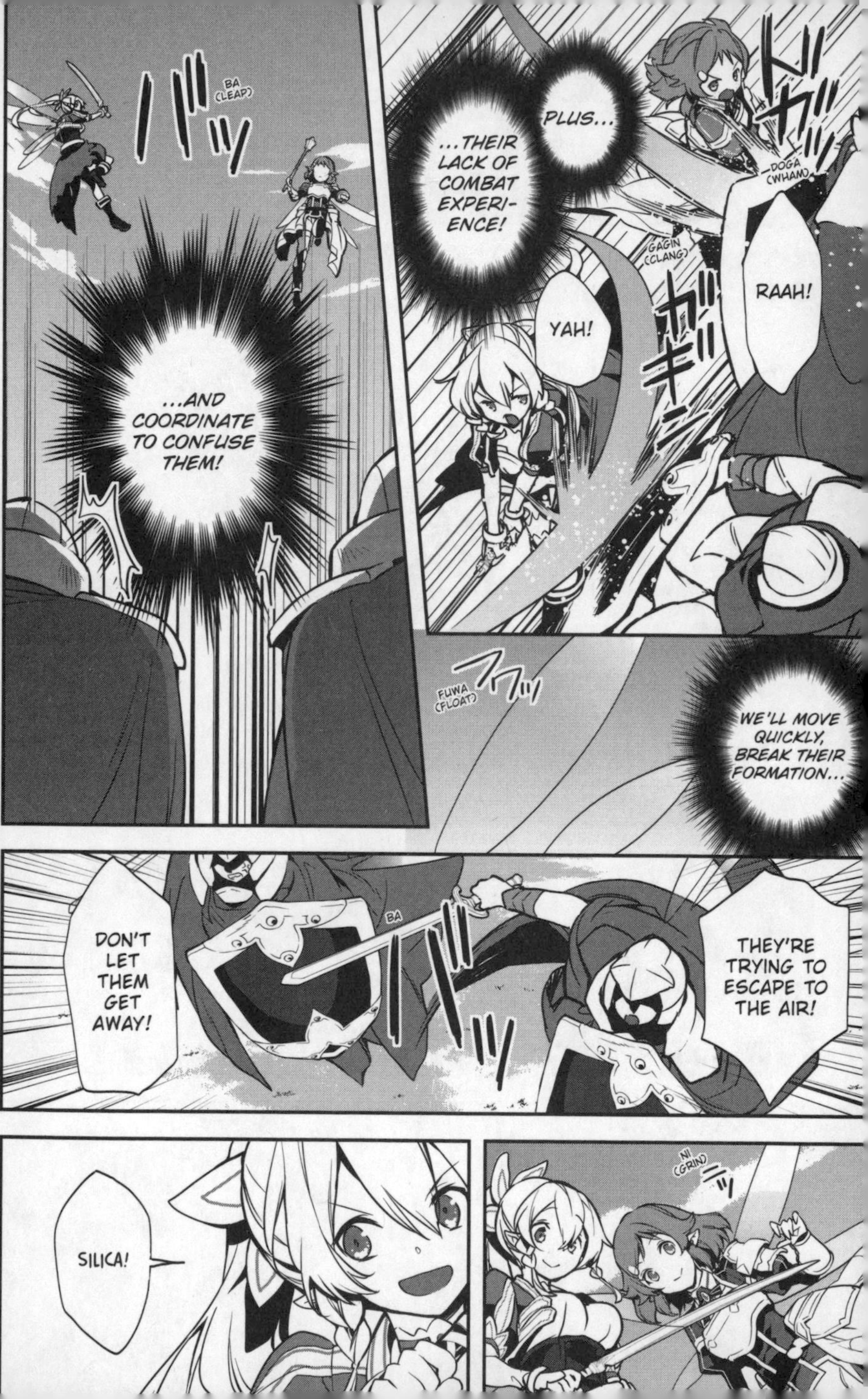

FUWA (FLOAT)
WE'LL MOVE QUICKLY, BREAK THEIR FORMATION...
BA (LEAP)
...AND COORDINATE TO CONFUSE THEM!
PLUS...
...THEIR LACK OF COMBAT EXPERIENCE!
DOGA (WHAM)
RAAH!
GAGIN (CLANG)
YAH!
THEY'RE TRYING TO ESCAPE TO THE AIR!
BA
DON'T LET THEM GET AWAY!
NI (GRIN)
SILICA!

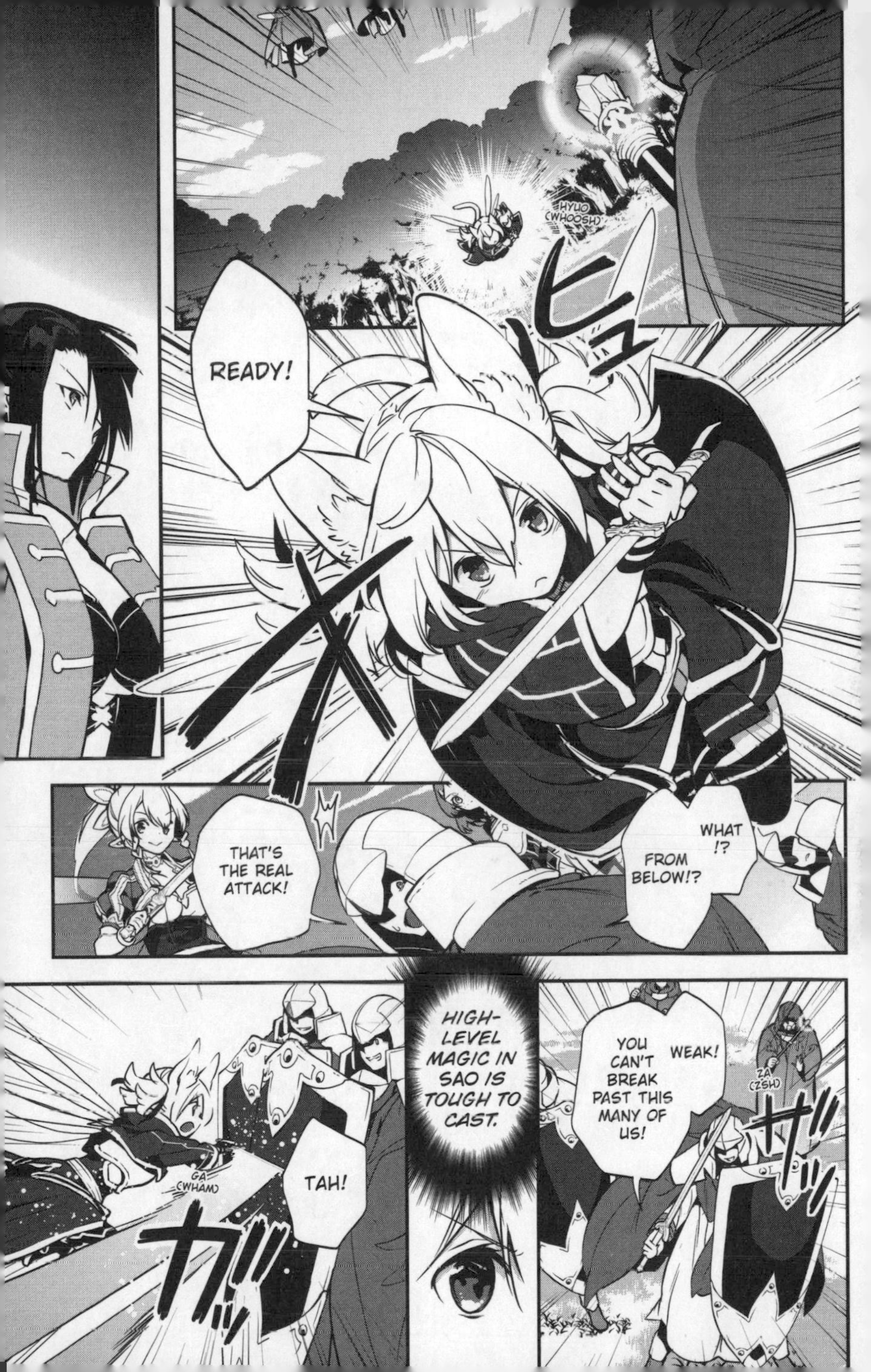
HYUO (WHOOSH)
READY!
WHAT!?
FROM BELOW!?
THAT'S THE REAL ATTACK!
HIGH-LEVEL MAGIC IN SAO IS TOUGH TO CAST.
WEAK!
YOU CAN'T BREAK PAST THIS MANY OF US!
ZA (ZSH)
TAH!
GA (WHAM)

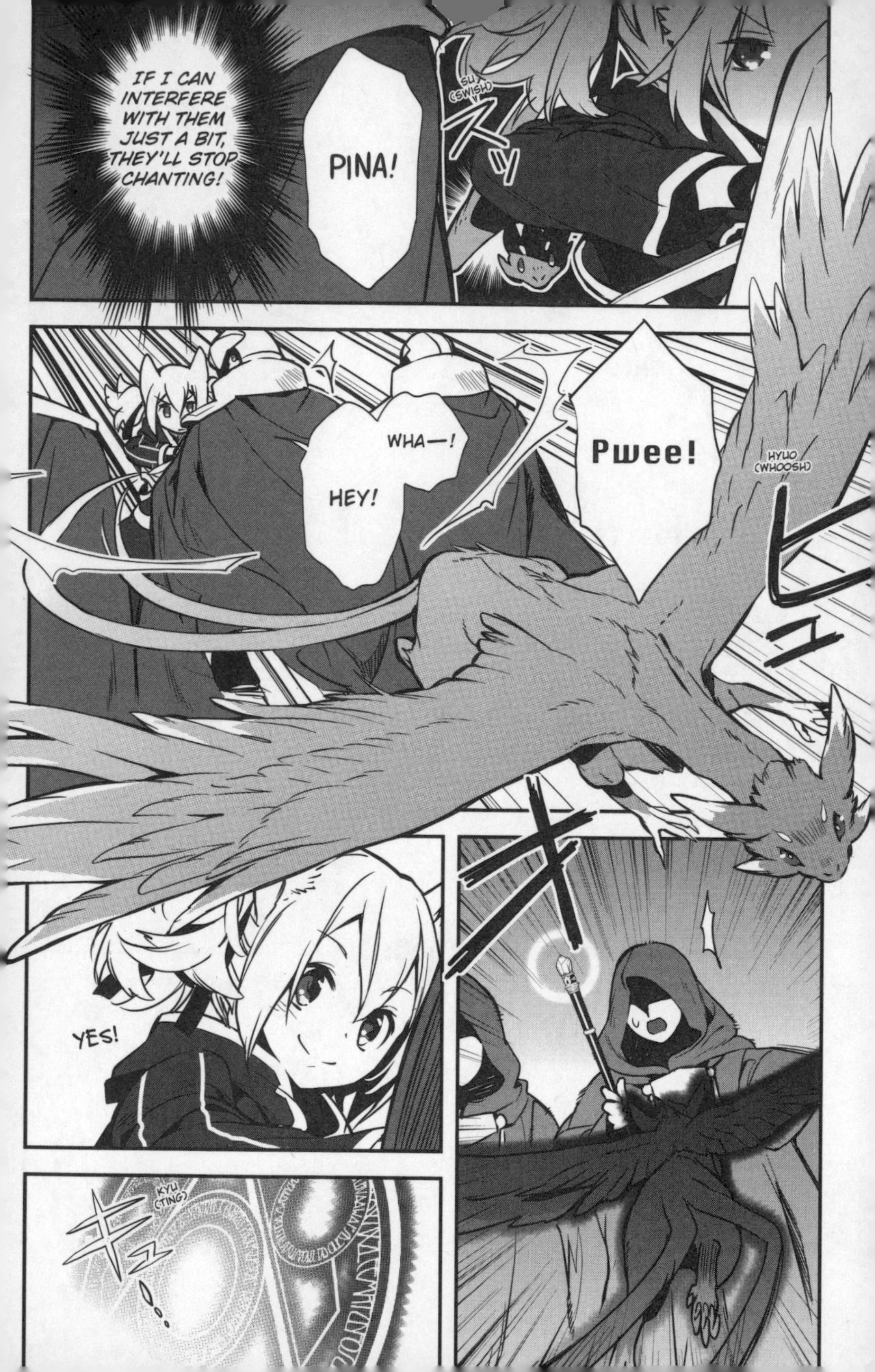
IF I CAN INTERFERE WITH THEM JUST A BIT, THEY'LL STOP CHANTING!
PINA!
SU (SWISH)
WHA—!
HEY!
Pwee!
HYUO (WHOOSH)
YES!
KYU (TING)

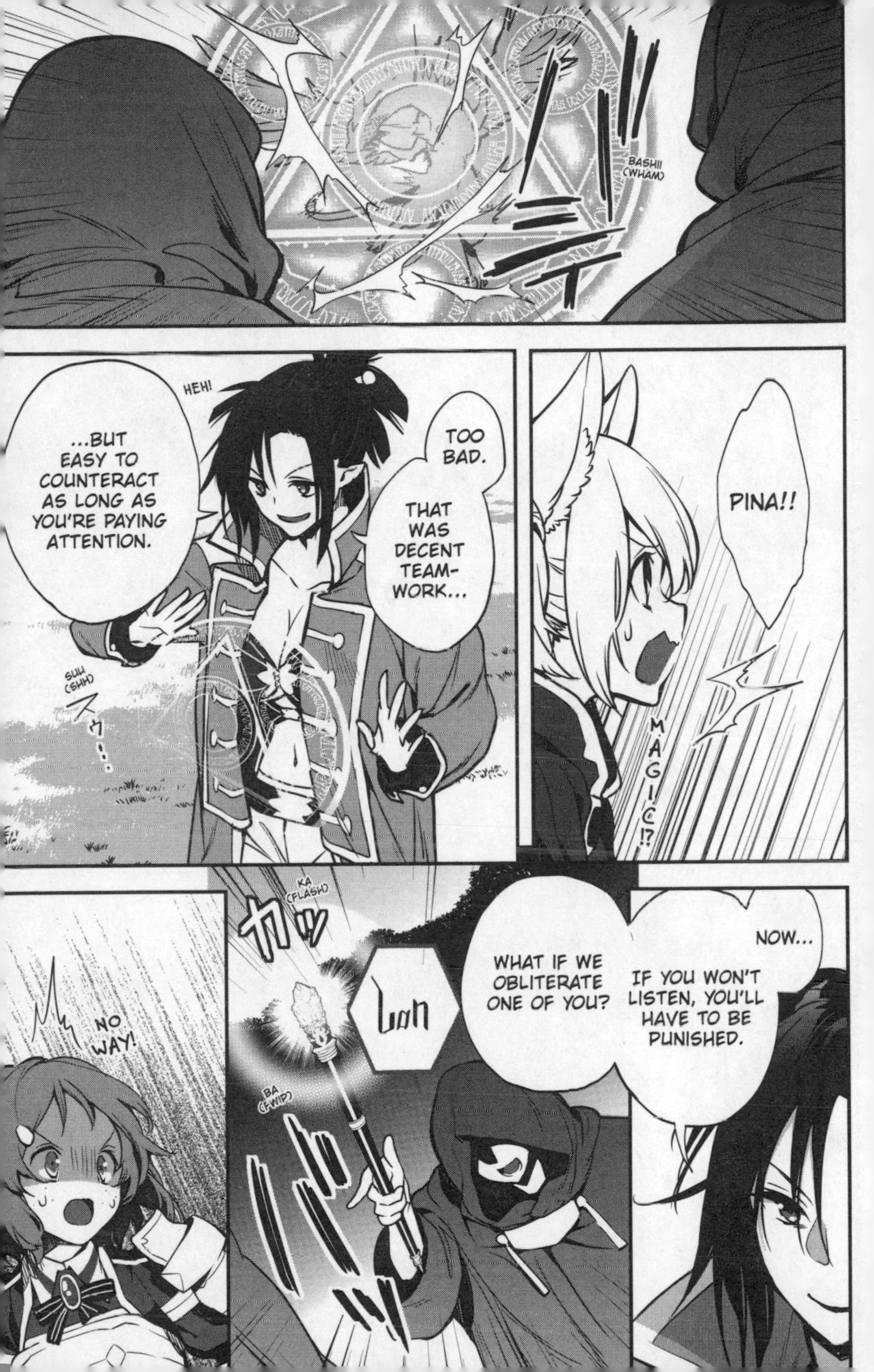
BASHII (WHAM)
PINA!!
MAGIC!?
HEH!
TOO BAD.
THAT WAS DECENT TEAM-WORK...
...BUT EASY TO COUNTERACT AS LONG AS YOU'RE PAYING ATTENTION.
SUU (SHH)
NOW...
IF YOU WON'T LISTEN, YOU'LL HAVE TO BE PUNISHED.
WHAT IF WE OBLITERATE ONE OF YOU?
KA (FLASH)
BA (FWIP)
NO WAY!

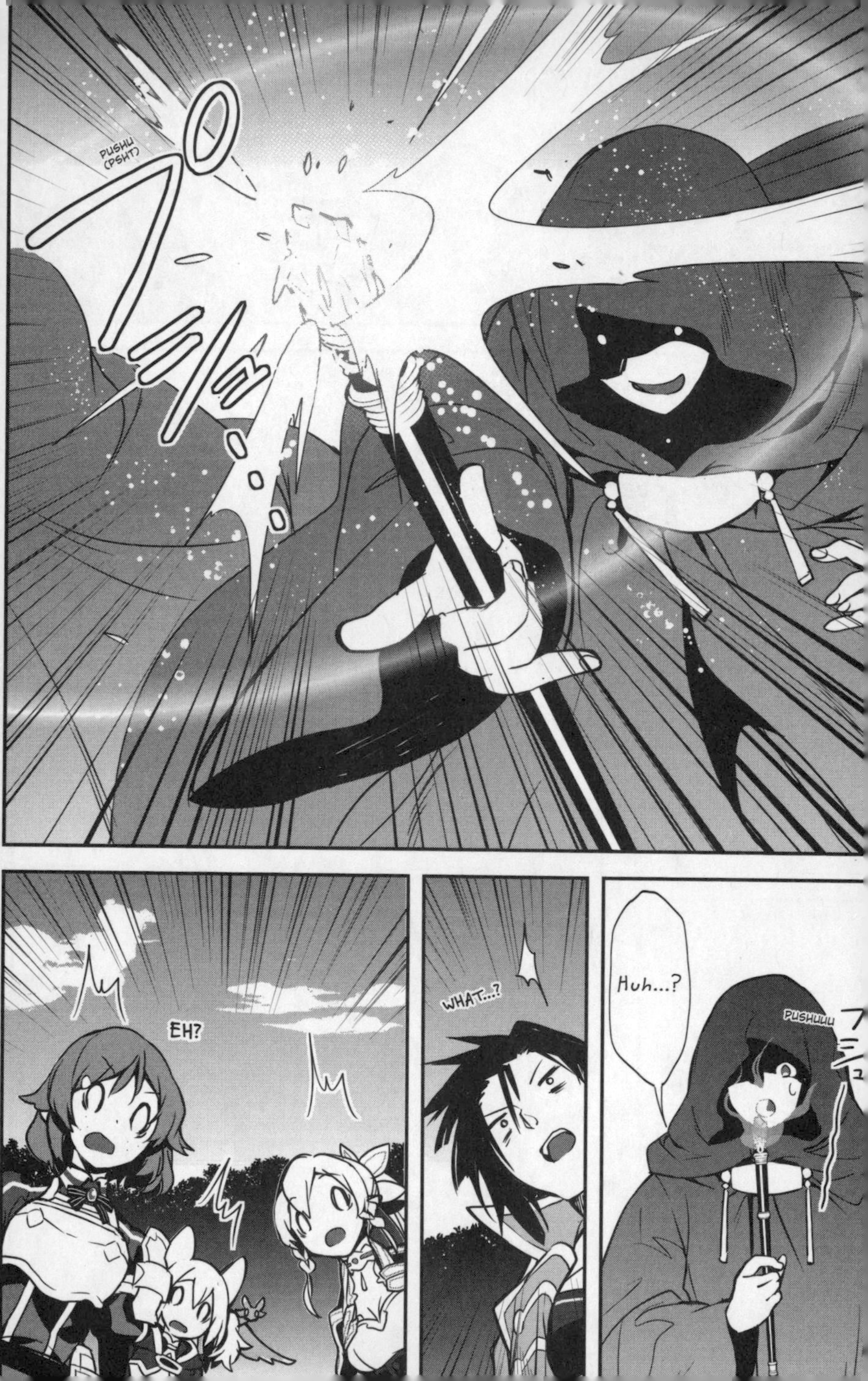

PUSHU (PSHT)
Huh...?
PUSHUUU
WHAT...?
EH?

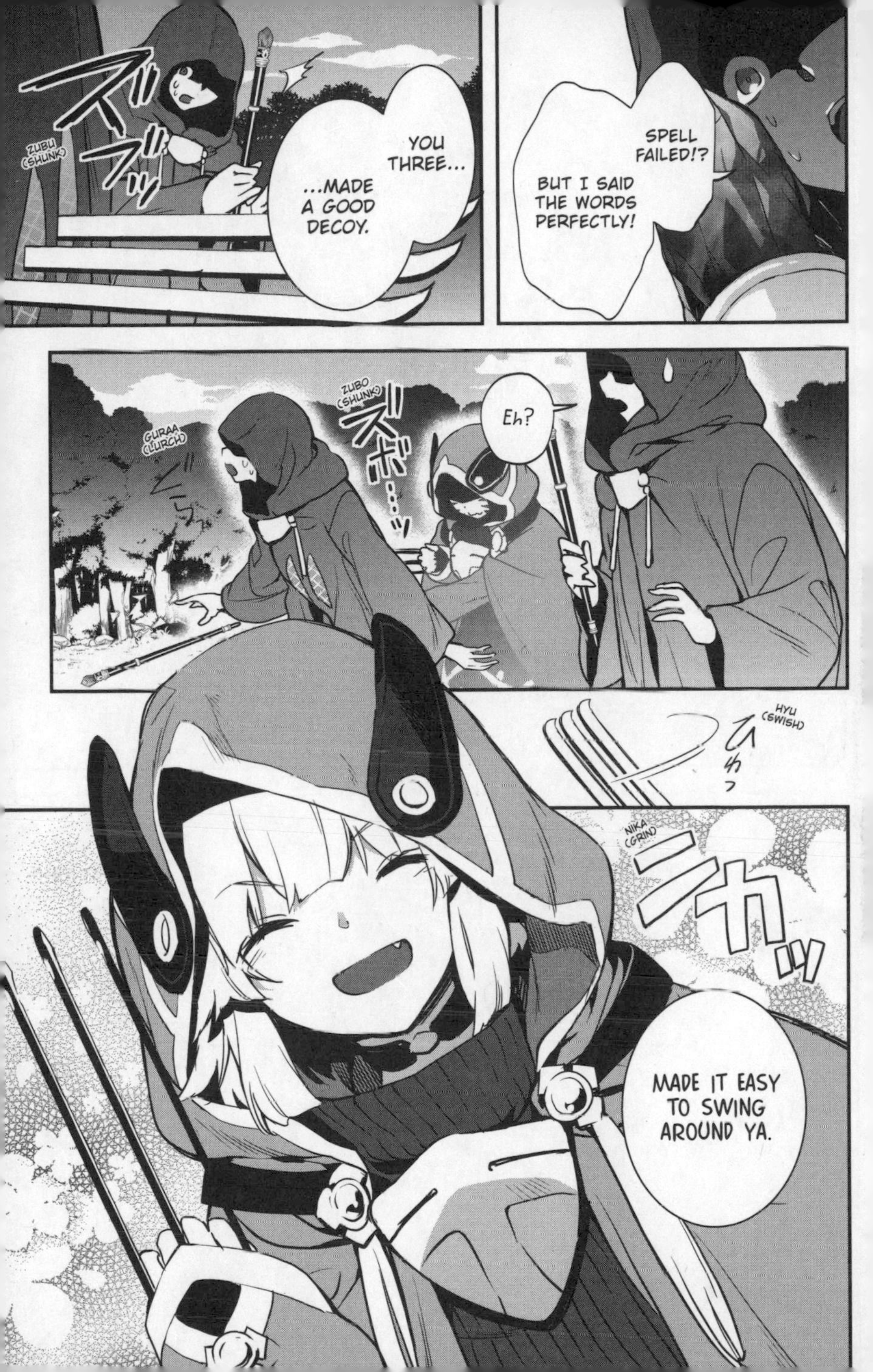
SPELL FAILED!?
BUT I SAID THE WORDS PERFECTLY!
ZUBU (SHUNK)
YOU THREE...
...MADE A GOOD DECOY.
Eh?
ZUBO (SHUNK)
GURAA (LURCH)
HYU (SWISH)
NIKA (GRIN)
MADE IT EASY TO SWING AROUND YA.

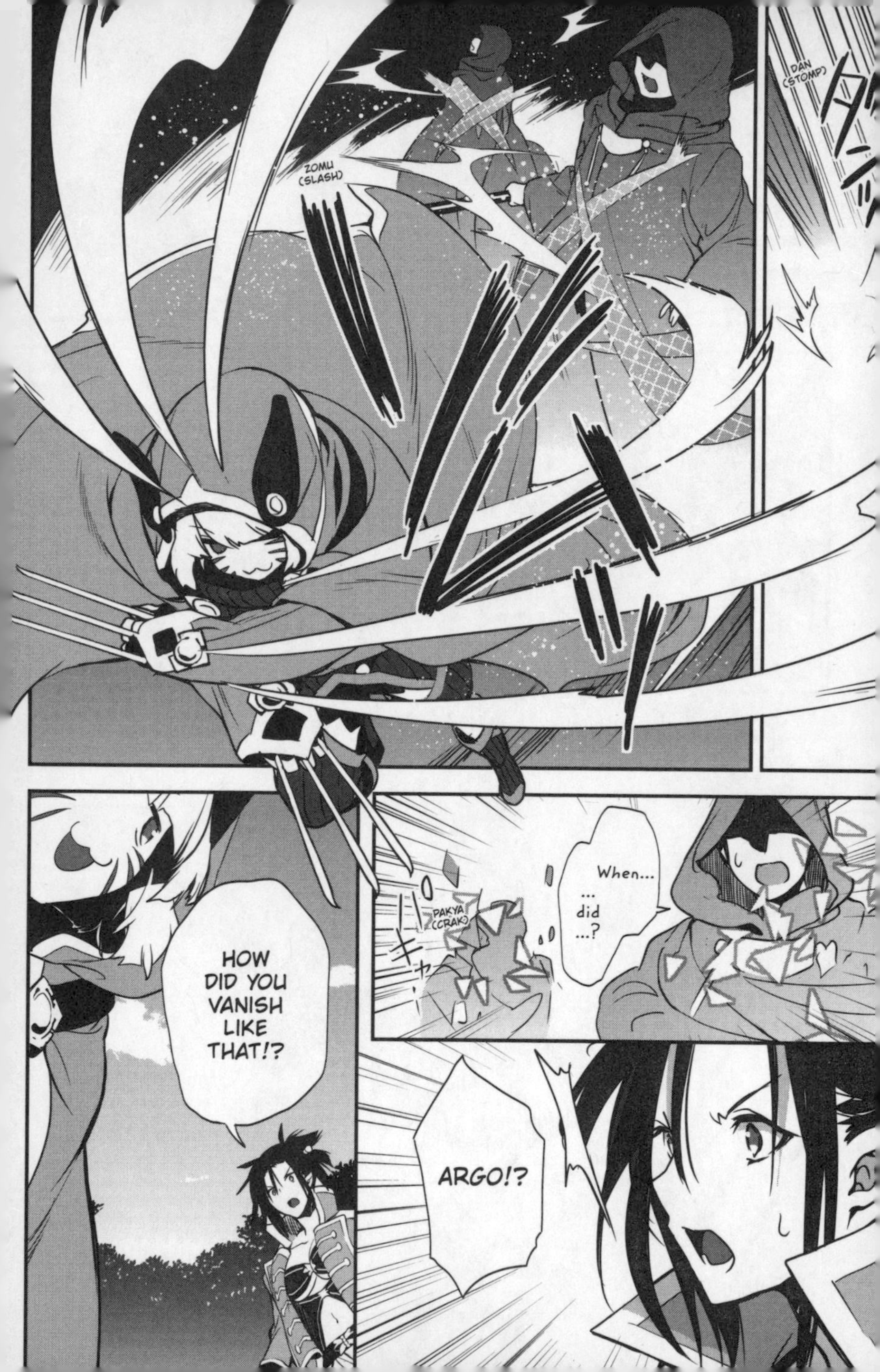
DAN (STOMP)
ZOMU (SLASH)
When...
... did ...?
PAKYA (CRAK)
HOW DID YOU VANISH LIKE THAT!?
ARGO!?

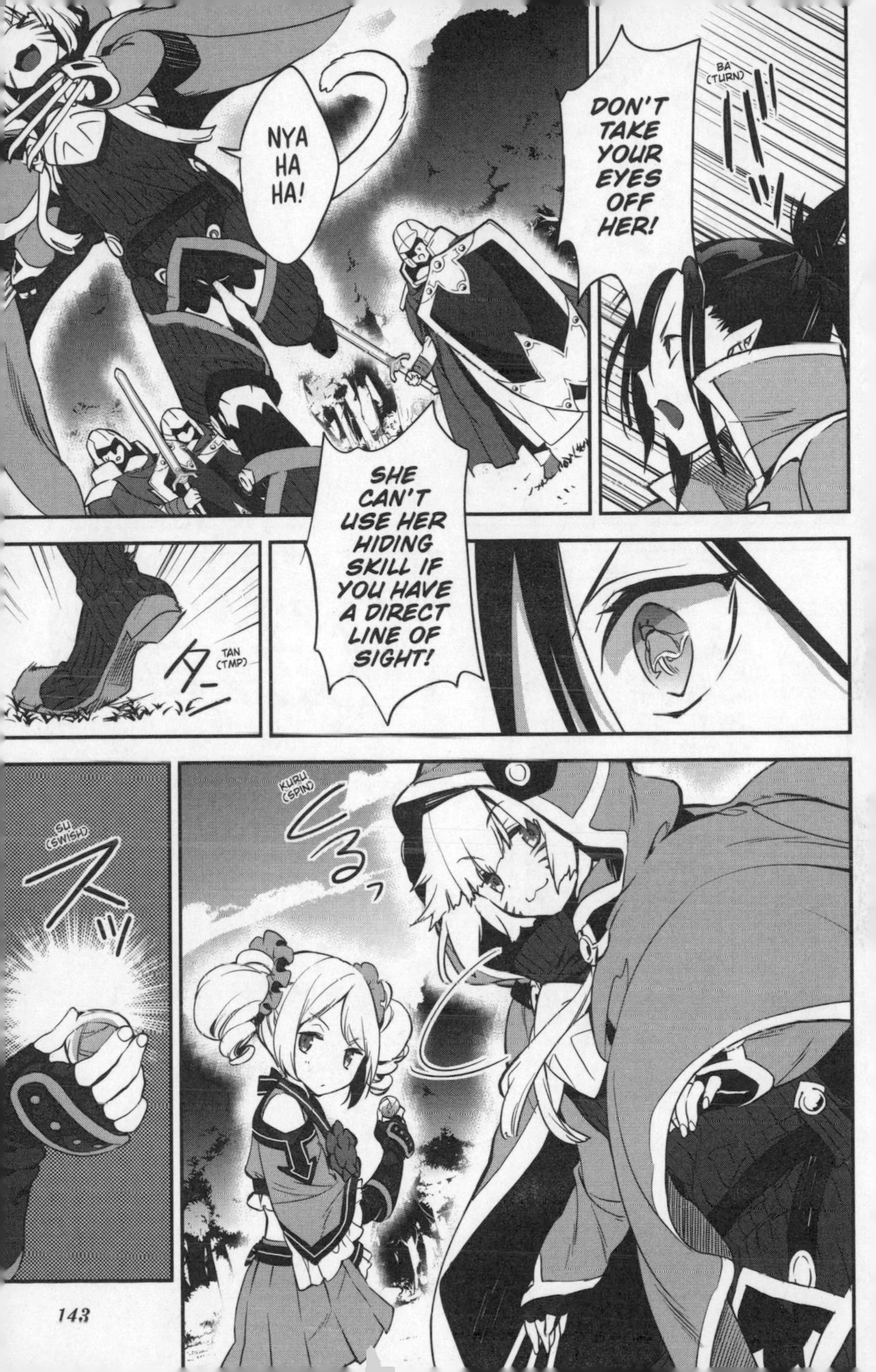
BA (TURN)
DON'T TAKE YOUR EYES OFF HER!
NYA HA HA!
SHE CAN'T USE HER HIDING SKILL IF YOU HAVE A DIRECT LINE OF SIGHT!
TAN (TMP)
KURU (SPIN)
SU (SWISH)

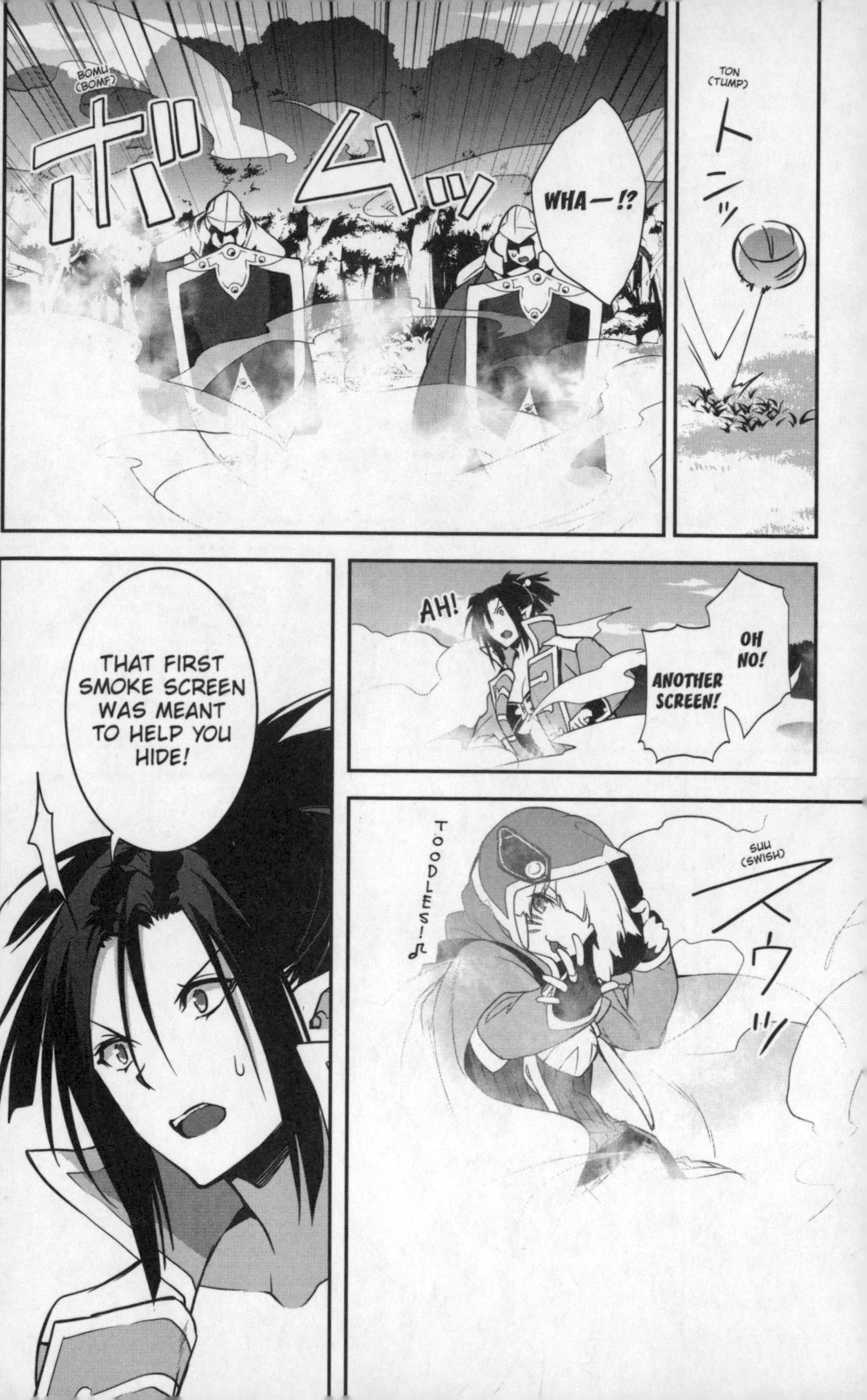
TON (TUMP)
BOMU (BOMF)
WHA—!?
OH NO!
ANOTHER SCREEN!
AH!
THAT FIRST SMOKE SCREEN WAS MEANT TO HELP YOU HIDE!
SUU (SWISH)
TOODLES!♫

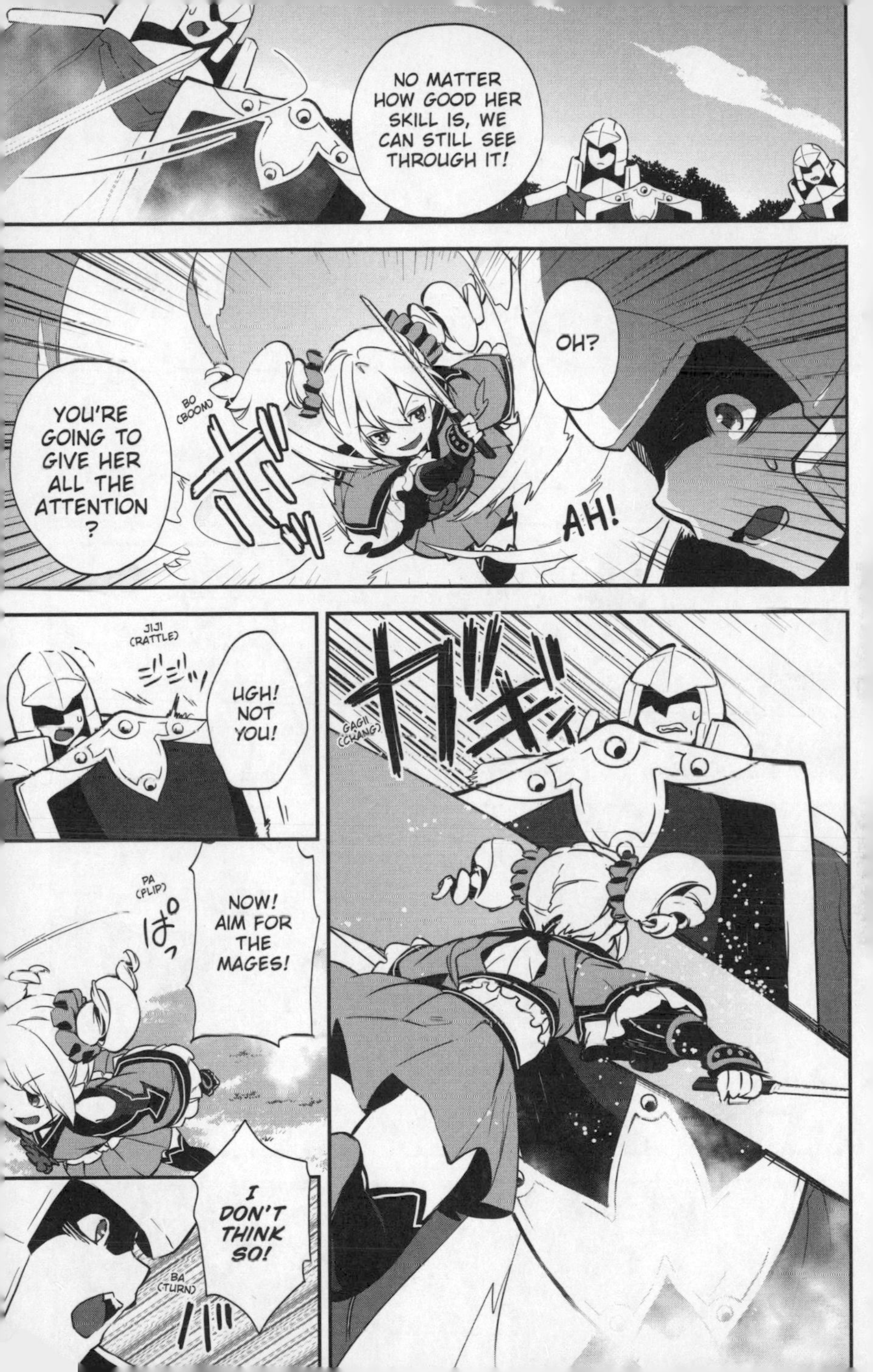
NO MATTER HOW GOOD HER SKILL IS, WE CAN STILL SEE THROUGH IT!
OH?
BO (BOOM)
YOU'RE GOING TO GIVE HER ALL THE ATTENTION ?
AH!
GAGII (CHANG)
JIJI (RATTLE)
UGH! NOT YOU!
PA (PLIP)
NOW! AIM FOR THE MAGES!
I DON'T THINK SO!
BA (TURN)

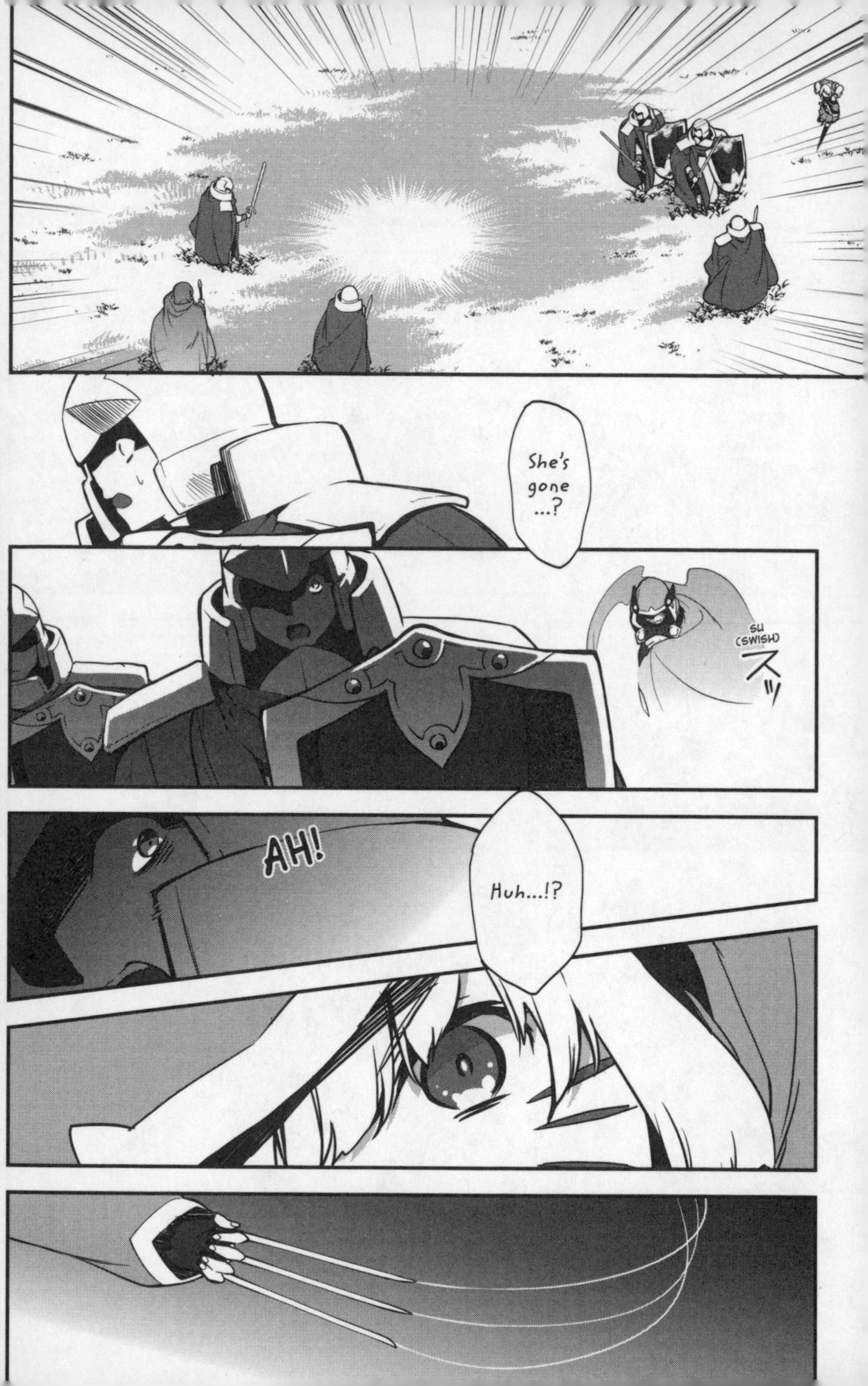
She's gone ...?
SU (SWISH)
スッ
Huh...!?
AH!

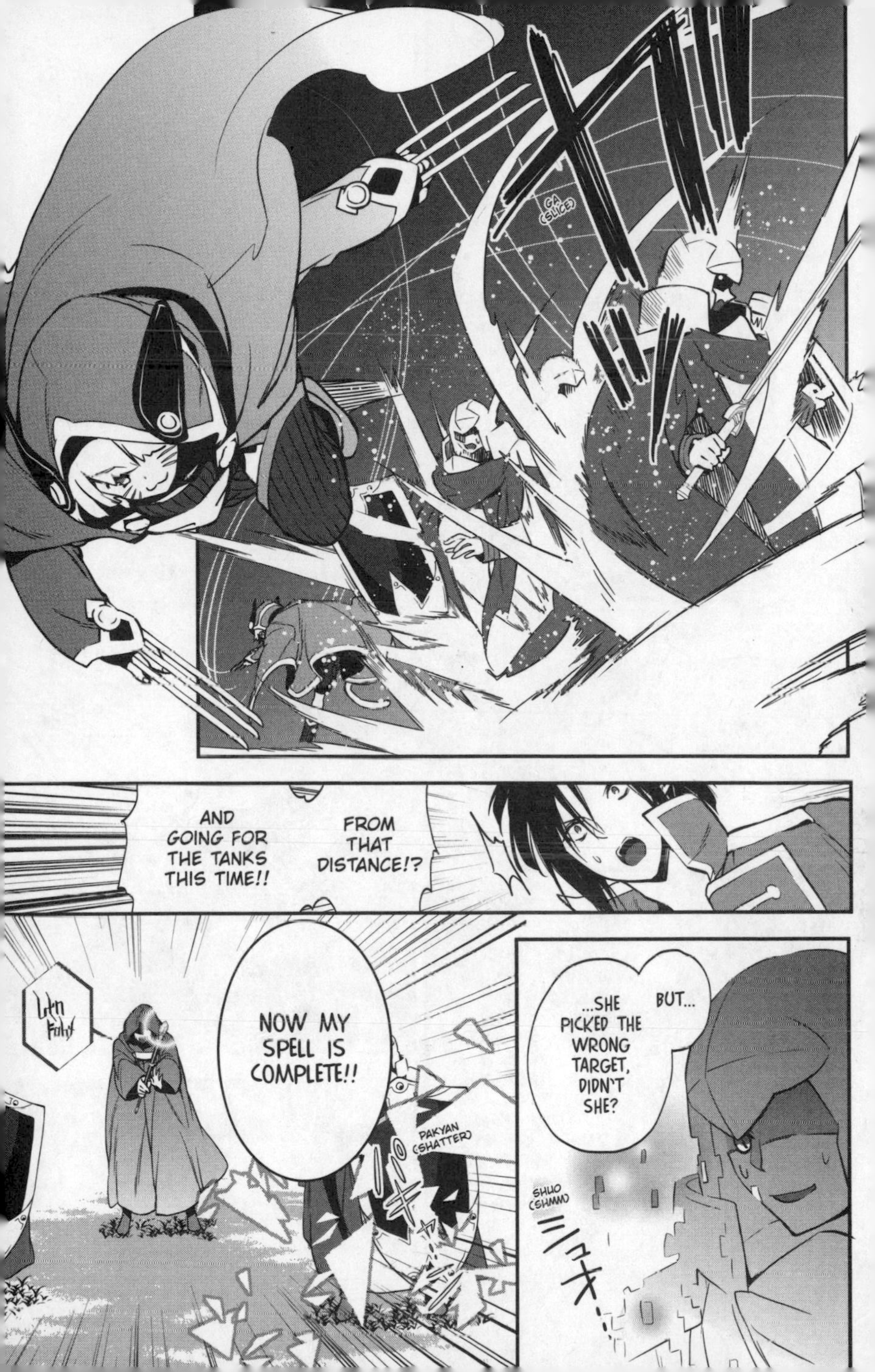
GA (SLICE)
FROM THAT DISTANCE!?
AND GOING FOR THE TANKS THIS TIME!!
BUT...
...SHE PICKED THE WRONG TARGET, DIDN'T SHE?
SHUO (SHMM)
NOW MY SPELL IS COMPLETE!!
PAKYAN (SHATTER)

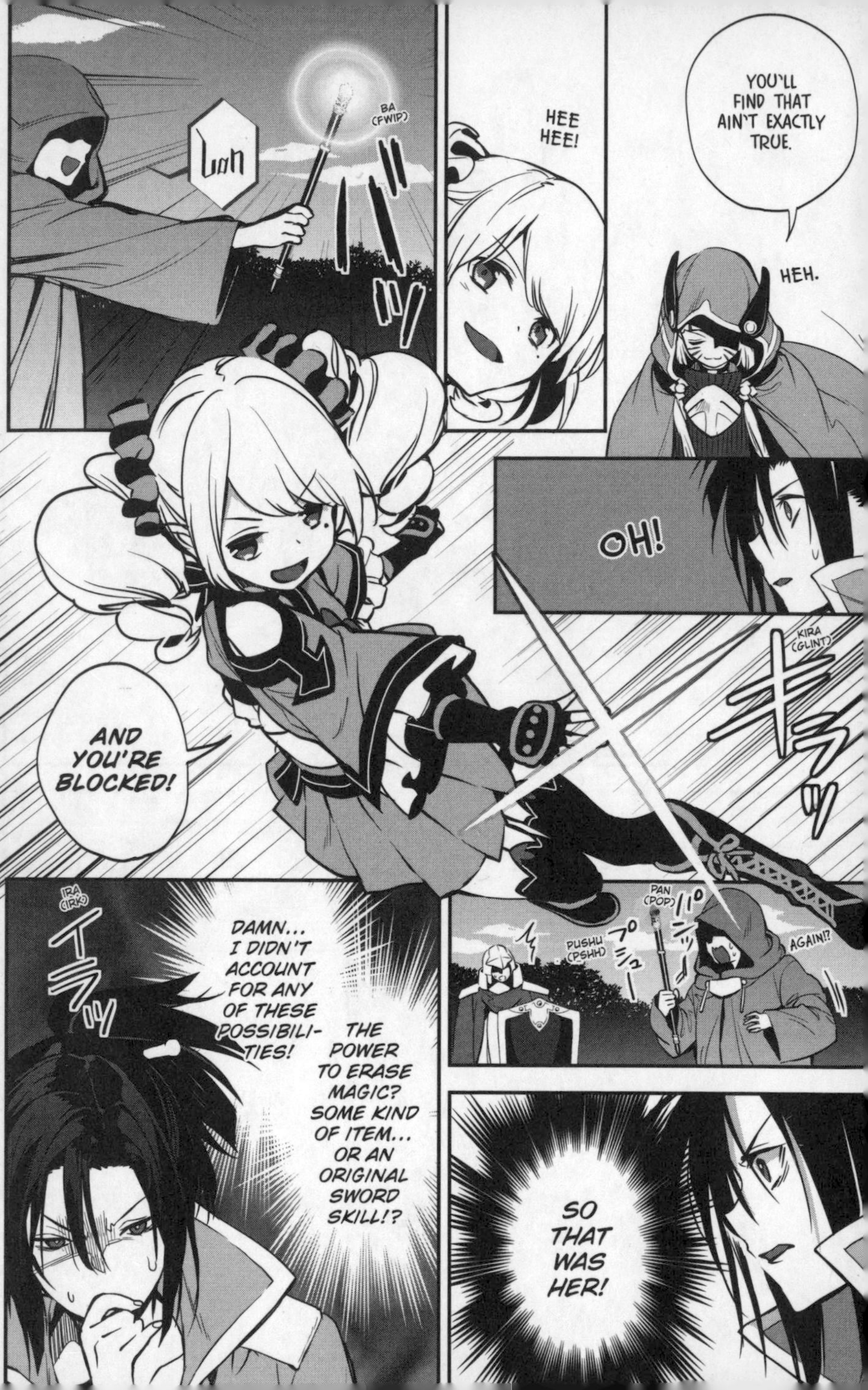
YOU'LL FIND THAT AIN'T EXACTLY TRUE.
HEH.
HEE HEE!
BA (FWIP)
OH!
KIRA (GLINT)
AND YOU'RE BLOCKED!
AGAIN!?
PAN (POP)
PUSHU (PSHH)
SO THAT WAS HER!
IRA (IRK)
DAMN... I DIDN'T ACCOUNT FOR ANY OF THESE POSSIBILI-TIES!
THE POWER TO ERASE MAGIC? SOME KIND OF ITEM... OR AN ORIGINAL SWORD SKILL!?

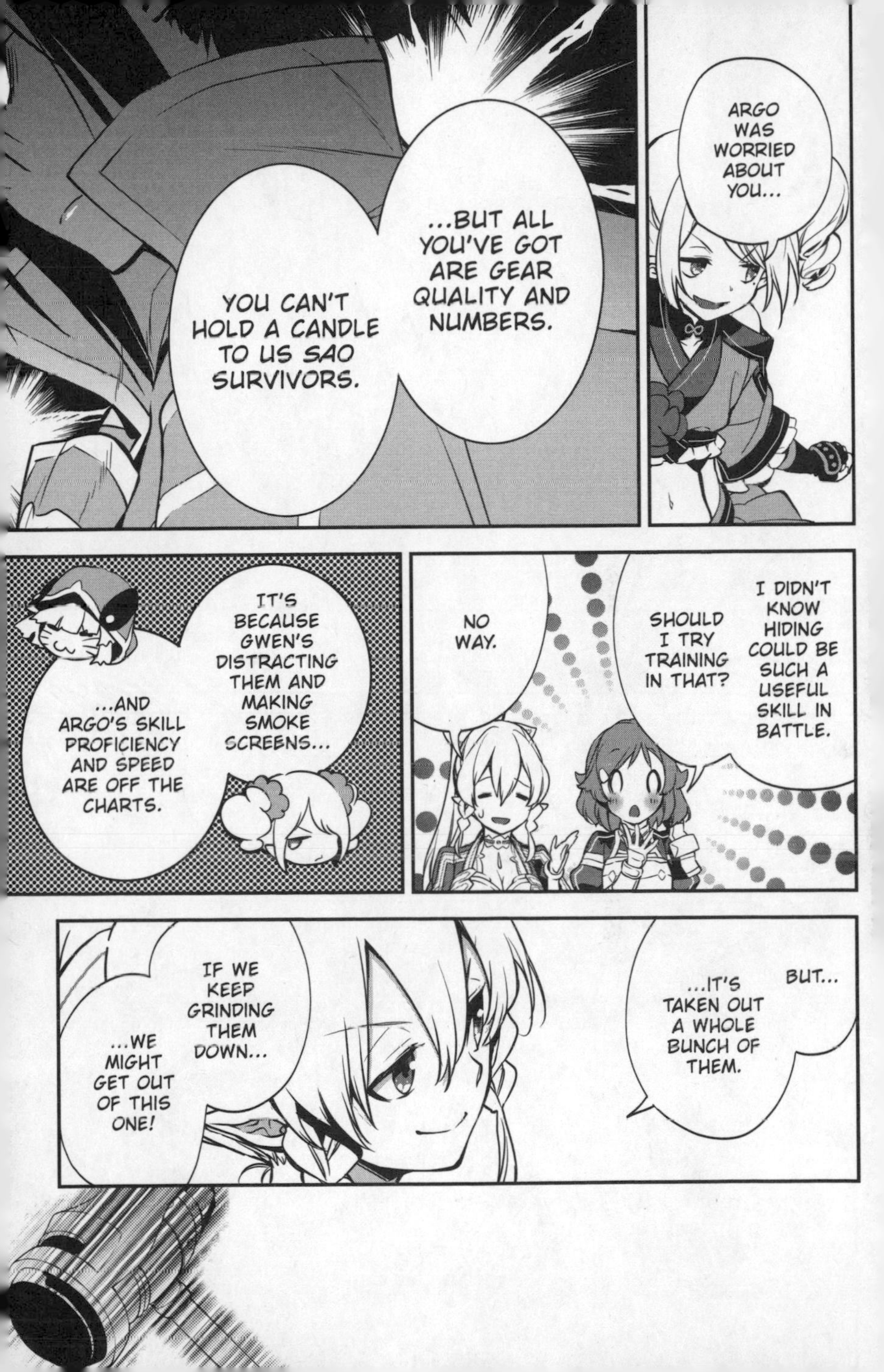
ARGO WAS WORRIED ABOUT YOU...
...BUT ALL YOU'VE GOT ARE GEAR QUALITY AND NUMBERS.
YOU CAN'T HOLD A CANDLE TO US SAO SURVIVORS.
I DIDN'T KNOW HIDING COULD BE SUCH A USEFUL SKILL IN BATTLE.
SHOULD I TRY TRAINING IN THAT?
NO WAY.
IT'S BECAUSE GWEN'S DISTRACTING THEM AND MAKING SMOKE SCREENS...
...AND ARGO'S SKILL PROFICIENCY AND SPEED ARE OFF THE CHARTS.
BUT...
...IT'S TAKEN OUT A WHOLE BUNCH OF THEM.
IF WE KEEP GRINDING THEM DOWN...
...WE MIGHT GET OUT OF THIS ONE!

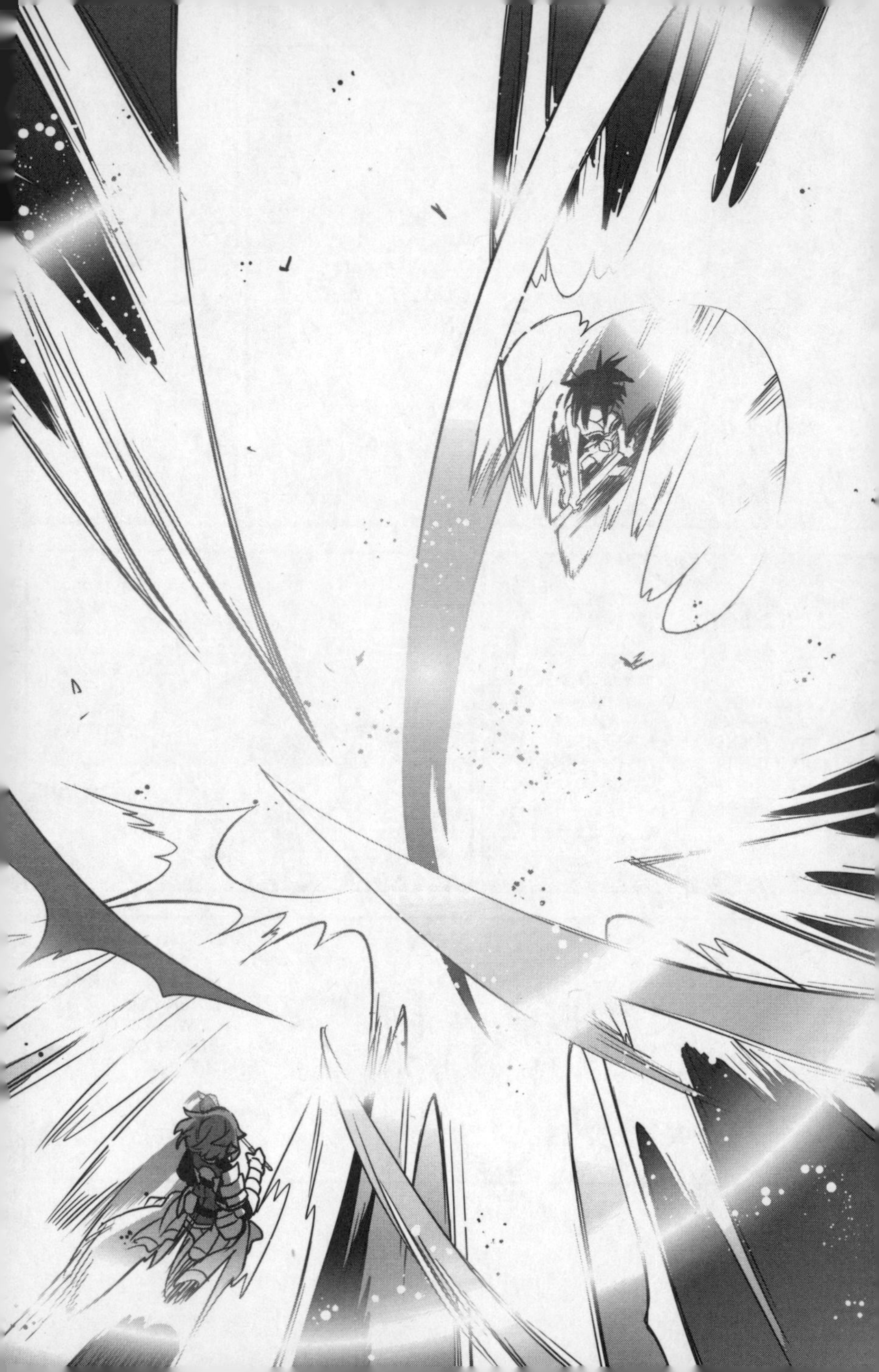

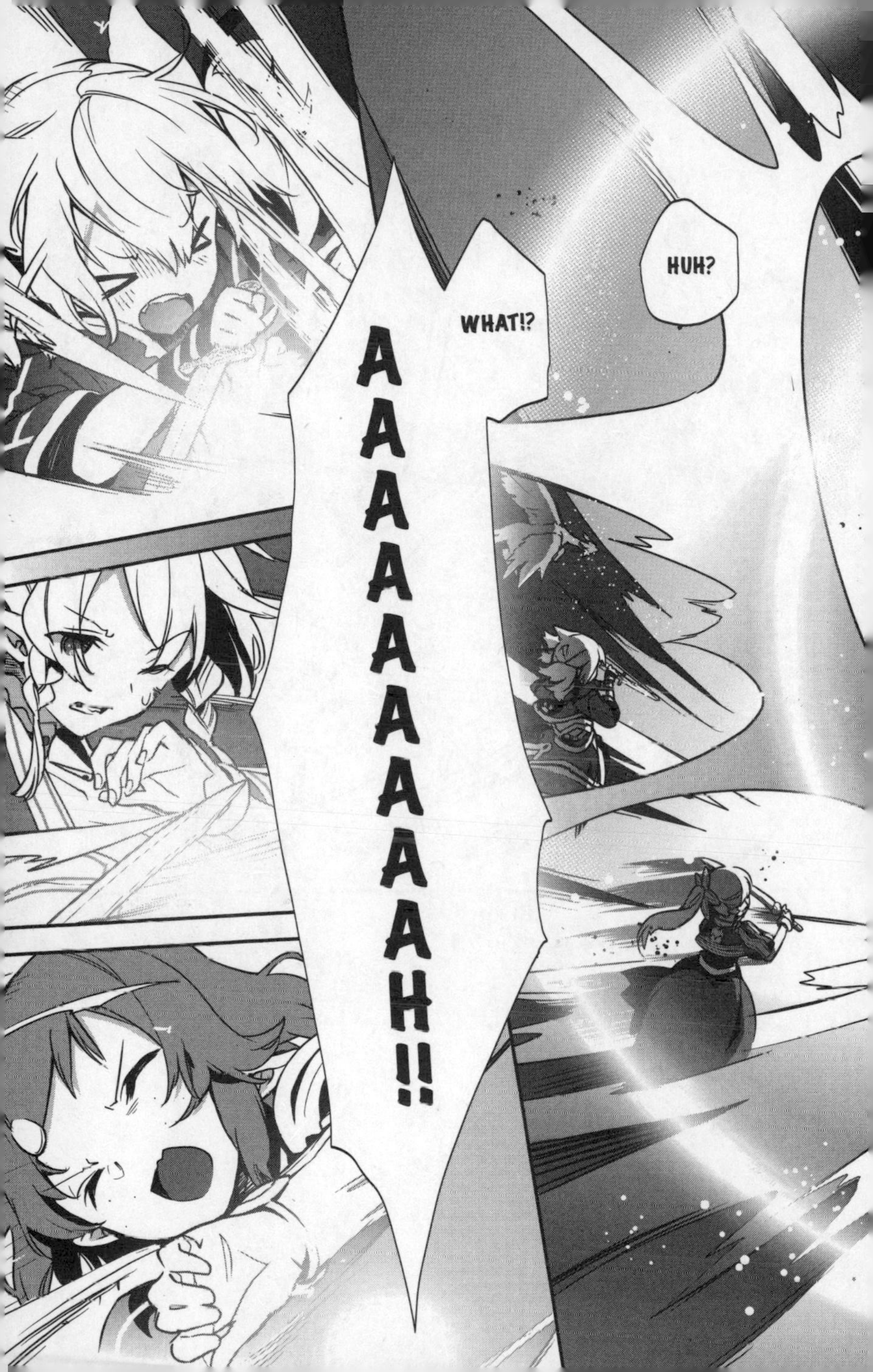
HUH?
WHAT!?
AAAAAAAAAH!!

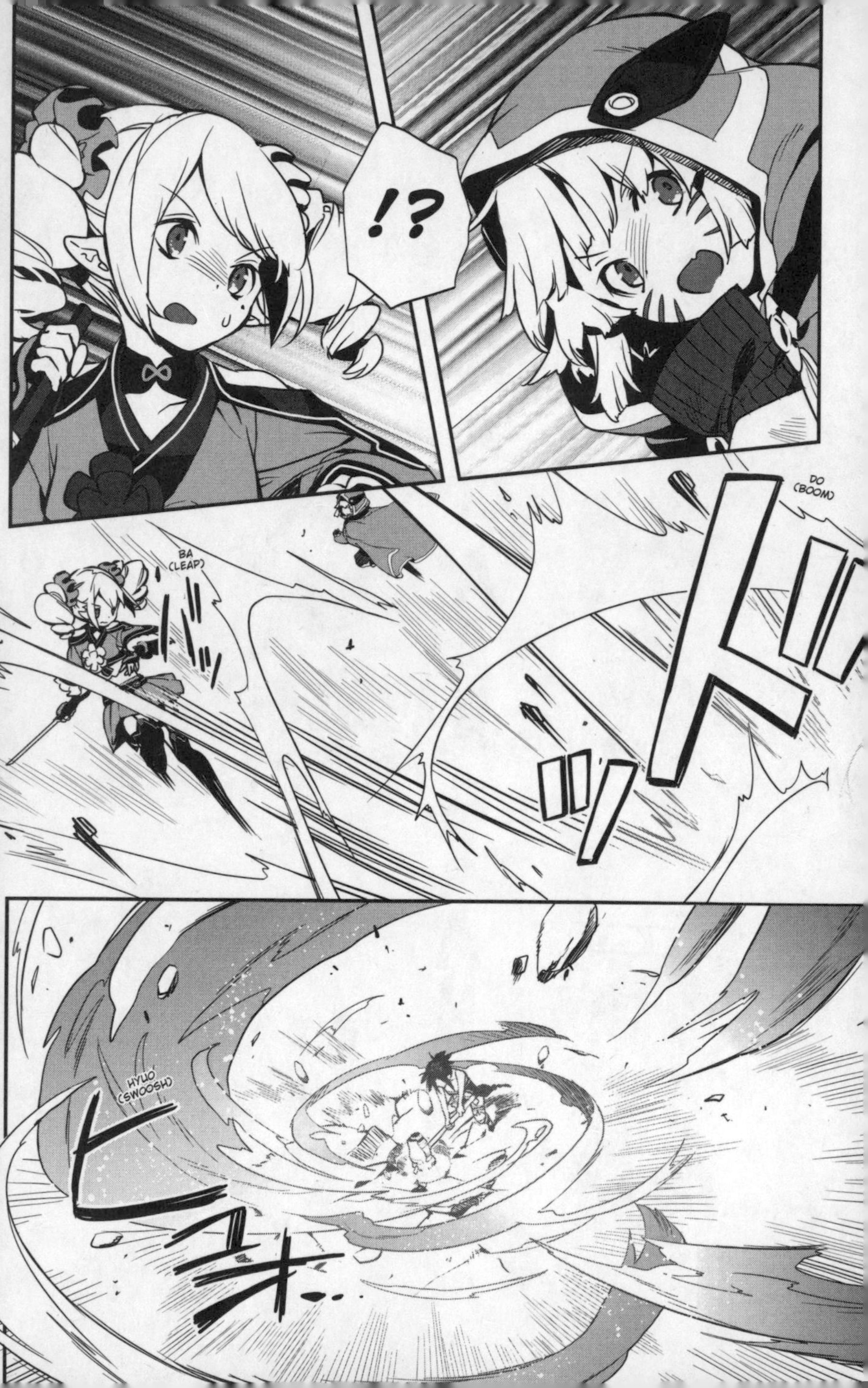
!?
DO
(BOOM)
BA
(LEAP)
HYUO
(SWOOSH)

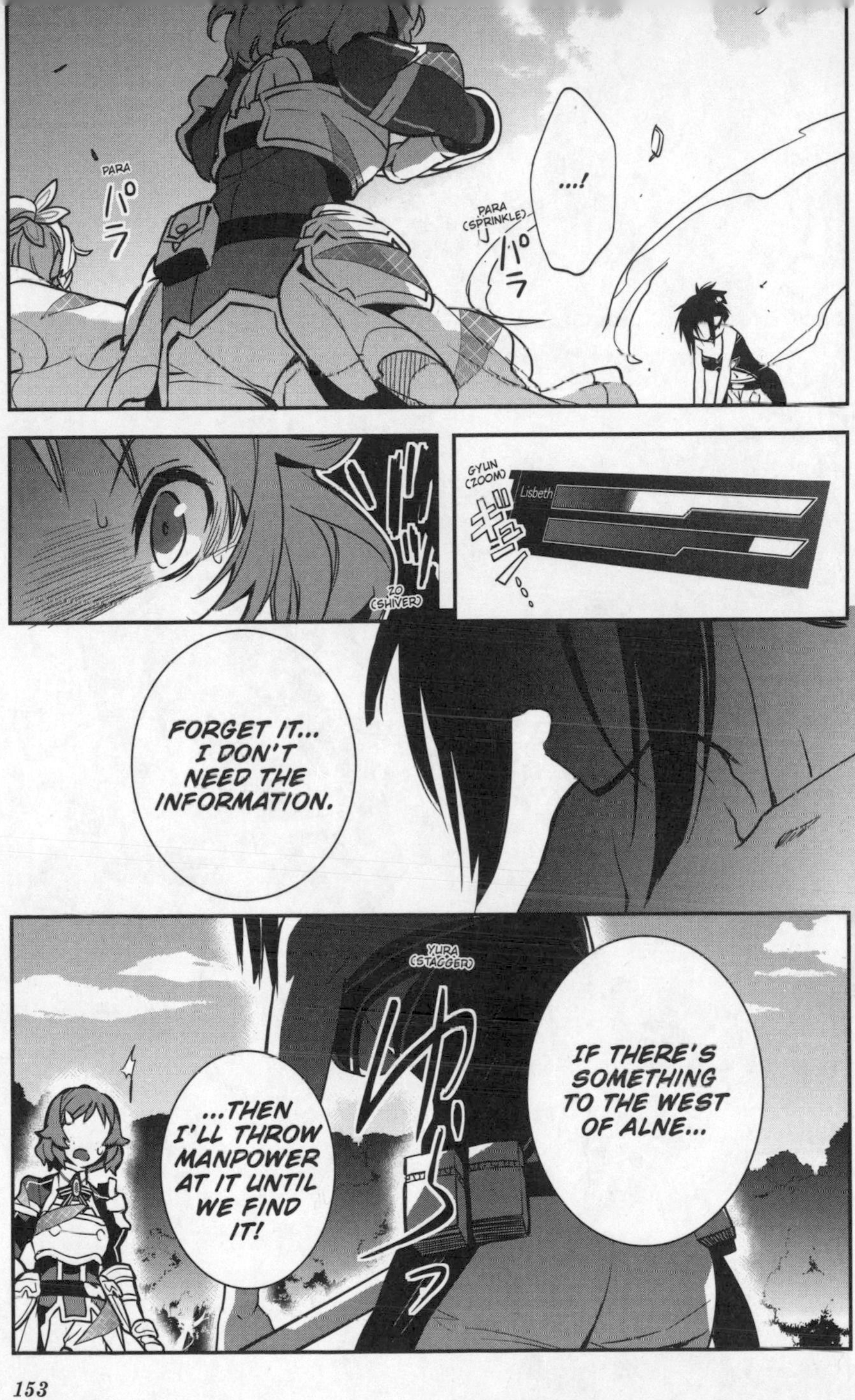
PARA
パラ
...!
PARA (SPRINKLE)
パラ
GYUN (ZOOM)
Lisbeth
ZO (SHIVER)
FORGET IT... I DON'T NEED THE INFORMATION.
YURA (STAGGER)
IF THERE'S SOMETHING TO THE WEST OF ALNE...
...THEN I'LL THROW MANPOWER AT IT UNTIL WE FIND IT!

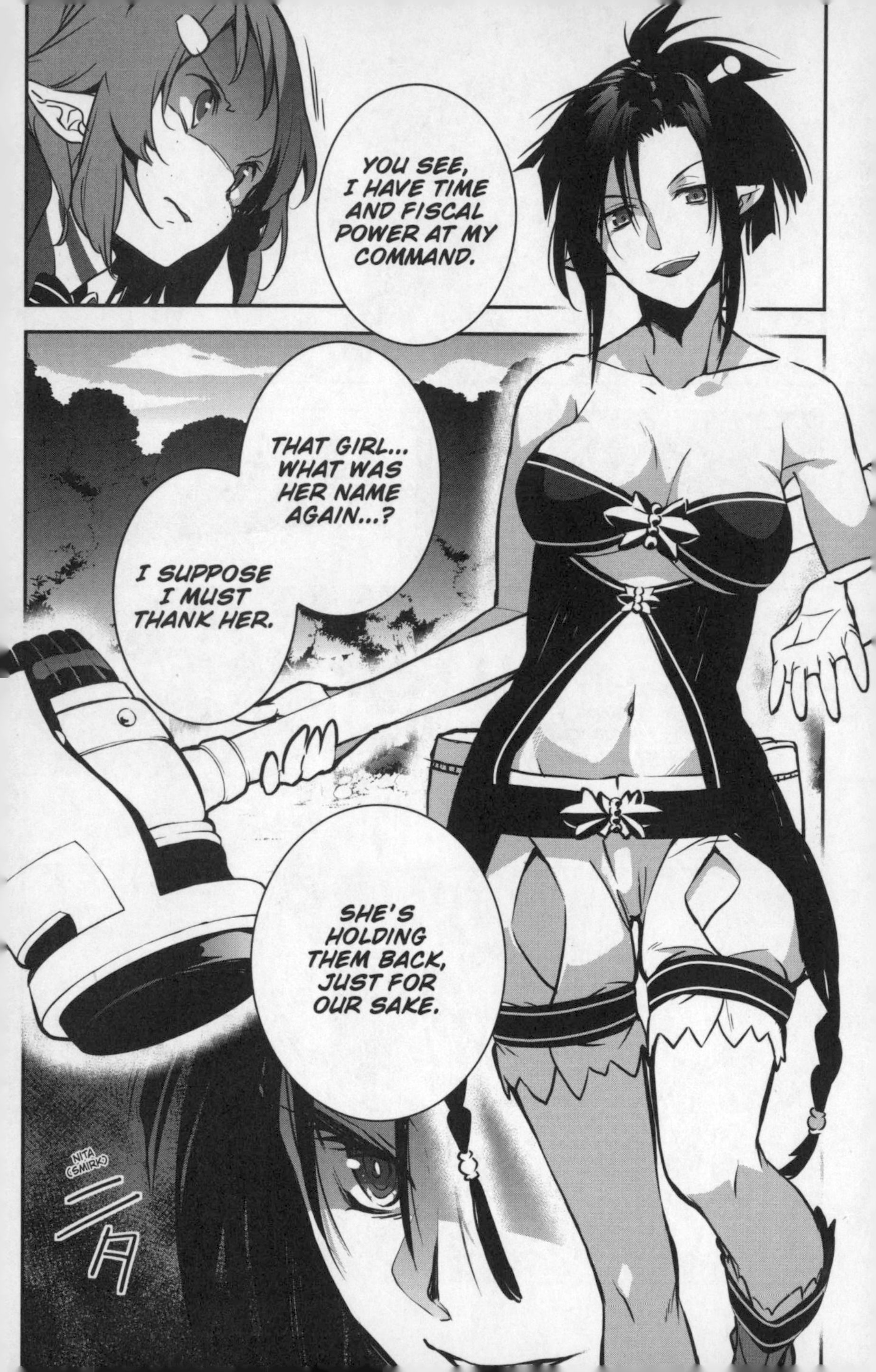
YOU SEE, I HAVE TIME AND FISCAL POWER AT MY COMMAND.
THAT GIRL... WHAT WAS HER NAME AGAIN...?
I SUPPOSE I MUST THANK HER.
SHE'S HOLDING THEM BACK, JUST FOR OUR SAKE.
NITA (SMIRK)

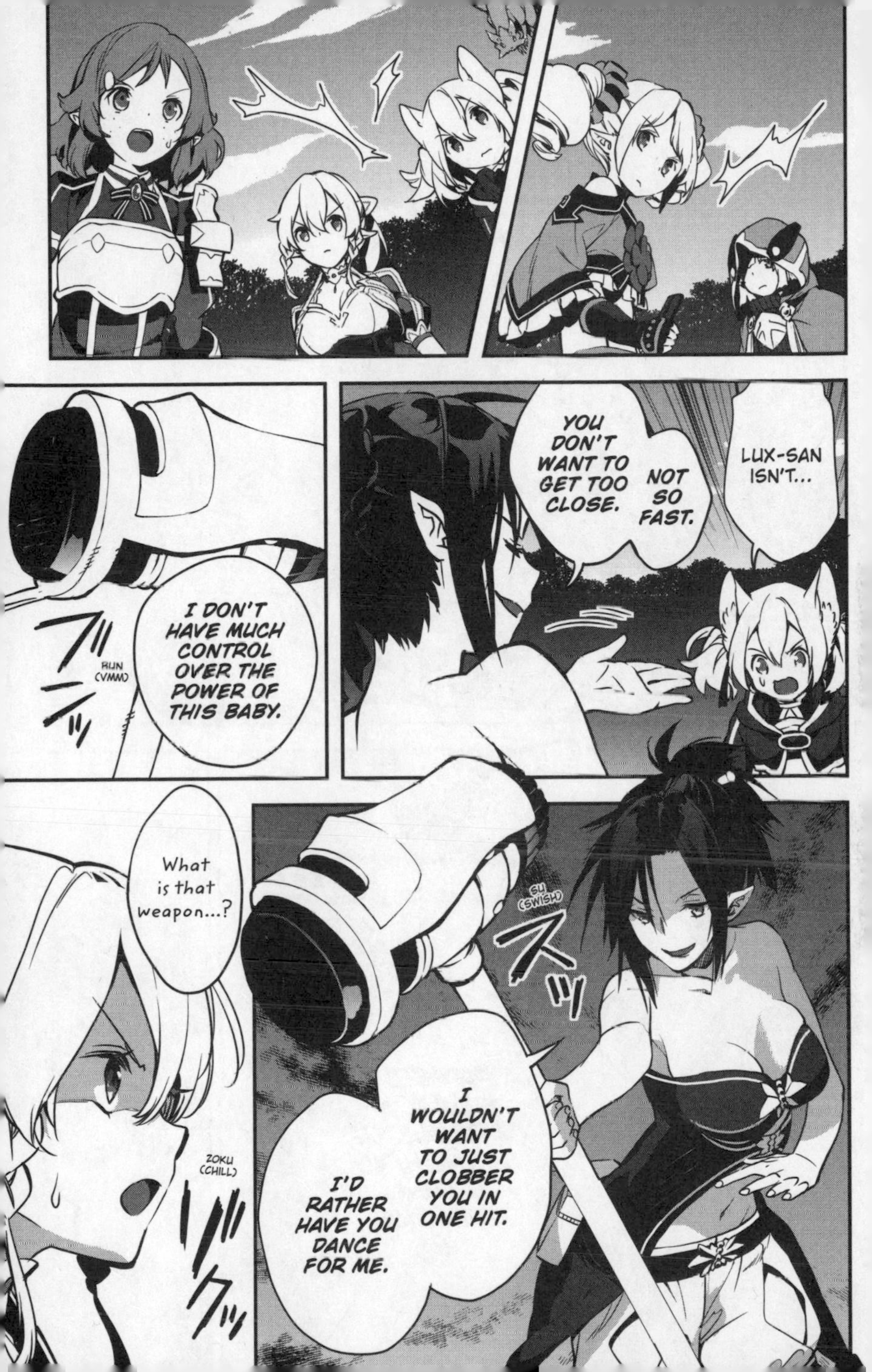
LUX-SAN ISN'T...
NOT SO FAST.
YOU DON'T WANT TO GET TOO CLOSE.
I DON'T HAVE MUCH CONTROL OVER THE POWER OF THIS BABY.
BUN (VMM)
SU (SWISH)
I WOULDN'T WANT TO JUST CLOBBER YOU IN ONE HIT.
I'D RATHER HAVE YOU DANCE FOR ME.
What is that weapon...?
ZOKU (CHILL)

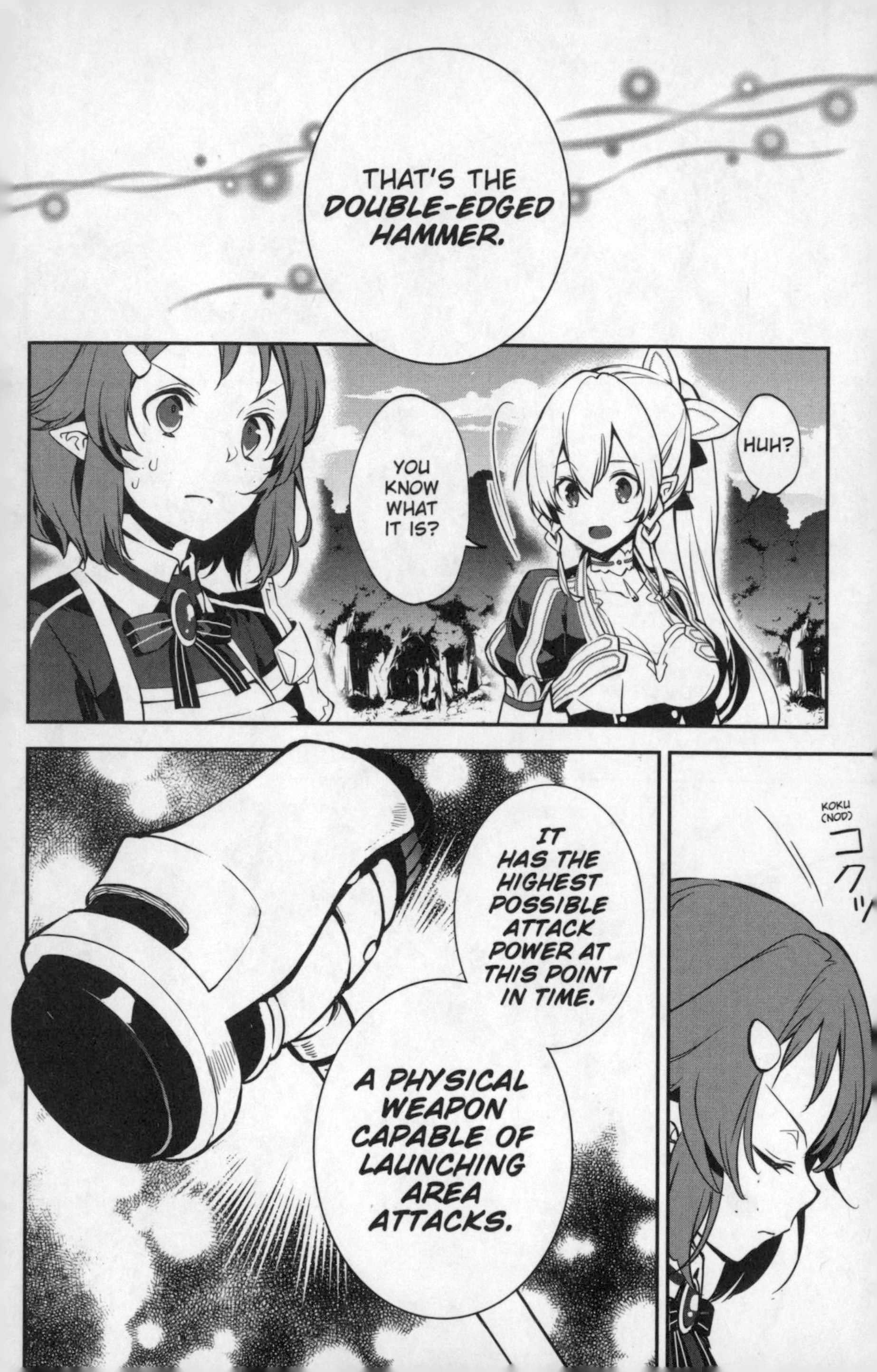
THAT'S THE DOUBLE-EDGED HAMMER.
HUH?
YOU KNOW WHAT IT IS?
KOKU (NOD)
IT HAS THE HIGHEST POSSIBLE ATTACK POWER AT THIS POINT IN TIME.
A PHYSICAL WEAPON CAPABLE OF LAUNCHING AREA ATTACKS.

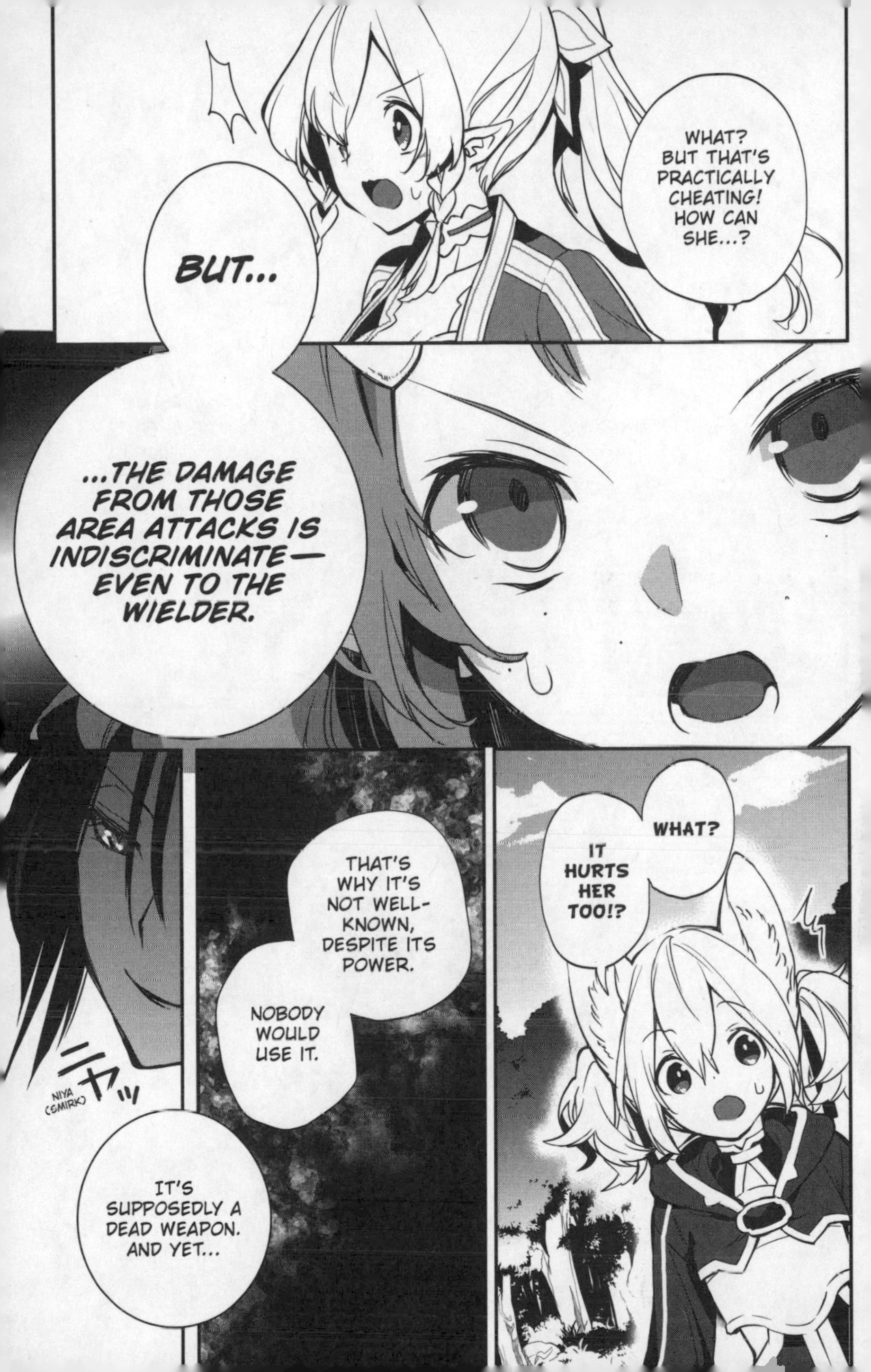
WHAT? BUT THAT'S PRACTICALLY CHEATING! HOW CAN SHE...?
BUT...
...THE DAMAGE FROM THOSE AREA ATTACKS IS INDISCRIMINATE—EVEN TO THE WIELDER.
WHAT?
IT HURTS HER TOO!?
THAT'S WHY IT'S NOT WELL-KNOWN, DESPITE ITS POWER.
NOBODY WOULD USE IT.
ニヤッ
NIYA (SMIRK)
IT'S SUPPOSEDLY A DEAD WEAPON. AND YET...

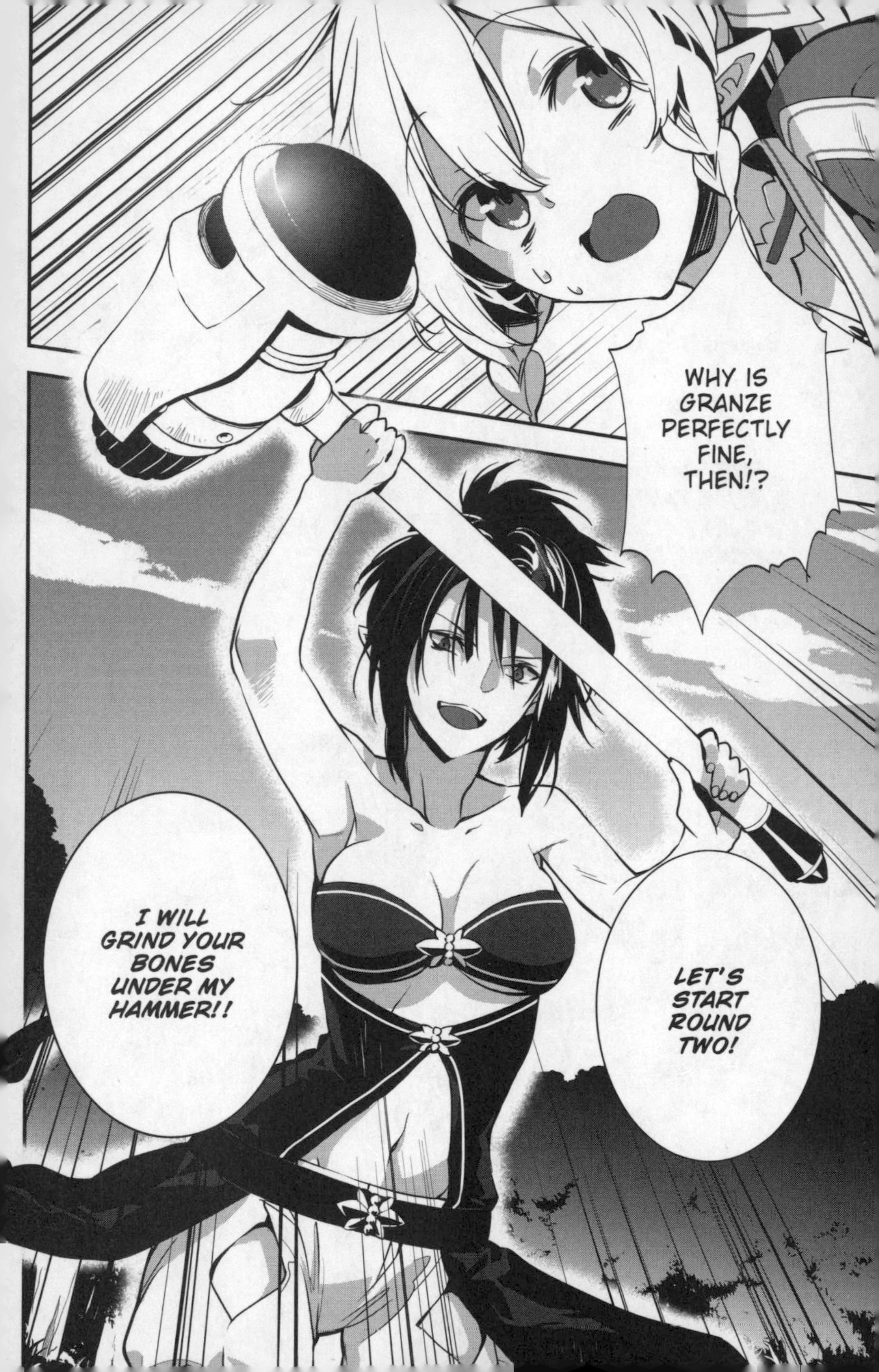
WHY IS GRANZE PERFECTLY FINE, THEN!?
LET'S START ROUND TWO!
I WILL GRIND YOUR BONES UNDER MY HAMMER!!

SWORD ART ONLINE

GIRLS' OPS

APRIL 19TH

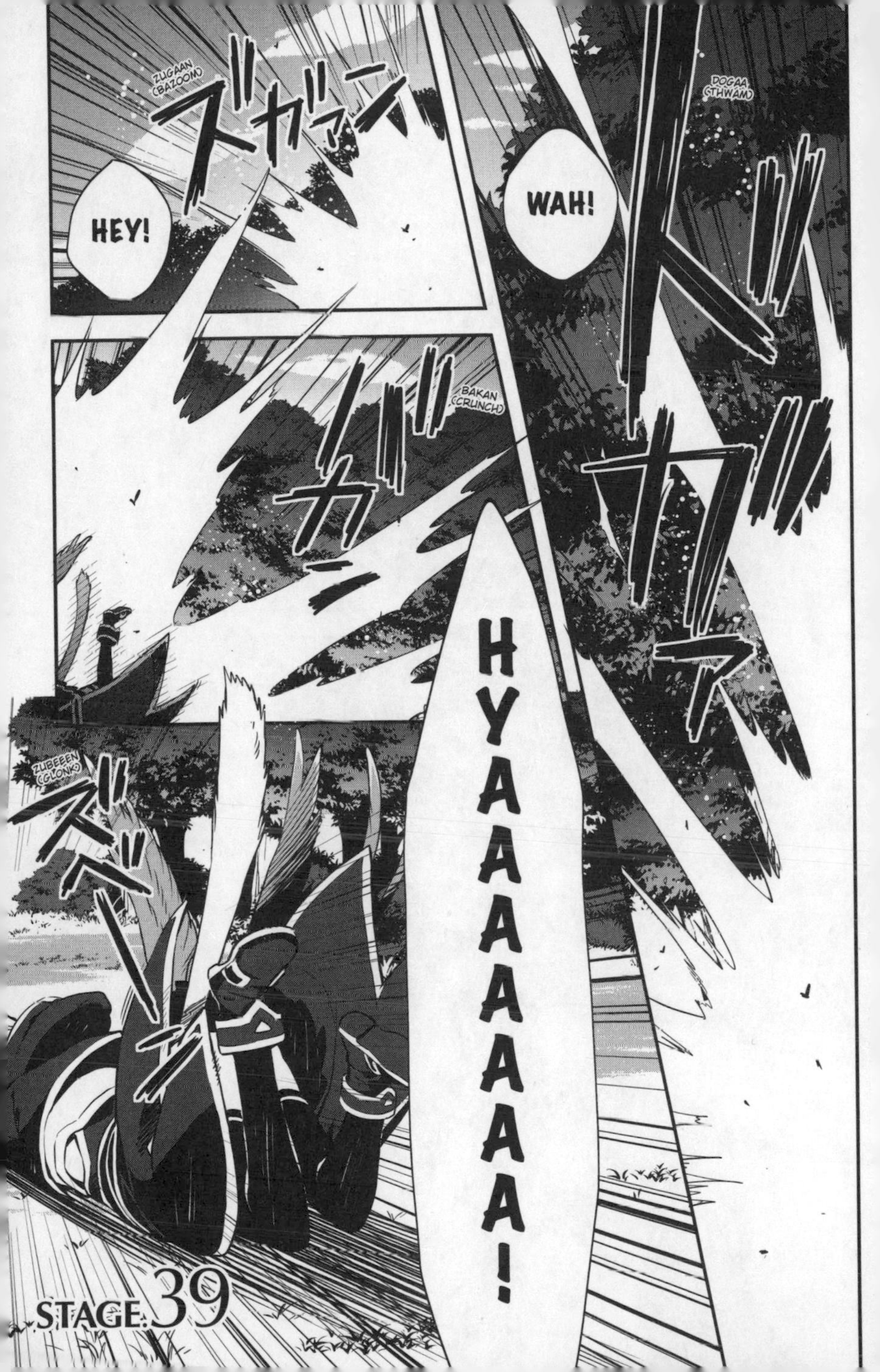

DOGAA
(THWAM)
WAH!
ZUGAAN
(BAZOOM)
HEY!
BAKAN
(CRUNCH)
HYAAAAAAAI!
ZUBEEEN
(GLONK)

STAGE 39

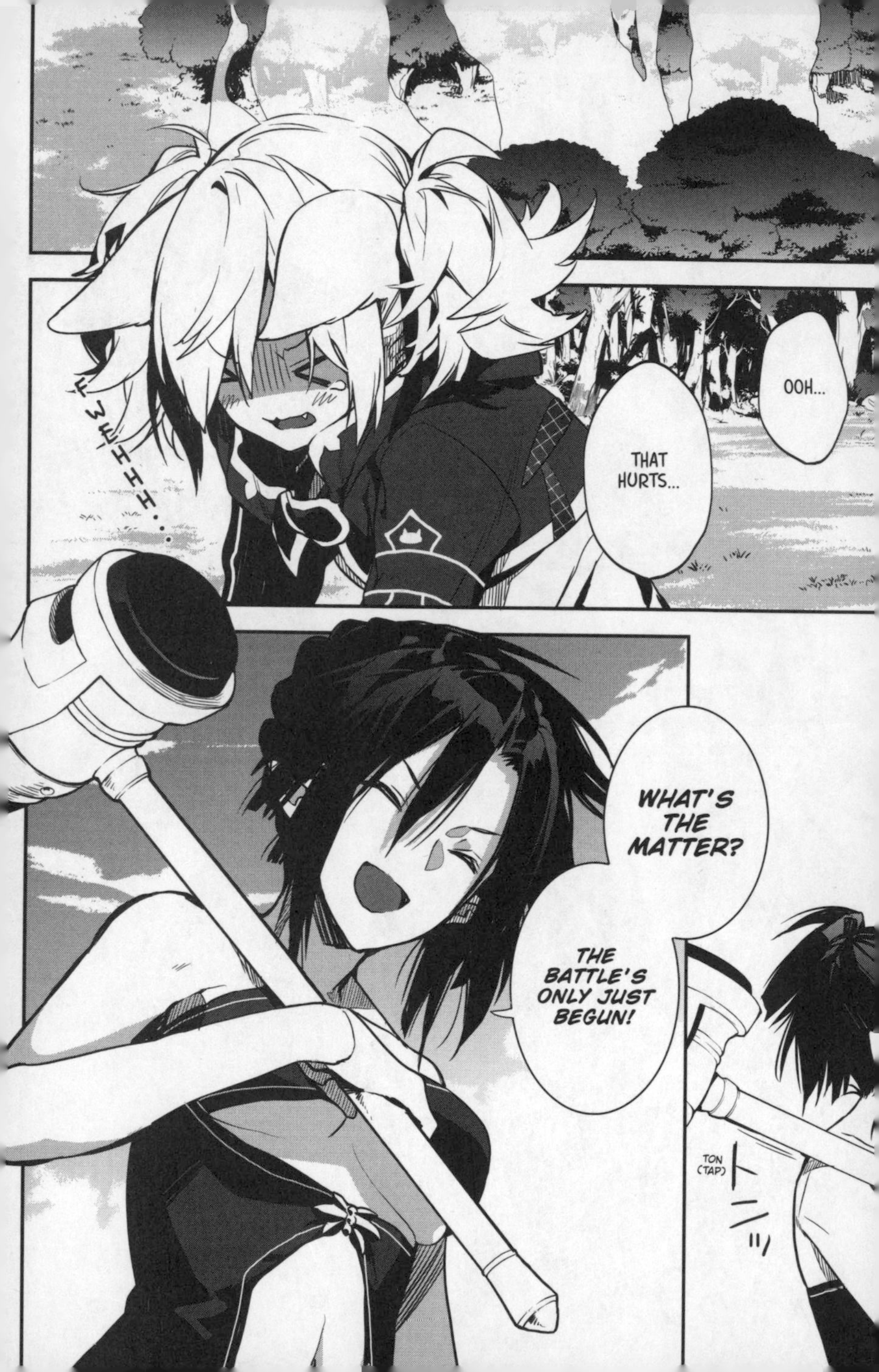
OOH...
THAT HURTS...
FWEHHH...
WHAT'S THE MATTER?
THE BATTLE'S ONLY JUST BEGUN!
TON (TAP)

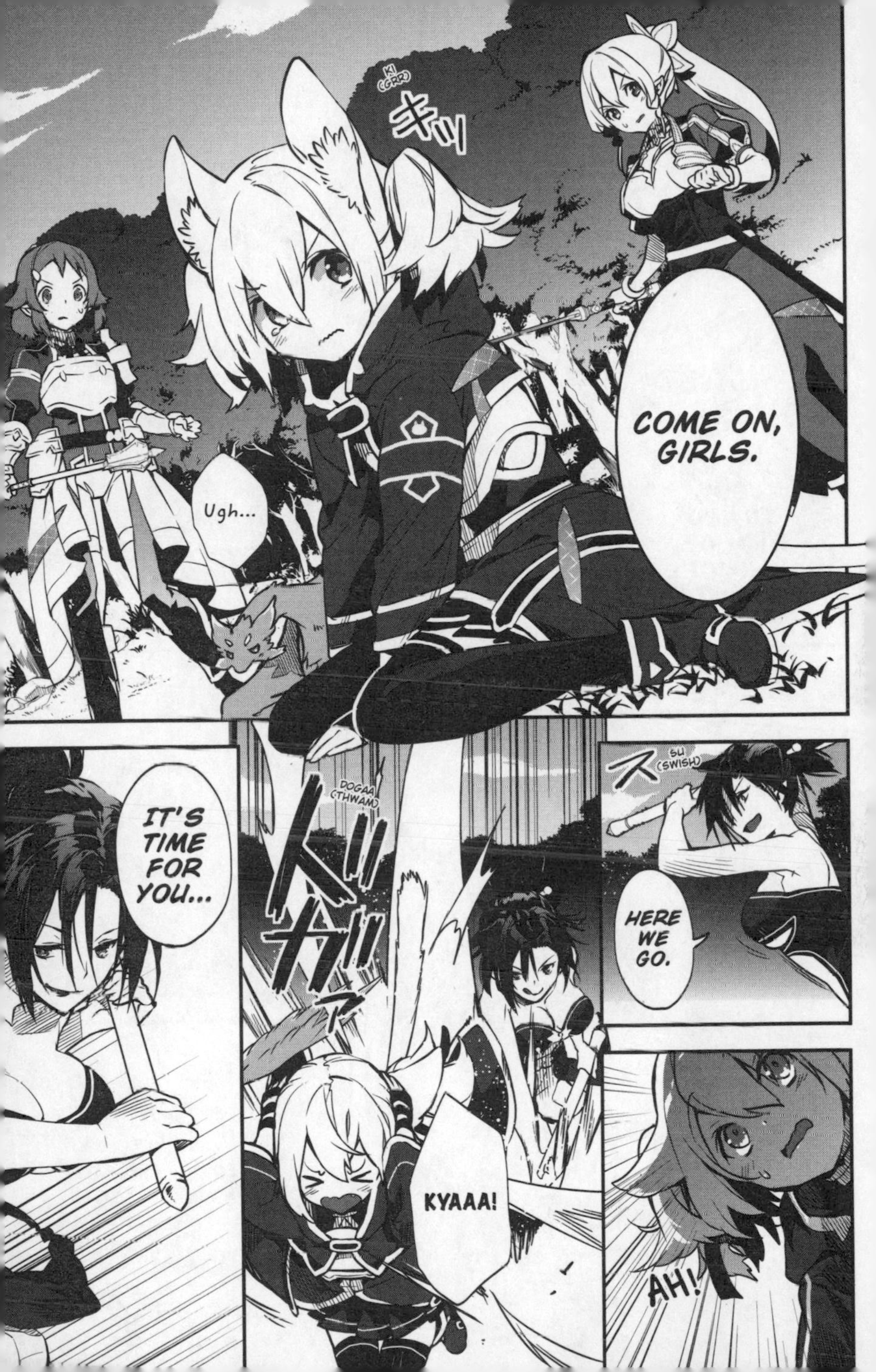
COME ON, GIRLS.
KI (GRR)
キッ
Ugh...
SU (SWISH)
ス
HERE WE GO.
DOGAA (THWAM)
ドッガッ
IT'S TIME FOR YOU...
AH!
KYAAA!

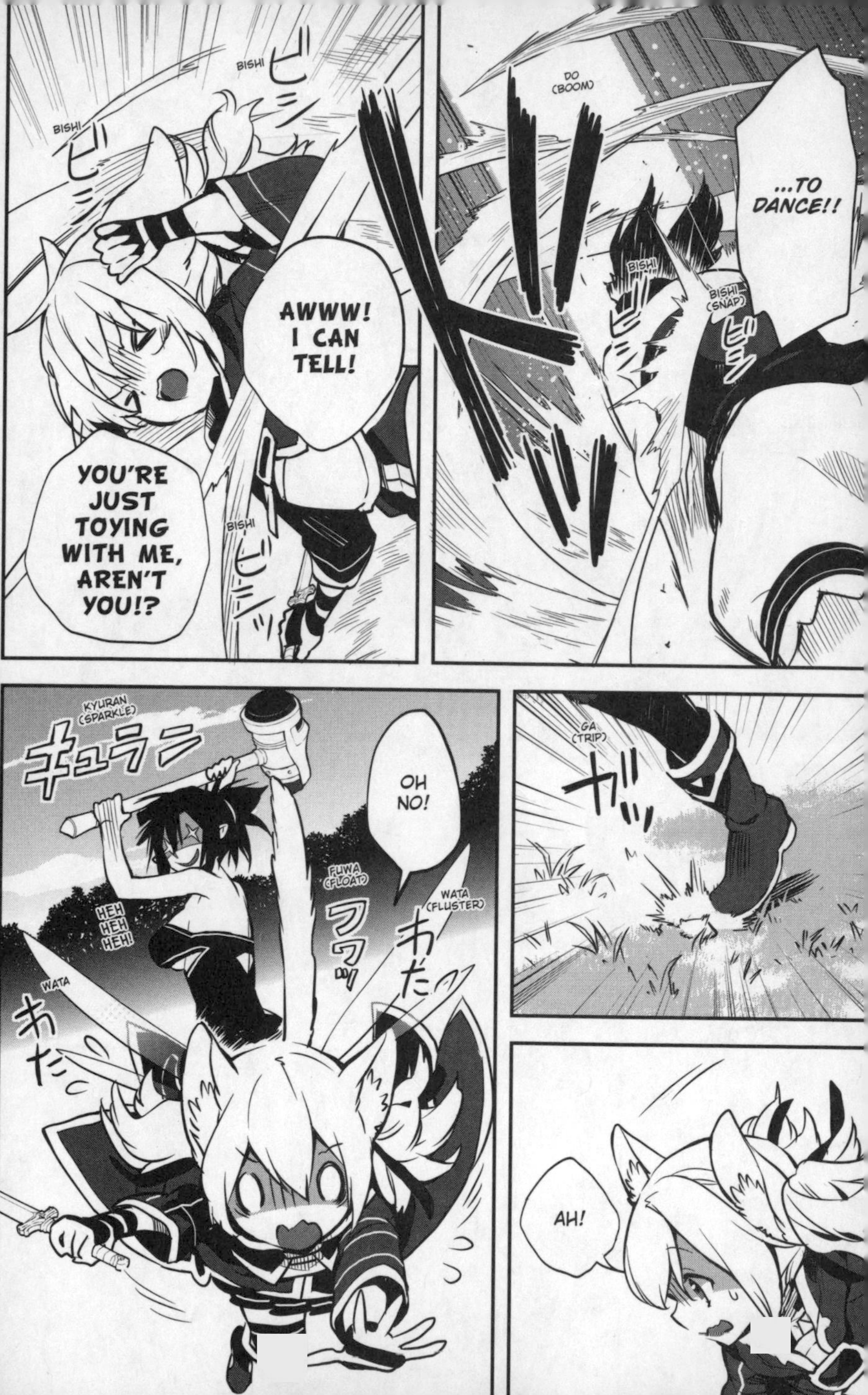
DO (BOOM)
...TO DANCE!!
BISHI
BISHI (SNAP)
BISHI
BISHI
AWWW! I CAN TELL!
YOU'RE JUST TOYING WITH ME, AREN'T YOU!?
BISHI
GA (TRIP)
AH!
KYURAN (SPARKLE)
OH NO!
FUWA (FLOAT)
WATA (FLUSTER)
HEH HEH HEH!
WATA

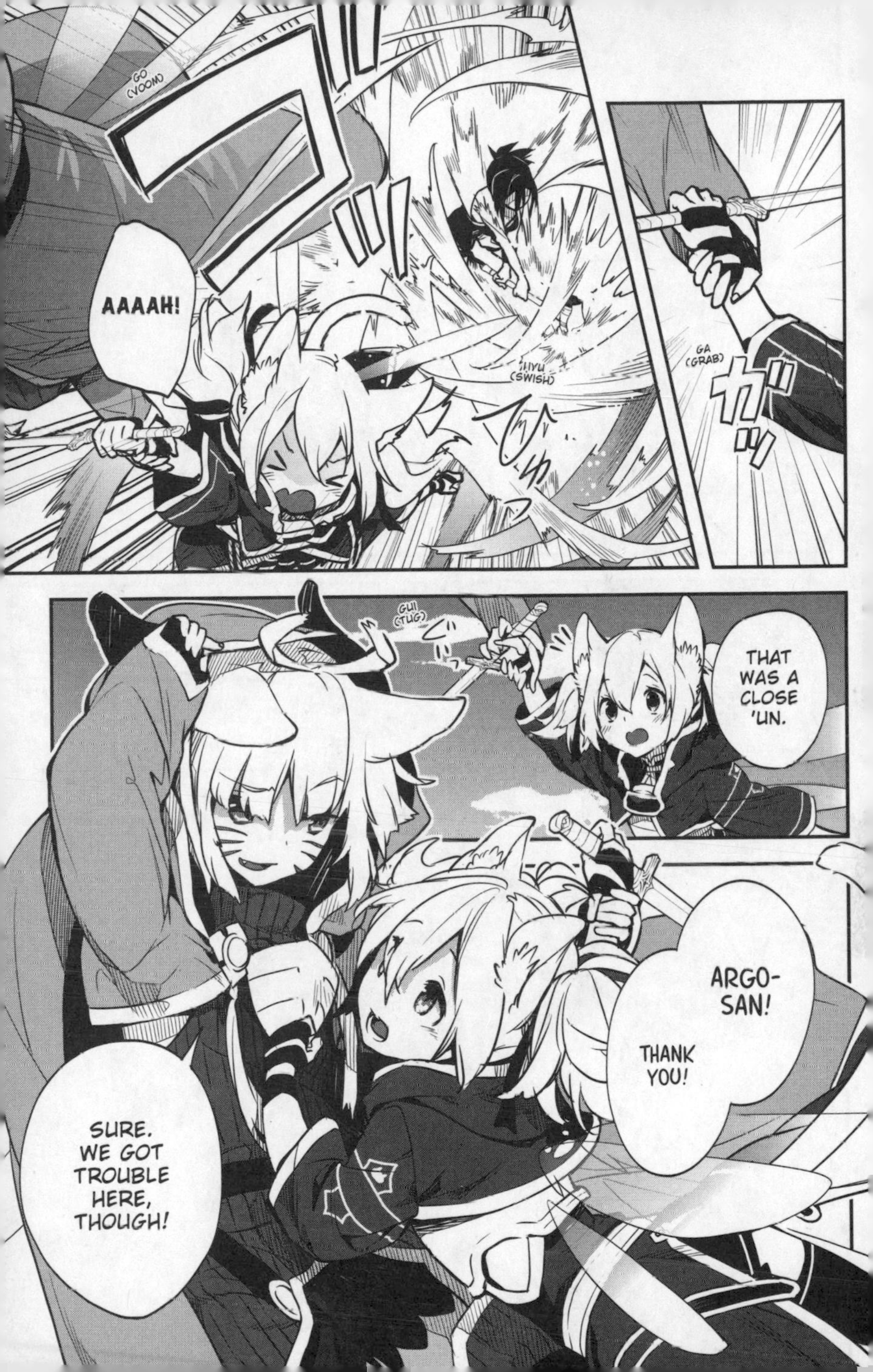
GO (VOOM)
AAAAH!
HYU (SWISH)
GA (GRAB)
GUI (TUG)
THAT WAS A CLOSE 'UN.
ARGO-SAN!
THANK YOU!
SURE. WE GOT TROUBLE HERE, THOUGH!

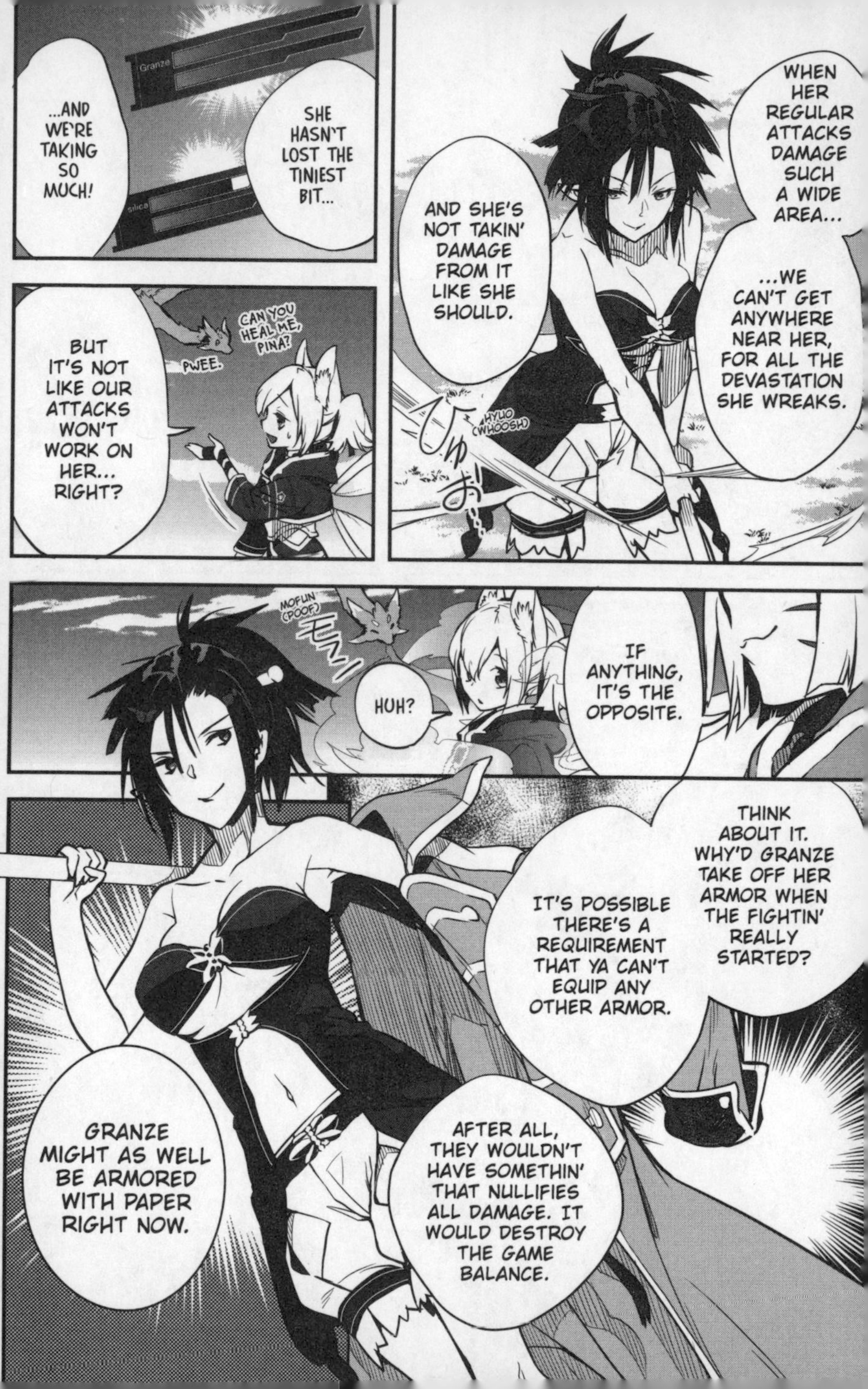
WHEN HER REGULAR ATTACKS DAMAGE SUCH A WIDE AREA...
...WE CAN'T GET ANYWHERE NEAR HER, FOR ALL THE DEVASTATION SHE WREAKS.
AND SHE'S NOT TAKIN' DAMAGE FROM IT LIKE SHE SHOULD.
HYUO (WHOOSH)
Granze
Silica
SHE HASN'T LOST THE TINIEST BIT...
...AND WE'RE TAKING SO MUCH!
CAN YOU HEAL ME, PINA?
PWEE.
BUT IT'S NOT LIKE OUR ATTACKS WON'T WORK ON HER... RIGHT?
IF ANYTHING, IT'S THE OPPOSITE.
HUH?
MOFUN (POOF)
THINK ABOUT IT. WHY'D GRANZE TAKE OFF HER ARMOR WHEN THE FIGHTIN' REALLY STARTED?
IT'S POSSIBLE THERE'S A REQUIREMENT THAT YA CAN'T EQUIP ANY OTHER ARMOR.
AFTER ALL, THEY WOULDN'T HAVE SOMETHIN' THAT NULLIFIES ALL DAMAGE. IT WOULD DESTROY THE GAME BALANCE.
GRANZE MIGHT AS WELL BE ARMORED WITH PAPER RIGHT NOW.

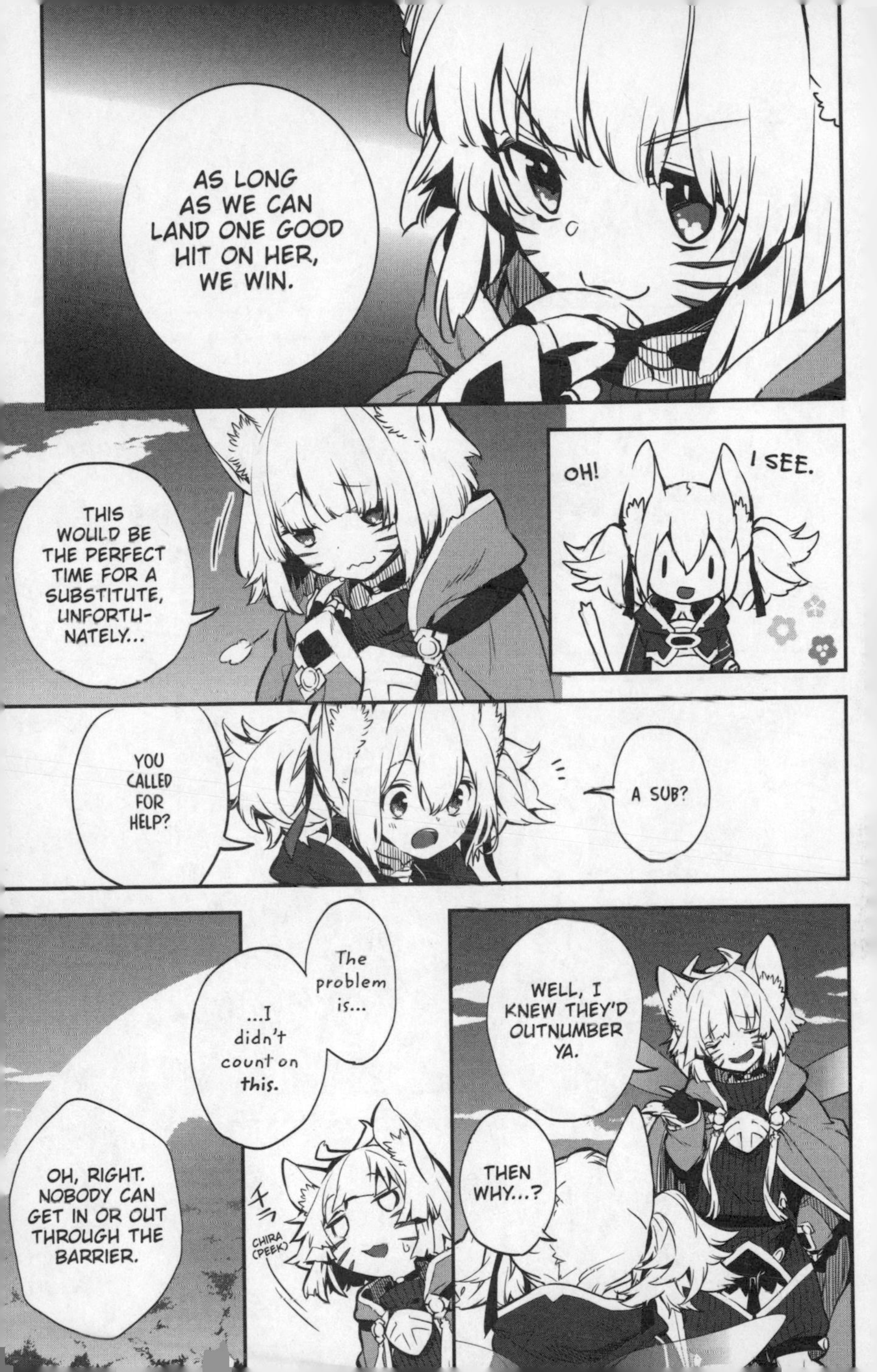
AS LONG AS WE CAN LAND ONE GOOD HIT ON HER, WE WIN.
OH!
I SEE.
THIS WOULD BE THE PERFECT TIME FOR A SUBSTITUTE, UNFORTU-NATELY...
A SUB?
YOU CALLED FOR HELP?
WELL, I KNEW THEY'D OUTNUMBER YA.
THEN WHY...?
The problem is...
...I didn't count on this.
CHIRA (PEEK)
OH, RIGHT. NOBODY CAN GET IN OR OUT THROUGH THE BARRIER.

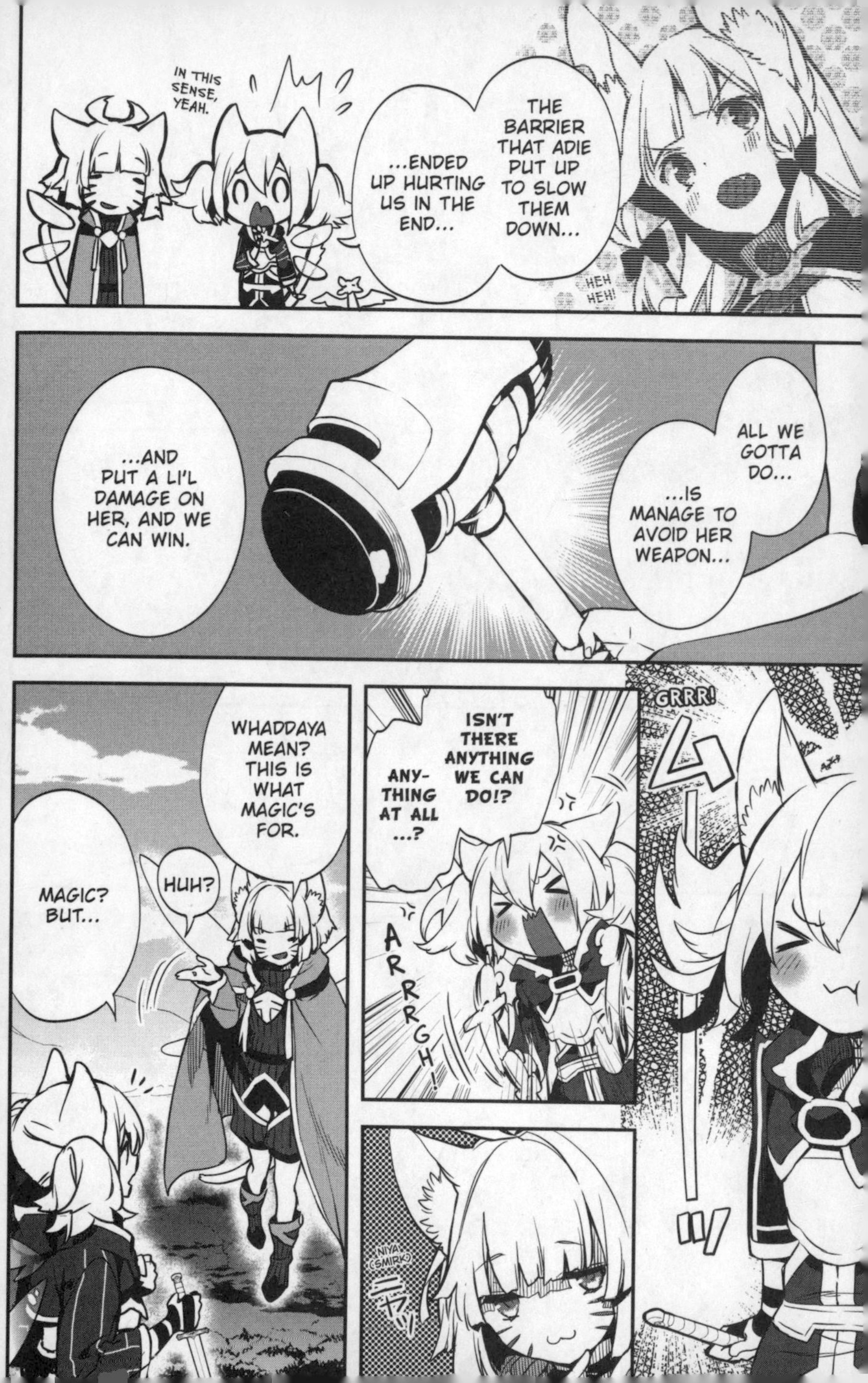
HEH HEH!
THE BARRIER THAT ADIE PUT UP TO SLOW THEM DOWN...
...ENDED UP HURTING US IN THE END...
IN THIS SENSE, YEAH.
ALL WE GOTTA DO...
...IS MANAGE TO AVOID HER WEAPON...
...AND PUT A LI'L DAMAGE ON HER, AND WE CAN WIN.
GRRR!
ISN'T THERE ANYTHING WE CAN DO!?
ANYTHING AT ALL ...?
ARRRGH!
WHADDAYA MEAN? THIS IS WHAT MAGIC'S FOR.
HUH?
MAGIC? BUT...
NIYA (SMIRK)

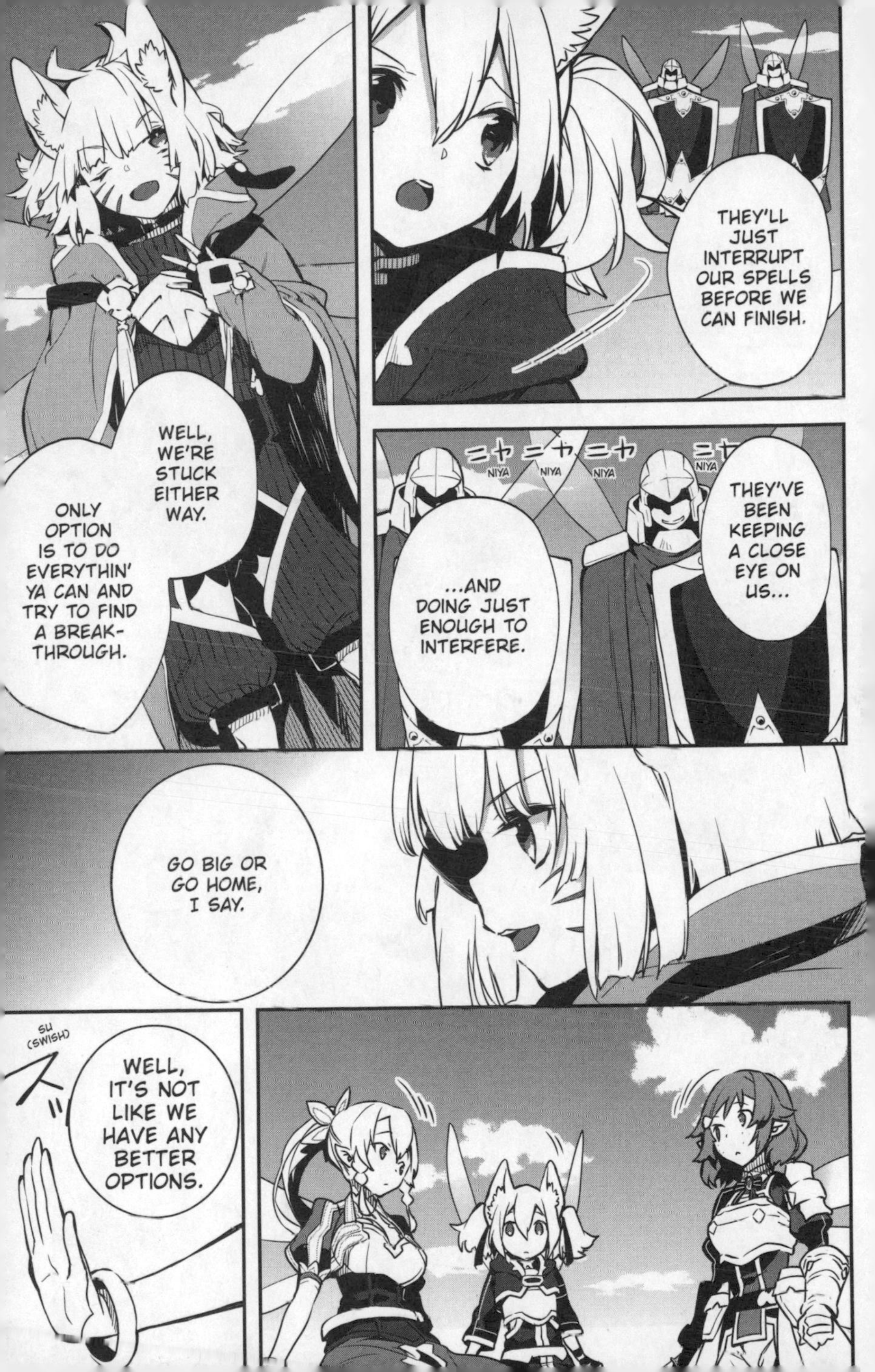
THEY'LL JUST INTERRUPT OUR SPELLS BEFORE WE CAN FINISH.
ニヤ ニヤ ニヤ ニヤ
NIYA NIYA NIYA NIYA
THEY'VE BEEN KEEPING A CLOSE EYE ON US...
...AND DOING JUST ENOUGH TO INTERFERE.
WELL, WE'RE STUCK EITHER WAY.
ONLY OPTION IS TO DO EVERYTHIN' YA CAN AND TRY TO FIND A BREAK-THROUGH.
GO BIG OR GO HOME, I SAY.
スッ
SU (SWISH)
WELL, IT'S NOT LIKE WE HAVE ANY BETTER OPTIONS.

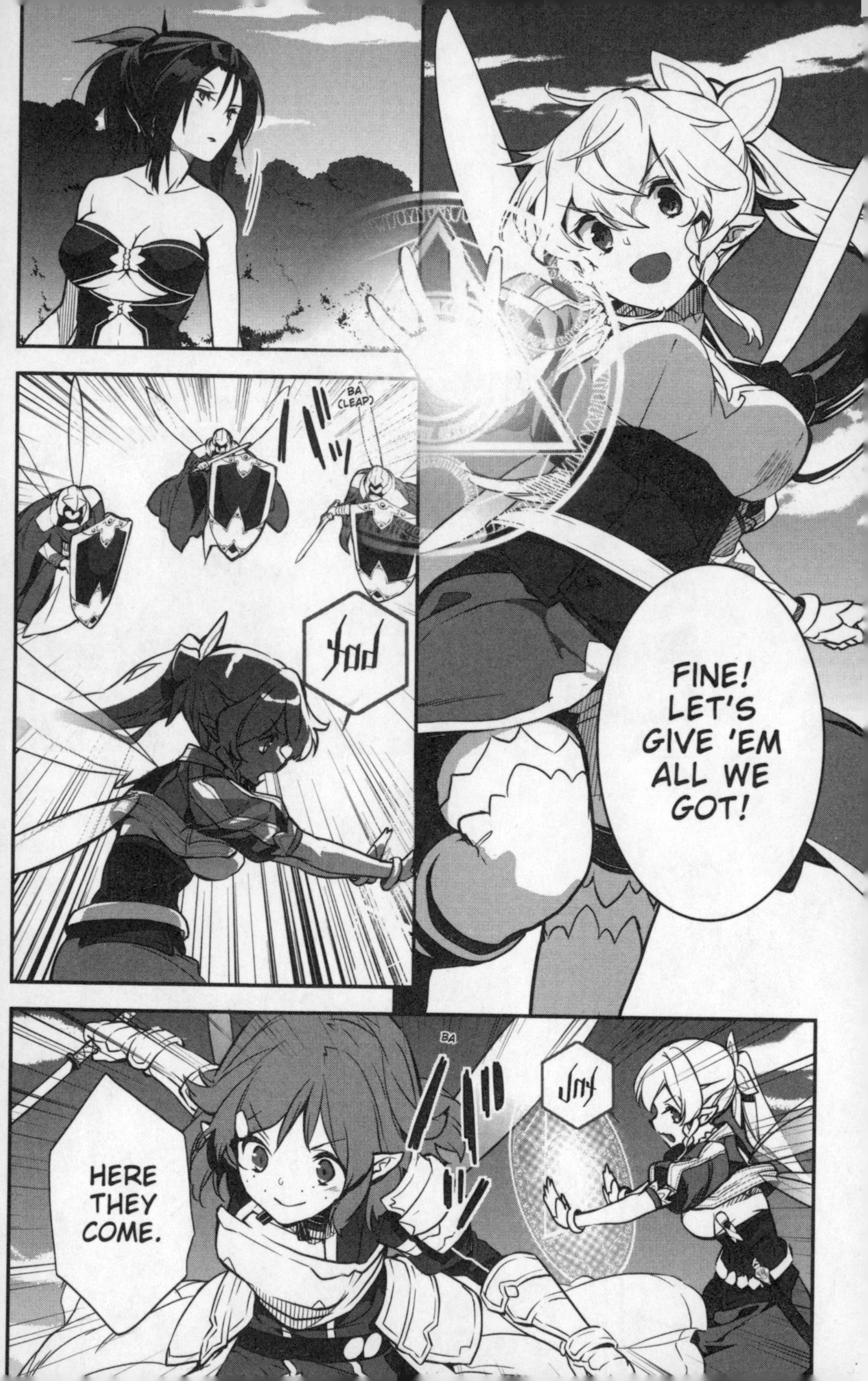
FINE! LET'S GIVE 'EM ALL WE GOT!
BA (LEAP)
BA
HERE THEY COME.

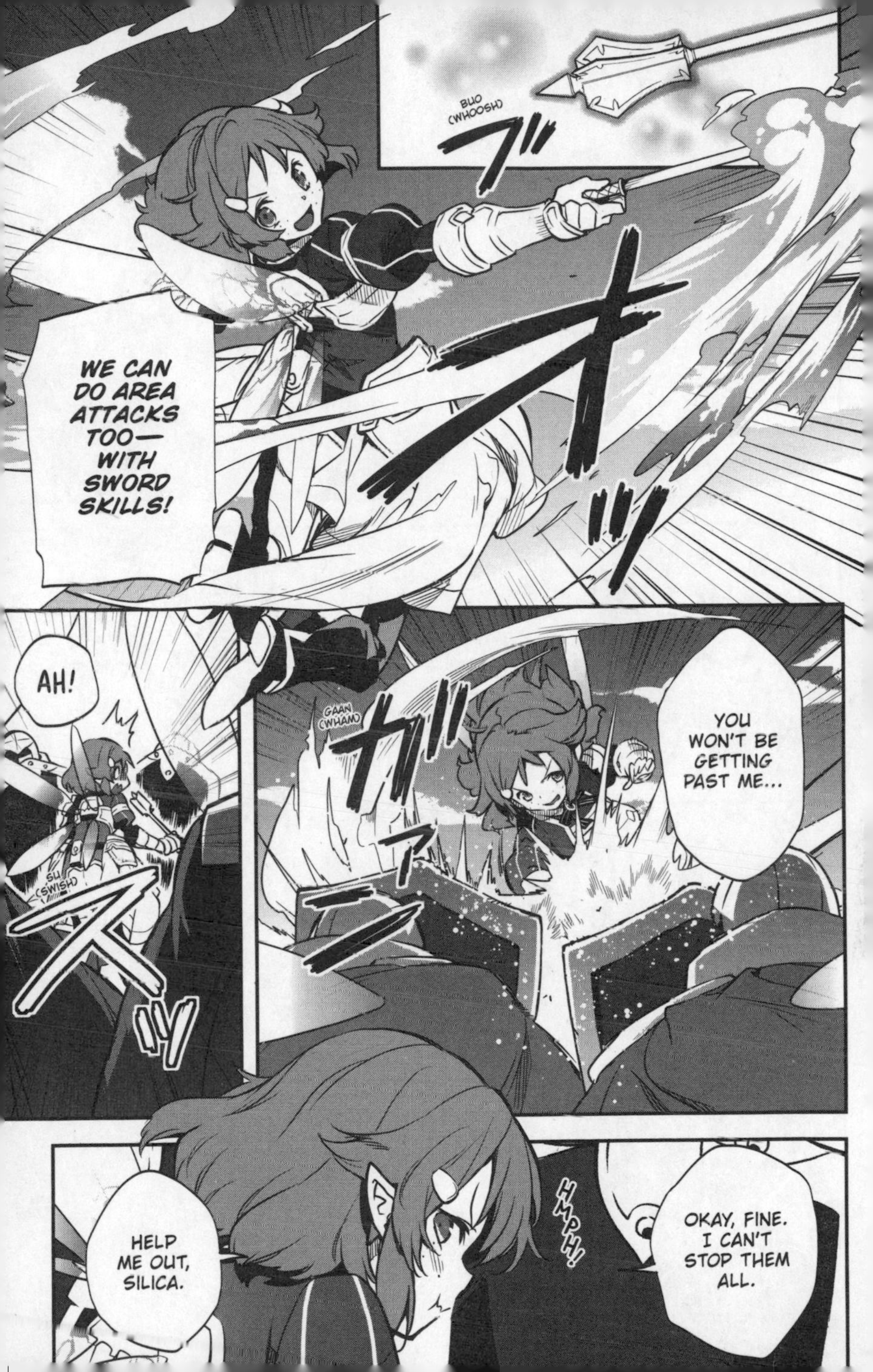
BUO (WHOOSH)
WE CAN DO AREA ATTACKS TOO— WITH SWORD SKILLS!
YOU WON'T BE GETTING PAST ME...
GAAN (WHAM)
AH!
SU (SWISH)
OKAY, FINE. I CAN'T STOP THEM ALL.
HMPH!
HELP ME OUT, SILICA.

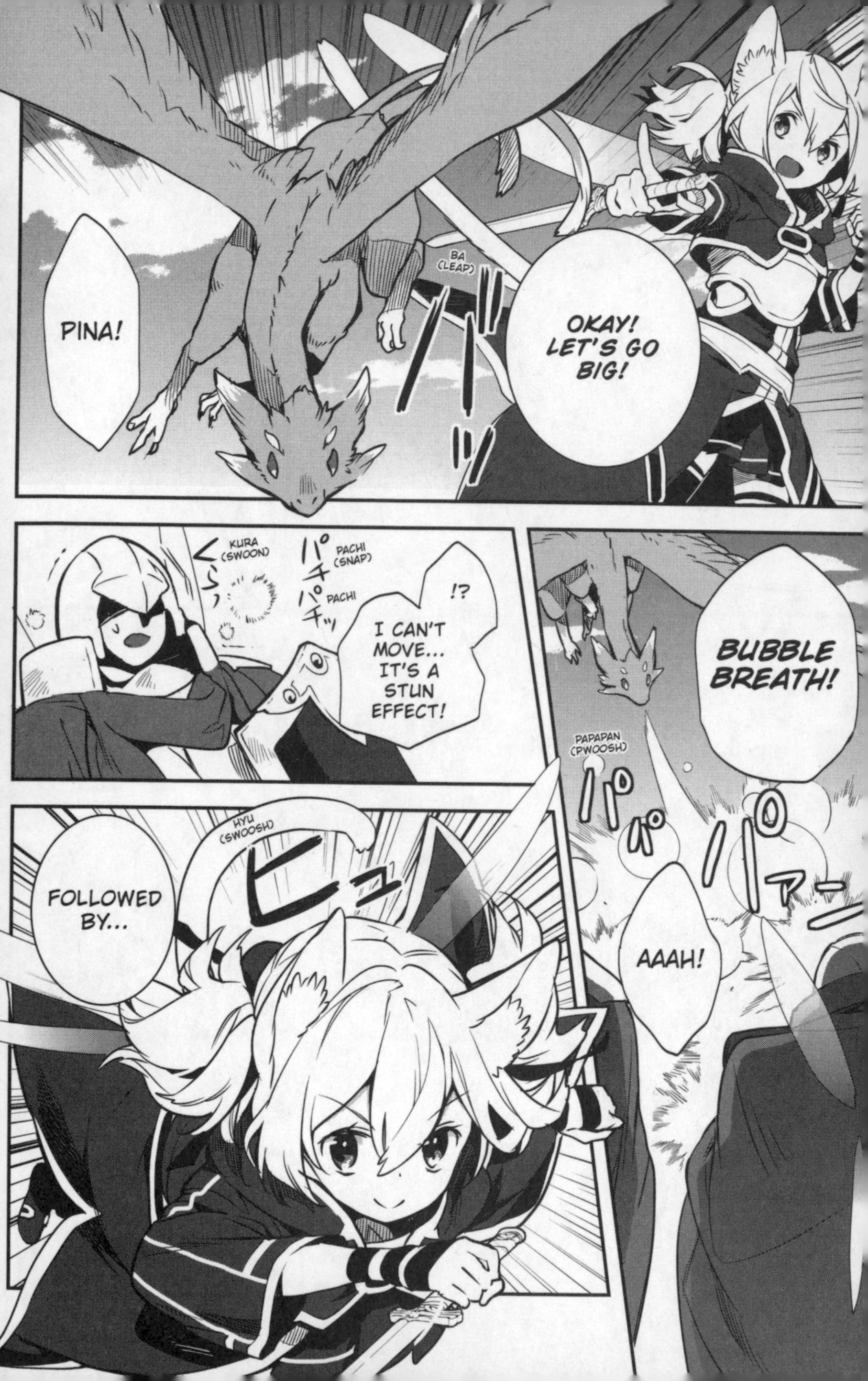

OKAY! LET'S GO BIG!
BA (LEAP)
PINA!
BUBBLE BREATH!
PAPAPAN (PWOOSH)
AAAH!
PACHI (SNAP)
PACHI
!?
I CAN'T MOVE... IT'S A STUN EFFECT!
KURA (SWOON)
HYU (SWOOSH)
FOLLOWED BY...

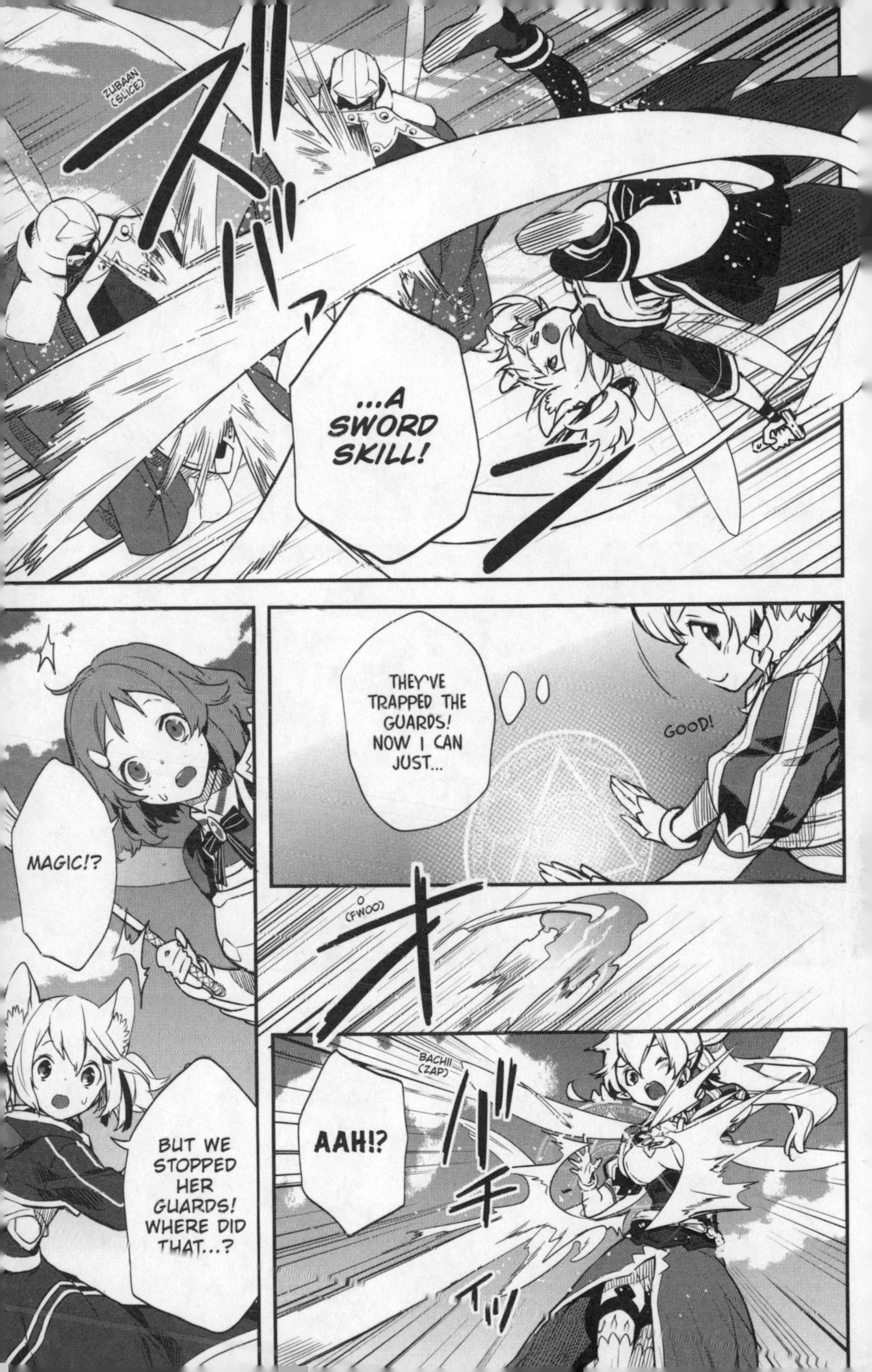
ZUBAAN (SLICE)
...A SWORD SKILL!
GOOD!
THEY'VE TRAPPED THE GUARDS! NOW I CAN JUST...
MAGIC!?
O (FWOO)
BACHII (ZAP)
AAH!?
BUT WE STOPPED HER GUARDS! WHERE DID THAT...?

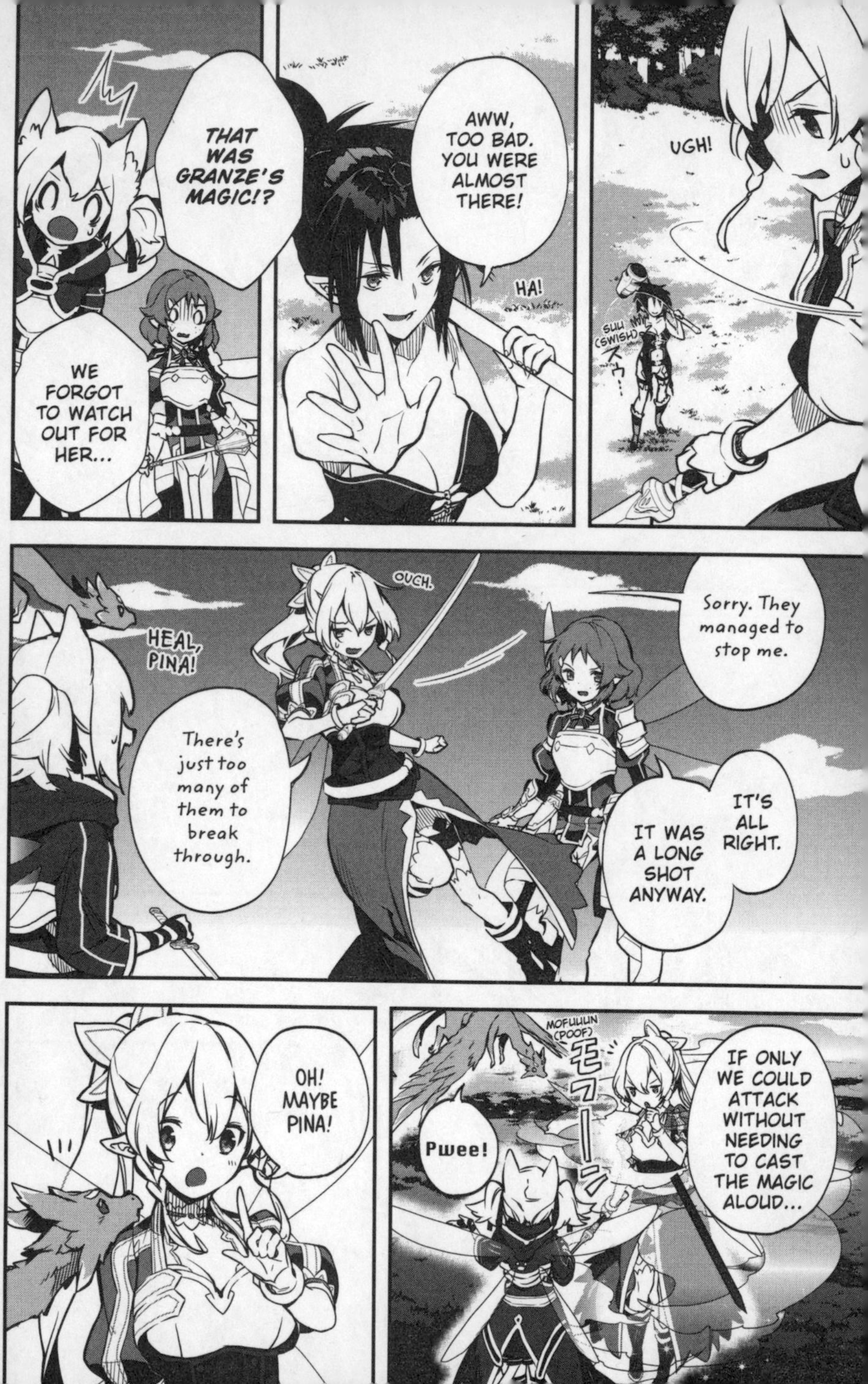
UGH!
SUU (SWISH)
AWW, TOO BAD. YOU WERE ALMOST THERE!
HA!
THAT WAS GRANZE'S MAGIC!?
WE FORGOT TO WATCH OUT FOR HER...
Sorry. They managed to stop me.
OUCH.
IT'S ALL RIGHT.
IT WAS A LONG SHOT ANYWAY.
There's just too many of them to break through.
HEAL, PINA!
IF ONLY WE COULD ATTACK WITHOUT NEEDING TO CAST THE MAGIC ALOUD...
MOFUUUUN (POOF)
Pwee!
OH! MAYBE PINA!

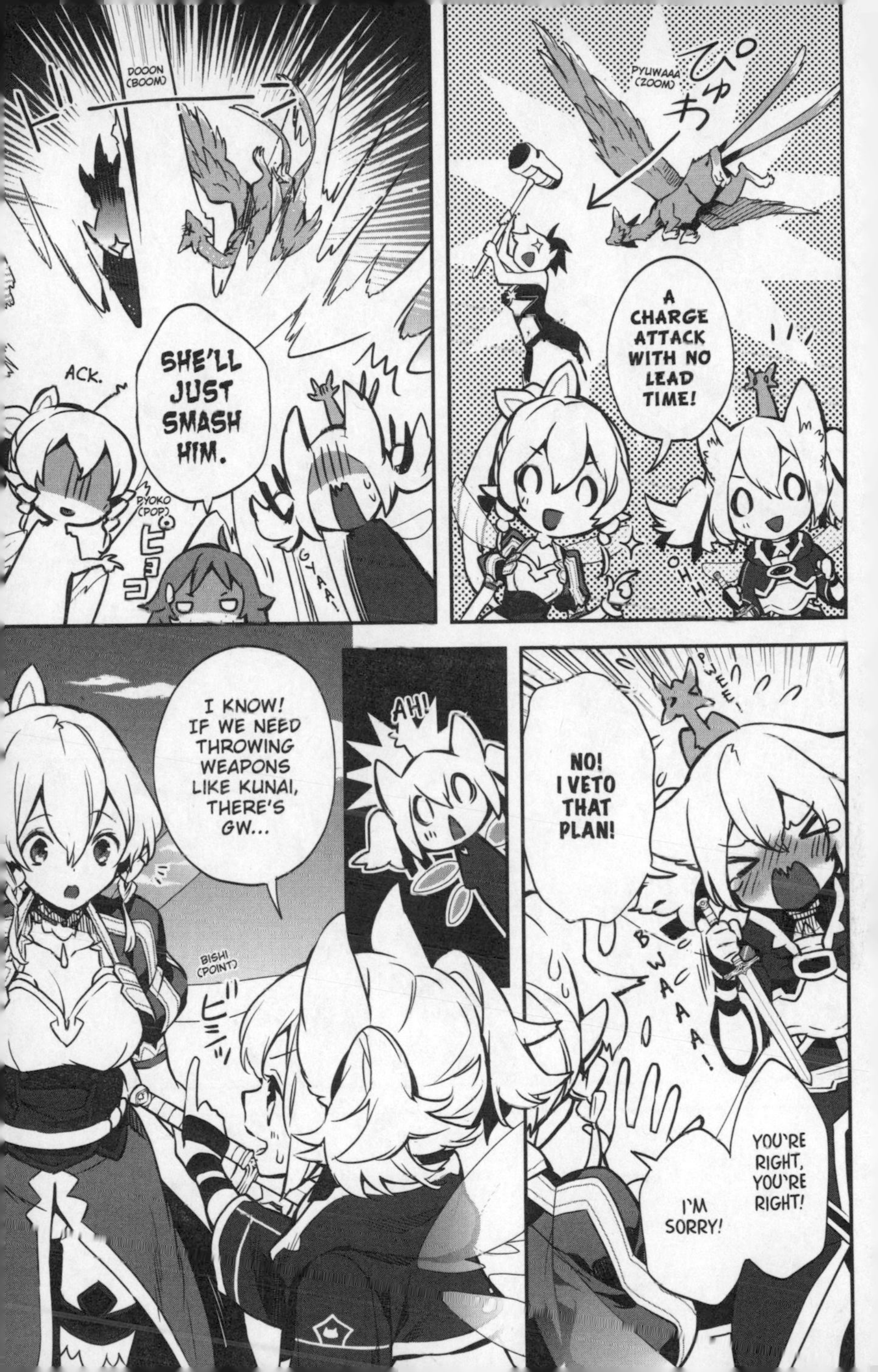
DOOON (BOOM)
ACK.
SHE'LL JUST SMASH HIM.
PYOKO (POP)
GYAA!
PYUWAAA (ZOOM)
A CHARGE ATTACK WITH NO LEAD TIME!
OHH!
I KNOW! IF WE NEED THROWING WEAPONS LIKE KUNAI, THERE'S GW...
BISHI (POINT)
AH!
PWEE!
NO! I VETO THAT PLAN!
BWAAAA!
YOU'RE RIGHT, YOU'RE RIGHT!
I'M SORRY!

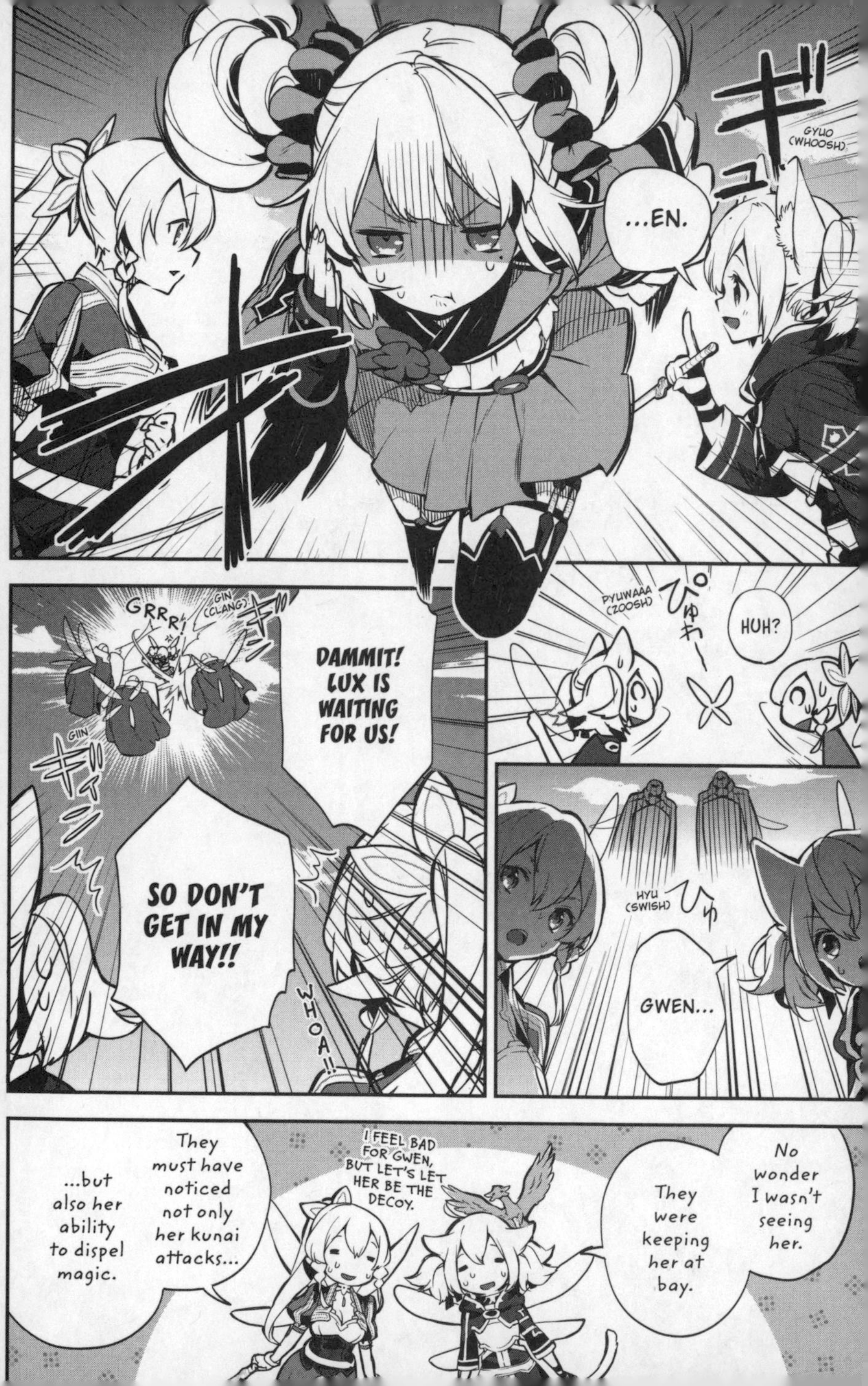
GYUO (WHOOSH)
...EN.
PYUWAAA (ZOOSH)
HUH?
GIN (CLANG)
GRRR!
GIIN
DAMMIT! LUX IS WAITING FOR US!
SO DON'T GET IN MY WAY!!
WHOA!!
HYU (SWISH)
GWEN...
No wonder I wasn't seeing her.
They were keeping her at bay.
I FEEL BAD FOR GWEN, BUT LET'S LET HER BE THE DECOY.
They must have noticed not only her kunai attacks...
...but also her ability to dispel magic.

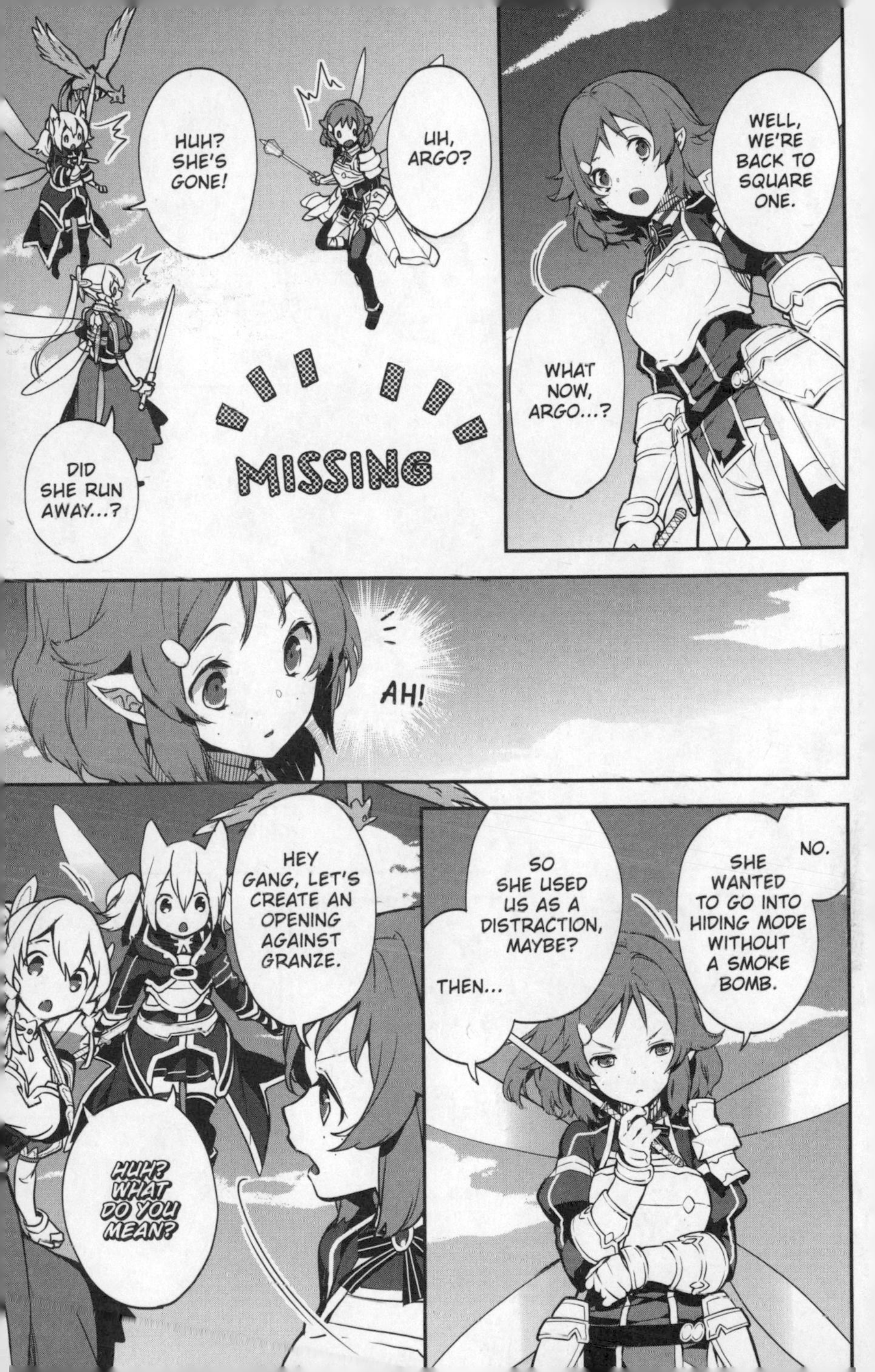
WELL, WE'RE BACK TO SQUARE ONE.
WHAT NOW, ARGO...?
UH, ARGO?
HUH? SHE'S GONE!
DID SHE RUN AWAY...?
MISSING
AH!
SO SHE USED US AS A DISTRACTION, MAYBE?
NO.
SHE WANTED TO GO INTO HIDING MODE WITHOUT A SMOKE BOMB.
THEN...
HEY GANG, LET'S CREATE AN OPENING AGAINST GRANZE.
HUH? WHAT DO YOU MEAN?

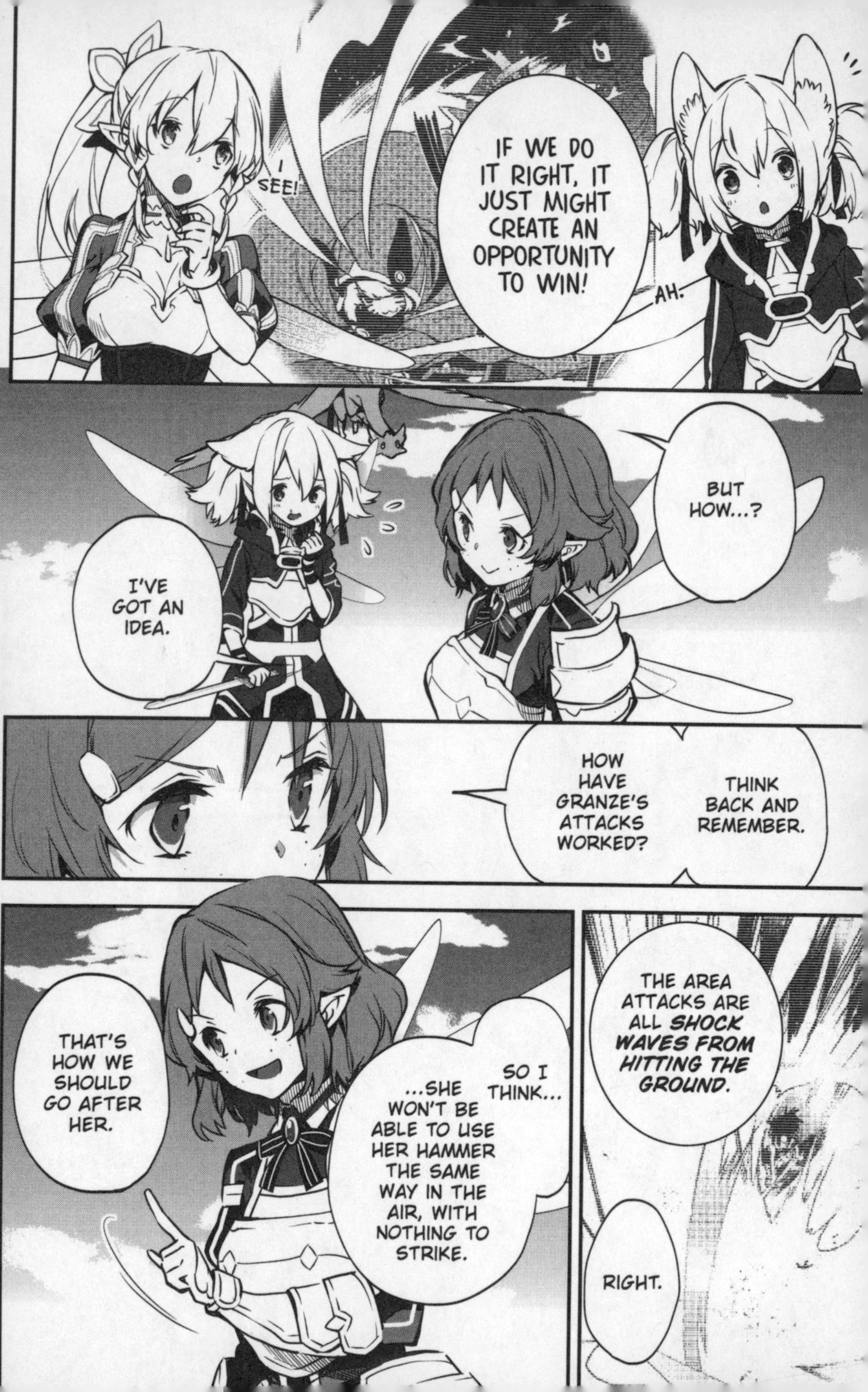
AH.
IF WE DO IT RIGHT, IT JUST MIGHT CREATE AN OPPORTUNITY TO WIN!
I SEE!
BUT HOW...?
I'VE GOT AN IDEA.
THINK BACK AND REMEMBER.
HOW HAVE GRANZE'S ATTACKS WORKED?
THE AREA ATTACKS ARE ALL SHOCK WAVES FROM HITTING THE GROUND.
RIGHT.
SO I THINK...
...SHE WON'T BE ABLE TO USE HER HAMMER THE SAME WAY IN THE AIR, WITH NOTHING TO STRIKE.
THAT'S HOW WE SHOULD GO AFTER HER.

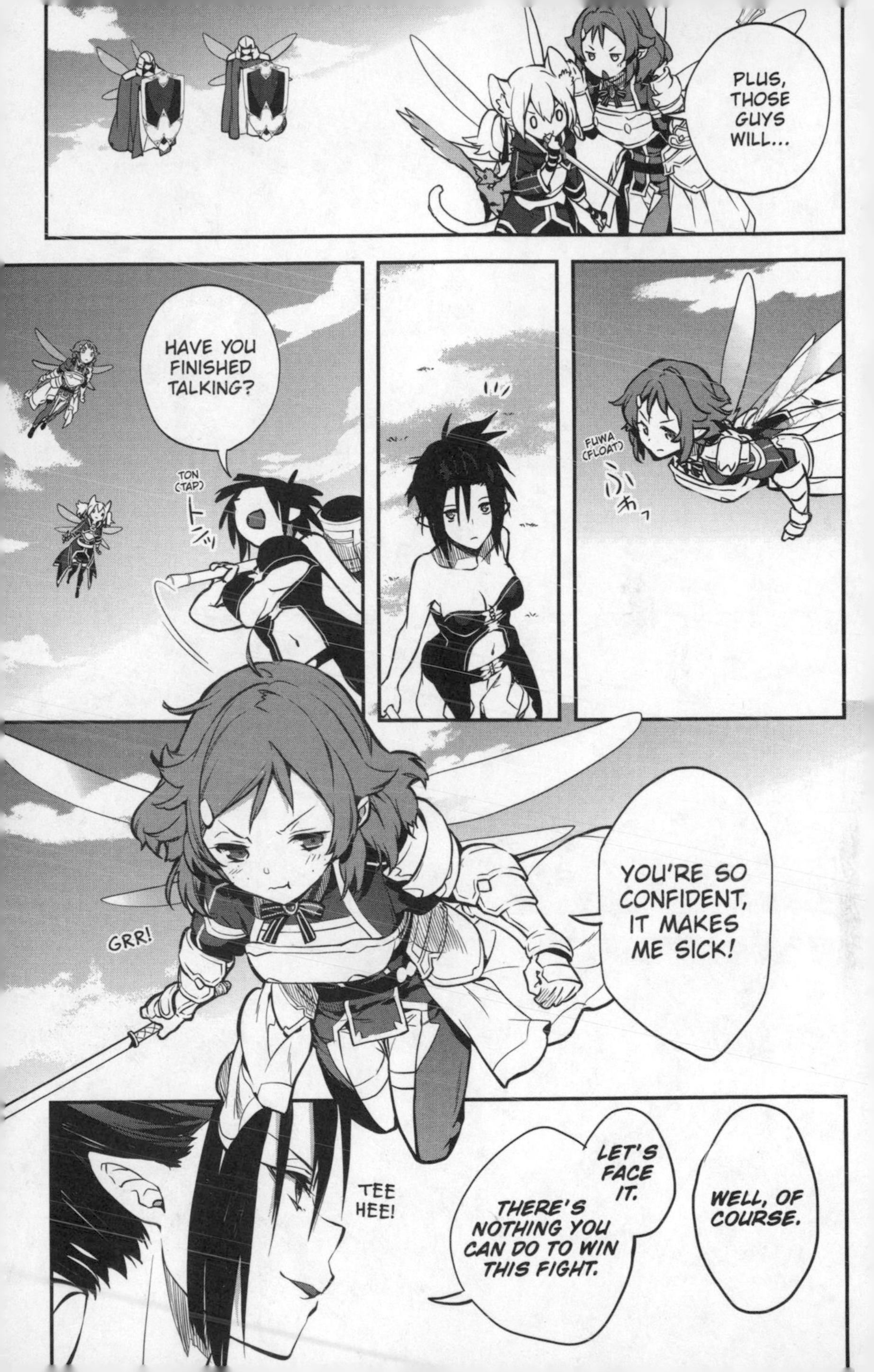
PLUS, THOSE GUYS WILL...
FUWA (FLOAT)
ふわっ
HAVE YOU FINISHED TALKING?
TON (TAP)
トンッ
YOU'RE SO CONFIDENT, IT MAKES ME SICK!
GRR!
WELL, OF COURSE.
LET'S FACE IT.
THERE'S NOTHING YOU CAN DO TO WIN THIS FIGHT.
TEE HEE!

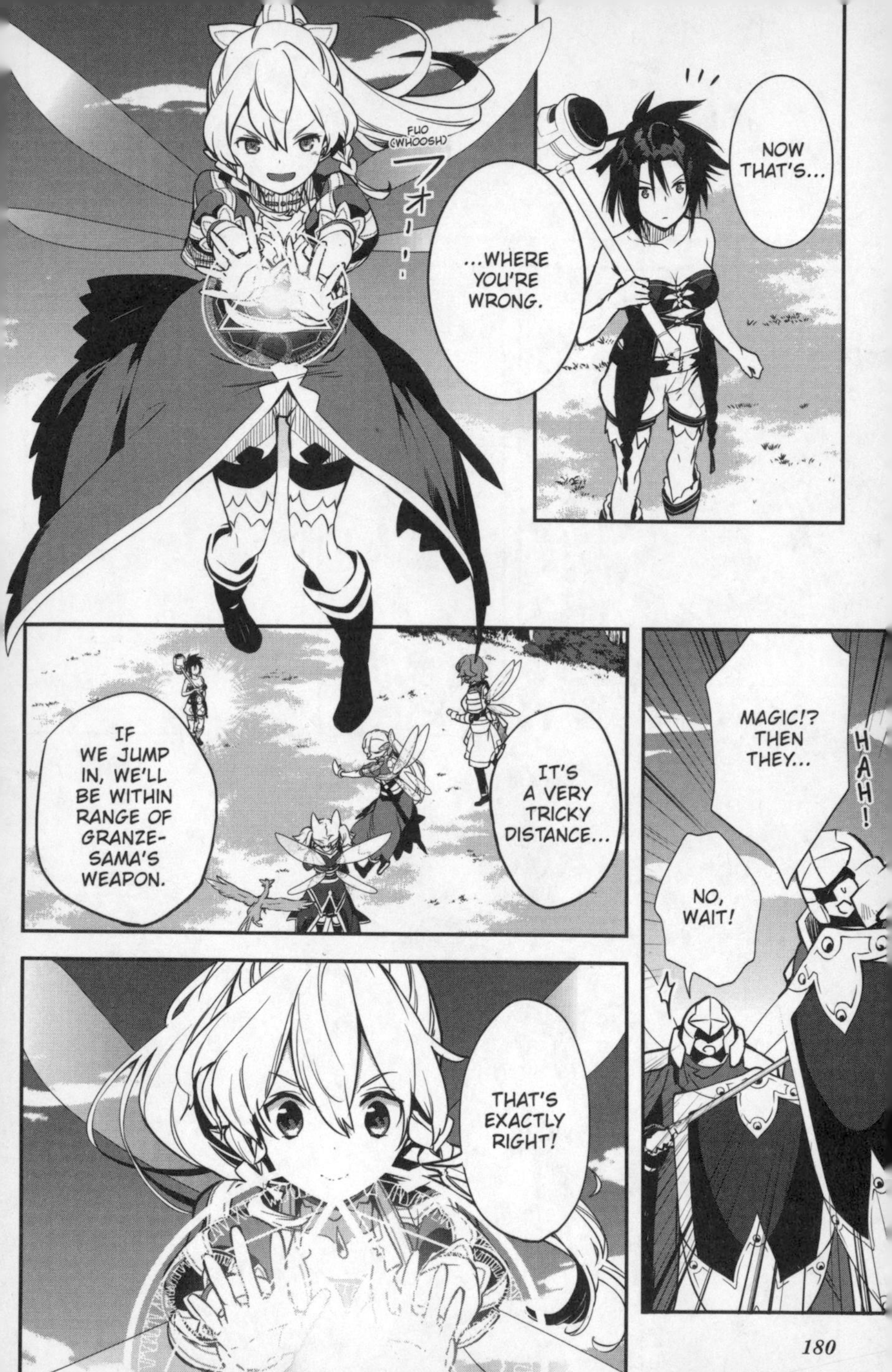
NOW THAT'S...
...WHERE YOU'RE WRONG.
FUO (WHOOSH)
MAGIC!? THEN THEY...
HAH!
IT'S A VERY TRICKY DISTANCE...
IF WE JUMP IN, WE'LL BE WITHIN RANGE OF GRANZE-SAMA'S WEAPON.
NO, WAIT!
THAT'S EXACTLY RIGHT!

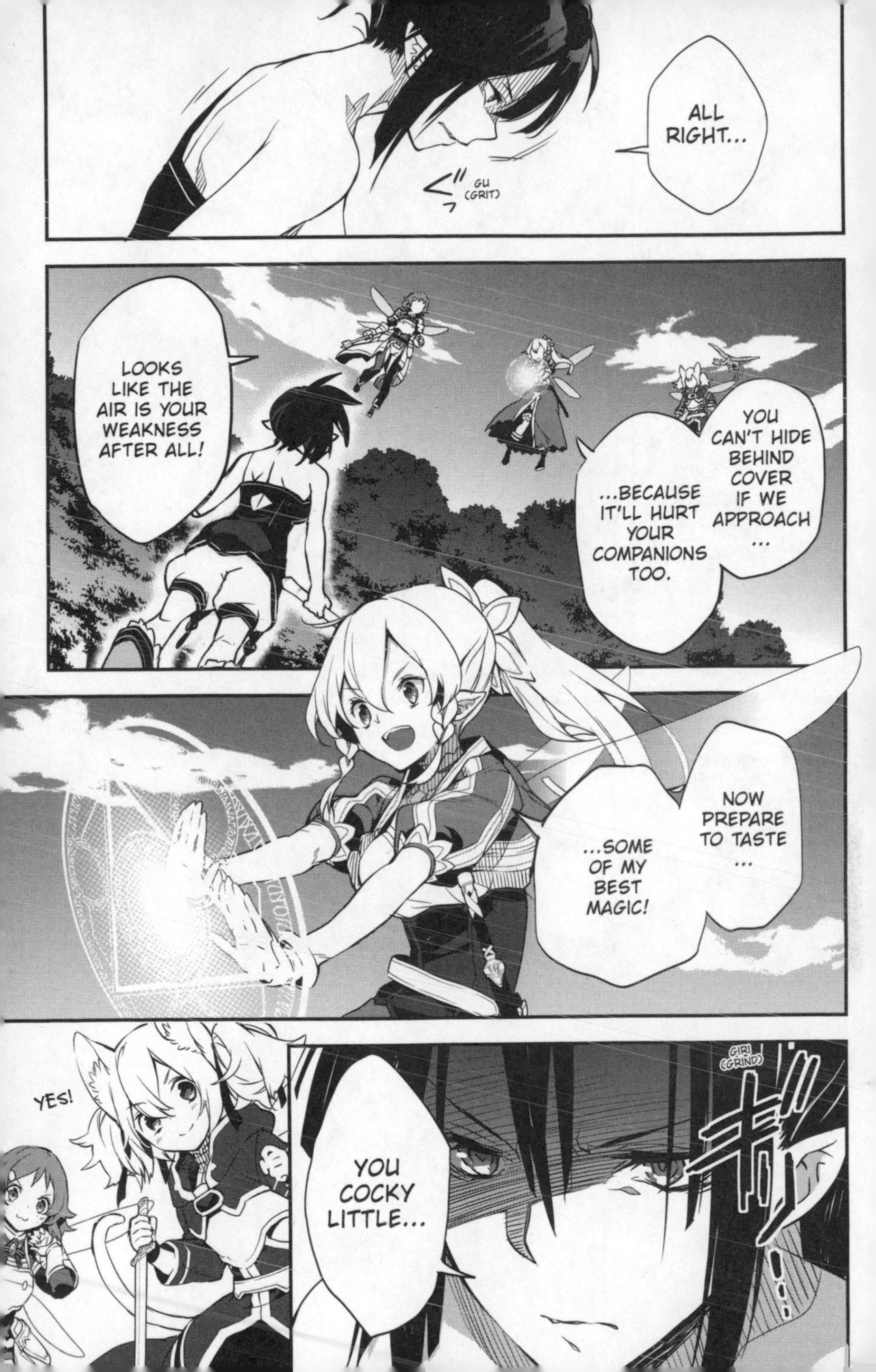
ALL RIGHT...
GU (GRIT)
LOOKS LIKE THE AIR IS YOUR WEAKNESS AFTER ALL!
YOU CAN'T HIDE BEHIND COVER IF WE APPROACH ...
...BECAUSE IT'LL HURT YOUR COMPANIONS TOO.
NOW PREPARE TO TASTE ...
...SOME OF MY BEST MAGIC!
GIRI (GRIND)
YOU COCKY LITTLE...
YES!

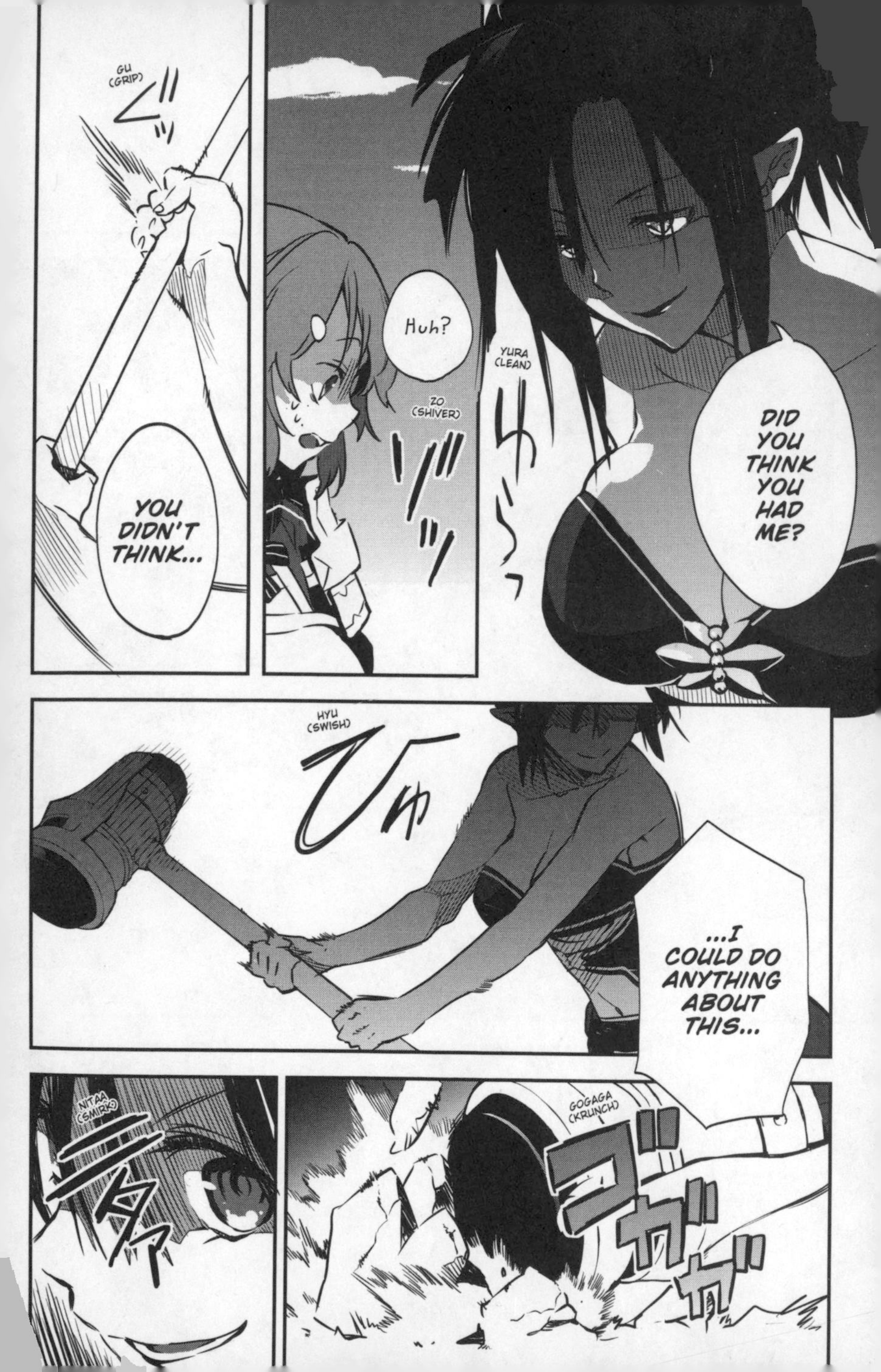
YURA (LEAN)
DID YOU THINK YOU HAD ME?
ZO (SHIVER)
Huh?
GU (GRIP)
YOU DIDN'T THINK...
HYU (SWISH)
...I COULD DO ANYTHING ABOUT THIS...
GOGAGA (KRUNCH)
NITAA (SMIRK)

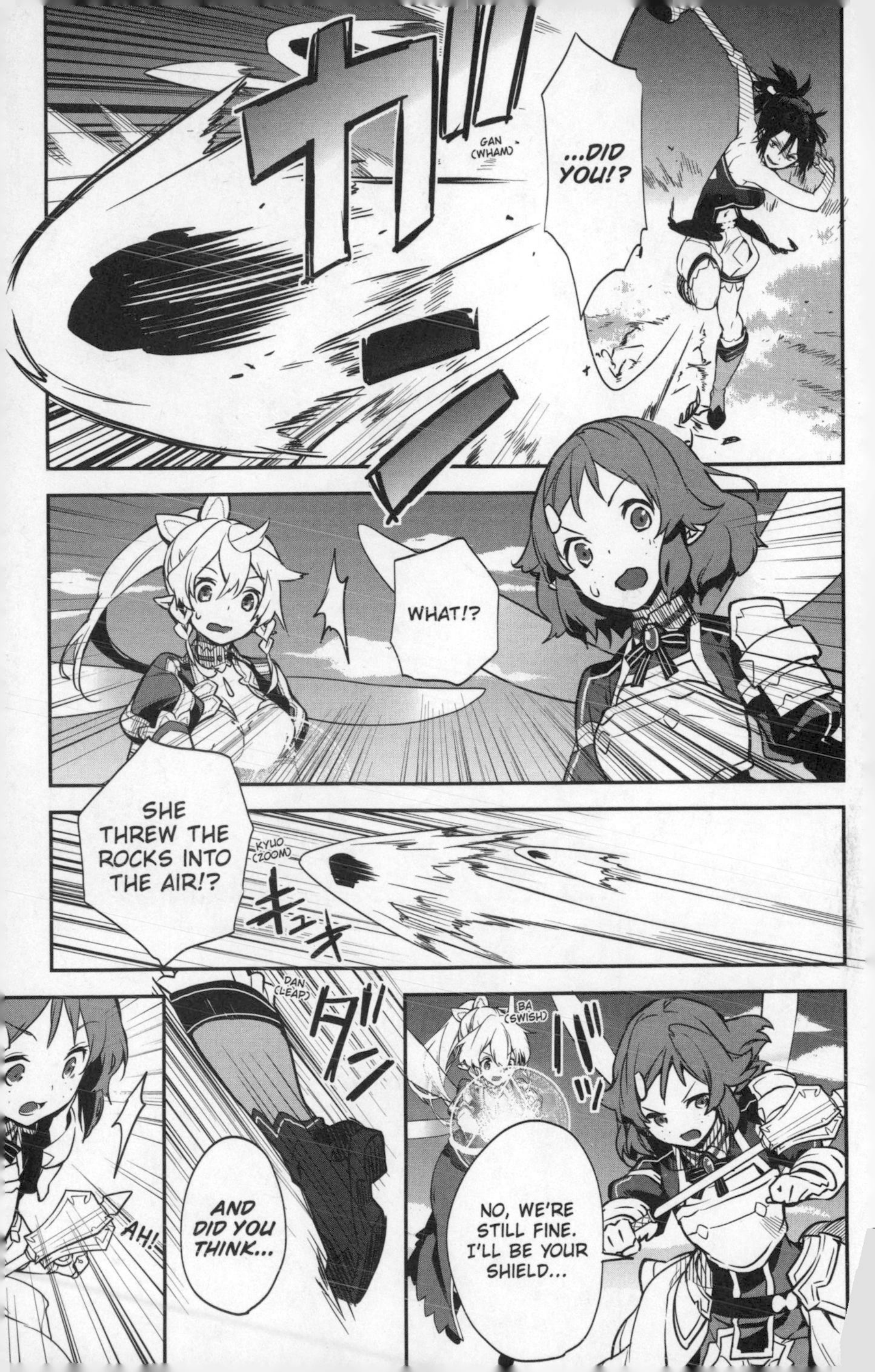
...DID YOU!?
GAN (WHAM)
WHAT!?
SHE THREW THE ROCKS INTO THE AIR!?
KYUO (ZOOM)
BA (SWISH)
NO, WE'RE STILL FINE. I'LL BE YOUR SHIELD...
DAN (LEAP)
AND DID YOU THINK...
AH!

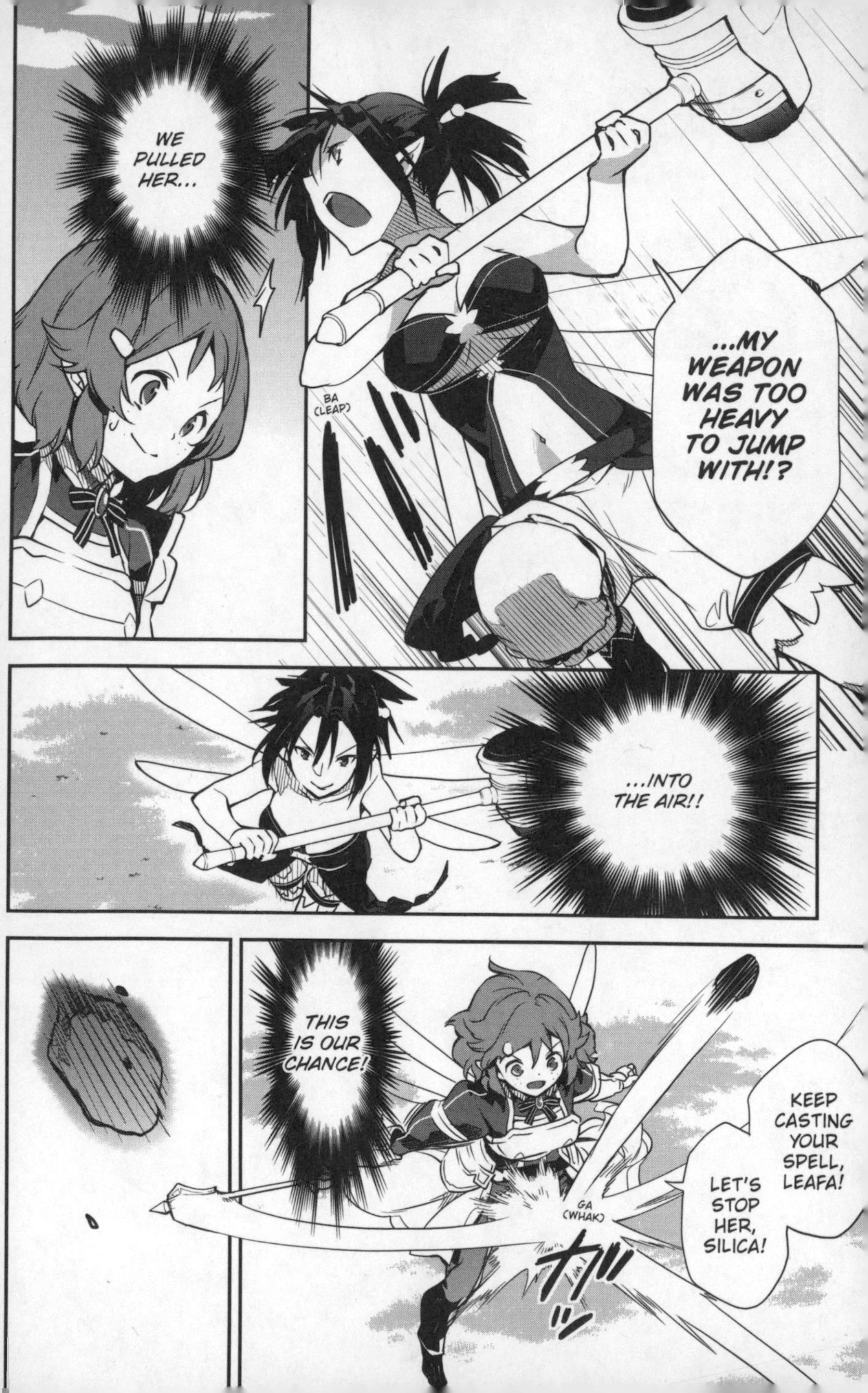
WE PULLED HER...
...MY WEAPON WAS TOO HEAVY TO JUMP WITH!?
BA (LEAP)
...INTO THE AIR!!
THIS IS OUR CHANCE!
KEEP CASTING YOUR SPELL, LEAFA!
LET'S STOP HER, SILICA!
GA (WHAK)

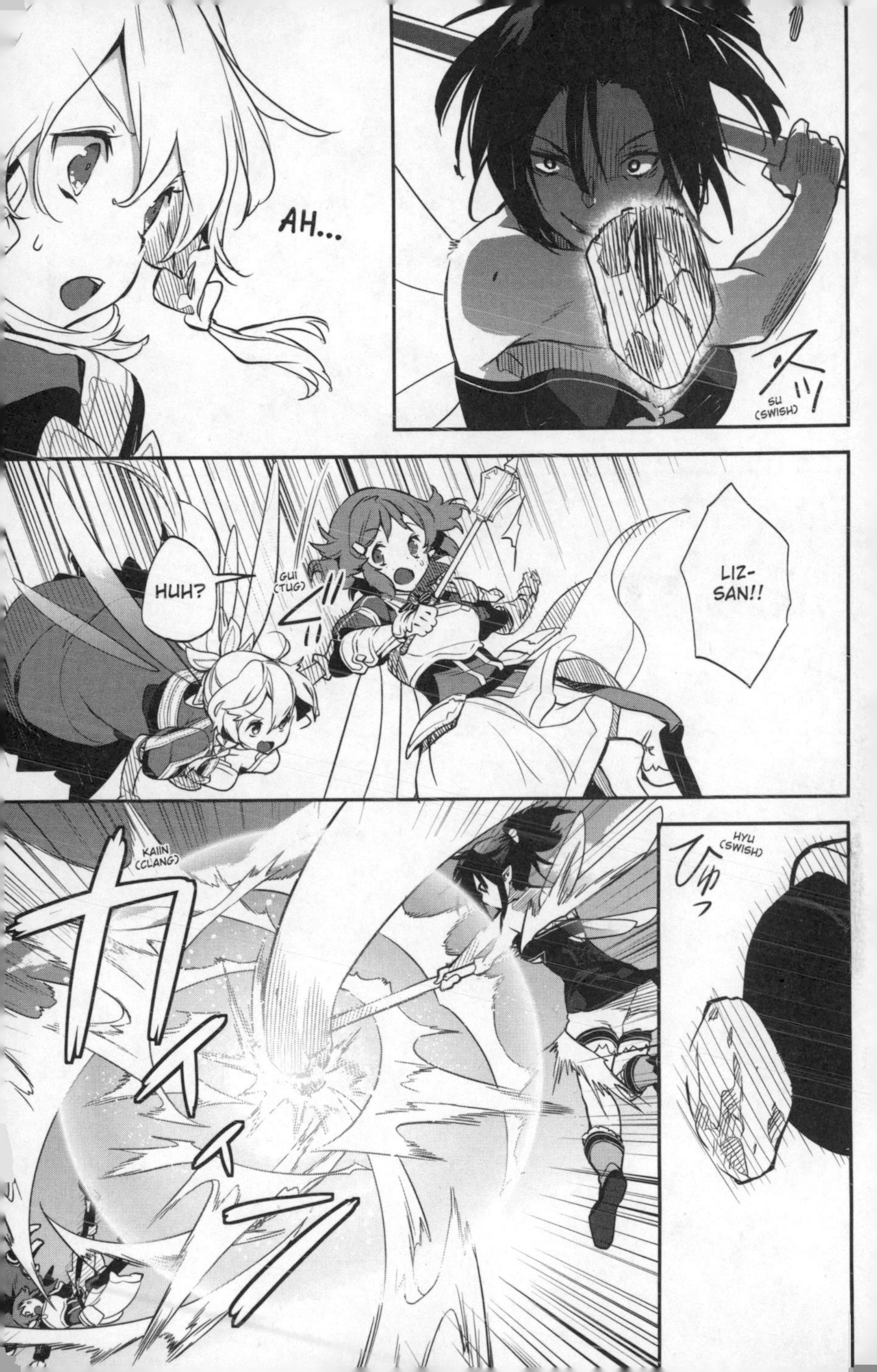
SU
(SWISH)
AH...
LIZ-
SAN!!
GUI
(TUG)
HUH?
HYU
(SWISH)
KAIIN
(CLANG)

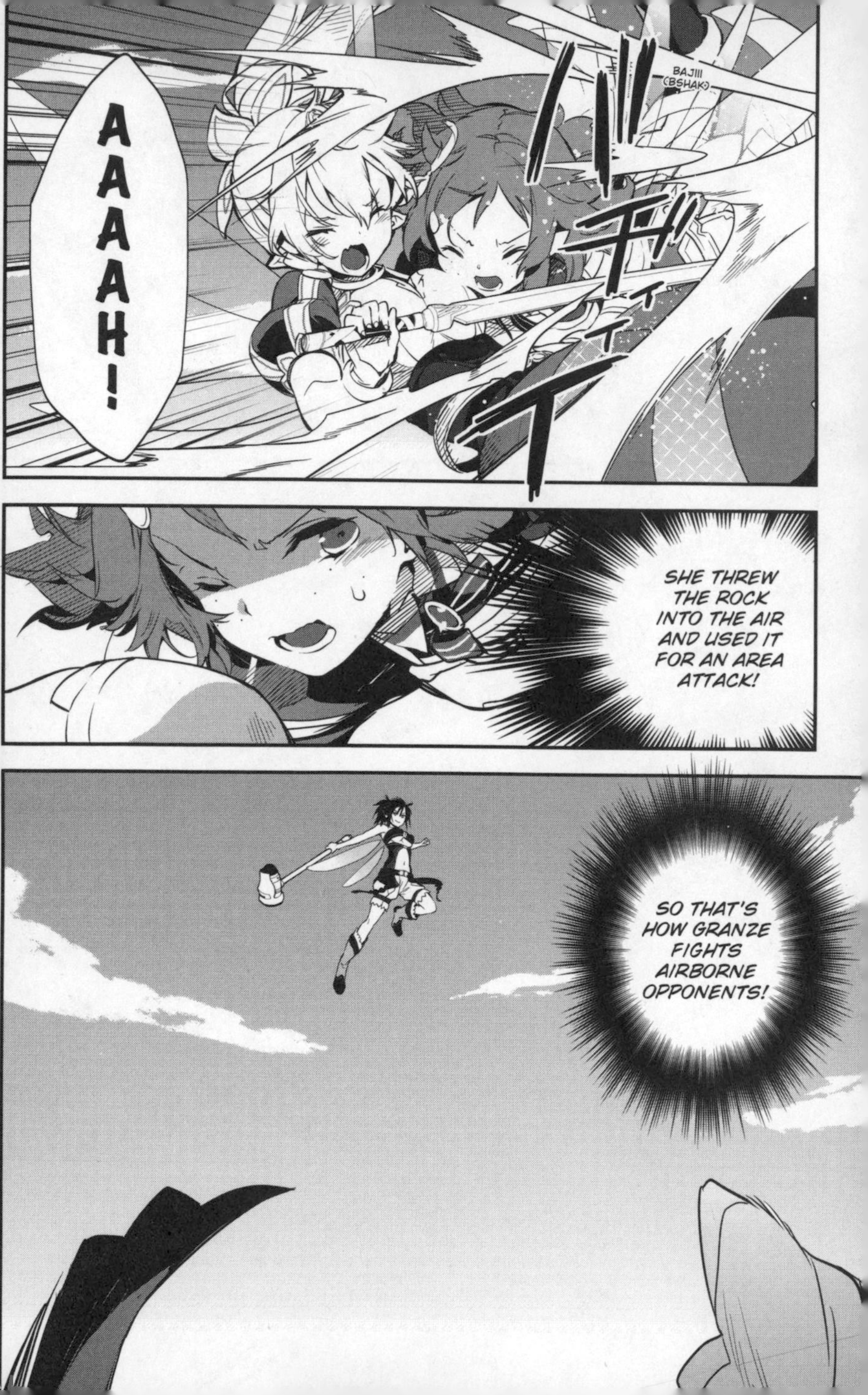
BAJIII (BSHAK)
AAAAAH!
SHE THREW THE ROCK INTO THE AIR AND USED IT FOR AN AREA ATTACK!
SO THAT'S HOW GRANZE FIGHTS AIRBORNE OPPONENTS!

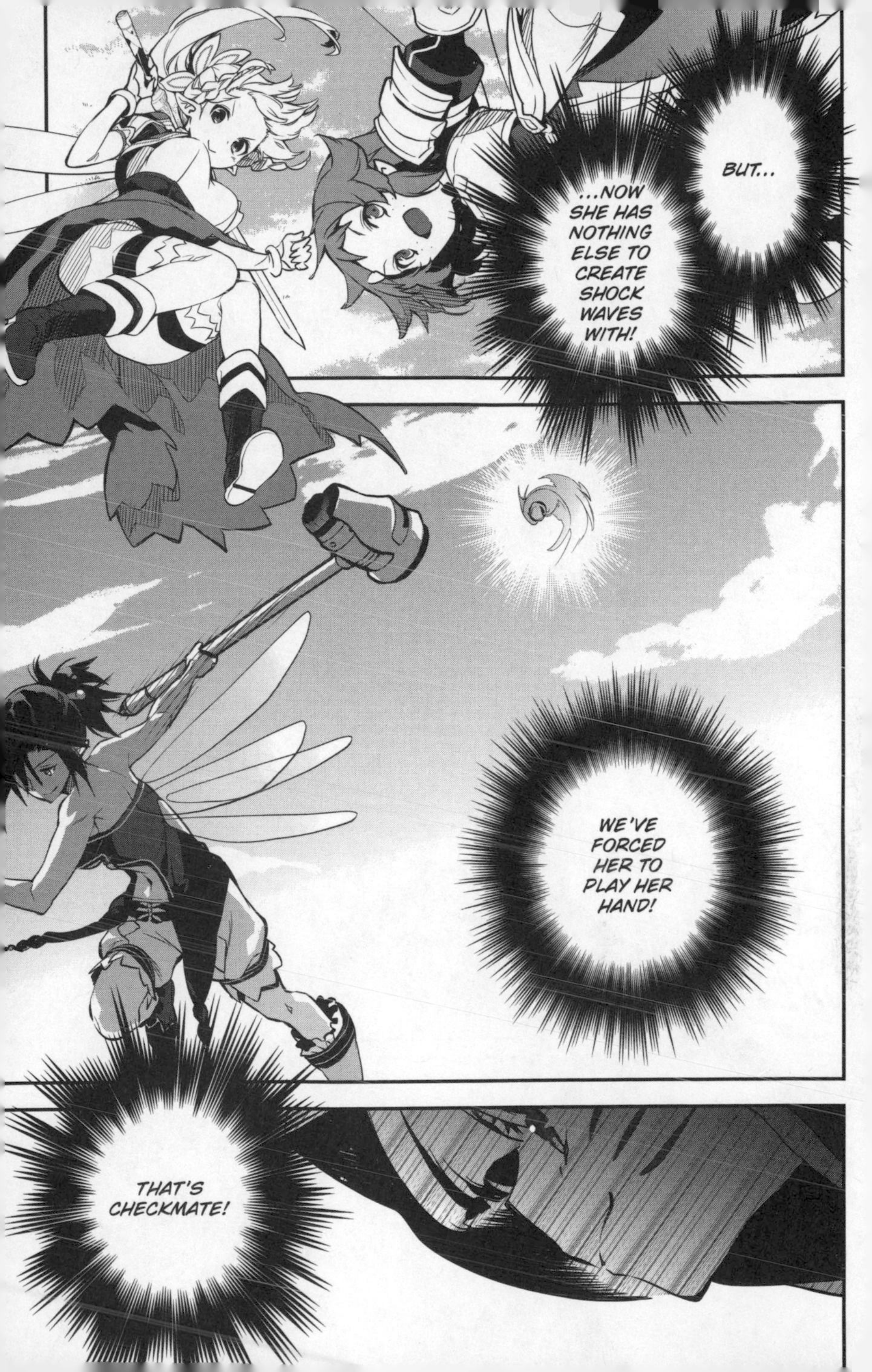
BUT...
...NOW SHE HAS NOTHING ELSE TO CREATE SHOCK WAVES WITH!
WE'VE FORCED HER TO PLAY HER HAND!
THAT'S CHECKMATE!

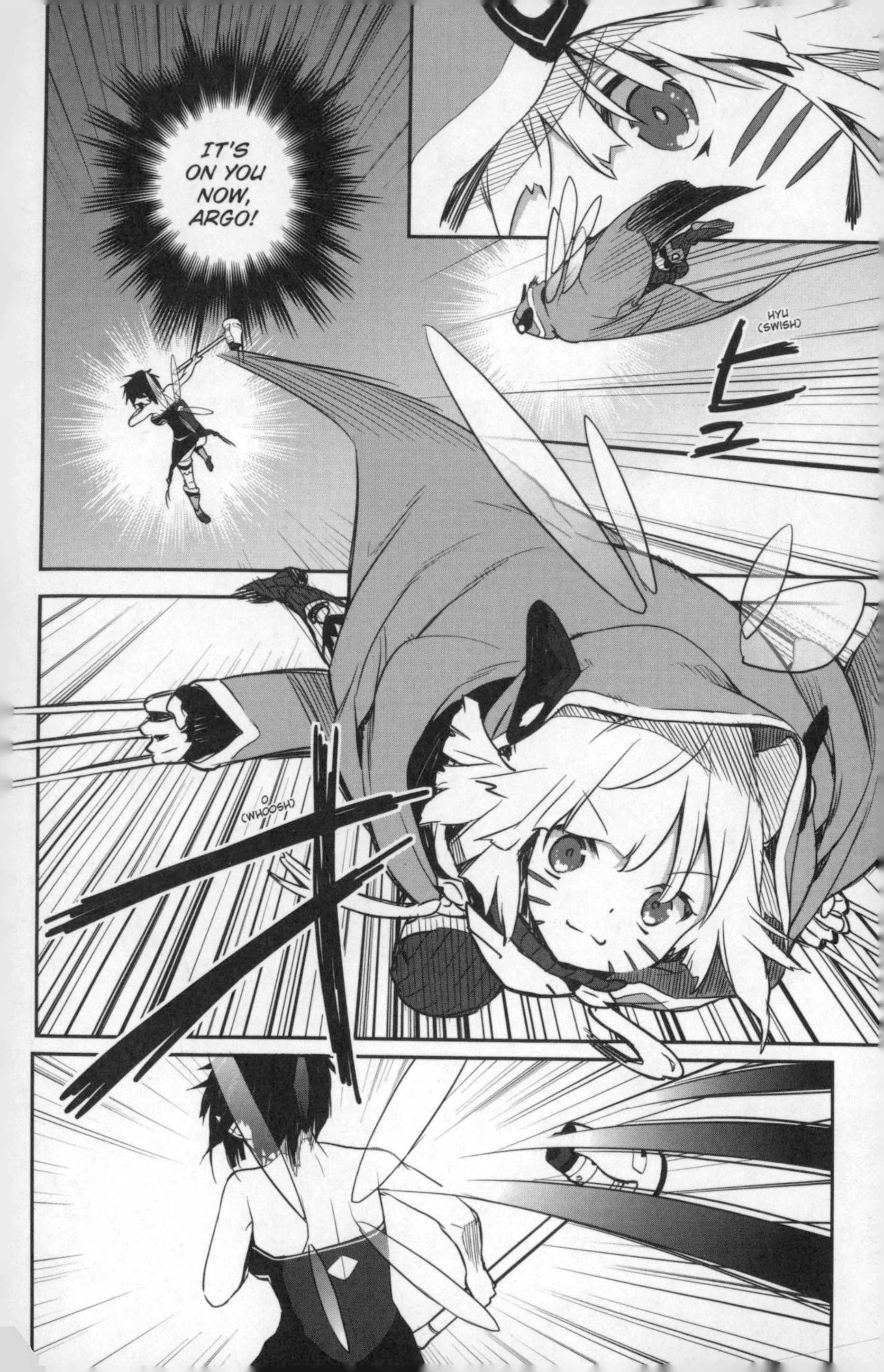
IT'S ON YOU NOW, ARGO!
HYU (SWISH)
ヒュ
O (WHOOSH)

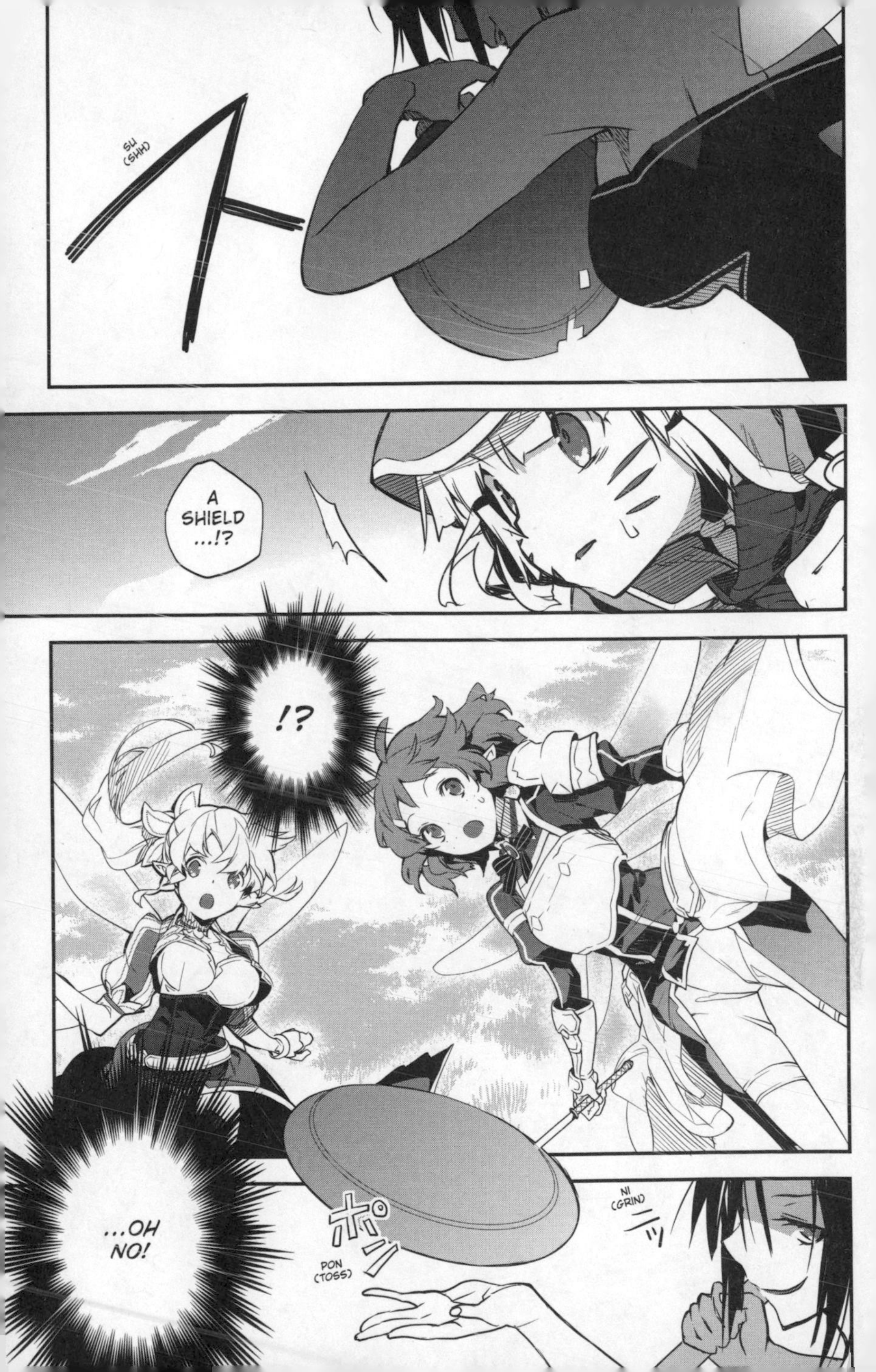
SU
(SHH)
A SHIELD ...!?
!?
NI
(GRIN)
PON
(TOSS)
...OH NO!

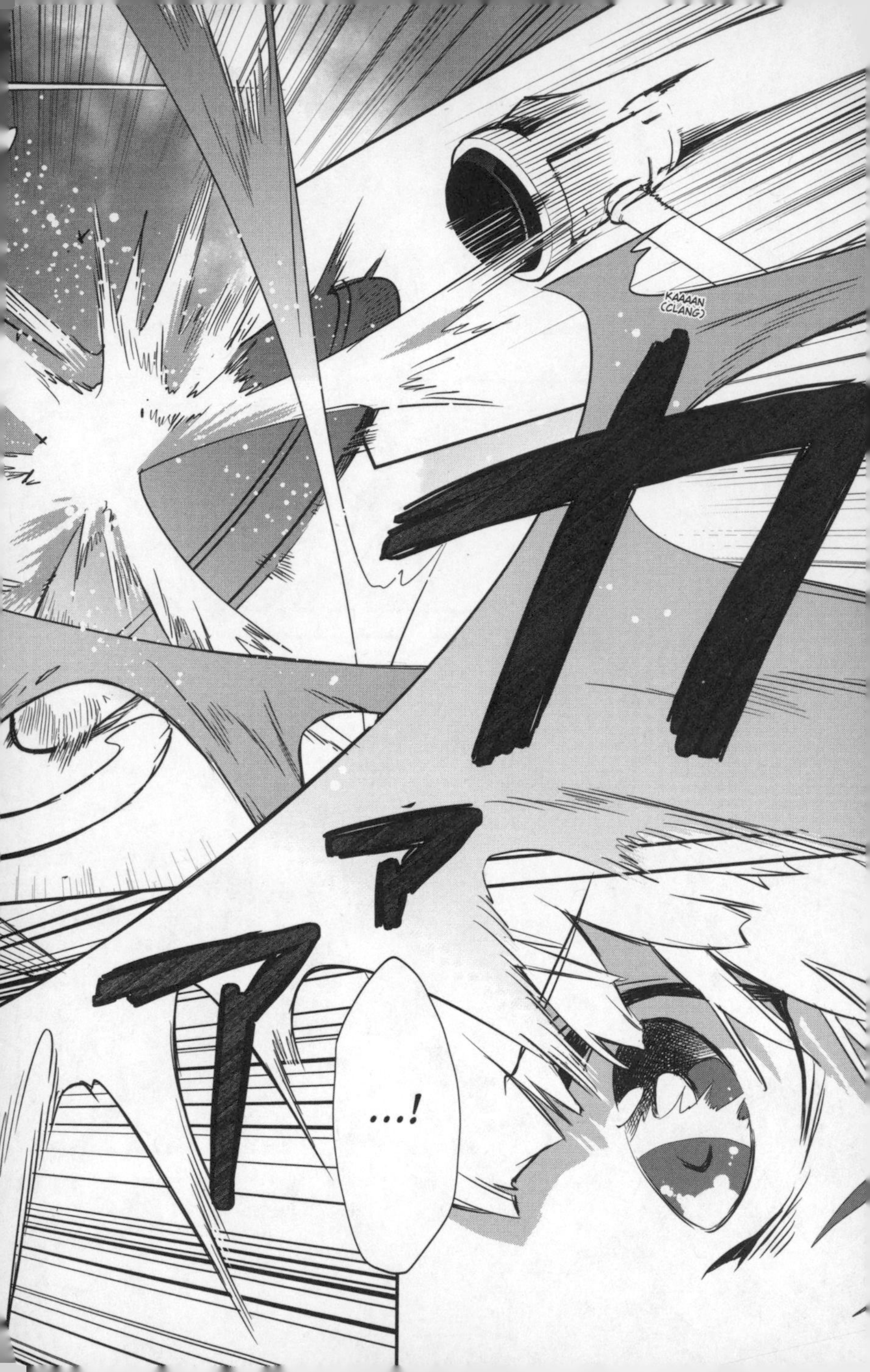
KAAAAN
(CLANG)
カァァ
...!

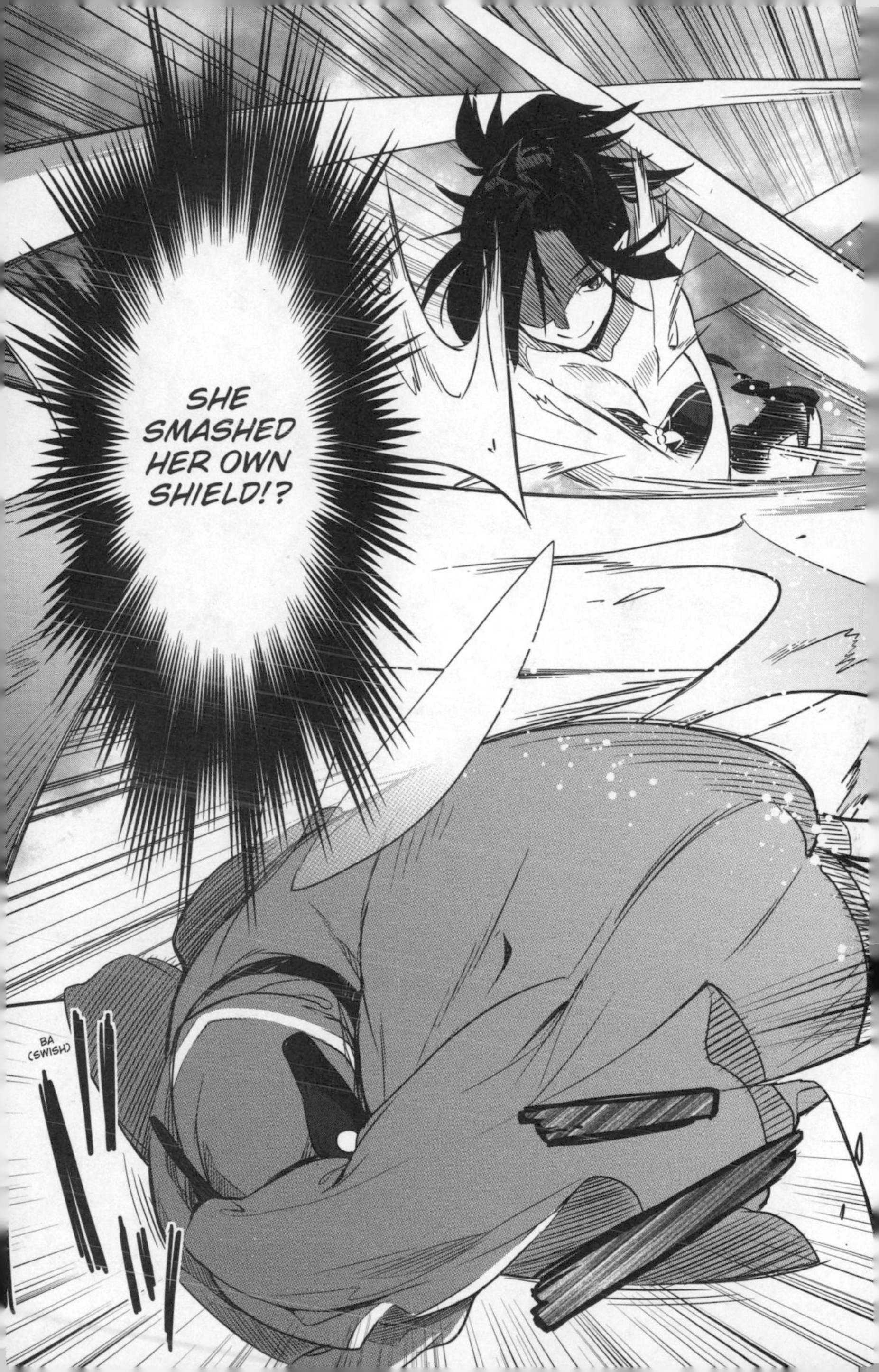
SHE SMASHED HER OWN SHIELD!?
BA (SWISH)

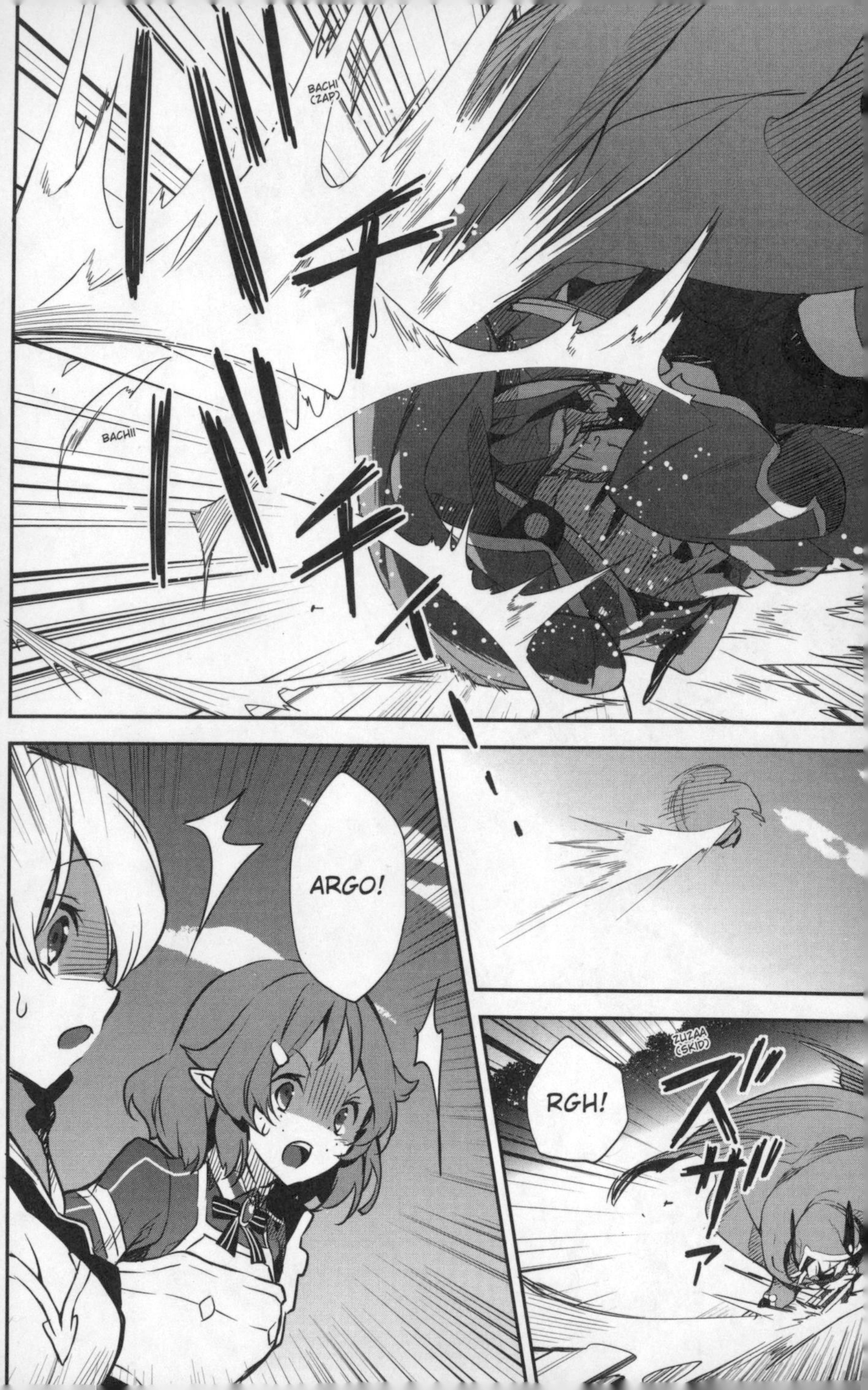
BACHI (ZAP)
BACHII
バチバチィ
ZUZAA (SKID)
ズザァ
RGH!
ARGO!

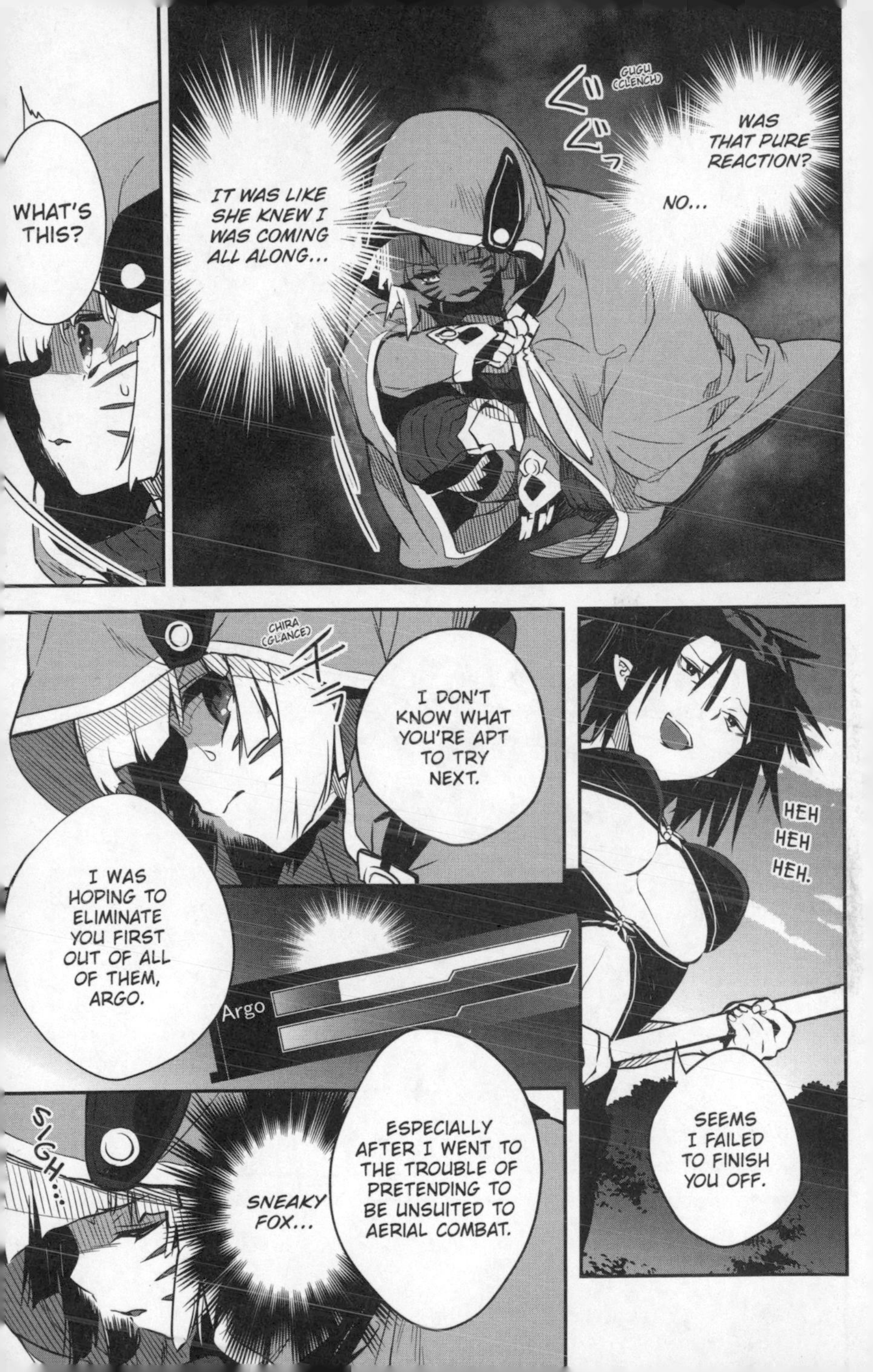
WAS THAT PURE REACTION?
NO...
GUGU (CLENCH)
IT WAS LIKE SHE KNEW I WAS COMING ALL ALONG...
WHAT'S THIS?
HEH HEH HEH.
SEEMS I FAILED TO FINISH YOU OFF.
CHIRA (GLANCE)
I DON'T KNOW WHAT YOU'RE APT TO TRY NEXT.
I WAS HOPING TO ELIMINATE YOU FIRST OUT OF ALL OF THEM, ARGO.
Argo
ESPECIALLY AFTER I WENT TO THE TROUBLE OF PRETENDING TO BE UNSUITED TO AERIAL COMBAT.
SNEAKY FOX...
SIGH...

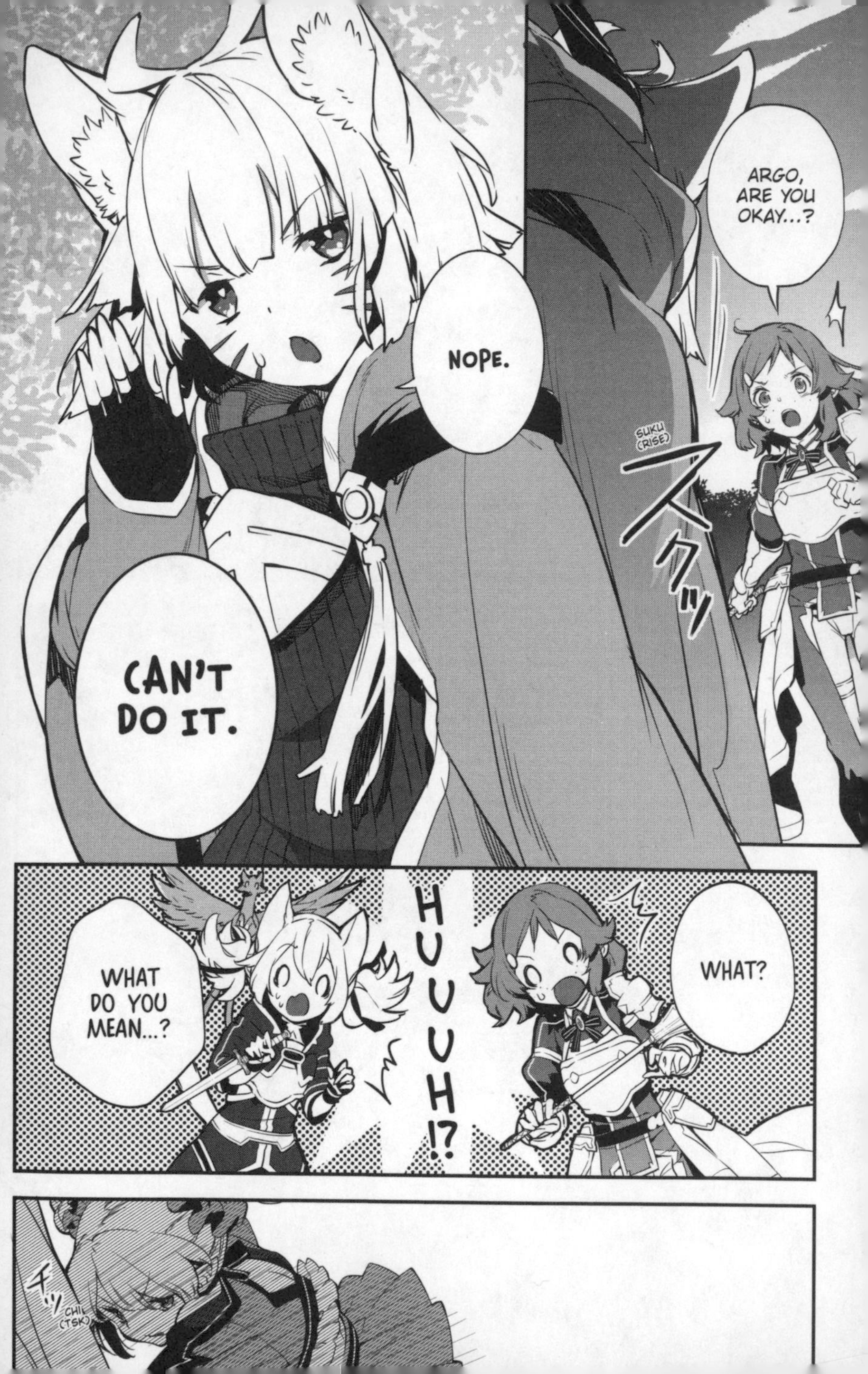
ARGO, ARE YOU OKAY...?
SUKU (RISE)
NOPE.
CAN'T DO IT.
WHAT?
HUUUUH!?
WHAT DO YOU MEAN...?
CHI (TSK)

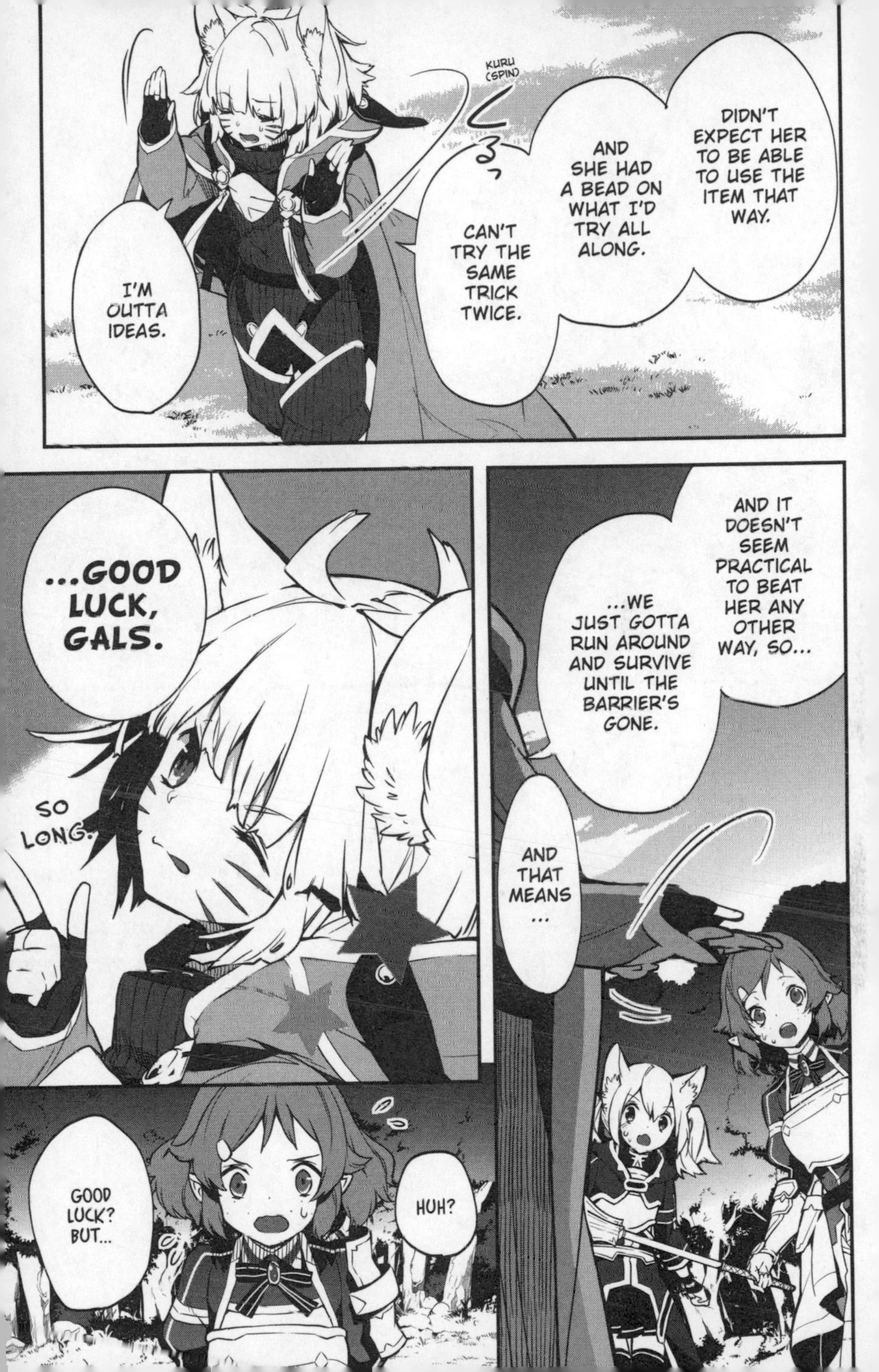
DIDN'T EXPECT HER TO BE ABLE TO USE THE ITEM THAT WAY.
AND SHE HAD A BEAD ON WHAT I'D TRY ALL ALONG.
KURU (SPIN)
CAN'T TRY THE SAME TRICK TWICE.
I'M OUTTA IDEAS.
AND IT DOESN'T SEEM PRACTICAL TO BEAT HER ANY OTHER WAY, SO...
...WE JUST GOTTA RUN AROUND AND SURVIVE UNTIL THE BARRIER'S GONE.
AND THAT MEANS...
...GOOD LUCK, GALS.
SO LONG.
HUH?
GOOD LUCK? BUT...

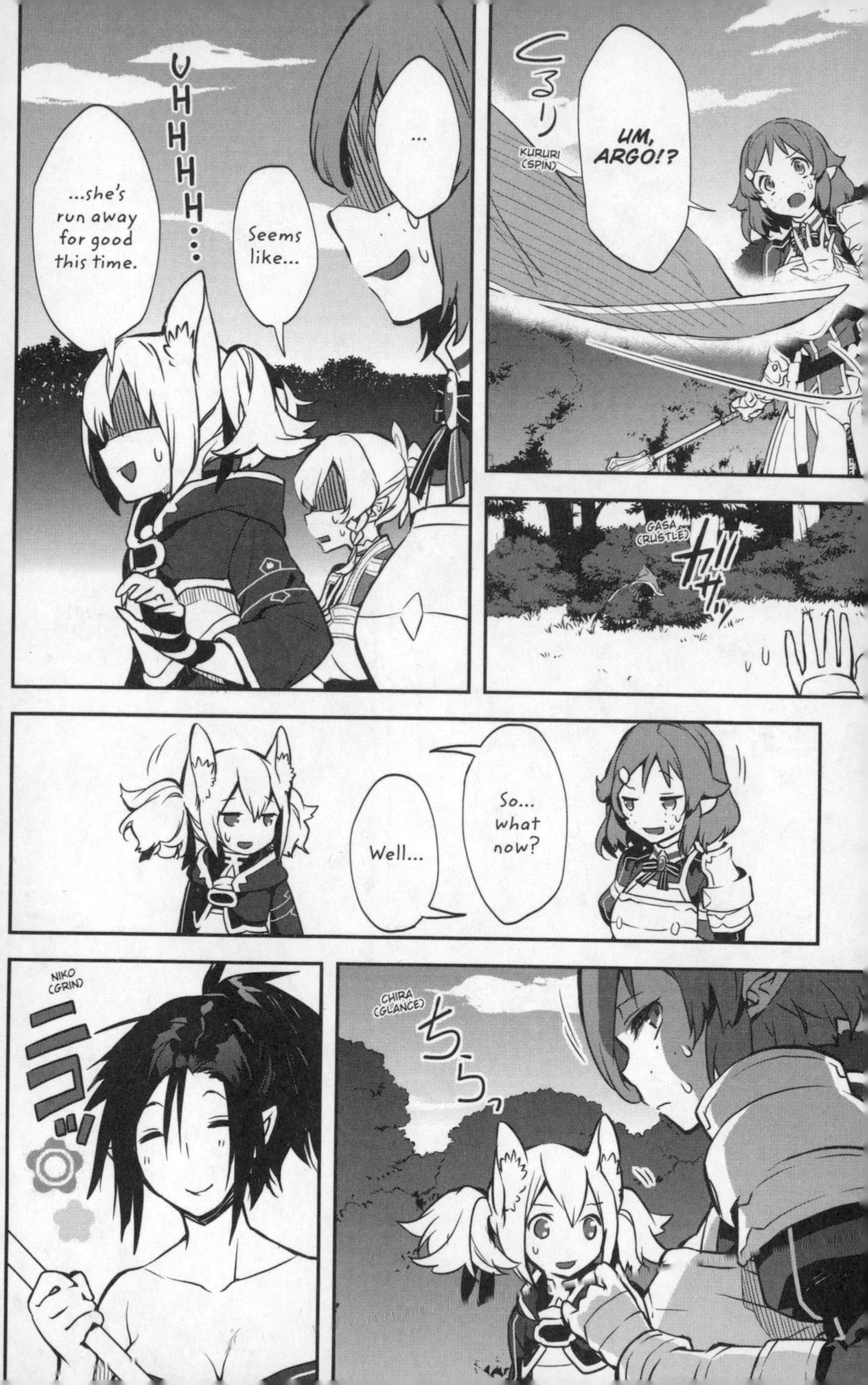
くるり
KURURI (SPIN)
UM, ARGO!?
...
Seems like...
...she's run away for good this time.
UHHHH...
GASA (RUSTLE)
So... what now?
Well...
CHIRA (GLANCE)
ちらっ
NIKO (GRIN)

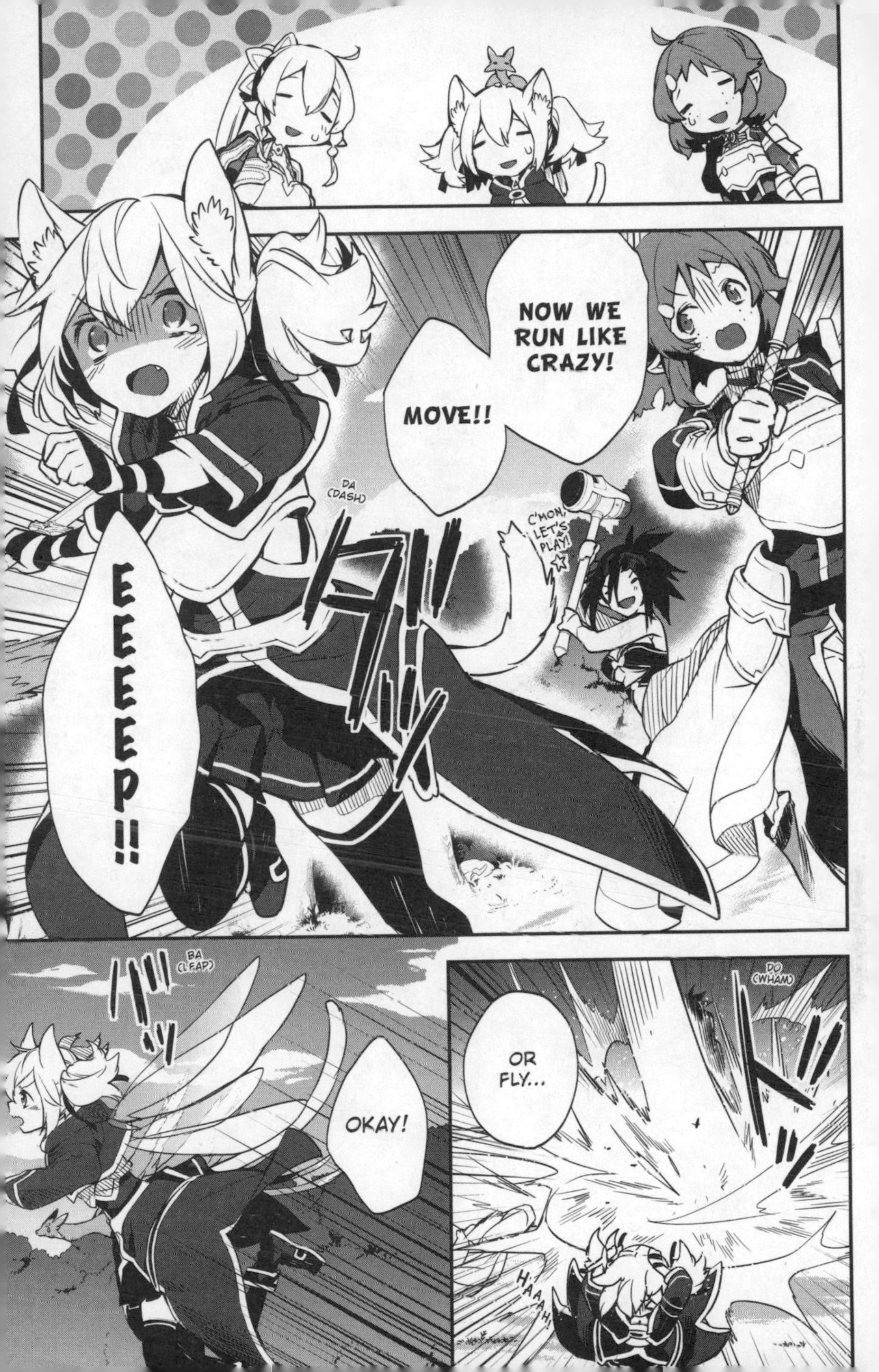

NOW WE RUN LIKE CRAZY!
MOVE!!
C'MON, LET'S PLAY!
DA (DASH)
EEEEEP!!
DO (WHAM)
OR FLY...
HAAAH!
BA (LEAP)
OKAY!

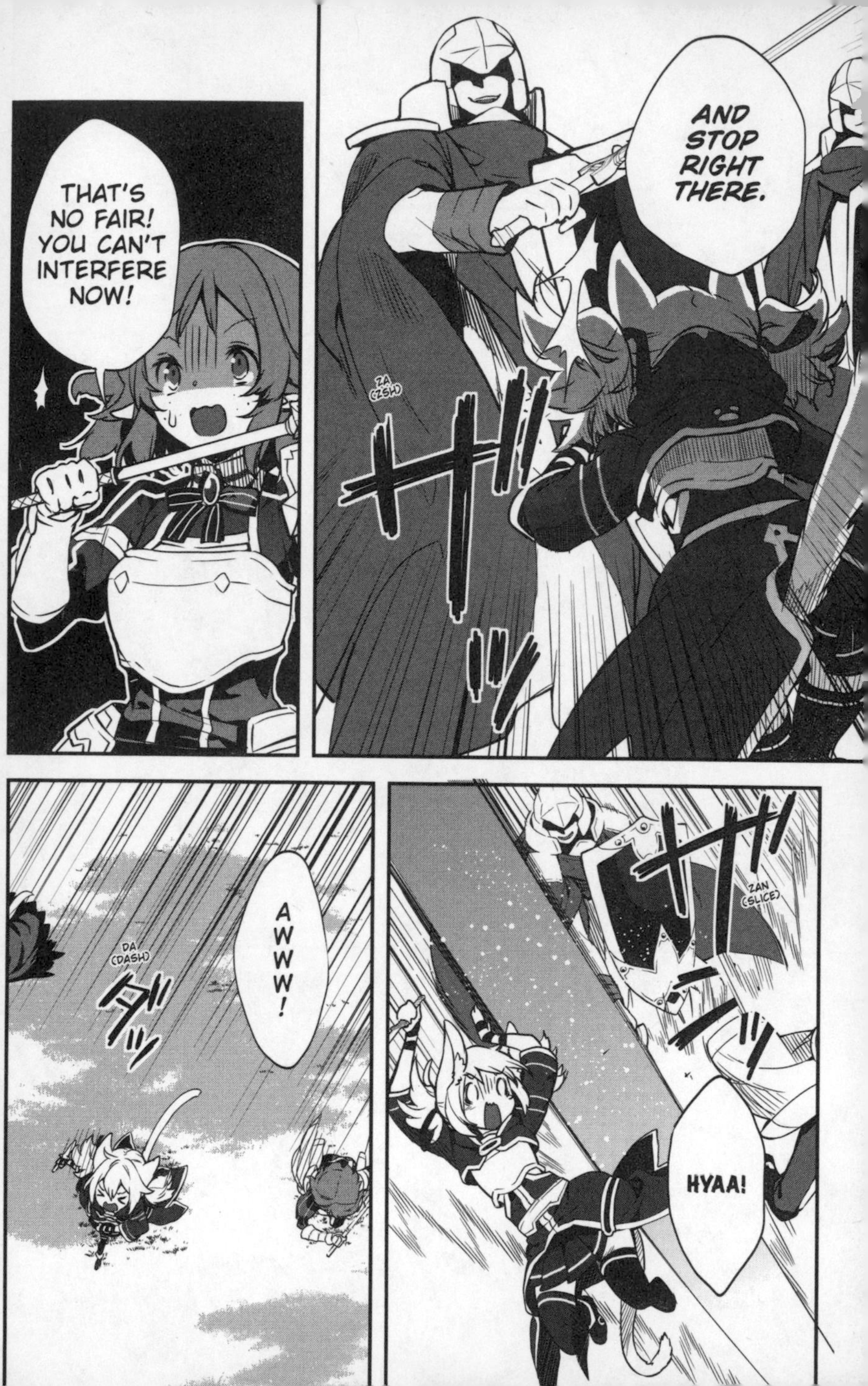
AND STOP RIGHT THERE.
ZA (ZSH)
THAT'S NO FAIR! YOU CAN'T INTERFERE NOW!
ZAN (SLICE)
HYAA!
AWWWW!
DA (DASH)

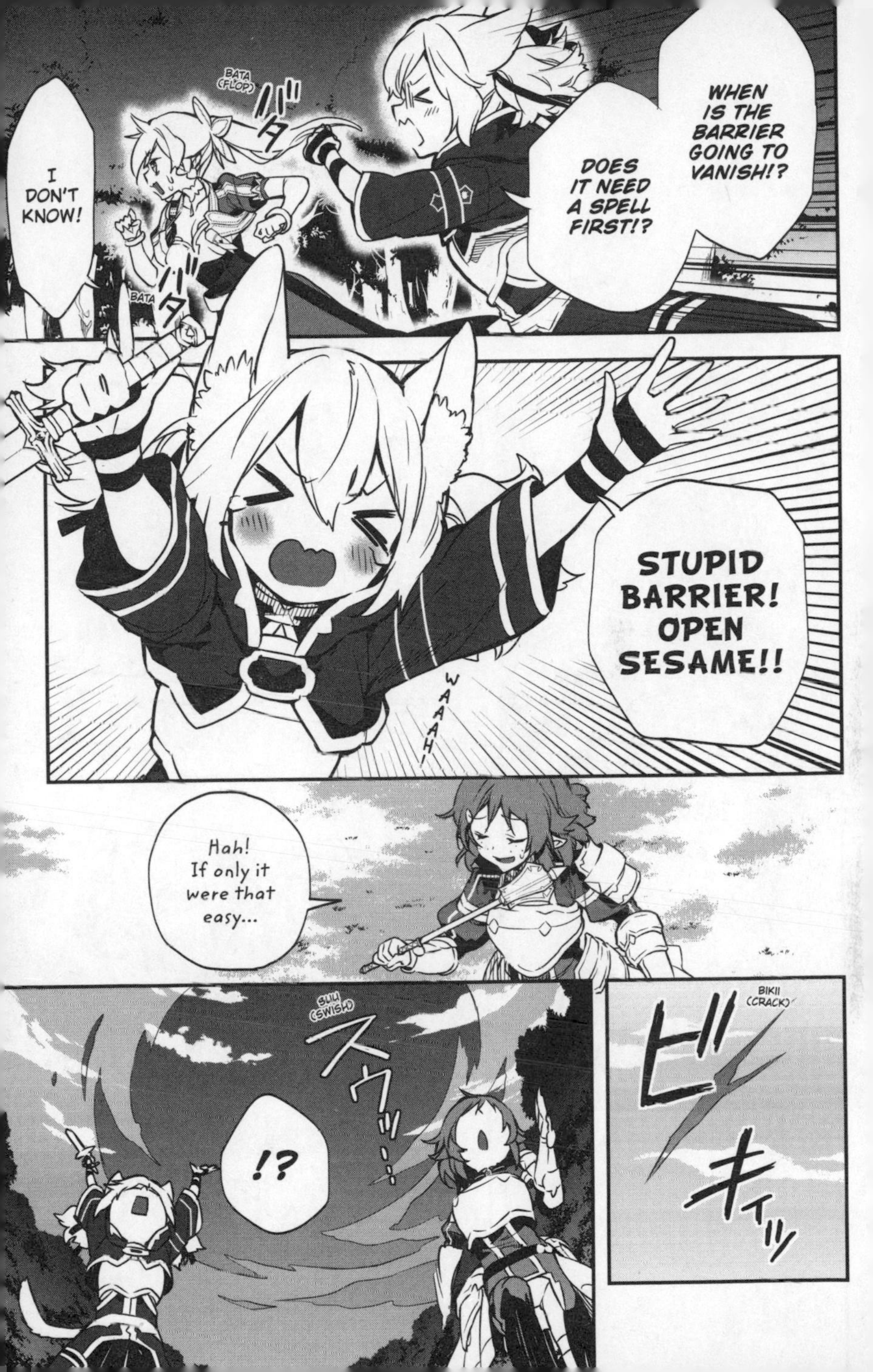
WHEN IS THE BARRIER GOING TO VANISH!?
DOES IT NEED A SPELL FIRST!?
BATA (FLOP)
I DON'T KNOW!
BATA
STUPID BARRIER! OPEN SESAME!!
WAAAAH!
Hah! If only it were that easy...
BIKII (CRACK)
SUU (SWISH)
!?

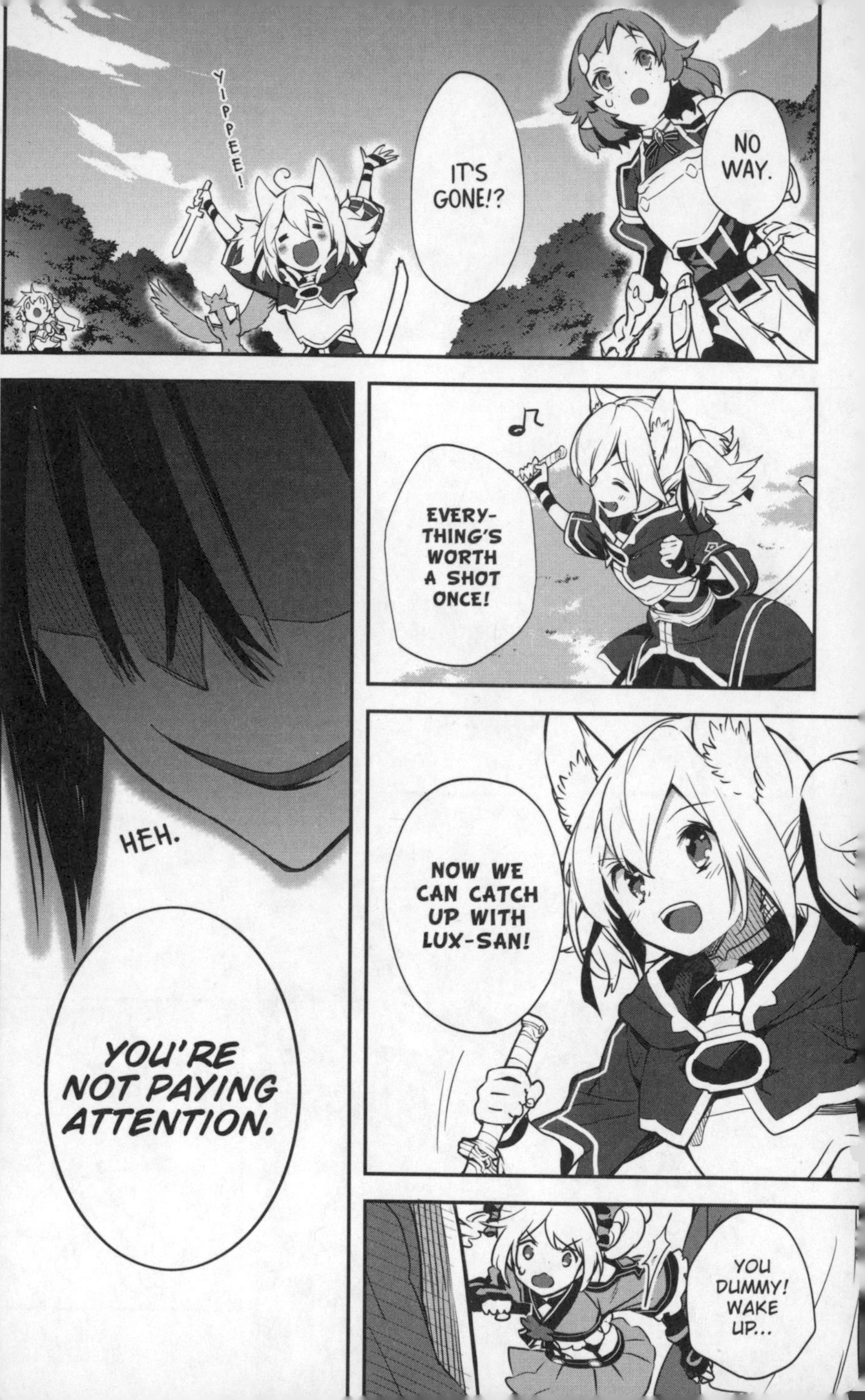
NO WAY.
IT'S GONE!?
YIPPEE!
EVERY-THING'S WORTH A SHOT ONCE!
HEH.
NOW WE CAN CATCH UP WITH LUX-SAN!
YOU'RE NOT PAYING ATTENTION.
YOU DUMMY! WAKE UP...

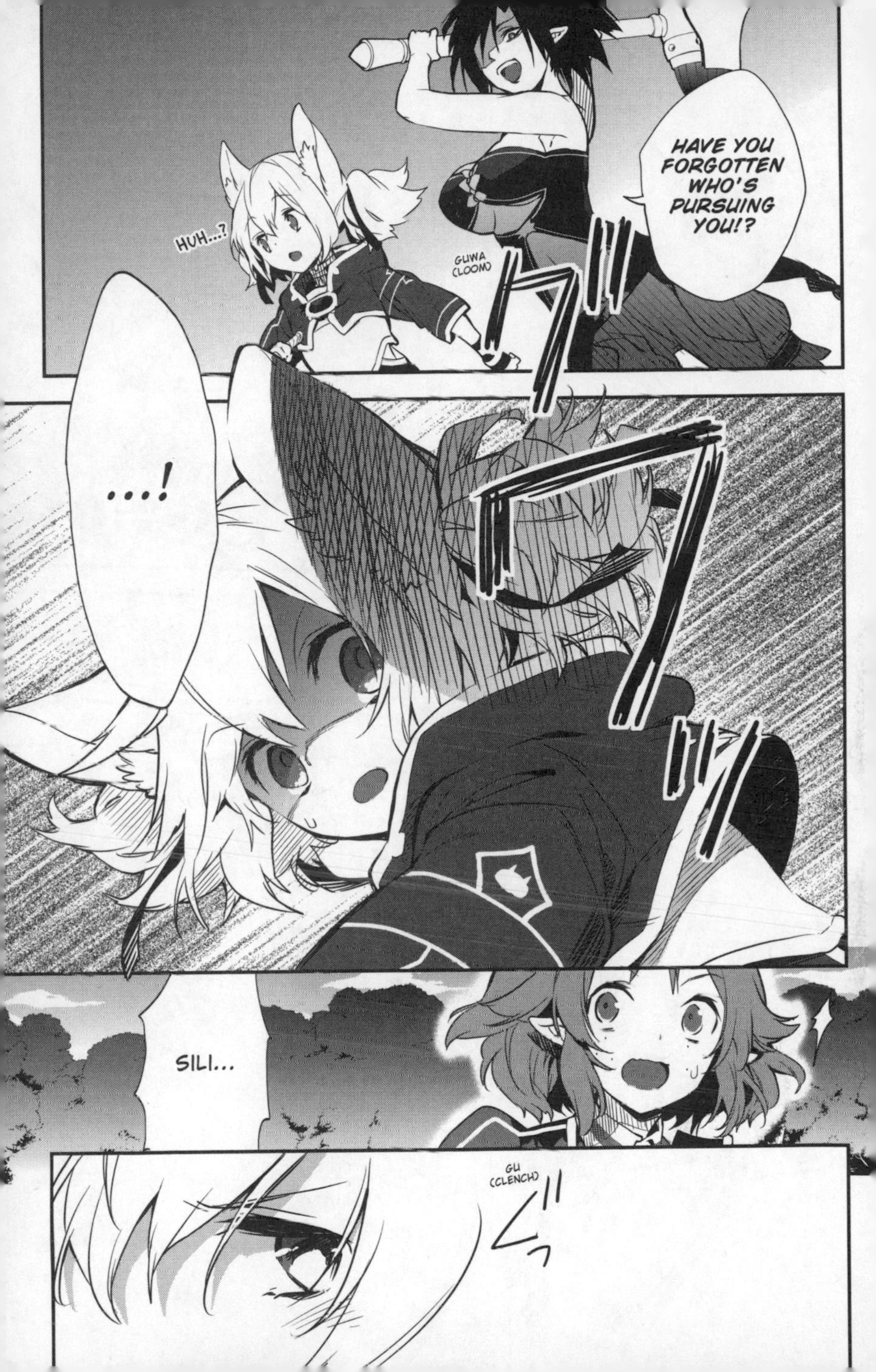
HAVE YOU FORGOTTEN WHO'S PURSUING YOU!?
HUH...?
GUWA (LOOM)
...!
SILI...
GU (CLENCH)

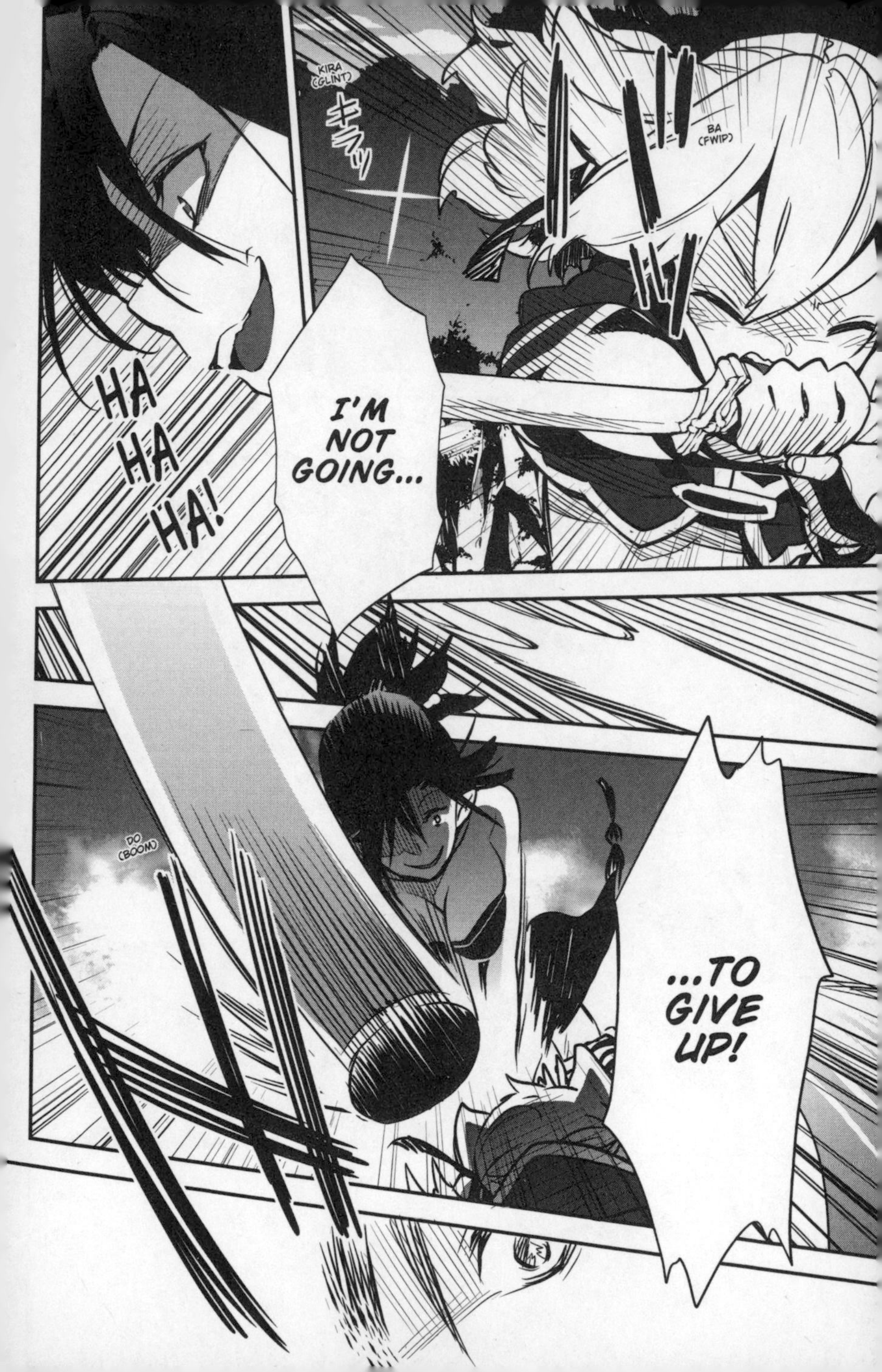
BA (FWIP)
KIRA (GLINT)
HA HA HA!
I'M NOT GOING...
DO (BOOM)
...TO GIVE UP!

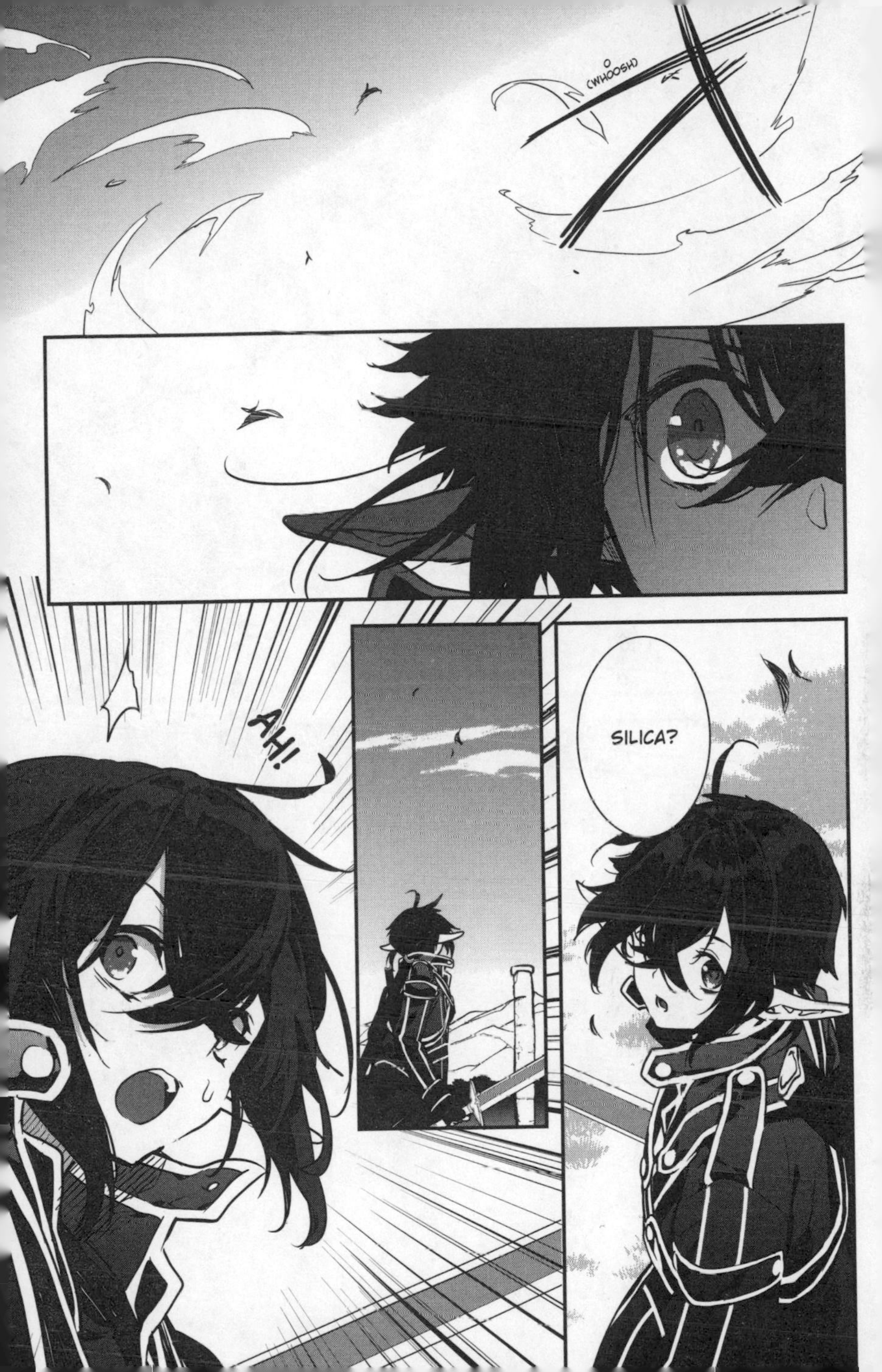
(WHOOSH)
SILICA?
AH!

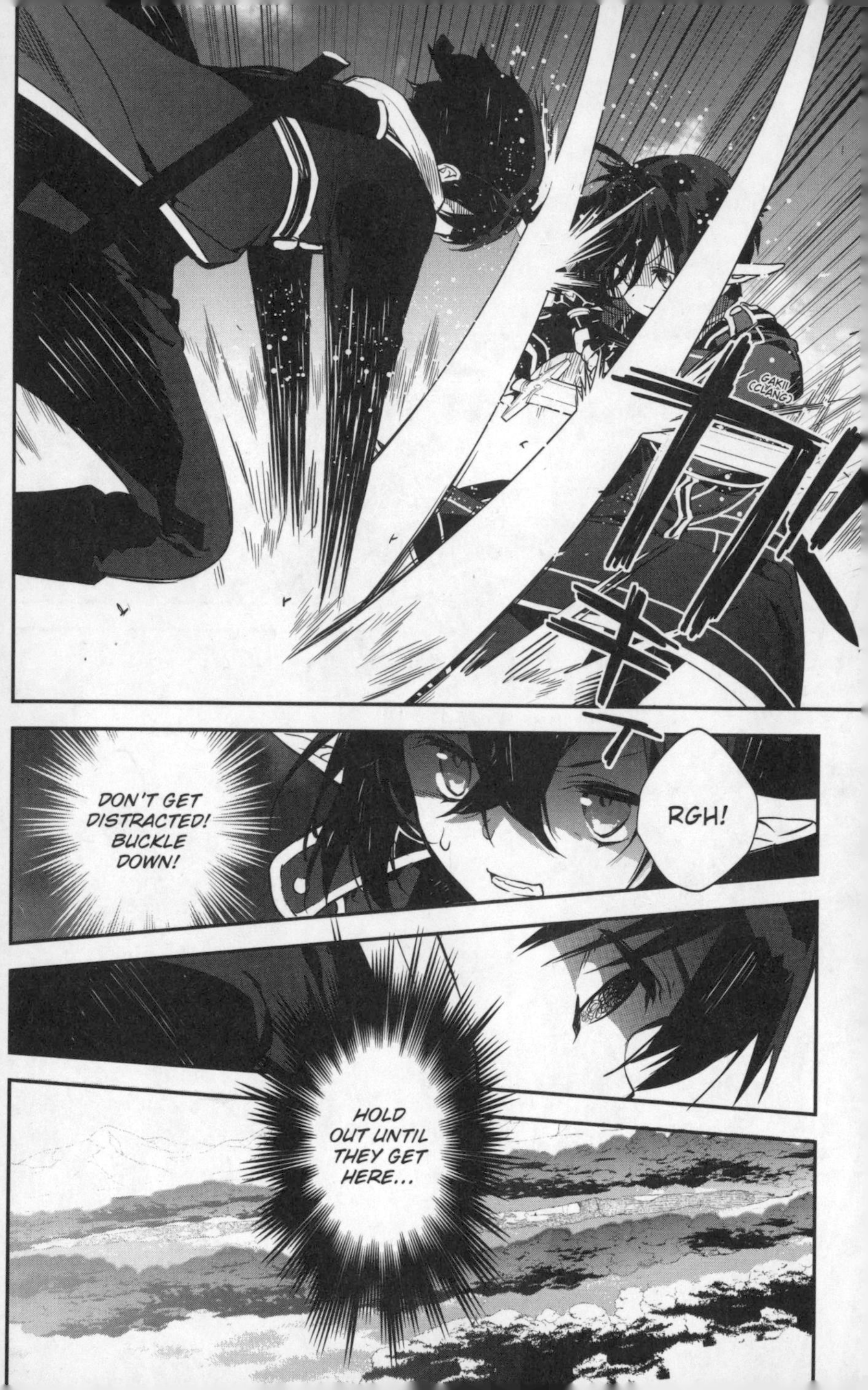
GAKI (CLANG)
RGH!
DON'T GET DISTRACTED! BUCKLE DOWN!
HOLD OUT UNTIL THEY GET HERE...

SWORD ART ONLINE

GIRLS' OPS

SWORD ART ONLINE
GIRLS' OPERATIONS

To be continued in the next volume!

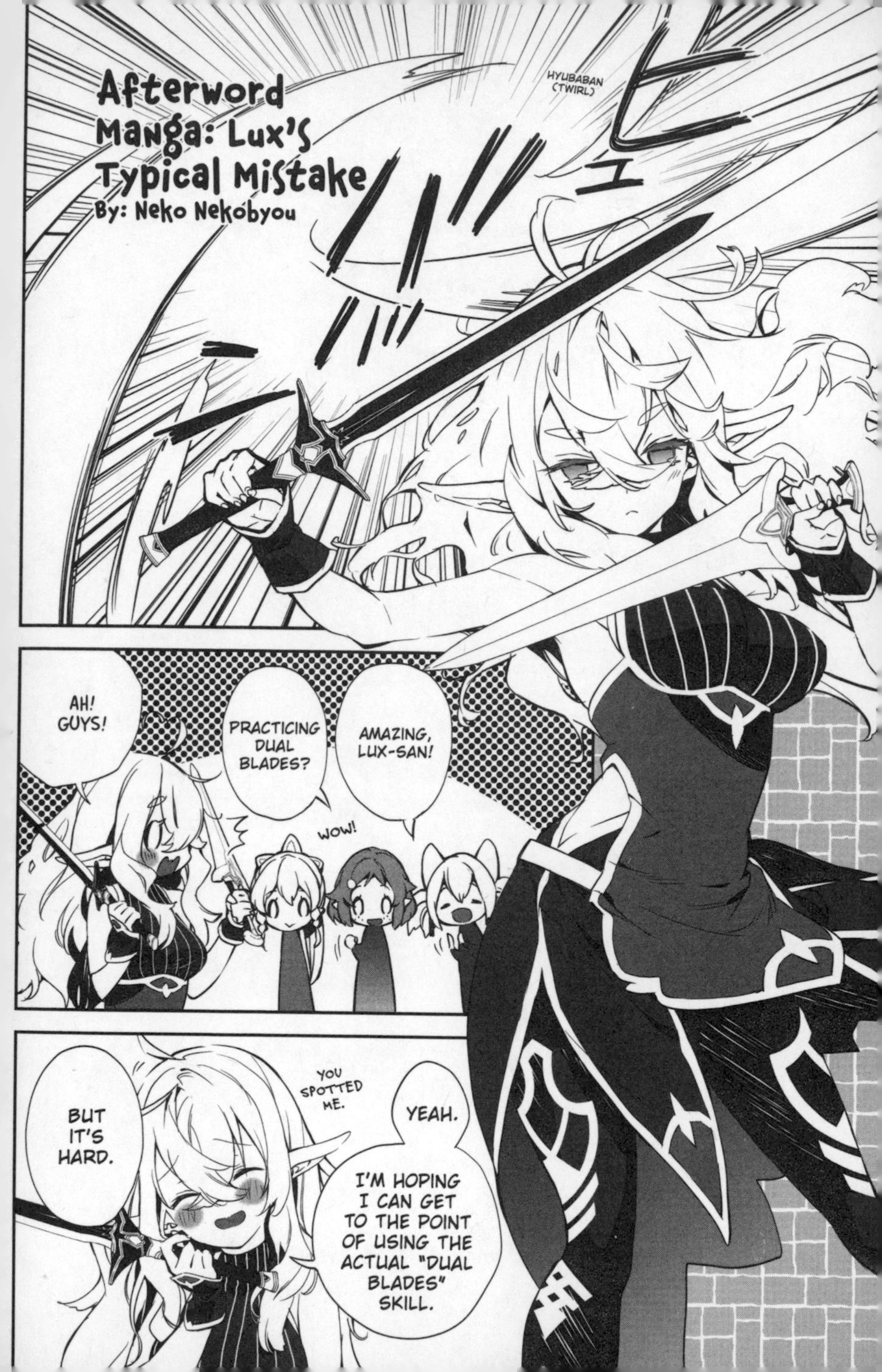
Afterword Manga: Lux's Typical Mistake
By: Neko Nekobyou
HYUBABAN (TWIRL)
AMAZING, LUX-SAN!
PRACTICING DUAL BLADES?
WOW!
AH! GUYS!
YOU SPOTTED ME.
YEAH.
I'M HOPING I CAN GET TO THE POINT OF USING THE ACTUAL "DUAL BLADES" SKILL.
BUT IT'S HARD.

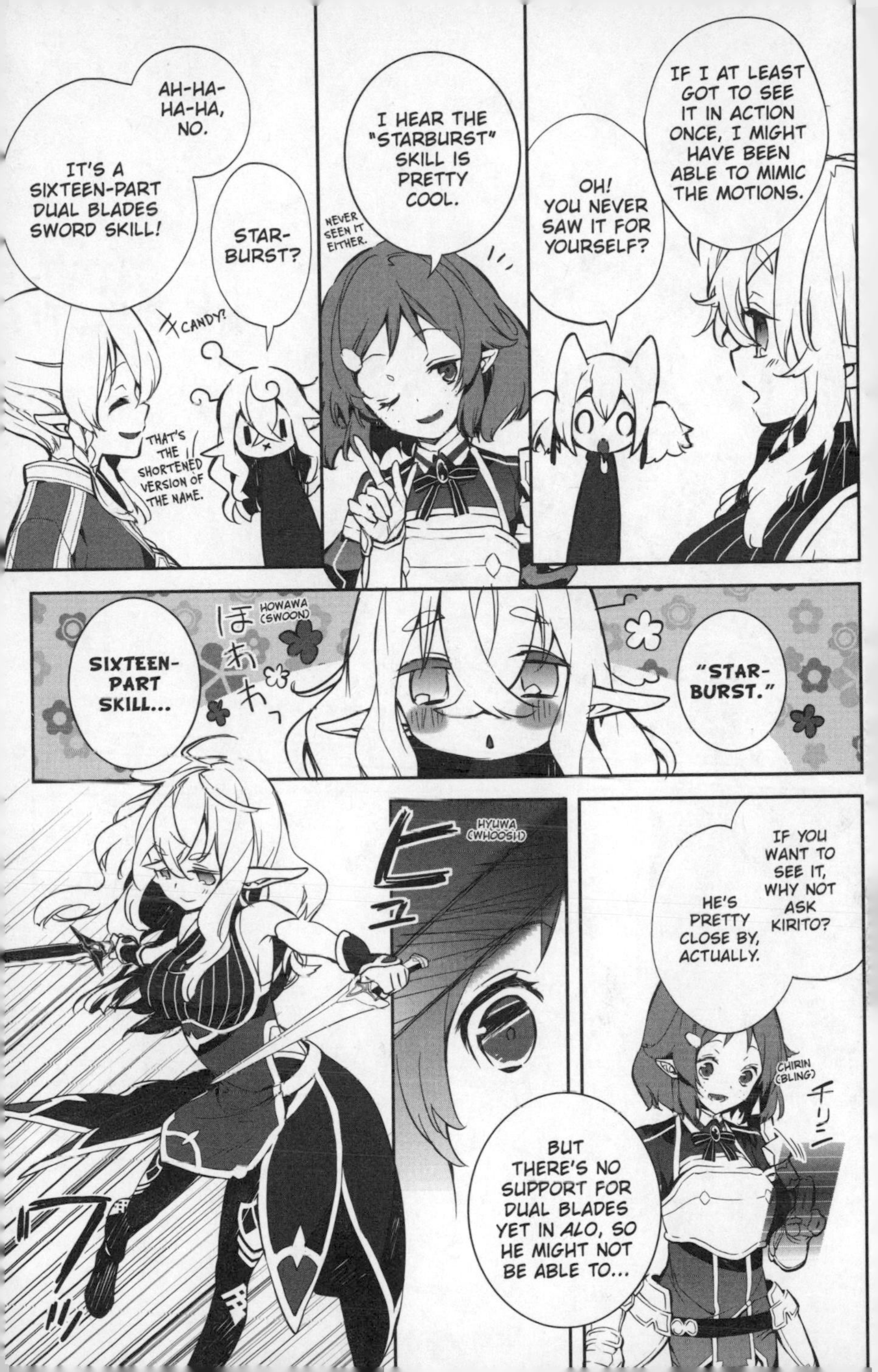
IF I AT LEAST GOT TO SEE IT IN ACTION ONCE, I MIGHT HAVE BEEN ABLE TO MIMIC THE MOTIONS.
OH! YOU NEVER SAW IT FOR YOURSELF?
I HEAR THE "STARBURST" SKILL IS PRETTY COOL.
NEVER SEEN IT EITHER.
STAR-BURST?
CANDY?
AH-HA-HA-HA, NO.
IT'S A SIXTEEN-PART DUAL BLADES SWORD SKILL!
THAT'S THE SHORTENED VERSION OF THE NAME.
"STAR-BURST."
ほわわっ
HOWAWA (SWOON)
SIXTEEN-PART SKILL...
IF YOU WANT TO SEE IT, WHY NOT ASK KIRITO?
HE'S PRETTY CLOSE BY, ACTUALLY.
チリン
CHIRIN (BLING)
BUT THERE'S NO SUPPORT FOR DUAL BLADES YET IN ALO, SO HE MIGHT NOT BE ABLE TO...
ヒュ
HYUWA (WHOOSH)

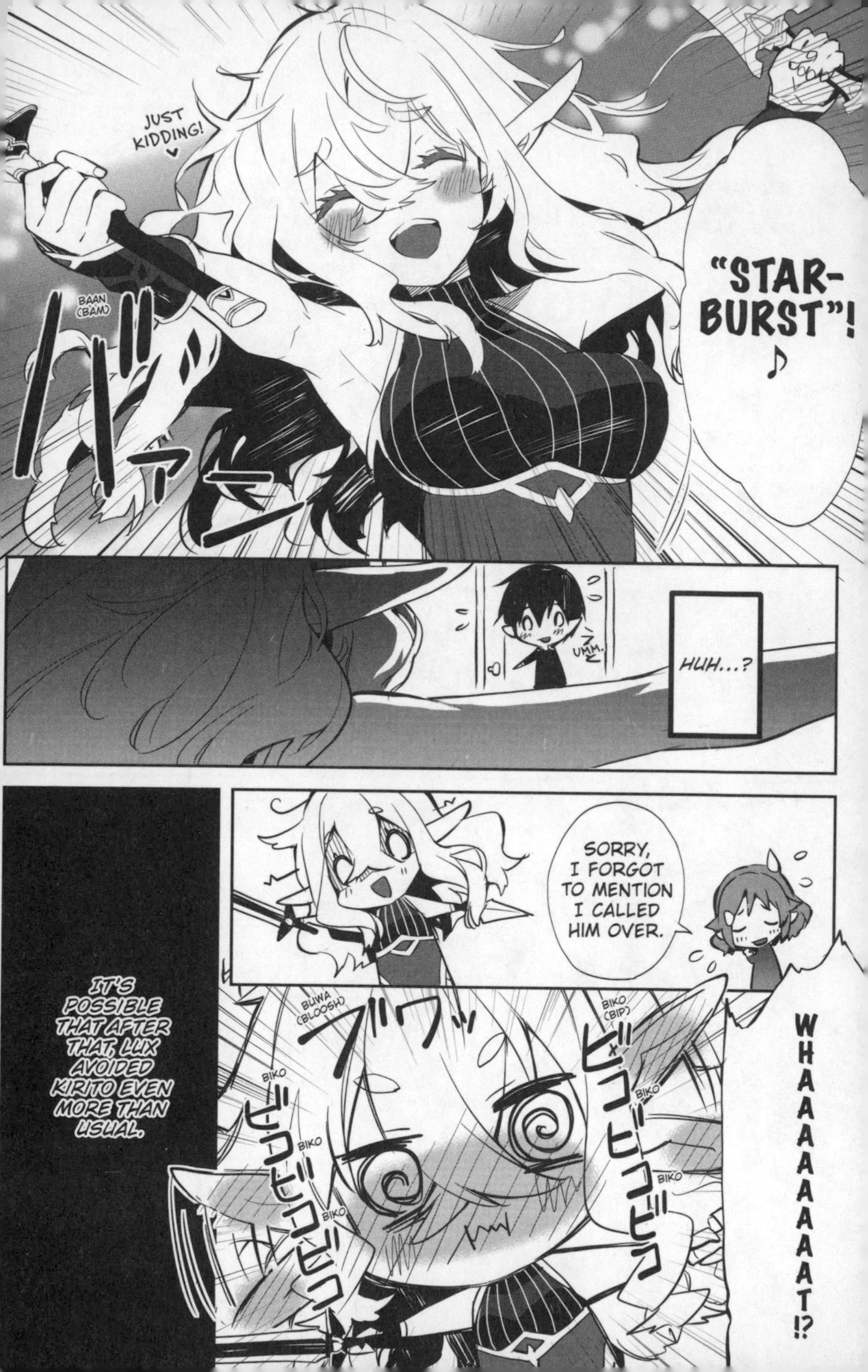
"STAR-BURST"! ♪
JUST KIDDING! ♥
BAAN (BAM)
HUH...?
UMM.
SORRY, I FORGOT TO MENTION I CALLED HIM OVER.
WHAAAAAAAAAT!?
BIKO (BIP)
BUWA (BLOOSH)
BIKO
BIKO
BIKO
BIKO
BIKO
IT'S POSSIBLE THAT AFTER THAT, LUX AVOIDED KIRITO EVEN MORE THAN USUAL.

Special Thanks!!

YAJI

REKI
KAWAHARA-SENSEI

ABEC-SENSEI

KAZUMI MIKI-SAMA

TOMOYUKI
TSUCHIYA-SAMA

AKIRA
FUNAKOSHI-SAMA

EVERYONE WHO READS
THIS BOOK!

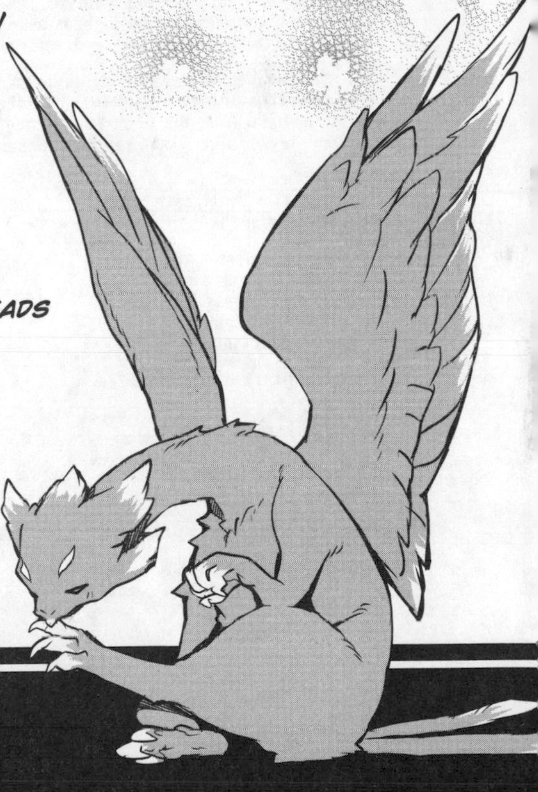

SWORD ART ONLINE: GIRLS' OPS 7

ART: NEKO NEKOBYOU
ORIGINAL STORY: REKI KAWAHARA
CHARACTER DESIGN: abec

Translation: Stephen Paul
Lettering: Phil Christie

This book is a work of fiction. Names, characters, places, and incidents are the product of the author's imagination or are used fictitiously. Any resemblance to actual events, locales, or persons, living or dead, is coincidental.

SWORD ART ONLINE: GIRLS' OPS
© REKI KAWAHARA/NEKO NEKOBYOU 2020
First published in Japan in 2020 by KADOKAWA CORPORATION, Tokyo.
English translation rights arranged with KADOKAWA CORPORATION, Tokyo,
through Tuttle-Mori Agency, Inc., Tokyo.

Yen Press
150 West 30th Street, 19th Floor
New York, NY 10001

Visit us at yenpress.com
facebook.com/yenpress
twitter.com/yenpress
yenpress.tumblr.com
instagram.com/yenpress

First Yen Press Edition: May 2021

Yen Press is an imprint of Yen Press, LLC.
The Yen Press name and logo are trademarks of Yen Press, LLC.

The publisher is not responsible for websites (or their content) that are not owned by the publisher.

Library of Congress Control Number: 2015952589

ISBNs: 978-1-9753-2585-5 (paperback)
978-1-9753-2586-2 (ebook)

10 9 8 7 6 5 4 3 2 1

WOR

Printed in the United States of America